When Geese Fly South

~A Novel~

Tennessee Gunns

BURKWOOD
Media Group

Burkwood Media Group, PO Box 1772, Albemarle, NC 28001

www.burkwoodmedia.com

Printed in the United States of America

Dedication

Once again
to
Debra, Drew, and Carson.

Acknowledgements

The creation of a novel does not happen without dedication and a team of good people, who make books available for all cultures. In 2021, *Saddles of Barringer* and *When Geese Fly South* were accepted and approved by Columbia University, located in New York, New York for the Pulitzer Prize for literature competition.

For me, special thanks goes to Burkwood Media. The talented team in Albemarle, and Charlotte, North Carolina has a vision to ensure my work is available to an evolving readership and finds strategic ways to partner with major retailers like Walmart Books, Amazon Books, Goodreads, Barnes & Noble, and many other relevant bookstores; they ensure my work remains relevant, shepherding the marketplace in coffee shops, libraries, and on social media. Each day, I say a prayer for your families and presence in my writing career.

Additionally, I think my family and friends in California, Utah, West Virginia, Virginia, North Carolina, South Carolina, Pennsylvania Maryland, Georgia, Louisiana, Florida, Oklahoma, Texas, Rhode Island, Tennessee, and the ones in South Africa, as well. A hug for you now and see you soon. I have been lucky with friendships and support.

One
The Big Guava

In the fall of 1999, he packed his bags in angst and left The Big Guava to write what he'd heard about for decades and to understand the truth of the story. Turned in the keys to his beachside apartment in Tampa, Florida, headed for the mountains of the Shenandoah Valley, to where his career in journalism found its origin. The lastingness of that framework in his life was made immortal, far more adventurous than what he'd first expected.

THE PEN OF A WRITER

A year earlier, he'd carved out a decent name for himself as a Tampa Bay sports columnist, where he'd acquired traits from his mother, who made good stories come to life as a North Carolina news columnist herself in the 70s. However, the newspaper's charm eluded his father, who despised anyone associated with education and especially with an aspiration to express literature. His father's passion was to scurry from righteousness and the love of family when he could and became no better for it.

In the Big Guava, his job as a sportswriter included tracking down top seeds and scoping out hot-headed coaches for interviews, especially the egotists, who used the media for their own glory. Another class of so-called coaches existed, though, the ones who opposed what sportswriters printed, which was the dead truth of what happened.

Being a good sportswriter was a cakewalk in Jason Laramie's book. To him, writing was as easy as a sacrifice fly or a foul shot from fifteen feet. He was known for landing interviews with big-name players, lining up high school coaches and key players who transitioned from Friday-night heroes in the media, and later joined big-time college programs across the country.

"The realization of journalism wasn't a field I'll grow wealthy at age twenty-one," said Jason. However, he was on his own and supported himself, which was measureless inside his playbook. Jason saw himself being a sportswriter for magazines and working his way into sports broadcasting or crunching numbers as a sports analyst in ten years. Nothing else satisfied, like being at the ballpark, twenty-feet away from a ninety-nine mile an hour fastball that gets jacked out of the park from home plate, toting a camera to capture the moment and holding a locker room pass was vital to his job. Being amid the big game was no different to him than being in the middle of a forest fire, where he knew something was about to happen and it did in sports, year after year.

After lunch at a Cuban restaurant on October 15, 1999, the bulldog senior editor at the *Tampa Bay Times*, Tommy "Top" Hunter, called Jason into his office for a meeting. Known as a good reporter in his heyday, who had dug deep in the trenches of journalism, spent 444 days on the Iran Hostage Crisis in Tehran and won the Pulitzer Prize for Beat Reporting. Equally he was known as the Terminator, dropping sportswriters on the spot for missing the smallest details of the game and the backdrop. Thus, Jason Laramie, broad and confident, assumed his time as a "Rookie Cub" writer in The Big Guava had come to an end. Something bigger. Better.

He stepped into his office for an update. This time it felt more like the still air of a funeral home and less like a celebration of weekly events. Since he was not known to edit the Obit column, it was something more personal.

He told himself, "I'm the only one in his office." The meeting was abnormal for a pigskin celebration and some barbeque. Speaking frankly, he added, "What's going on, Top?" He turned with a big smile. "Are you firing my butt for shouting at that good-for-nothing umpire in St. Pete last Saturday night?"

"Jason, that was my brother, Tony."

His head jerked backwards. "I'm an ass. Sorry that he's family."

"He mentioned the jackass in the stands from the *Times*, by the name of Jason Laramie, who hated his guts." Top Hunter leaned forward as he often did. "Did you get his bad calls on video? No one loves ragging his car-hood-sized strike zone more than I do."

"Nope." He drew the big strike zone in the air with his hands. "But I'll be there next weekend to watch the "Blind Umpire" do his thing again on Saturday."

Top Hunter didn't laugh, though. He seemed preoccupied. Jason's boss looked like someone had hit him in the gut with a foul ball.

Folding his hands together, Top removed his glasses and adjusted his lopsided bow tie. "Jason, you won't be at St. Pete next week for another game. You've been promoted, called up the line, to the next team, way, way up."

"What are you talking about, boss man?"

"The investigative team likes your wild-ass writing style and crazy North Carolina way of thinking and your style of nosing around." Top shrugged. "I'm sending you to them, the big guys need a good pen."

"Them, who?"

"Third Floor Newsroom."

"I'd rather harass your blind brother on weekends."

"This is something that will fatten your career and pad your pockets, writer."

"Third Floor, huh?" Jason snapped his fingers. "Fred, o' what's his name, Hughes."

"Yeah, that's him. He can be a jerk, at times, though."

"I work for him now, huh? I'll clean out my desk."

"Spoke of you as an ace writer. I agreed. Lied through my teeth, of course." Top laughed. "Nah, I told 'em 'Hell of a writer, that Laramie kid,' that's how I said it to Hughes, anyway. First time he ever recruited one of mine, though. Strange. Told him, you're the best of the best, if he needed a sportswriter in the Great South." Top leveled his gaze at Laramie. "That's the bad part."

"The bad part, sir?"

"Do you know what your weakness is, Laramie kid?"

He was 21 years old and cocky. In his head, he had zero weaknesses.

"You don't know jack about investigative reporting. And more importantly, kid, you gotta be the 'clam in a sea of dark hats,' if you know what I mean."

"Hey, don't forget about that high school coach in Ocala, I busted paying players from some fake account he'd created to land star players in Central Florida from unnamed contributors," he reminded him. "All they wanted was points on the board. That's all."

Top Hunter tapped his hand on the desktop and stood. He laughed, and so did Jason. The last one they'd have together in the office before he left dust on his desk and saw his new big shot boss.

"I'm sure your next assignment will be bigger than coaches padding pockets of jet-fast running backs on the gridiron."

Then he became curious. "Why did the investigative team need my journaling hand? What's the scoop, Top? I'm a big boy. Talk. My heart can handle it."

"You're headed to the majestic Shenandoah Valley."

"But I'm a salty beach bum." He couldn't deny his inquisitive nature. "There's beach babes in my boat on weekends. I can't go to Virginia."

"Suntan lotion and seagulls, you're my kinda guy, Laramie."

His sunglasses flew off his head. Laramie sprang up and rolled up his dress shirt, and unwrapped the leather band from his arm. "Look at this native tan, face and legs are the same shade as my butt."

"You'll burn your Scots-Irish ass at St. Pete Beach." He waved his arm.

"I'm in the ocean too much to move north, sir. Fred Hughes can't make me move north. No sweater. No snow boots. I have no desire to live in a valley, either. Come on, Top. I'm not goin' to Virginia."

For ten minutes, he had a hundred reasons why he couldn't take the job.

"Top, you can pick another rat writer!" Jason stood when he wouldn't take his side.

Top Hunter picked up the phone. "Hughes? Laramie's on his way up to the Third Floor right now, stiff arming rookies to take the position. Yeah, he's in."

"You lied, Hunter." Jason walked out.

"Laramie!" yelled Top, stepping into the hallway, "I'm tryin' to get you up the ladder, son. Don't screw this deal up!"

"I'll give Hughes a piece of my mind."

***

Fred Hughes stepped outside his office and handed a note to his copy intern, who was on the phone when Jason Laramie was in the elevator. Becca hung up.

"When Laramie gets here," said Fred, "send him in, Becca."

"I suppose he's one of us now. No longer selling his soul for pigskin and popcorn and chasing sorority babes on weekends. The young man wants to be a real journalist, huh?"

Mr. Hughes walked back to his door.

"Allegedly, that is," said Becca, "he's chasin' sorority sisters. He's a handsome man. Got those soft ocean blue eyes, long blonde hair and he rolled up in a new Jeep today."

"I wish he typed as fast as he drives."

"Laramie could've played D-1 ball, though," Becca said while checking her face in a small mirror, "too much boozing, they say." She tapped her long fingernails over the lid of the printer. "I've heard he can take the top off .....off a jammed printer in less than ten seconds. Hmmm? He's my kind of guy."

"Becca," said Hughes, leaning out his doorway, "we just bought that printer three days ago, come on, it couldn't be broken."

Jason walked beside Becca, grinning and chewing gum.

"My printer is jammed," she flirted while winking and sliding her hand down her hips. "Could you be a gentleman, hmmm?"

"I could take that top off," he replied, "see what's down inside the machine."

"Please do." Her voice hummed.

"Is that Laramie's grizzly bear voice, I hear?" asked Hughes, pounding on his desk. "Damn it! I'll need a fresh cup of coffee, Becca."

Becca leaned her head on his shoulder. "Call me after work," pressing her number into his chest. "I love Jeeps, Jason."

Sweet notes of perfume ran inside his nose, like a runaway train. His pocket jingled. Did she just slap my butt?

Lifting her chin, eyes closed, lip set. They had lunch together once under a live oak, two weeks prior to his kiss.

Footsteps down the hall caused her to pull away and release a long sigh, watching his broad shoulders and butt disappear into the office of Mr. Hughes.

"Sir, you wanted to see me?"

"Come in, Laramie." Fred Hughes crunched his hand with his manly linebacker grip.

"Finally, I meet the man of this glorious operation, Lord Hughes."

"Take a seat, smartass."

His keys jingled. "Hurry, hurry, boss man, Becca is waiting."

"Don't get too comfortable, though." He held up a waste basket. "Trash that ugly tie, too."

"Becca likes my Big Guava, I bet? I'll keep it."

Hughes flipped a column of facts in his lap.

"Here, read this headliner of the *Dominican Today* loud enough for Becca to hear that hound dog voice she tells her girlfriends about at lunch. Then pack your bags, buddy."

"New Orleans, I bet?"

"You gotta be Volt Hendricks or Ringo Bare to land in New Orleans, Laramie." Hughes snorted out a laugh. Shouting, "The Shenandoah Valley, kid."

Hughes pulled the long string on the blinds and an endless baby blue sky opened up. Jason thought how the tide was lonely without him, the waters called him to the beach on weekends. Did he need anything more?

"Support local, boss."

"I love the Big Guava sunshine, don't you, Laramie?"

"I'll keep my shirt on."

His eyes ran across the pages, soaking up the story like water on a sandy beach.

"Laramie, that story should get you motivated, shake you, and make your blood pressure spike to the moon, big guy."

Jason read: "Three Americans murdered in Santo Domingo: Moby Steel, 20; Raymond Taylor, 83; and Myrtle Taylor, 80, former residents of Mount Jackson, Virginia." He tried to find the hook. "Shenandoah County, huh? What's this ink about, boss? I don't do murder trials."

"Virginia."

He stared at Hughes again. "Mount Jackson, tucked away in a big valley."

Still confused, he locked his eyes on his boss.

"Send the new guy, Plummer, to scout Virginia. Becca needs to tour my condo this weekend."

"No, no, no. I picked you."

"Jesus, I'm a sportsman." He crunched the newspaper and made it into the basket. "I don't do crime."

Hughes rolled his leatherback chair in Jason's direction, tapping his pen.

"From what little I've found out, the two men were linked to Andy Oliver Vineyards. Now does that sound familiar?"

"You mean, my uncle's vineyard?"

"Weston Laramie." Hughes had a picture of his uncle after they'd reeled in a Blue Marlin together in 1993. "That's right, he's my college roommate. We go back."

"I've never met my uncle."

Hughes fumbled through a stack of papers on his desk. Turning up empty, he shouted, "Where's my notebook on Andy Oliver and Weston Laramie, Becca?"

"You mean, the good looking man who sent us a bottle of Andy Oliver for Christmas?" Becca touched Jason's round shoulder. "Why? Does Jason Laramie need an assistant?"

Hughes waved her away with a newspaper in his hand. He turned to Jason.

"Ever read Mickey Spillane's novels, Jason?"

"I read *Black Alley* a couple years ago when I was laid up with the flu. Why?"

"You remember the story?"

"Yeah. Hammer almost died from a gunshot wound in New York and then went to recover in Florida for eight months," he said, getting uncomfortable. "His friends and family thought he was dead. He headed north to Manhattan to resume his life. He met an old Army buddy, Dooley, on his deathbed, he stole and hid 89 billion dollars from the Dons of the Mafia. The mob are looking for their inheritance. Wounded Mike Hammer, takes on the mafia in New York. That's it?"

Becca made chill bumps run down his neck.

"He's the man for the job, Mr. Hughes."

Jason didn't know if she meant he was the man for the investigation or the one to remove the top off her...her jammed printer. He hoped for a third option.

***

Fred Hughes turned his back to Jason and kept talking.

"Listen," said his boss, "there's a backstory of murder at Andy Oliver Vineyards and I want it before the big guys from New York or Washington blast it on the front page. My investigative nose tells me, the three, who were murdered, fled south from your uncle's vineyard the month before." Hughes slapped his big hands together before the start of the game. "Like geese, they got out of town and fast, to the Dominican Republic and were killed. I need the big, ugly story. You're my insider from now on."

Becca massaged his neck.

"That's hot, hot stuff, Hughes."

The assistant removed her hands and left the room. Hughes turned and faced Laramie.

"You're a quick study, Laramie," said Mr. Hughes, clicking his pen a half dozen times. "Might take you a year or more to wrap it up, but I want it done right. Don't flub this up, like you did that locker room cheerleader scandal last month. Don't tamper with witnesses in beginner Spanish, either."

His heart pounded when Becca walked up behind him again.

"I have to go north and investigate like Mike Hammer, huh?"

"Your uncle may be involved in something big or he may be clean as a whistle. If I was his nephew journalist, I'd see what's going on and write the damn story myself." Hughes rubbed his gray beard and mustache into his face, back and forth, and nodded until he had Laramie convinced.

"I'll write it."

Becca screamed, "Yes, yes, yes!"

Jason shifted his pants. Then shoulders.

"I got this story, but I need a year or two and more money."

"The big secret here, Laramie." He batted the newspaper in his hand and paced around his office. "You want the big secret? You want to know why you are here in my office?"

His eyes followed Hughes.

"The crime is public, but this assignment is covert. They call it "When Geese Fly South." Came down from way, way above my damn head, hit me like a rock, too."

"I'll keep the story under my North Carolina hat, boss." He went forward and grabbed a baseball from Fred's desk. "Why do they need my side of the story, anyway?"

"Let's talk in a few months, Laramie."

"I may need a per diem and a good computer or Becca as my assistant."

"That's me, eager Becca, the copy intern."

"Can she?" said Jason.

"Nope. She stays in Tampa. Here's my cell, hot shot. For God sake don't get busted or let anyone know what you're writing." Mr. Hughes popped his arm. "Here's the worst part."

Hughes shut the office door. Laramie pressed his sweaty palms against his slacks and tugged his collar a few times.

"What's up, sir?"

"I gotta let you go freelance on this story. Sorry, bud."

"You brought me up here to fire me? Take that column and stick it, Jack." Jason jumped up and left his big office, like a pitcher who got pulled.

"When you're finished with this big story, Laramie," Hughes shouted down the hall, "I'll buy the first copy, you hear me?"

Jason felt like he was cut from the team. Pulling Becca from her chair he landed one on her; lit her lips up with a second kiss, too.

"We're not co-workers anymore. I'll pick you up at five." He kept on walking.

"Learn Spanish, Laramie," Hughes hollered. "You'll be back here next year to thank me for sending you to Andy Oliver, kid."

The flip of his chin wasn't his normal baseball sign of Southern Hospitality.

***

TO THE COMMONWEALTH STATE

Jason Laramie's only experience with investigative reporting came from popular television shows, like Matlock and the dreaded Rockford Files. Old school.

But being his last name was Laramie, his boss thought he'd have no trouble milking a story out of his uncle in a few months, perhaps. All he knew for now was that the victims, Moby, Myrtle, and Raymond, had left Andy Oliver Vineyards just two weeks prior to being killed. At the time of the murders, they were on the payroll of their new boss, well-known Southerner Mickey Starr, Savannah's seafood king and owner of The Famous Tobacco Barn.

Jason figured he'd start by meeting Mickey Starr in Savannah and investigating what he knew. He belted down a typewriter, gold pen, and some paper inside the passenger's seat of his Jeep and turned the key.

"That's all you'll need...journalist," said a familiar voice.

"Top Hunter, what the hell are you doing here?"

"Came to wish you good luck. That's all you'll need in the Shenandoah Valley." Top gave him a brand new map and a long, hard stare. "You're pissed off, aren't you? You goin' drive off and not talk to me?"

"Damn right, I'm pissed off."

"I don't blame you, Jason." He opened his car door. "Let's grab some Mexican food and talk about Andy Oliver."

He slammed the Jeep door. "If you're buying; I'm out of work."

"You got it."

At the nearest Mexican establishment, they talked for two hours about what the former sportswriter could expect in Virginia. Then he got to the point.

"The reason you're pissed, well, it's because you didn't get to date Becca."

"Wrong. We gettin' married, Dad! I love your daughter. Becca, she's a fine woman."

His eyebrows nearly popped off his head.

"I'll kill you, playboy!"

"No, no, none of that. We never even talked." He held the truth from him. "And yeah, that's half the reason I'm pissed."

"You write this story, 'for I kill ya." Top said, "I'll see that my daughter Becca drives you around in her convertible when you get back to Florida, though."

"I've seen all of Tampa I want to see. Time to move on, boss."

"Well, you write the story first and don't get busted," Top said. "Becca might want to visit you in Virginia soon."

"She might, Dad." Jason grinned. "Might take months before I get a good lead."

Top and Jason walked to the parking lot.

"Listen, this is big stuff," Top removed his glasses from his big ears. "I'm not sure what you might have to do to get it down on paper, but be careful."

He nodded and grinned. Confused.

"I'll call you soon, Top."

"Don't call me, just send me a copy. And don't call Becca, either, until you have typed the last word."

He spun gravel and made a dust trail out of the parking lot. "I'll marry Becca!" Jason shouted through his hands.

The loud exhaust muffled his voice. Thank God. Top was known to carry a weapon because Becca needed her "printer top" removed pretty often from guys. Jason raked his thin beard and headed into a hornet's nest in the mountains. He glanced into the passenger's seat. "What the heck?"

A big note.

Writer Laramie,

Here's $25,000 as a down payment. The man who wants this story investigated and written asked me to hand it to you personally before you left The Big Guava. There's more money when the last chapter is wrapped up. The clock is ticking... Don't write us a goat choker.

Your friend,
Top Hunter

PS: Becca said to tell you, she needs help taking the top off her printer.

OUT OF ROUTE

His investigations were somewhat out of route — in Savannah. Jason drove to The Famous Tobacco Barn where he saw Mickey Starr leaning against his classic truck. He handled a long cigar outside the paddock at sunset, and a plane had just landed, where a lady stepped out in a pumpkin colored dress, followed by two gentlemen in white dress shirts. They talked to Mickey for a moment in a field of golden grass beside Tobacco Road. The blonde hopped into a white limousine while one man drove away in a restored Chevy truck. The other man was Mickey Starr, who drove away in a yellow convertible Cadillac. With dark glasses and a ballcap, Jason parked in the shadows underneath two live oak trees and saw the grandeur of The Famous Tobacco Barn, found on the cover of several books and magazines. Mickey Starr and Tipp Starr had surely made the property wonderful. Horses. Barns. Oktoberfest. Carnival. Then the writer turned the Jeep around and beelined to downtown Savannah for a seafood dinner. After three beers at Moon River, he mustered up the courage to make a call. The phone rang three times before anyone answered.

"Hello."

"Uncle Weston?"

"Good evening. Andy Oliver Vineyard."

"This is your nephew."

He stood against a brick wall at the Crystal Parlor, where he could see the waitress place a creamy crab stew on his table alongside a dark soda and she waved at him.

"The one my brother keeps bragging about, who lives in Tampa."

"Jason Laramie, the sportswriter. Yeah, that's me."

"You still got chickenpox, kid?"

"No." He laughed. "My father sent you my picture in the summer of '86."

"Just pulling your leg, what can I do for you?"

He didn't look forward to asking him but he said it anyway.

"I was wondering, if you have an extra room for a while?"

"How long?"

"Not sure."

"I knew one day you'd have the balls to visit your uncle for the first time. Listen, if you are anything like your father, then, I don't have a doghouse for you to sleep in, just stay in Florida and keep your Wild Turkey and chickenpox."

"My father's a jackass. I'm not."

Sniffing. "Since you have good judgement, I have a room. When will you be here, James?"

"Three weeks."

"Hope the Yankees are in the World Series in October," responded Weston succinctly. "Look forward to meeting you, James."

"Jason. My name is Jason," he said. "Jason Laramie."

"I have plenty of work at Andy Oliver." Weston pressed the phone deeper into his ear. "If you need work, that is?"

"I'll take it." He thumped his head against the glass. "What type of work?"

"Have a safe trip, James."

The phone went dead.

IF IT WASN'T FOR PETER PRICE

Seven hundred miles north of The Big Guava, in Troutman, the Jeep Jason drove overheated in North Carolina. Smoke billowed from underneath the hood like a bullet ripped through the radiator hose. He parked on the shoulder of Interstate 77 and could see a well-lit truck stop at exit 42. A stocky man stepped out of a burgundy antique Land Rover and walked toward his Jeep.

"Young man, you're far, far from Florida with that chimney of smoke polluting this perfect Carolina air. Anyway, son, my name is Peter Price."

He greeted him with a strong handshake, hoping he wasn't a serial killer.

"Jason Laramie. Trying to get to Virginia."

The man removed his ball cap, scratched his soft sandy hair, curled a good sized grin, and walked around the vehicle with his flashlight.

"I can fix an American car, but I won't work on those foreign jobs. Yeah. And I'll fix the broken keys on that typewriter 'cause my wife is a school librarian. Those things I have come to understand from kids who intend to pawn typewriters."

"Can you fix this Jeep?"

"Looks like you knocked the ASDF off the typewriter when you loaded it into that cheap cardboard box." He stood and glared through the plastic window of the vehicle. "I've seen ugly kids in the passenger's seat, dogs in the passenger's seat, plants in the passenger's seat, and saw a chimp once when Eastwood came to town, but bless your little heart...why do you have a broken typewriter in your vehicle?"

"Typewriter needs fixin' too?" He adjusted his accent. "I mean, it's broken and is in need of repair, Mr. Price."

"You write those summer romance books like the Sparks fellow, kid? Everyone is reading historical fiction again." He sniffed. "Wait!" Snapped his fingers. "You headed to Virginia, you must be John Boy Walton, from Walton's Mountain, up in the Shenandoah hills somewhere?"

"No John Boy. If you can fix the Jeep and the typewriter, I'll grab a hotel for the night, sir and pay you well?"

Mr. Price locked the hood tight.

"I don't do hanky-panky work, Slim." He laughed at Jason. "You're a big time writer, I bet?"

Jason rubbed his chin which hadn't been shaved since the morning he was last employed in Tampa.

"It's a good story, though." He told the mechanic. "I'll mail you a copy when I'm done, Peter."

"I'm too busy to study the past again, kid. I lived it. Watch the rest on a documentary channel and stay amused in funny pages."

The next morning, Jason grabbed a cab to Mr. Price's garage on Eastway Drive, downtown Troutman and hoped he was a real mechanic.

"You're in luck, kiddo. Had the matching parts in the warehouse. So I fixed your Jeep and it's ready for the Commonwealth State."

He walked around the vehicle, touched the paint, checked his face in the side mirror and massaged his mustache with pride before he offered a price.

"Good runner since the radiator has become smokeless, huh, Laramie?"

"A writer has to have wheels to track down stories, like John Boy."

"Would you consider selling this Jeep?"

"Nope." Jason handed him cash for parts and labor.

Suddenly, he looked down into the passenger's seat, and like some miracle the typewriter was repaired, too. Jason pressed ASDF, which functioned smoothly as if it did inside the factory, years earlier. With a repaired Jeep, he had five hours until the first pitch of the World Series.

***

Monday night, he reached Skyline Drive. Compared to the heat he'd left behind in the Sunshine State, the brisk air of the Shenandoah Valley felt like opening a refrigerator door in October when he climbed from the vehicle. From what he'd watched on television and in photographs, up close and personal, was the only way to see that part of Virginia, abstract and pure. Naturally, elegant, made by God. Jason had never witnessed mountains so serene, earthly and rustic, like a sour apple smell covering the ground after a cold thunderstorm.

THE INFLUENCER

Jason's grandfather, Harvey, married Annanetta and had two boys, first Weston and then his father, Victor. The Army moved Harvey around the countryside often, transferring the soldier from Ft. Drum to Ft. Leonard Wood to Ft. Campbell to Ft. Hood then finally, in 1974, he proudly retired after twenty years, where he exited as a First Sergeant at Ft. Bragg, North Carolina. Later, they moved to High Point, North Carolina, where Weston and Victor graduated from high school.

From the pictures Jason had in a family album of his Uncle Weston Laramie, a tall and handsome man, held a defined jawline and was born with a cleft chin. He sported a thick mustache, dimples, and shiny dark brown hair. Jason's mother said Weston was as fascinating as he was good-looking. His father said he saved every penny he ever made. Weston was an amateur boxer, famous as a street fighter, they said. At eighteen, he kicked a ten foot basketball rim with his right foot and impressed recruiters at High Point University. Gifted with gab, Weston had talked his way through anything, parking tickets, social events, car deals, and even held a part-time job in real estate, and that was most of what Jason knew about him from his nosey mother. His passion was to make wine, the kind found at weddings.

Top of his class in '74, his scores rang the bell of a number of colleges and especially with Harvey's brother, Dr. Elmer Laramie, a viticulture professor at the University of California, Davis. The summer after high school, Weston hopped a bus in High Point, headed for Davis, California, where he was introduced to winemaking and the Japanese language, by his Uncle Elmer.

After college, he bought a home in the small country town of Mount Jackson, Virginia, and started with the first vine and row and a few rose bushes. The man was well liked by everyone he met, that is, other than his brother, Victor, who hated anyone successful and had a few dollars to spare.

Jason's mother once spoke of how people disapproved of Weston dating a Japanese lady, Sorano Tanaka; one of the sweetest people this side of Hollywood. But his mother also said Sorano was the most beautiful lady she'd ever met.

"What happened to them?" Jason rolled thoughts through his head.

His mother told him how Sorano's business propelled her into television and radio. She was a delightful woman, dedicated to her career as an upscale restaurant designer, just like Weston had poured his life into winemaking. Business, not family, was their similarity; "getting the early edge in life," was their divide. Sorano, wealthy, beautiful, and social, warmed his uncle's heart from first sight.

Weston, on the other hand, was raised as a military brat, hopping from one military post to the next. When it came to love, Weston and Sorano were young and wild about each other. Danced on weekends. Swam in the river afterwards. They traveled between North Carolina and Virginia, trailing onto Long Island on holidays; a relationship rich in acceptance, they were inseparable and dynamic. Wherever Sorano was, Weston was beside her. Not everyone approved of an American with a Japanese lady in 1977. Traditional values, in the Bible belt, and even on Long Island impacted their love life.

Jason could never pull their whole story from his mother. Were they engaged? Why didn't they marry and have kids like a normal couple did?

When Jason saw an old photograph of them at Monticello in his mother's family scrapbook, he set out to investigate their relationship.

Jason's uncle had been absent from family reunions since he was born. His heavy workload and extensive travel kept Weston in shape in the vineyard. He'd heard a hundred stories about his travels to France and Italy from his mother and father, who spoke of all the stickers on his old luggage bags, places he'd been and his passport was stamped over twenty five times by the time he was thirty-two.

Jason's mother, Iris, the nosiest person in the world, had an exceptional gift for gossip, and if he didn't know better, he thought his mother had a secret crush on her brother-in-law, just like lots of other women did.

Followed up with his grandfather to confirm all he'd heard was true, a man of mystery lived, and the story made Jason curious, especially as a writer. If Weston's stories were true, he would be compelled to write down what his mother said and gather his own observations, in time and in person. She knew a great deal about writing, having been a columnist for a local paper in Greensboro, North Carolina for a decade. She had turned Jason to God and to his God-given talents. Thus, journalism was in his veins. When Weston heard Jason wanted to become a writer, he mailed a typewriter from New York City to High Point, North Carolina for his nephew's sixteenth birthday, the same one Peter Price had repaired. It was the one he worshipped in the passenger's seat. If his uncle meant for his gift to piss off his father, the plan worked. Jason's father hated the machine because the clicking interrupted his military television shows.

Jason's high school English teacher thought his work had merit, though. Many of the stories he'd written were about Weston and Sorano. No one else. His uncle had looks and charm. What happened? Why did he live alone?

Two

"Welcome to Shenandoah County"

From his home, the bedrock of the Blue Ridge Mountains, tall and wide, towering from golden mountain to golden mountain, lured people with cameras, they said, formed by molten magma and solidified, rolling into the sky, stretched like clumps of dough on a chef's table. Green valleys of spring became harvest in autumn, like footprints underneath God's sovereignty, which stood evident to everyone, like pyramids did in Egypt. Full and meandering were rivers and streams, filled with bass and trout and big green frogs, too. Lakes were home to ducks and geese, alive in their natural element. Land where the game occupied valleys and hillsides, made Shenandoah County a desirable place from the first settlement until now, a place of multi-culture and diversity. Native to modern times, the area had less than a thousand people who were blessed with spectacular views across the countryside, in that part of Virginia, where they met, fell in love, and raised their families.

Land only God could have shaped with His fingertips, Jason thought as he crossed into Shenandoah County. As he drove through the winding country roads to his new home at Andy Oliver, he was reminded of a relevant slogan, "Virginia is for Lovers," and looked forward to meeting his amazing uncle for the first time. If luck would have it, for him, at least, he would uncover the story he felt honored to write for Hunter and Hughes.

When his feet splashed water across the soil of the Commonwealth with great anticipation in October 1999, it was truly autumn, the landscape was yellow with maples, green with loblolly pines, golden brown oaks and colors of dark red were stunning, and many other trees were unknown to him. Redbuds, hollies and apple trees outlined his uncle's property, all in all, Jason was surrounded by beauty in the Shenandoah Valley. Giant mountains appealed to travelers, filled with earth tones and beaming warm natural light touched the golden hillsides first. No better season to visit Andy Oliver Vineyards, than in the fall, to toast a glass of wine with him.

Soon there would be more leaves on the ground than in the treetops, and a steady rain blew in from the south the first time he'd witnessed his white two story farmhouse. Blue covered the skyline and puffy cotton clouds rolled above his head for most of the drive. Jason imagined clouds hanging on strings from heaven and on that evening, for him, it was much different than the Florida landscape. He thought about the paintings of Bob Ross and Bob Timberlake and others and why the scenery captivated their canvas. The county was serene where people in larger towns talked of vacationing there and folks in the country wondered what happened in bigger cities, such as Orlando, Austin, and Omaha and the like. Each one envied a different place, a different time, and so did he, a flood of curiosity was unsettling to Jason.

With great uncertainty, he anticipated the role of an apprentice at Andy Oliver Vineyards, traveling by default, which humbled him to pieces. Weston needed his help, he felt. Though his hands were without calluses as most writer's protected themselves in that way, Jason's desire was to work beside him, take it all in, and one day meet the famous Sorano Tanaka. He promised himself that much, but he was there to investigate and later, write about the victims of an international crime, just the thought made him conscious and a better person.

His uncle lived not far from the North Fork Shenandoah River where tire swings hung from large oak trees and sycamores branched out over the riverbanks and where three generations were found swimming and fishing on weekends. Jason had a desire to be among them, in the midst of the sun and fun, hurling himself into the depth of the cold, clear water. His first hope for Weston was that he would become his good friend. His uncle's concern for his whereabouts would be the same as his own parents, he predicted, holding him back from all the adventures and mishaps that were hidden in that part of the mountains.

Without payment or rent required, Weston's back room was vacant, a bit sentient, the one he had built in the early 80s after he had broken up with Sorano, hoping she'd change her mind and return to Shenandoah County. When the wind blew like ice in the winter, the air was cool and fresh, at times, and it's funny what a Tampa writer imagined, but a good place to experience life and write, he thought.

"Each morning, a pot of hot coffee on the stove," he said, "Fresh water existed in hand dug wells, which flowed enough water from the majestic mountains for a lifetime of good coffee, writing and reading books."

Chickens, fresh brown hen eggs, scrambled or fried, beside dark bacon and a gracious slice of ham on a long farm table as well, meaning he was a traditional cook, without fancy pans and pots atop a gas stove and an old iron skillet, one he favored did most of the work in the kitchen, he just knew it. His thoughts were shaped with elevation and fantasy, where fresh air filled his lungs and his calloused bare hands fought the day, but he would have been teasing him to say it aloud. Weston didn't mind a good laugh, though, but not in the beginning. However, brewed humility was his preferred cup of tea and it kept him active. Jason came to realize, he didn't care if he ate or slept as long as he worked daylight until suppertime or when he decided to ring the dinner bell and rest.

After Jason lost his job, half drunk, lined with hundreds inside his palms, sporting a typewriter was a lethal combination for an aspiring writer. Unsure if he'd made the right decision to stay with him or not. However, his choices and friends were few and limited. One option was to crowd himself with his seventeen year old sister on a military post in Heidelberg, Germany under the care of his unpleasant parents. That was not considered.

Some folks said he was crazy to leave the Sunshine State behind. To become a better writer he needed to travel and soak up the clock, see the world, and if he passed on Germany, well, he'd miss the boat on a once in a lifetime opportunity to go abroad and see Europe and date a German tart. Though, unsure, he wouldn't have changed his decision about his trip to the beautiful Shenandoah Valley. Nothing at all. In a town, less than three thousand people reported on the 1990 census and yet purposeful and natural, the place was where he planned mountain stories and listened for the next great whopper to tell to his grandchildren, if he found a wife, that is. Jason dreamed his day job was simple, to feed a horse, stack firewood and tend to the chickens or something of that matter, the Walton's Mountain life perhaps.

TRAVEL LIGHT, TAKE FASTER STEPS

He pulled into his uncle's driveway with one bag of luggage, a baseball cap and a good working typewriter in a cardboard box. When he got to Virginia, he told himself, "I'll buy a newspaper, catch up on current events, and be one of the locals telling stories inside a month."

"Uncle Weston!" He knocked. "Ridge Laramie, you home?" Door eased open.

Most of the town's people called his uncle by his nickname, "Ridge," the only man in the town of Mount Jackson who had hiked the Appalachian Trail from Georgia to Maine in less than fifty-five days, which was something outstanding among any generation and it made him famous in Shenandoah County. His nickname stuck, like a big time boxer or professional athlete, he was notorious. No sooner did he return home from the wilderness than a certain fame surrounded his vineyard. That's when he started to expand the vineyard of Andy Oliver, of which became the reason for this book. His uncle planted his first vine in 1980.

While the rest of the world lived in Reagan's trickle down economy and recession, Uncle Ridge Laramie built barns, planted vineyards, and studied the business of grapes. Later, he made an outstanding wine and it sold and sold. Ridge ordered oak barrels for his warehouse, equipped Andy Oliver with a gravity flow system, slapped on grape labels, and shipped his brand across the country.

An avid baseball fan, Weston didn't care for any team other than the pinstripes on Brooklyn. He had grown up listening to games on the radio and watching Mickey Mantle, Yogi Berra, and a slugger named Joe DiMaggio who was his favorite player of all time. He followed no team but the Yankees. To him, no other team existed but the one from Brooklyn.

In his mid-forties, thick in the shoulders, the football player type, he walked upright, like a true champion. With a giant smile he showed a mouthful of teeth.

"Hey, there's my bloodline, the famous photojournalist from Tampa, Florida." He stood and examined his features. "Get in here. I was in the back organizing your room."

They didn't hug. Awed and feared the legend of Shenandoah, Jason stepped inside the farmhouse.

"Good to finally meet you, sir."

"You look good." He stepped back. "Wait! That long beach bum hair, is that woven into some Jamaican dreadlocks? Should I pull the mop and see? Has it ever met the barber's hand?"

"Don't touch it. It's my magic hair."

"Good luck. Might have a mouse inside of that mop."

He placed his glasses on his nose for a closer look.

"I'll cut my hair if you cut that goatee." Jason hit his arm. "You look like Waylon Jennings, Uncle Weston."

"And you look just like a younger version of your father's fine looking brother."

He hoped that was true.

"This is your new home for a season, James."

He didn't tell him that he didn't want to be there.

"Call me, Jason."

"Well, whatever."

He examined his new room. No pictures. No television. One radio. A flat top guitar signed by Johnny Cash leaned against a chair in the corner, and a handful of classical books and some old vinyl records were stacked on a high dresser. Mattress was soft and fat and the sheets were the color of cotton.

A new computer, printer and white paper sat on a wooden desk by the bed. Other than a white metal bed, a mismatched wooden nightstand and a small, dusty trunk placed by the foot of his bed, the room had a frontier home design. Jason found out later, his uncle meant for the room to be without distraction, a blank canvas, built for a writer.

"Here's a clothes basket."

"What day do you wash clothes?"

"You won't believe this one, nephew." He placed a stack of white towels on Jason's bed. "Dang it! My chocolate maker caught my maid making love with one of my butlers underneath the grotto, where the waterfall makes a loud splash into the saltwater pool." He walked over to the window and his head tilted to the blue sky. "I got so mad that I discontinued my laundry service. Shipped the two lovers back to Hefner, out in Hollywood. Can you believe that?"

He grabbed his nephew's shoulder and laughed until the joke was no more.

"How does a guy as old as Moses catch a glowing blonde each month?"

"Hey, I can't figure Hollywood out. Wash your own damn clothes, Amigo!" He chuckled. "About this room, thought you'd add your own touch, make it a good writer's room. Paint palm trees and coconuts on the wall, have a cool glass of Absinthe, like Hemingway did."

"I'm not a painter." He raked his hand over the top of the dusty trunk.

"Paint a picture on the wall or make a memory of the place," Weston said. "I call Andy Oliver home. I hope you will as well."

From Jason's beautiful hillside window, the view went for miles across the long, wide valley. "I like Andy Oliver. Lots of room to breathe in a country town."

He cocked his head in disbelief. "You don't like it here, do ya?"

"It sucks. There's no ocean. No sand. No beautiful women." He rolled his hands and laughed. "Not much here." He scanned the items in the room again. The wooden walls had nails but no pictures. Drab and dusty, the place was okay and it needed something, a woman's touch.

"Your father didn't tell you this was the Hillside Hilton, did he?"

"Nope. He pretty much, ah, well, he hates you. But my mother loves you, said how tight you are with a dollar and that you'd teach me more about business in a year than any graduate school could."

The warm evening sun made its way into his room.

He stood steady. "You are afraid of good instruction, huh?"

"I can learn more from you than I can from an overrated professor who shouts about journal articles and how lovely his thirty something girlfriend is on the beach, when they stay in Rio for a week, globetrotting on sabbatical."

"Takes both academics and experience to win in business. Any man who sells education short, well, he's a fool, Jason. He's not a leader, either."

"It was my mother, who encouraged me to stay here and a few others."

They found their way into the kitchen, upscale and welcoming, the most elaborate room in his home. Weston poured two glasses of his best red wine, a Pinot Noir, the town fell in love with since the early '80s.

"How's my damn brother, Victor, anyway?"

"He's almost retired from the Army. Three years left in service."

They sat at a long bar and drank and talked about good fishing spots. Talked about his brother, rolled one story after another until he became upset with Victor all over again. Then Jason followed him to his oak bookcase and they spoke of the sincerity of Mark Twain and the modernism avant-garde movement of James Joyce, and had something in common other than knowing his father. Weston returned to his favorite seat at the bar, pointed to the high countryside behind his home and relaxed. Jason felt comfortable, but knew his uncle had a strong temper and had educated himself beyond his reputation as a winemaker. His first meal was brown beans, cornbread and a tomato sandwich. No meat.

"Three more years, huh? Lucky bastard, he was the wiser brother, our father said."

"What about my payroll since I'm a new hire, building a good retirement plan at Andy Oliver, I bet?"

"Payday is on Friday. You'll sleep less here than in Tampa. My golden rule, I don't pay if you are late." He told him with a hard look. "This isn't a nine to five candy striper job."

"Do they still have candy stripers?"

His uncle just looked at him, cracked a few jokes and talked about his uncle in California, how he married a wealthy candy striper when he finished his undergrad degree.

"You look like my brother," he slapped both his shoulders. "And you're growing a mustache, too. For God's sake shampoo that damn mop on your head and get a crew cut." He pushed his shoulder into the living room. "You got whiskers like a Siamese kitten. I'll get you a lollipop from the bank on Friday after your haircut." He laughed, holding his gut. "Some dark fabric has attached itself to your lip, young man."

"I'll have a goatee like yours by Halloween."

"You may need some hair removal gel, like the young girls in the Hamptons who use that stuff on their soft, long legs before they hit the beach."

"They may need some help." Jason rubbed his tanned face, smooth as a volleyball and knew it would be in style soon, if he decided to look like his uncle.

"Well, this house isn't the White House or Martha's big mansion in Nantucket, now is it?"

"Nice place, though. The living room has Japanese curtains." He scanned the kitchen from where he was seated in the corner. "Kinda raw and primitive-like, manly."

"Primitive?" His uncle widened his eyes. "Fine as a room at the Ritz."

"Look at the dust you've collected."

Weston rested his hand over his heart and nodded.

"Part of my famous historical habitat collection. Natural and pure."

His nephew stood in the doorway restless. Was he kidding, and why was he not married with rugrats and a playground in the front yard? He couldn't figure him out, but he was a popular man in the Shenandoah Valley, even as far as Tampa, more people knew him than he did the sportswriter. He'd been hit in the heart a few times over the past two decades, at least, that's what his mother said about him when he was in college.

He owned a country farm, forty eight acres of rolling hills and hardwoods connected to a steady river nearby and logged countless hours amid pristine vines and his evenings were spent in the cellar or tasting room with customers. A nearby road was paved into town, one that was unknown to Jason when he first arrived. For his lack of knowledge on the subject of geography, he was given a map and had a pen to find his way down winding country roads and to town and to the next town, if Jason needed to travel further.

He handled luggage, walking to where he had a spare bed.

"How's the music in this town, radio stations, I mean?"

"We have country and hard rock in Mt. Jackson," said Weston. "We prefer George Strait and Willie Nelson in this town." He snapped his fingers and walked into the living room. "Oh, yeah, tonight, hmmmm...the Yankees and Braves play in the World Series." He ran into the kitchen, plundered through the cabinets, swung doors until he had boxes in his hands. "Got popcorn and peanuts, but no cotton candy." Holding up the snacks, "We're not a carnival ride, kid."

He surveyed the home, plundered and flipped through magazines. Boredom.

"I need to run to town, check things out."

"Yeah, go, test that Jeep in these hills," snapping his fingers louder than he'd ever heard anyone before. "Hey, we're goin' watch the game together, right?"

"Yeah, of course," crossing his arms, "don't eat all the popcorn."

"Do you have a guitar shop in Mount Jackson?"

Weston turned completely around in the kitchen with an empty glass in his hand. "Music shop is on the corner."

Jason stood with his hand on the door. "You don't play a guitar autographed by Johnny Cash, sir."

He turned to his nephew like he'd cussed him out and stomped on his prize grapes. "In this house, we watch baseball, too, thank you very much."

"I didn't see you as the baseball type, Old Man."

"You gotta glove, sonny."

"Nope. But I have written about baseball."

He fell against the wall laughing. "Anyways, we have some time before the first pitch," trying to catch his breath. "I have some work to do in the vineyard, sinking posts and cutting the grass."

"I'll cut the lawn and then head to town."

"The lawn?" He laughed. "We have grass and bushes in Virginia. We don't have lawns or tinsel trees."

"Okay. I'll cut the grass and chop the bushes."

"Deal. I'll work in the vineyard. Glad you can do something."

At sundown, the lonesome streetlight was like a ray of hope with character and contentment in its glow at the farm house. A glimmer of light, the only familiar sight from the city he left behind, of which he became addicted to the post and light and bugs for his thoughts. Three red stained log cabins stood a football field away from the lawn tractor he used for cutting the grass.

The farmhouse was like an island inside the vineyard.

"You have vines that span forever across this land." He took the keys to the tractor. "But not a lawn, huh?" Weston rolled his eyes, ready to strangle his neck. "I can handle it," grinning. "By the way, thanks for having me over."

"You haven't been here long enough to thank me, kid." He removed his glasses and covered his eyes with his Yankees cap.

They worked for a while. His uncle meant to callous his hands, and it happened about the time the sunset and the sweat rolled off Jason's back but the grassy lawn was mowed. Later, his nephew drove to town and bought a few things for his empty room, so he'd have it when he needed it.

"You missed the game."

"It's just one in the morning."

He stood and sniffed. "Are you drunk, townie? Are you taking drugs?"

No answer was given.

Jason stumbled into his guest room. Eyes red as fire, closed with little help, jerked the cover. Ten minutes later Weston opened the bedroom with a mouthful of wrath. The young man was knocked out. With a bright light to his back, his parental silhouette stood over his limp body and he thought of Victor's high school days and found Jason was no different, he told himself. Then the house became dark sometime after the owl stopped hooting and filled his claws from the garden.

The alarm blasted the writer's ears off at five o' clock. Still dark, his uncle rushed into the room. The door slammed, it became personal.

"Get the hell out of my bed!"

His eyes opened. Between Jason and Weston was a cold bucket of water in midair. The thought of a cold river rushing at him sobered him quickly. "Stop it! Damn it!" He shivered under the sheets. "You're crazy, just like Dad said."

"You'll learn, just like my brother did when he came home drunk in high school. He was covered in an ice bucket bath from my father's hand."

A second time, he drew the ice bucket backwards and the metal handle held under his intimidating grip, he swayed with force and motion, then realized it was empty. In a rage, his uncle pulled the curtains back with his unoccupied hand, hoping the sun was up, but it was too early.

"Damn it!" Cold and wet, he sat up straight and shivered in a pool of water and ice cubes, shouting back at him. "You're a nut, man!"

"You're headed to Germany on the next flight out of town, and take your big whiskey bottle with you!"

"I don't have money for an airplane."

"I do." He cocked the bucket again, and threw it down the hall. Metal rattled. Echoed. "Stay with your *Daddy and Mommy*, be a big kid in your Heidelberg treehouse."

"Why do I need to leave?"

"You are a drunk ass punk kid who doesn't take direction, walking through life like it's a damn joke. You're not even a serious writer or you'd take notes and listen."

He slung the last drop of water on his head from his hands. His shirt was soaked, legs turned blue, and jumped inside the bathroom, locking the door.

"I don't need your help," he shouted through the door. "My friend Sherrill will help with the vineyards, and I can hire the Thompson twins, down the street, if I have to rely on reckless boys to work my vines."

"Are you firing me?"

"Your duffle bag is packed, the old trunk is in the back of your Jeep, and it's started, so get, get, get the hell out of here."

In jeans and tennis shoes and a jacket, his nephew raised his hands to surrender. "Let's start over." He walked into the living room fully dressed. His uncle was as serious as a man under deep confession on Sunday. Casting out aggression, his poppy red eyes targeting him the same as his father did when he was under an uncontrollable rage, but he didn't thrash him.

"Here's your hat. Go, get off my land!"

"Alright, yeah, yeah, man." He walked out of the house with his shirt untucked. Mad as hell, he slapped the Jeep with one last word. "You're a nut, man." *Ridge Laramie is crazy.* He told himself.

"I don't put up with foolishness from a brat kid, who is too much like his daddy."

To drive this way or that way? Beach or mountains? Virginia or West Virginia? He thought of his cousin who lived in Hillsboro, near Cranberry Glades, West Virginia or he could turn to a friend who rented an apartment in Virginia Beach. He unfolded the map, one his uncle had pitched on the floorboard, then headed South on I-81, cut east on Highway 211. The sun warmed his face, as he drove through harvested farms and fields spotted with rolled hay, continuing eastward on Highway 522, Jason stopped for fuel at a sports bar in an old Civil War town, Culpeper. Two men talked about a baseball game in a bar. He missed it. The round bartender moved like molasses and said, "Hernandez got the win."

"Rivera saved the Yankees," said the man on the bar stool. "Took it from the Braves."

"Did Clemens pitch?" He asked the strangers, wiping a steamroller headache from his eyes.

They both spun in his direction, rolled their eyes. Disguised perhaps? Well, he wasn't a huge Yankees fan to begin with or was it that he was late for the game and dodged rules?

"Heck of a game, kid, you should have seen it," said the bartender. "What's your name, son?"

"Jason Laramie."

Two guys spoke low to each other.

"This Laramie kid doesn't have any money to bet on the Braves tonight, Tony."

"Here's twenty-five grand," he slammed his bet on the counter, "says the Braves swept the Yankees in the next four games."

"I stand corrected," the bartender held the money. "I'll keep the money in the back until the Series is over, boys. You win, Laramie, you take fifty-grand home. Deal, boys?"

The writer spent the next four nights at the sports bar, shirt sweaty and nervous, pitch by pitch. By the third night, he was down three games. The Braves had to win the next four games before he could recoup his money.

Jason rented a room for a few days in Culpeper to divide his differences and hoped the atmosphere was clear back at the vineyard. By Saturday at five in the morning, Jason lost another thousand trying to arm wrestle his money back. Through the glass window he could see his uncle, gripping a bread roll in one hand and a fork in the other, stuffing his mouth. He knocked.

"Uncle Weston, I can see you." He tugged and pushed on the doorknob and heard the lock rattle. "Open up."

"I can see you. Selling Acapulco Gold or are you drunk?"

"Unchain the door... please. I'm sorry. I don't do drugs!"

He chuckled from the kitchen, finished the water first and cleaned his food.

"Thought you'd be a Heidelberg drunk and raising your right hand to Hitler."

"I need to work."

From outside, he felt the warmth of the fireplace, the first of the season for him, and smelled the fresh, salty bacon. His profile was all he could see when he looked over his shoulder and went back to eating.

"This is a winery business." He rolled his kitchen chair back. "We work, kid. Run along, get back to your cocaine crowd in Tampa." He walked over to the door, strolling reluctantly.

Reached in his shirt pocket, withdrew a picture, and pressed it to the glass of the door. "Who's the Japanese lady in the picture with you?"

"Did you steal my picture? Drunkard and a thief."

The writer stood with his hand against the glass. "Found it in the dusty trunk, stacked under dozens of postcards and letters from Japan and New York City." He raised his voice. "Can you let me in the house .....please?"

"I haven't spoken to her in years."

Her face brought back too many promises.

"She's too good for you, anyway, Uncle Weston." He grinned at him, grinned as if he had the upper hand. "You are too old to catch a lady like that again."

"That's bologna. Still got it all like Bogie and Bacall."

He unhooked the door as Jason held the picture. Weston snatched the picture from his hand as fast as the hammer fell on a wooden mousetrap and placed his glasses on his nose. Sat and examined other pictures in his living room, curling a smile on his face and laughed to himself. What he prized more than anything, he held in his possession.

Jason told himself a good story should be brewing.

The writer unpacked while his uncle was lost in the picture, before he changed his mind. He sat under a lamp with a good cup of coffee and munched on crispy bacon, leaning back and stretching his arms in the kitchen. Jason planned to make it his home, at least for a while, until his assignment ended. The writer hoped to hear more about the lady and finish the dessert in his fridge.

His eyes caught something. "Where'd you get that scar on your neck?"

"I was knocked around in a bar fight."

"Big city boy set these country folks straight, huh?" His uncle closed one eye behind his glasses. "That's the best way to make friends. Get to a new town, start a bunch of trouble."

His nephew didn't say a word. Weston turned his attention back to the picture that fit comfortably inside his palm. While staring at the wall, Jason predicted how memories flooded his mind when the photo hit his hand. Beautiful. Dark eyes. Dark hair. Slim. Full of life.

"I might have overreacted with the bucket of ice water."

"No. I should've shown respect. It's alright." He chewed. "Good BLT."

"My meals haven't killed anyone yet."

Questions rolled in the writer's head about her and him.

"Could the Japanese lady cook?"

"Sorano Tanaka was one of the best cooks in the Big Apple."

Jason smiled and felt compassion for him.

"I've never been to New York."

He kept his eye on the picture.

"This picture was taken in October of 1977. Show me you want to work here and I'll take you to the Big Apple." Weston nodded several times as if he wanted to say something more about her. "Long and beautiful hair. She was envied by women from Shenandoah County to Times Square." His thumb stroked the face in the photograph. "Prettiest woman I'd ever seen," he mumbled to himself. "Ten years ago, I checked each room twice, combed closets, checked the tool box and the trunk for this beautiful photograph, and you've found it. I haven't lived in that moment in twenty years or so."

"She's a lovely woman, you can bet that much." Jason was hungry all the time and chased a chocolate pie with fresh coffee. Roosters crowed. Toasted his cup of coffee as the sun blazed through the window, of which he was not going to be disturbed from his meal.

"More beautiful than any lady I have seen."

Stirred the cloudy milk into his coffee cup and aimed his spoon at the stove. "How was the eggs, toast and jam? Knew you'd be back today and hungry as a big bear, kid."

"Felt like an uncaged animal at your breakfast table. Lost my manners."

From where he stood in the doorway, the mountains were in peak color. Clouds slid across the sky, west to east, shifting, and slowly dancing. Peaceful. Orange. Brown. Golden mountains. In the distance, the sounds of big trucks rolled freight along the highway.

"Dad said you'd fallen in love with an Asian chick from New York."

"He's always been in my business." Weston hammered his fist against the door. "You work the next three days for free since I had to hire someone to fill your boots while you were in Culpeper livin' it up like a sailor, fighting and playing cards, Victor-Jason."

"That's not fair. I'm broke. Not a dime to my name."

"They said Tony bought a yacht betting against some dumbass kid from Florida."

The writer shaped his ball cap and followed him to the front porch where he loved to stand as an overseer and gaze at what he'd built, he predicted.

"How'd you know where I was staying?"

He sipped his coffee. "You called your father, kid." He leaned against the post, with a toothpick in his mouth. "My brother cussed me out for kicking you out. "I'm worried sick about my son, Weston!" he shouted. "Hanging up on him was easy." He turned toward his nephew, "You one of those mama's boys they talk about on that Jerry Springer channel?"

"No, not me. Ha-Ha-Ha." And then he was curious, to understand a question his parents never knew, so he asked him, "Did you consider Sorano as a wife?"

He sniffed. The sunshine had a wonderful glow behind the mountains. Grabbed his sunglasses and keys, glancing at his nephew, back and forth, still, sighing, and turned without an answer.

"Get in the truck." He slammed the door and drove to the vineyard. "You'll work alone if you ask too many questions."

"That's my job as a reporter, to ask questions, you see, find out the facts."

Turned on the radio and gave him an evil eye.

"Did Top Hunter send you up here to hound me?"

"Of course, he did." He lifted his chin.

"About the murders, I bet, for a good story?"

Hurt. Mind fogged. Raged on the inside.

"He sent the best writer to Andy Oliver."

"You need to be in Savannah beating down Mickey Starr's door for answers and not bothering me."

Jason rolled the window down, refreshing and cool, air hit his face. Clammed up.

"Do you miss the Japanese lady?"

"I miss her dearly."

"How'd you meet?"

"Met in High Point, North Carolina when the Yankees played the Dodgers in the '77 World Series. Hell of a game, too. She loved Virginia more than North Carolina. Loved the mountains, hiking trails, and mostly the migratory birds, soaring through this big valley," he said while parking the truck.

"You mean, she loved the fall of the year?"

"When the geese fly south, that was her favorite time of the year."

"You can see the geese better from Mary's Rock atop that mountain, part of the Appalachian Trail, if you ever want to hike it?"

"We could drive it, old man?"

His uncle laughed. "You drive the Blue Ridge Parkway and hike the Appalachian Trail."

Later, Weston scooped two mason jars with ice and poured orange juice over the ice, sliding a slice of orange on the rim of the glass. Appreciating the extra steps that Weston took to make him feel at home, Jason held up the jar by the handle.

"Can we drive the Blue Ridge Parkway sometime?" Toasting his mason jar to Weston, the jar must have been placed in the ice box the night before to be that cold to the touch at lunch. "You can tell me about Moby Steel, Raymond and Myrtle when we drive."

"They were great people until they turned against Andy Oliver. Something persuaded them, though, money perhaps or the promise of money?"

"How did they double cross you?"

He never told his nephew. Instead he had another plan.

"Here, my boy," walking through rows of vines. "Let me take you to see Andy Oliver Vineyards and some of the gang. I'll tell you about that famous pub in High Point, the one where I met Sorano and she couldn't keep her hands off of me."

"You wish."

"I like my version over hers."

By the end of the day he'd been introduced to the winemakers and the friendly viticultural team in Mount Jackson welcomed him aboard. Everyone was friendly except Sherrill. The oldest employee, the one with sparse gray hair atop his head, touched his face and head often, turning his tiny hands inside his wiry silver beard and kept to himself. Sherrill Taylor made Jason repeat each name, important and meaningful, names of those from each department before he was allowed to sample wine or take a three hour tour. Andy Oliver meant the world to Sherrill and so did Weston, he'd do anything to protect the winemaker, a rare breed among social circles.

As the winery grew, expansion came and more workers were added on Easter Sunday in 1998, learning customers and standards until Sherrill was satisfied with their knowledge and behavior. Weston had hand selected all fifteen workers, not based on experience, but on their traits and behaviors. Four-hundred and twenty-one applications were combed by Sherrill, and it was said, the last three workers had waited two years to work for Weston Laramie. He was far more admired than Jason knew, so each day he learned something new, gaining an endless respect for his uncle's rapport with people. From the first week, he discarded every negative word his father told him as a teenager about Weston Laramie. Later, and within his first month, Jason realized being at Andy Oliver was time well spent and he'd wasted years listening to his father. None of it was the truth. Jealousy burned through Victor's veins and his adversary was Weston, and he knew it, too.

"Despite what happened in the Dominican Republic, the best of my life is poured into Andy Oliver." Weston's voice was broken, eyes were dark but sincere, and in that moment, he had an unforgettable, and rare vigor in his face.

After a short time, Weston felt Jason had earned the privilege to spend the day in the largest tasting room in Virginia, a spectacular place to sample reds and whites and learn, and his nephew favored the Moscato over the others. The sweet flavor caught his attention over the rest of the bottles and made people laugh, something he'd missed in Tampa with Becca, and he felt like family.

His first introduction to what Top Hunter and Becca already knew about Andy Oliver, known as the best wine on the East Coast. That day, uncle and nephew, mentor and student rode the burgundy hippie van for the first time together back to their house as the thunder rumbled and lightning cracked along the mountaintops, and the sun fell behind a dark curtain of mountains.

Later, after two bottles of Andy Oliver, Weston spoke of how he met Sorano Tanaka and they laughed until they cried, glued to story after story. Then, they became friends, he spoke of the two Irish brothers who owned the pub in 1977. The murders were never mentioned. More admiration grew inside of Jason. Friends.

The next day, Jason trimmed and styled his hair. Weston grinned. His nephew was unsure if he was pleased or not, because the haircut did not take place inside the town barber shop where Weston parked his van. His nephew walked next door to the beauty shop, while Weston and a gang of veterans left him a gift inside his Jeep.

"What do I need with a six pack of nail polish?"

Men were bent over on the street laughing.

"It's a new wave of grooming, Jason," said one man from the barber shop.

That night he painted a flower on Weston's van. Even.

Three
The Irishman's Pub, 1977

The powerful Yankees team from Brooklyn won over one hundred games by October and made the World Series in 1977. Because of a sign he read, **We love baseball as much as beer**, so without delay, Weston rushed inside the crowded pub and found a vacant table with two chairs.

His uncle said, "Other than Yankee Stadium, there's no better place to watch a baseball game than The Irishman's Pub in downtown High Point, North Carolina."

At the same time, streets were packed with fashionable women, dressed to the nines, strolling in earth tone colors and stylish suits, drawing crowds of people as they walked by the shops and store fronts. Men drooled in admiration and imagination, in a town humming with culture and beauty, following his hunger, Weston Laramie was in the midst. Large crowds packed the streets for the High Point Furniture Market, where companies made bids on furniture, fabrics and anything related to home decor was bought and sold. Fabric designers and sales reps mingled with the locals to relax and grab a bite inside restaurants after hours. Long limos. Luxury vehicles. Sports cars. Small buses. The Market brought big sales and the town boomed and busted at the seams with people from all walks of life, together for less than a week.

In his early twenties, long before he was known as a legendary hiker, Weston Laramie combed his long, sandy blonde hair with a colored brush, and dressed in bell bottom jeans, spent his extra time at the same table with his close friends Frank and Emma. She'd been sitting on Franks' lap for much of the evening.

Emma winked at Frank, then he stood, buttoned his thick green Army jacket and for him, it was the signal to leave.

"Emma wants to be a mother," said Frank. "What can I say?"

She leaned on Frank, tugging on his arm and shirt.

Weston stood and threw up his hands.

"Come on!" shouted Weston. "Who walks out during game five of the World Series, anyways?"

"The Yankees are getting their ass handed to them," said Frank, who emptied his mug. "She wants me. Sorry, Wes, duty calls when the Yankees are behind."

Frank Wagner held open the pub door for Emma. The door swung open, wide, smoke fogged the room, from cigars and cigarettes, when Frank and Emma left. Then, Weston waved to his friends, who complimented him often as friends do. He knew Frank well enough to say he would join the Army by Thanksgiving. With his eyes on the entrance, a thin and radiant Japanese lady stepped inside the pub, a bit uncomfortable at first, and her dark eyes were hunting for a chair. Only two seats were left inside the pub, and they were at Weston's table. The man stood and acted cool. Then, out of the blue, Weston waved her over like he was part owner of the pub and knew her from college or somewhere else. In a surprise, her tiny hands waved at Weston laughing as if they knew each other. He turned his hand to the vacant seat beside him.

She politely accepted his suggestion.

"Koko ni seki ga arimasu," said Weston as he stood beside his chair.

"I'm Irish, sir." said the lady, stretching her smile. "I'm not Japanese."

Weston liked her from the start. He predicted she was in her mid-twenties.

"I'm Japanese, young lady." said Weston, who took her coat.

"This is a great view of the game. You speak Japanese well."

"Certainly," he said. "Watashi ga yarimasu. Why, yes, I do."

"Now I have a man to speak in my native tongue."

"What's your name?"

"Sorano Tanaka."

Instantly they'd become friends, he was damn happy and satisfied, with less time being spent watching the baseball game than he'd originally planned. They were hung up in conversation as if they'd studied Japanese together in college.

His hand raised when she mentioned her name.

"Of the sky?"

Her thin arms touched his shoulder each time he spoke her own language and she leaned on him, something unlike females of her culture did in the 70s.

"Yeah," her mouth dropped, "Of the sky." Amazed, she stared into his sky blue eyes. "How do you know what my name means?"

Leaning in close, he whispered something.

"Chichi wa watashi ni kotoba o oshiete kuremashita."

"Your father is a wise man to teach you about Japanese culture."

"What's your name?" Her head leaned toward him many times.

"Weston Laramie."

She covered her lips with a napkin when she laughed and told him her middle name. Her face was pale, like porcelain, and in a tender way, blinked her colored eyes at him. At times, the crowd was wild, just like in most professional sports and it was no different in High Point. She held her long black hair to the side of her face. Black. Shiny. Straight. Remarkable. The way she softly rolled her lips around after she had spoken, gained his attention, and he became excited the more questions she had for him.

"It means western town," her mouth turned into a wide grin. "Studied Old English myself, Laramie."

The crowd stopped talking, glued to the broadcast when the star of the Yankees stepped up to the plate and positioned his foot into the batter's box.

"My favorite catcher is at bat," she screamed at the television, "Come on, Thurman Munson!"

"Munson," said Weston, "He's from Akron, Ohio. Good player, too."

They talked between pitches and during commercials, spoke of baseball and travel and how long she was in High Point. Sorano sat on the edge of her seat, watching Don Sutton shift into the stretch position, pitched one ball, cutting low and inside. Thurman Munson swung.

"He hit it!" said Sorano, her hands raised above her shoulders.

Patrons in the bar stood to see the ball fly long and far, even Dodger fans watched the television with curiosity. Sorano locked arms with Weston and through her eagerness, she jumped, cozily hand-in-hand, wrapped close with her new friend. He did the same.

"Good hit." Weston's feet left the ground.

"It's out of the park!" screamed Sorano. She hugged him as if she'd known him all her life, from school, from work, from somewhere else. Everyone calmed down and took their seats when Munson's feet touched home plate.

"We needed that one," Weston told her.

She was a true fan of baseball, holding her hands together, and shaking her legs in excitement.

"Good left field shot," said Weston. "Munson is a Hall of Famer in my book."

She released his left arm when Munson tipped his hat from the front of the dugout. Weston didn't mind being close to her, close enough to kiss, and smell her sweet perfume, or gazing at her face either.

"Reggie Jackson's up next," said Sorano. "He's a lefty, like me."

"The pitch is belt high, Reggie," announced Weston. "There's the swing."

Sorano stood and grabbed his arms and backed up two steps, more strength in her comfort and trust toward him than with the first homer.

"It's going, going, it's gone!" she shouted.

The baseball was blasted over the right field fence.

She hugged him again.

"Out of the park, Weston, that's two in a row!"

Fans were elated. Dancing, jumping, and shouting around their tables. Drunk. Happy. Friendly. The place was a madhouse. The entire pub rocked in excitement, more Yankees fans than Dodgers occupied the pub, in motion, too. For obvious reasons, Weston didn't want to be anywhere else. She high fived tables of people she didn't know, new friends and old buddies of Weston's, smiled and drank in celebration. Some from college. Some from work.

"It's back to back home runs." Her lungs released a deep sigh of relief.

Every time a homerun was scored Joe Kelly sold more beer.

"Sorano, I could use a beer to celebrate."

She nodded her head after they settled down.

"Me too. Something from Sapporo, Japan, please?" catching her breath, seeing her hometown play well in the World Series made her thirsty after she finished her water. She leaned on his shoulder. "Japanese beer reminds me of my family and friends in Tokyo."

Weston stood and flagged the red headed bartender, who was a longtime friend, the owner, one of the Kelly brothers.

The old man shuffled around in a green flat hat and green shoes and quickly acknowledged Weston's hand above his head. He was being served by the Irishman himself, who raised his thumb and nodded about him being with a pretty lady.

"Could you put two bottles of Sapporo on my tab, Joe?"

"You like Japanese imported beer now, Laramie?"

"I love all beers equally."

"I bet you do, Laramie. I bet you do, 'cause of the lady on your arm, Weston, huh?"

"He's a smart man." Placing her hand inside Weston's, she raised her arm over her head, straight-faced and winked at Weston. "Lovers for life, Weston. It's official." She told the men.

Joe and Weston laughed as much as Sorano did.

Did she smell my cologne and go crazy? Weston thought.

The pub owner grinned at Sorano's blissful face over his shoulder and her next words were to Weston. The lady, natural and pure, sat up tall and with great confidence, and spoke to him, still hand in hand.

"Dha mugai fuar le do thoil." said Sorano, who laughed at him.

Joe Kelly took off his flat hat and placed his cover on his chest.

"Weston, at your table is a keeper, sonny boy," he said in an Irish accent. "Not all women are elegant and smart, especially the ambivalent ladies you have brought here." He turned to Sorano, and said, "Beoir bheorach fuar le do thoil." The bartender tipped his hat. "Two cold Japanese beers, coming right up and they're on me, Joe Kelly style."

Joe Kelly walked behind the bar, stared at Weston and Sorano and told his brother, Jim, from Dublin, Ireland about Weston switching beers. Jim laughed over the noise of the customers, his twin brother shuffled across the room, dodged people, and rushed two beers to Weston's table to find out for himself if his brother was a lunatic and to see the Japanese lady up close. Jim had to see it with his own Irish green eyes.

The old bald Irishman, Jim, sat the beers on the table and removed his checkered green flat hat, in honor of Weston's new friend and prepared his lips for a comment.

"An bhfuil sé fíor go labhraíonn tú mo theanga?" said Jim Kelly.

"It's true." She lifted her beer high. "Next time we'll have a pub crawl, Kelly."

The old man's jaw dropped, he twisted his head at Weston, who shrugged, and Joe Kelly raised his hand above his waistline, and said in a low, deep Irish accent, "The lady drinks here anytime she wants to pub crawl, Weston."

Jim and Joe stood at Weston's table.

"They'd love her in Dublin, Laramie," said Joe Kelly, who wrinkled his round face and scratched his hat when he laughed. "But she's an honorary Colleen too, who is too good for your life, Laramie."

Weston found out she was fluent in Gaelic and Spanish, along with Japanese and English. He needed to know about her.

Disappointed in the team from Brooklyn, she rolled the ends of her hair in the last two innings and accidentally used the "F" word. Weston grabbed his stomach when she let it slip and nearly fell on the floor. One home run from Munson, two homers from Reggie Jackson and an extra run wasn't enough to close the gap as the hot Dodgers claimed the fifth game.

"It was good meeting you, Sorano Tanaka." Weston hugged her neck in a gentlemanly way. "Enjoyed the night with you and I hope you did as well."

In a soft sweet voice, she said, "Well, are you going to ask me out to watch Game 6 at this table?"

"Well, well, then, how about we have an official date, right here, at The Irishman's Pub for the sixth game?" Weston's eyes sparked with an interesting fire of hope. "I know you'd like to see the Yankees win big tomorrow, how about that date, Sorano?"

"Watashi wa sore o watashi no yorokobi da to omotte imasu."

Sorano answered in her own language, the top of her head was under his chin, lifting herself under his eyes when they stood, being crowded in the ninth inning as people pressed them close, and he held her hands inside his jacket. Somewhere amid the nearness escaped a fresh, cool smile only inches from his face, optimism erupted, and not because of the Kelly brother's words, but in her desire to be with him.

A sizable tip was placed on the table for Joe and Jim, who were still fascinated by Sorano's knowledge of the Gaelic language and when they walked near the door of The Irishman's Pub together, Jim said, "Weston, you will do well with her." Joe spoke close to his ear, in private, said, "Love needs you both."

"He's already in love," Jim told his brother.

Still dark, Sorano scanned the parking area and noticed luxury vehicles parked in front of the pub.

"Look," said Sorano, "there's a new burgundy Kombi van," with her hand in the direction of the vehicle. "I've always wanted to drive one of those hippie vans."

"Let me see your hand."

Under the lamp post was where he cupped her hands.

"What's this?"

"It's the key to my home."

He blew his cool breath into his hands and looked away. The man held his laugh in as long as he could behind his hand, then a grin expanded on his glowing face.

"This is the key to my hippie van, now go drive it."

"The burgundy Kombi belongs to you?"

"Let's go for a ride, gal." He pulled her arm.

"Well, Weston," running ahead of him, "let's cruise High Point."

By the time Weston finished the sentence Sorano was ten steps ahead of him, distancing themselves from the curbside of The Irishman's Pub, headed straight to the Kombi van. That lady spent half the night chugging around High Point, up and down rolling streets, handling winding country roads with ease. Then racing down West Green Street, West Russell Ave, past the university area where Weston spent his college days "as sober as a priest," were the words he used with her. That was until his Uncle Elmer introduced him to the art of winemaking in Davis, California, one hot summer in the mid-70s. Weston dropped her off at her hotel lobby. She promised to meet him after work at The Irishman's Pub for the next game. He held her face in a long intimate kiss. She didn't want to let go. Weston left about two in the morning.

Tables at The Pub were packed with baseball fans for Game 6. Weston arrived early to claim his favorite table and calm his nerves with a pint, where he had more questions and time to pace his thoughts.

Yankee fans booed Steve Garvey, who tripled off Mike Torrez in the first. Weston waited at the same table where Joe Kelly and Jim Kelly teased him when they saw him seated alone after an hour, deep in disappointment. He checked his watch about the time Burt Hooten walked Reggie Jackson in the bottom of the second. Talked himself out of leaving when Chris Chambliss belted a bullet out of the park to tie the game at 2-2.

By the time the bottom of the fourth rolled away, Weston downed his third pilsner pint. Crowded and smoke filled, packed inside the tight room, he waited in anticipation, and hoped there wasn't a cultural divide between him and her. Beads of sweat rolled off his forehead. Dodger fans turned belligerent with one another, out of control because of the close turn of events. Weston was alone as he turned down offers from single ladies who wanted to watch the game with him. Maybe they want my seat, he thought?

In the fourth inning Sorano walked inside.

Springing from his seat like a runner, Weston rushed to her side, and escorted her to the table.

"Watashi wa gēmu no hotondo o noga shimashita," were his first few words.

"Reggie Jackson, your favorite player is up to bat next," said Weston holding her hand. "You haven't missed it all. There's five innings left."

Side by side, as if they were still seated in the Kombi van or in the lobby of the hotel, she sat next to him.   He massaged her palms.

The next batter stepped to the plate and the crowd drew their attention when they started chanting REG-GIE. REG-GIE. REG-GIE. Clearing her eyes, Sorano stood and screamed for her home team, "It's going, going, it's gone, out of the park."

"Over the fence again!" shouted Weston as they raised their hands in good spirit. Yankee fans stood. Chanted. Cheered. No place was more ecstatic than The Irishman's Pub during Game 6.

"Mr. October did it again!" She shouted, hugging and kissing Weston's cheek.

"That's his first homerun tonight, it's 5-3," announced Weston.

In the bottom of the fifth inning, Reggie Jackson smacked another pitch over the tall fence. The pub turned wild and Joe and Jim loved the atmosphere that baseball brought to their fine establishment.

In the seventh inning stretch, small framed Joe Kelly climbed atop a ladder, legs draped and seated himself in a cheerful mood. Everyone waited to hear the oratory of the owner.

He pressed his flat hat against his chest, and said, "My brother and I gotta share some horrifying news, lads," sniffing. "We're out of brew. No more good beer on tap, the well is dry, brothers and sisters." He poured the last Irish beer into a mug to show his customers the bad news. "Finished the last drop, myself. Just like the captain goes down with his ship, so do I drown with a pint of pilsner."

"What? Boo. Boo. Boo! You suck, Joe. You suck, Joe!" The angry crowd chanted. "Are we really out of beer, Joe?" asked a round man at the bar.

"We're all out of the good Irish beer, you'll have to drink American brew from here on out, lads. I'm sorry."

"USA. USA. USA." The crowd chanted.

Little Joe Kelly was a small firecracker but charmed people, and led the group in "Take me out to the ballgame....take me out to the crowd...buy me some peanuts and crackerjacks...I don't care if I ever get back. Let me root, root, root for the Yankees." The song went on for a while.

Handing out peanuts and crackerjacks was his brother Jim.

Then Joe climbed down from the ladder and opened the American taps, where he played "Taps" over the speakers as if someone had died, pointing at the last bottle of Irish brew, wiping his eyes. By the eighth inning, regardless of what team fans cheered for, Joe Kelly made everyone feel at home in The Irishman's Pub.

In all the excitement of the game the sweet lady from Westbury, New York, wrapped her thin striped scarf around the base of Weston's neck and pulled him close. To his surprise, she kissed him in front of everyone, it was a good one, for his memory bank and lips. He opened his eyes.

"What was that for?"

"For being such a true gentleman, giving me this seat for the World Series," she whispered into his ear, "so the brunette with the big eyes and whisky sour can't befriend you as long as I'm this close."

"Roxanna?" He glanced over her shoulder. "She puts on a red dress for anyone who will keep her crystal tumbler full of whiskey."

"Well, you're a good lad to have around, Weston Laramie." She kissed him again.

Chugging half a beer, Weston wondered what was next.

"Why were you crying earlier?"

"The cab driver dropped me off after work, just to the right of the entrance and I looked up, and screamed when a man on his motorcycle blocked the front door.

"Is he here?"

"I'm not sure. His neck and arms are tattooed, black leather jacket and a black bandana was tied around his head."

Weston stood. "Is he here?"

"No." She turned in every direction. "He has a black braided beard, up to no good, who has no interest in sports." She examined the pub. "Some gang banger redneck stalking ladies and intimidating people."

Weston clenched both hands and raised up.

"I know the man, but I don't see him." Red spotted his face. "That guy was here three weeks ago during the playoffs. This isn't the first time he has harassed a lady."

"The lady in the red dress, I bet?"

"He held her down against her will three years ago. Never got penned for it."

"Help me look around again." Weston was the only man standing. "I'd like to find him, give him a message."

"Sit down, Weston, watch the game."

Sorano jerked his arm several times before he submitted to the game.

"Okay. I'm good, cool, back in the game."

She rolled her thin lips, said, "I remember his bilious grin."

Weston had seen the man she described a few times after he was released from jail. Banned from the establishment by the Kelly brothers after the incident, been in trouble at the pub a dozen times.

"He must be here somewhere."

Weston stopped watching the game for a moment. His face was cold and stern and he walked to the restroom, knowing he'd find the man in a dark alley, toking on a joint or selling weed to some teenagers behind the trash bin.

"No." She scanned the faces of a hundred men inside the pub before she gave up. "I haven't seen him yet."

"How'd you get past him?"

"Three men walked up to the door, they cursed each other and the man rolled his motorcycle around the side of the building, tapped the handle bars with brass knuckles and acted as if he hated the world."

"Did he say anything or do anything else?"

"He drove across the street on his motorcycle the last time I saw him."

Weston lifted the mug to his lips and watched the television.

"Hope the cops get that slime off the streets. I'm going outside for some fresh air."

"No. Let's watch the game, Weston, please?" Flagging her hand at Joe Kelly. "Weston would like to sample your finest American beer, Mr. Kelly."

"That's the Weston Laramie that I know and love, my boy. The prodigal son hath returned," Joe Kelly said in his Irish country accent.

"Yes, he's back. Pour one from Saint Louis and one from the Rockies, please," placing her hand over her heart, "I'm buying his brew tonight."

Joe Kelly threw the towel over his shoulder and chuckled his way behind the bar and poured, turning from the television to the mug and back again. Never spilled a drip of brew, steady as a doctor in an operation.

"That's the kind of date I love," shouted Joe Kelly with a deep throaty laugh. "Ha-Ha-Ha, my lady. I love it. But Weston will never let you pay. I'm sorry, he's just too good of a man for it."

She wrapped herself inside his arms until the bottom of the eighth inning. Sorano leaned forward with her eyes on the batter's box.

"Reggie's up to bat again," she said, grabbing Weston's arm.

The crowd in Brooklyn chanted, so did Yankee fans in The Irishman's Pub, "REGGIE-REGGIE- REGGIE!"

What a phenomenal feat? Reggie Jackson swung, connected and blasted the baseball like a rocket to the moon. Dodger fans were slack jawed. On the other hand, Yankee fans rattled tables and cheered, jumped and shouted as Reggie Jackson belted an eighth inning home run.

"This is unbelievable," said Sorano. "Three homeruns in one game!"

The Japanese lady fell into Weston's arms.

"It's 8-3," said Weston. "Would you like to leave?"

"Let's stay until the end."

Hugging her, Weston was content where he was behind her. Undisturbed. Nor did he speak much in any language. She asked a hundred questions. He enjoyed the closeness more than the answers he'd given to her while they watched the last inning. Tucked away in the sleeves of his coat were her arms, rubbing his chest and arms. People exited the pub in discouragement that their team wasn't atop the scoreboard, but diehard Yankee fans stayed until the last pitch.

All of a sudden, Weston blurted out what was on his mind.

"Hadn't been in a serious relationship in two years or so, how about you?"

"More years than that for me. What was she like, your last lady friend? There's an image in my mind."

Weston didn't spread his humor or sugar coat his words to reflect speculation as much as he squared himself like an oak tree, dry and confident in his capabilities with any woman.

However, rare occasions occurred when he lightened the mood to make someone more comfortable and curious around him.

She was a lady who painted her face with a conservative touch, had jet black hair that shifted in the softest breeze and smiled after each sentence. She had a people pleasing personality.

The Irish pub became vacant, the two of them moved to the large bar in front of the television and he admired her beauty in the light and for who she was, her sweet nature. Weston closed his eyes, covered his face with his large hand. "I loved that Aborigines woman with all my heart."

She squinted her eyes when she saw his grin and realized he lied.

"Weston, I'd like you to be serious for once." She pushed his shoulder. "Ha-Ha-Ha," she laughed. "She was a shortstop, the bat girl type, huh, big boy?"

The Aborigines lover laughed enough for three people, fell onto the bar, face down, and felt his belly move when he laughed. She rubbed his back.

"I loved strawberry shortcake, Abby, I called her."

"Joe Kelly will let you use his phone to call her, I bet?"

"She was an angry lady with a short fuse, anyway."

Weston was stunned to meet Sorano, kind and fun-loving, laughing at his "Abby" jokes, who even laughed at his clean sense of humor. He asked himself, "Why is she hanging around me after two baseball games, anyway?" He didn't complain about it and began to doubt himself. Simple. Romantic. Sincerely. Weston hummed on the inside, fresh and wound up, after a gentle kiss smacked his cheek, like a belt from dodgeball class, and then, he understood what his college instructor meant by halcyon, a word he missed on his final exam the year before Sorano.

Still acting silly with "Abby" jokes, Weston and Sorano were the last customers left inside the pub. They toasted glasses with a shot of Cliff's Old fashioned and sang "One For My Baby and One For the Road," a little Sinatra song they both sang with the Kelly brothers. Not a drop of whiskey was missed as the Yankees celebrated being World Champs. Weston stood and so did Sorano, side by side, he touched her face, and adored his new friend, holding her close. He hoped she liked him. He even asked her when he walked away from Joe Kelly.

"For as long as you will let me, let me, let me, Weston Laramie."

To see if she had a desire to see him again, he spoke.

"Good. What are we doing after the game?"

"The furniture market ended for me today. Our company has a short meeting in the morning. I'm out of High Point until next spring," said Sorano, "Headed back to New York, by way of Virginia."

"Did you plan to rent a car?"

"That's my plan. My cousin runs a restaurant in Mount Jackson, Virginia," said Sorano, who adjusted her coat. "I haven't seen her in years."

"Is it a Mexican restaurant?" He finished his glass.

"Ha-ha-ha." She was coy. "No, Italian, smartie."

"I know the area well," he said. "There's a covered bridge, a good river with fish, and leaves should be at peak color, this time of year."

"Could you drive me in the new Kombi van? That is, if you're not busy, I mean."

"I'd love to drive you to Mount Jackson."

Weston tipped his friends, Jim and Joe, and said goodbye to the Kelly brothers. The two of them were arm in arm walking to Weston's van. All of a sudden she stopped.

"It's him sitting on his motorcycle. He's been waiting on me for hours."

The owner of the Irish pub had built some shelves in his storage room and watching Reggie Jackson made him a bit jealous of the batter. Weston picked up a board and struck the trash can to let him know she wasn't alone.

"Walk behind me." He told her.

The stocky man in a leather jacket lit a cigarette, and in a rush jumped off his motorcycle and walked toward Weston. His dark beady eyes locked on Weston as if he aimed to kill him with his brass knuckles.

"We'll fight," said Weston, taking the board in his right hand. "Just keep the van keys in your hand, whatever you do," he nodded. "So we can get out of here after it's over."

Pushing her toward the van, Weston said, "Hashiro, go. Run to the van!"

They split up. In the back of his mind, he wasn't sure if the lunatic would follow her to the driver's door or chase her, but he did neither. Anger inside the man raged, he wanted to cut

Weston's heart out, take him down, old-fashioned style, one slash at a time, and with redness in his face and eyes, he meant to end him, too.

"Watch yourself, Wes!" She called out to him.

"Yeah, Wesley, listen to your boss lady," said his hubristic opponent. "Be careful, Honey Pie. Ha-ha-ha." He raised his blade, step-by-step, the distance became shorter and shorter, turning the knife under his grip, like he intended to pour hell onto a man he didn't even know, just for being a man. They were the same size, having something to prove, each one. For only one man would gain recognition; the best fighter, an evil and acrid enemy, stood against Weston, and only one man would earn the win. Not always the good man, and not always the best fighter. Sometimes it was the lucky one, the one who could finish the other man with good fortune, pure and true, that was what Weston knew.

Like hot coals on his face, the man's character, cocky and lively, moving as his brother and father did during street brawls and bar fights, became a true reminder to him of how a fool acted, hanging between rage and violence. Weston was prepared and thoughts crossed his mind about other weapons he might have and madness so close to him, coupled with the innocence of the lady who waited for him, and that was enough.

His arduous plan was to draw him closer, far away from the van, and so close that he wasn't a threat to Sorano, yet close enough to surprise him.

"Please be careful." She nodded, tall and afraid, unlocking the door as fast as she could. Her eyes turned to him like a hawk. The engine hummed.

"I'm ready to, honey, baby," The man chuckled in his drunkenness, high as a kite, and he spoke with a raw, sloppy voice, raising his brass knuckles toward Weston and winking at Sorano.

The man paced toward Weston, drawing a long knife, side to side, up and down, slashing into the cool night air. Pills fell from his leather jacket and so did cigarettes, trailing as if bird seed and white sticks dotted the ground behind him and his motorcycle.

"She's a damn Jap lady, man!" The biker shouted, waving his fat Bowie knife, reflecting the only streetlight in the dark alley from the clean silver blade. "And you're a Jap lover! That breaks my heart and I'm kinda jealous, man, and headstrong, too."

The biker spat his cigarette from his lips, wiped his face with his brass knuckles and thumbed a scar above his right eye.

Weston couldn't tell if he was on drugs or just angry at the world for being different than he was. Evil jetted a red tint inside the whites of his eyes.

"She's Japanese-American." Weston sounded as he stood twenty-five feet from a man, who was sizing him up to kill him. God made her that way. He told himself.

"Hippie, are you ready to meet your Maker, you mophead, Jap lover."

"Jerk," sounded Sorano.

Weston heard the van running, glancing out the corner of his eye at Sorano, who slammed the door and her head eased out the window.

"Both of you Japs need to die."

"Is that you who smells like piss, motormouth?" asked Weston, making a dark laugh amid the back alley.

In a slow southern drawl, he said, "Doesn't matter. I'm goin' to kill you, take the van and the fine lady home with me."

Weston gripped the board in his right hand as tight as any baseball bat he'd ever held. The man charged him. Then, suddenly, at full gait, and good balance, Weston pulled and cocked the board, swung with every muscle he had and the lunatic dodged the board and laughed.

"Cut your arm, didn't I, Jap lover?" His opponent stood still when he laughed.

Sorano opened the door.

"You're bleeding, Weston." She had one foot on the pavement.

"Stay in the van!" Weston protected his arm, waving the other hand. His eyes never unlocked from his enemy.

The knife opened Weston's shirt and arm, the top of his shoulder turned red. The man staggered, off balance from a six pack of beer, turning inside his veins, stumbling his steps in a rage. The alley was made of soft gravel, dumped and unpacked, which didn't help Weston's footing as a boxer and batter, at that point. The lunatic adjusted his hat, snug, curled his upper lip until blood dripped and rotated the blade, tossing the handle from hand to hand, tapping the brass against the metal knife handle. The noise echoed. Weston heard the voice of his father inside him, calling and reminding him of his youth.

"Balance and power, son."

The biker swung high at his chest with the blade again. Weston jumped. Sorano stayed worried behind the wheel, wiping her tears and sweating. The board rammed low to the man's leg and downed him. The biker dropped and grabbed Weston's right leg and sliced his pants, missing his heel by only inches.

"Damn you!" The biker moaned, "I-I-I'll kill you. Damn you to hell!" He rolled in pain and kicked, screaming and groaning, "Ooooooo, my damn leg. I'll kill you and her!"

Sorano pounded the door and horn several times.

"Let's go, Weston! Get in, now!"

She gunned the van to where Weston stood, climbing into the driver's seat, he slammed his door. She touched his red arm. He pressed his hand on his wounded arm.

"Yeah, let's get the hell out of here." Weston told her.

He spun gravel, left tire marks, turned curves on Highway 74, racing until they topped the interstate, far out of sight.

"I need to care for you."

He said nothing and just drove. Then she cleared the fat tears from her wet face.

"Looks bad, Weston. Really bad."

Unbuttoning his shirt, he pressed his arm. "Feels deep, but I believe it's okay. Sorano, stay at my home tonight."

"Yeah, sure. Okay." She raised her chin. "Do you live alone?"

"I have a room at my parent's home, in transition now after college."

"What will your parents say when you bring home a Jap lady?" She leaned and laughed. "Honey Pie."

"My brother and parents are in California for two weeks."

"Good." She raised her eyebrows, swaying her head. "You got us out."

Tears were wiped away, brushing her cheeks with his sleeves and they became closer. The time was well after midnight. Nervous and shaking, she sat close to him in the kitchen, removed his torn shirt, rounded shoulders and strong biceps, tight physique everywhere else. Her fingertips pressed his skin, cold and clean at first, then cool, warm to the touch in a short time, nursing the wound with his Red Cross first aid kit. He'd kept one inside his backpacking gear since he'd bought the van.

"Looks pretty deep, Sorano." A small red and white gash was opened.

"You will have a scar. No need for stitches, though." She turned and walked away. "Are you in much pain, Wes?" Sorano queried.

"Not bad."

"Good. Can you take me to work in the morning, mophead?" laughing at him and holding his hand.

"Yes, you Irish speaking Jap-. You're lovely, just beautiful tonight."

She was close enough to smell his cologne. Then kissed him. She sat in his lap for the first time, arms around his neck and closed her eyes.

"We better call it a night, mophead," She whispered, smiling and massaging his shoulders.

The spare room his mother kept clean had low lights, the smell of cinnamon lingered, and kept it comfortable.

"Goodnight, lady."

Later, she woke herself up talking in her sleep.

He handed her a glass of water around two o'clock and checked her blankets.

"I didn't mean to wake you." She held his hand and tugged on his boxers.

"Sweet dreams, Honey Pie. I imagine I'm not the only one."

"Way ahead of you, Laramie."

What a fantasy? He waited a minute until she finished her glass, turned out the lights.

She leaned inside the doorway. Her outfit was flowery black and pink silken, shorts wrapped in lace and her robe covered her legs to the bend in her knee. Legs that had not seen much sunlight, slender and pale. Then her dark eyes warmed his face. After she waved her hand, no more words were spoken and he followed her to bed. Lights dimmed.

Four
Autumn, 1977

Immediately following the morning meeting in High Point, Sorano declined to take the airline out of Greensboro-High Point back to New York City with the rest of her co-workers, in lieu of riding with Weston to visit her family in Mount Jackson, Virginia. Once downtown and settled in her favorite spot in Shenandoah County, Sorano wanted to see the covered bridge she was amazed with as a teenager. She held her camera which was normally used for taking pictures of home decor and sights of New York and Japan, but this time was different for her. Private. Natural. Behind the camera, Weston caught her dark eyes sparkling in the midday sunshine.

For the first time in his life, Weston found himself snapping pictures of birds, flying birds for a lady. As many mountains as he'd hiked in North Carolina, the notion had never crossed his mind to capture the migration of fowl on camera, snapping an Olympus camera was of great value to her, more than him. She coached him on focal point, aperture, and depth of field, a crash course he passed the first afternoon in town.

Her words: "Try in some fashion, from time to time, to include the fall foliage and the covered bridge inside the frame of the shot, this is, if possible, when possible, make sure you snap some leaves in peak color, Weston. Now...um, you are a photographer, mophead."

His eyes sparked when she flirted with him and... there was a kiss or two when she walked within arm's reach and a few hugs and small notes tucked inside his pockets whenever she was close.

She'd assigned him to handle basic tasks. He was in charge of making a photo album full of wonderful birds for her collection, the one album she'd been adding to whenever she visited Mount Jackson, which seemed the same to him from year to year when he saw it for the first time. The beauty of the Shenandoah Valley was etched in her mind as a treasure she couldn't let go of, and for her, it had been that way all her life. Weston knew more about birds and cameras than he did about reading the mind of a woman, he felt. When he finished his photography session, he stood in a pair of gold rimmed, dark brown aviator sunglasses at the entrance of the historic Meems Bottom Covered Bridge, the place she visited more times than she had seen the Empire State Building.

"What are we doing photographing birds and bridges?"

She looped her arm around his thin waistline and under his shoulder.

"Wild geese?" he said. "I have seen geese fly south each year with an amazing spirit of dedication."

"Some of them, the strong ones," opening her arms, "fly up to seventy miles an hour, covering 1500 miles in a single day without stopping. That's amazing to think of for a bird." Sorano dropped her heavy camera until the next flock of geese made their way over the covered bridge. She stood inside the bridge, out of the sun, kissing him until she heard geese honking in the clear blue sky.

"Meems Bottom Covered Bridge, this is your favorite place to shoot photography in fall, I bet?" He hugged her. "I nicknamed you, Gachō ga minami ni tobu toki."

"When Geese Fly South?"

"You know Japanese well, Weston."

"Do you mind if I have this couple snap our picture?"

Laughing and looking over her shoulder, she said, "I'll load an extra roll of film just for you, mophead."

Her eyes danced when he hugged her and kissed the back of her neck, the spot just above the shirt and behind her soft long hair, made her eyes blink.

Standing at the edge of a golden hayfield, longer than a football field, Sorano walked up a gentle sloping pathway and handed the stranger her camera. Within a few minutes their new friend had snapped a roll of film. It was something to be remembered. Walking down a graveled road, Sorano photographed maple trees and large oak limbs, the ones that draped over the roadway made shapes and shadows on the ground. Limbs were captured on her camera and the Willow Tree touched the slow flowing river, more in a shifting fall breeze than any other season. He hadn't known anyone who embraced nature in a small community or handled big business in a large city as well as she did, soaking up life at her age.

Weston mumbled to himself, "She is an unbelievable woman."

With her second camera strapped around his neck, Weston stuffed his hand deep into his pockets. Then, to the north he heard something. They sat on a yellow blanket, her head on his legs, and for the rest of the evening they were propped up to see the northern sky. Happy.

"Sorano, here comes another flock of birds flying south for the winter, to a warmer place, I guess."

"They have a wonderful V formation, don't they?" She held up both hands to the blue sky overhead and waved, as if a reunion was in order with her old friends. "I wonder where they're headed this year or where they make their home when they finally land or get tired of flying south?"

"How did they learn to fly in a V formation?"

She walked over to him, locked arms, standing confident in her blue jeans and green sweater, hair still in a long ponytail below her shoulders, leading him to the Kombi van. Weston was lost when he stared into her shiny chocolate eyes. He fell in love for the first time in a long while. She placed her cameras inside the van.

Hand on his hips. In one swift karate move, she flipped Weston flat on his back.

"Wow!" grunting and moaning. "What was that for?"

Standing over top of him, smiling and surprised.

"I noticed you were falling," she smiled, "falling ...in love so I helped you get there."

He pulled her down to the ground beside him and tickled her.

"I fell in love the moment I saw you walk into The Irishman's Pub."

He'd never spent more than a few minutes of his life thinking about geese or waterfowl or falling in love, but after he met her, his eyes and ears and heart found hope. Something unusual and a cool reminder of what she taught him that autumn. They jumped inside the van.

"There's a bed and breakfast in town," she said, touching his arm as he drove. "I'd like to try the place, huh? I'm hungry."

"Me too. I love them both."

Weston followed her directions to Mount Jackson and was eager to find the bed and breakfast, grab some country cooking and relax.

"One room or two, lover boy?" She leaned against his shoulder, covered her face and giggled.

"The fall of the year is popular here, so we have ....um, just one room left," said the woman at the counter.

"You suggested bed before breakfast, Yankee lady." She laughed as loud as anyone could.

"Are you trying to seduce this Southern gentleman?" asked the desk clerk.

With painted fingernails against his skin, a familiar touch rolled down his spine and he cleared a thrilling knot in his throat, and became thankful for her, saying it more than once. Soft hands pressed his shoulders and neck, massaging each arm as they waited inside the dim lobby and any uncertainty he might've had disappeared when he turned to kiss her. Born genuine in that moment, racing hearts and climbing pulses, it happened, sure as the world. The thought of matrimony crossed his mind, and inside, a furnace of love brightened him, the gentleness of souls colliding, one to another, arrested by their own grandeur. Later, like a fine work of art, he imagined how he'd give her a wonderful life. Tighter with each turn, until the glorious mountains became a gatepost for the moon, together, as if nothing else existed.

Five
End of the Road

The day after Sorano flew home, Weston stayed in Mount Jackson and visited Meems Bottom Covered Bridge once more. Alone. He talked to himself as well as anyone else could, and listened to Mother Nature and spoke to God, while missing her.

"That's a ring-necked pheasant. Crow. Red-tailed hawk. Blue Jay." He named them. "Don't get distracted with the hawk," he told himself, staring into the Northern sky, and said, "Can you hear me, Sorano?"

Three beers later, he stood in front of his hippie van. Then carved a message on a large timber beam - **WESTON & SORANO.**

He carved the last letter into the bridge, which was against the law and he knew it. From the clear, blue sky, he heard honking overhead. Rushing to the end of the bridge, he ignored the less mechanical, and listened to nature, pure and skilled in flight. His life was inspired by her and for her, the honking of geese held his attention in the fall.

"More birds." He angled his head, blocking daylight, needing only a fracture of sunlight to view his target. "Long, dark dots moved across the brilliant blue valley sky, just like she said would happen." Blocking the sun with his hat, in Mount Jackson, he said, "I'll make a home for us here."

He sat in the van with the side doors open and watched what he had heard move closer and closer over the bridge, down further into the wide valley sky, the closer they flew the more he missed her. Then the birds passed overhead. Gone. Headed south like an airplane en route to North Carolina and even further to the Great South, out of the country, perhaps.

"More Canadian geese." He spoke low. Waving his beer can, stretching his arm as if he could touch their heads. Not just a dozen or two dozen honking geese, but he counted one hundred and seventeen geese that day flapping low under puffy cotton clouds. Graceful. Large. Determined.

"Where's Sorano when I need her?" he asked himself. Flapping their wings through the wide valley sky, graceful and powerful, headed south to somewhere far beyond Virginia.

She had coached him well enough to teach a college course on migratory birds, adding a new hobby to his list and left her camera behind for him, too. He expected she'd return for it in a few weeks.

"A goose will live ten to twenty years," he staggered around, speech slurred, and said, "A few of them will make it to twenty-five years of age."

"The large ones are fourteen pounds," said a gray haired police officer. "Son, public intoxication is against the rules in Mount Jackson," turning to his tag, "the same as it is in North Carolina, I bet." The officer was ten feet away.

"Most of the geese," Weston slurred the words, "are seven or eight pounds each, officer." Weston wiped sweat from his face. "You're wrong, Barney."

"Hop in the back of my squad car, loud mouth. I'll educate you about nature."

He took off running, but the policeman tackled Weston in less than ten steps. Other than on television it was the first time Weston Laramie had heard the full course of his Miranda Rights. Face down, pressed on the earth and one eye angled and arms cuffed.

"Wow! Look how glorious, a flurry of birds gained speed," said the police officer after he'd assured Weston as he cuffed him against the patrol car, that anything he said could be used against him. "I can't figure out how these big birds fly so well." He checked him for weapons and contraband.

The officer stuffed Weston's head inside the backseat.

"You can read about them in jail, Mr. Laramie."

"I have a card," said Weston.

"What kind of card, kid?"

"A get out of jail free card from a board game." Weston amused himself.

"They'll take your card and your picture at the station, hotshot." The officer started the car. "Be a good one too, something we'll keep in our office for a while."

About the time Weston was getting locked up, his younger brother, Victor, was trying to reach him to let him know he was an uncle.

"Brother," said Victor, "my boy's name is Jason Weston Laramie. He's a good-looking baby. Hey, Weston, give us a call."

He left a message for Weston at the Mount Jackson B & B, the place he'd rented until he found himself. One phone call was given to Weston Laramie, he called California. His parents were with his brother in High Point when Victor's wife had the baby earlier than expected.

"Uncle Elmer, I need a favor."

"Wes, what the hell have you done this time?"

"Can you get me out of jail? That get out of jail free card didn't work?"

"What? Can you call someone else, damn it, Weston?"

"No. I have only one call and you're my favorite old uncle."

"Yeah, dumbass, I'll get you out. Don't call me old again."

"After I get out of here, I have something private to discuss with you, okay?"

"What's next, did you steal a car?"

Later, his uncle said he'd listen to what he had to say but he only had twenty minutes. So, at a truck stop along Interstate 81 Weston called him at the agreed time.

"Do you think grapes will grow in the Shenandoah Valley of Virginia?"

"You want to grow wine grapes, Wes, build a winery?"

Weston stood positive, rolling dirt in his hand. "This soil is a breeding ground for good wine grapes."

His uncle was a well-known viticulture professional from southern California who advised several of the vineyards in Napa Valley and consulted as far north as western Oregon, where he was an expert in the number one cultivar, Pinot Noir.

"I'll stress to you, there must be a crumbly mix of sand, silt, and clay. Most of all, you must sweat to see grapes on a vine, my boy."

"I can see lots of grapes in this big valley, Uncle Elmer," Weston said, watching more and more geese fly south. The phone became silent. "Hello?" Weston tapped the end of the phone. "Are you still there?"

"Damn it, Wes, I'm thinking, taking notes in my office about the soil in Virginia," he yelled. "Don't bother me when I write. Here's what you can grow in the cool-climate of the Shenandoah Valley. Merlot. Cabernet franc. Cabernet sauvignon. Chambourcin. And Wes, it may take you seven years to produce a product."

"I need to get started soon."

"I'm writing down the good white wines. Hang on? I have studied the Shenandoah Valley for a decade. Riesling. Chardonnay," said his uncle, "And Viognier. Never forget the co-fermentation of Viognier."

"Forget the less economical wines, sir." Weston brushed his hands. "Can I grow Pinot Noir?"

"Grow it! Grow them all. Remember what I taught you. One life, one encounter. Cherish every moment of it and watch out for who comes to town. Some people will copy your craft, Wes."

"Thank you, sir," said Weston, holding the phone close. "Dr. Laramie, I met a Japanese lady, too."

Dr. Laramie ignored the comment.

"Do this before you head back to North Carolina."

"Yeah, I'll do it."

"Open a bank account in Mount Jackson. I'll be flying to Hawaii during Thanksgiving for a week. I'll wire the funds when I return."

"Okay. Thank you. I have one small favor," mumbled his nephew. "Could you get my Kombi van out of the impound yard? Sir, did you hear me, I met a beautiful Japanese lady?"

"I heard everything you said, Wes. I, personally, think being in love is a wonderful idea. Nothing better...but it's the best for you, kid. Bring her to California. Like to meet her. But Wes, I tell you not everyone else will feel the same way. WWII wasn't that far behind us, you know, Pearl Harbor was bad news."

"Thirty years or so."

"WWII ended thirty-four years and two months ago."

"You got the tattoos to prove it."

"There's a big damn tattoo on my back of how many men were lost at Pearl Harbor. Lived in the midst of war and it's hell. My comrades died. Friends, too. 2,008 Navy, 109 Marines, 218 Army soldiers. Plus 68 civilians, making a total of 2403 senseless casualties, bombed by 350 Japanese fighters."

"Why did the Japanese attack Pearl Harbor?"

"Land. Rubber. Oil. Japan needed the Dutch East Indies and more natural resources. That's why I say, not everyone will think it's a grand idea for a young man to date a Japanese lady, even three decades later."

"I'm in Mount Jackson, Virginia, though."

"I have a hearing aid. Heard every damn thing you have said to me. I don't sweat another man's problem. Women or wine. My God son, you've started off on the wrong foot in a town that doesn't even know you." His uncle laughed. "Lucky for you your uncle is a loaded professor and still teaches viticulture on campus."

"Lucky for me, my uncle understands women and money."

Resting his elbow on the phone booth, Weston leaned on the glass frame and felt his uncle would be the navigator and mentor behind the vineyard.

"You get the damn property as soon as the money hits your bank account. I'm a California silent partner now, the details of what I need will be in the mail once you get moved in, plant the first vine and fast. Yeah, for sure, I'll need a small cut for my good investment, Wes. I like a good bottle for dinner on Fridays, too."

Inside the phone booth, Weston became concerned and moved in repetition.

"The bad news," tapping his foot, "two suits from West Virginia are my competition. They want the land to build an eighteen hole golf course, big as The Greenbrier Resort, equipped with irrigation systems and a pool for the women, while the men play rounds. Sir, put the money on a wire, or we might miss the land."

"I'll have my attorney pull your van out of hock. You'll have wheels by sundown. Make us good wine, Wes, will ya?"

"I'll do my best."

"Call me on Friday, Weston. I'll have the money," asserted his uncle.

"Got a few dollars to spare."

"We'll talk Friday. Good deal. I'll let the landowner know it's sold."

In a rush, Weston hung up and could have touched the moon when he jumped. The rookie winemaker clenched his fist and jumped a half dozen more times and hugged a strange lady who was next in line.

"Mount Jackson is getting a first-class vineyard!"

"All I need is another wino in my family, sonny."

Weston left the phone booth, feeling like a champion. Van loaded, he headed south to High Point, North Carolina to load the rest of his belongings. Once home, he called his uncle, boxed his things and turned thoughts inside his young head, and drew up plans for what needed to be built in Virginia. After three days, he returned to the Bed & Breakfast in Mount Jackson. To his surprise, the "FOR SALE" sign on the land had been removed. He feared the two men in suits had beat him to the punch. Making the property their own, planning and zoning would soon see a golf course on the docket, he thought. The 48 acres of land was off the market, for sure. His next search was for the landowner, the agent, and that was Russell Clark, to knock him down, to ask a few questions and to locate his office within town. But the phone just rang off the hook. Weston wondered what had transpired in such a short time.

Three days in a row, Weston slept in his van and scoped out who could answer a few questions about the 48 acres of land on Conicville Road. On the pale evening of the fourth day he caught his own rough image in the rearview mirror. Dry lips. Dark eyes. Bummed out. Long hair. He caught a glimpse of something else; a man whose face he recognized. Russell Clark.

"There is a God," he said.

Weston followed him to an office door. His keys jingled about the time Weston pressed the door.

"I don't have any money for a bum in a hippie van, young man," said the land owner. "Go bother someone else."

"Isn't that ironic? I'm not here to beg," said Weston, shifting in a smart tone. "I'm here to buy something."

"You don't have any money or you'd be in a hotel." The man laughed.

"Who bought the land on Conicville Road?"

"I can't reveal my client list to a bum or anyone else."

Weston pushed him against the door.

"I'm going to ask you once more, who purchased the land we talked about?" He pushed him again. "Was it the suits from Harper's Ferry?"

"You're hurting me!"

Weston backed off as the man adjusted his collar and sport coat.

"A man from California closed the deal and wired the money on Monday morning. I guess that's what you want to know, boy?"

"Was it, Dr. Elmer Laramie?"

"How'd you know?" He nodded.

Weston adjusted his clothing.

"That's my favorite uncle, my other bum partner. I am Weston Laramie. You don't know me yet, Russell Clark, but you will someday." He curled a natural smile. "I'll be on Conicville Road, if you need me, sir. Good day."

"He told me you'd be here early to sign some papers," said the businessman, tapping his watch while he made coffee and offered Weston a plate of biscotti. "But I expected someone in a nice coat and some leather shoes, not a bum in hippie sandals." He made fun of Weston to his daughter, who aimed her long fingernails at Weston. "Jesus, this man doesn't even have a business suit, Shellie?"

The landowner made his way to his office desk and then leaned toward Weston with a sharp smirk. "Carolina didn't teach you to buy a shirt and tie, kid?"

"No. But I will turn water into wine for your pretty daughter, Russell."

"My daughter isn't interested in some bum who lives on a country stream. She graduated from George Mason, huh"" he blurted. "She's not engaged or looking for a man, either."

"I'm looking for a good man." She winked at him. "More cream for your coffee, Weston?"

"Yeah, sure." He walked over to Shellie. "George Mason, huh?"

The landowner flipped a business card in Weston's hand and laughed. Then Weston leaned out the window of his van. "I was here a few days ago looking for you, Russell. Your pretty wife said I should get some sandals and call her daughter for a date and I'll take her up on it now. Little miracles still happen to handsome men in sandals, who need a haircut, don't they, Russ?"

Later, parked on Conicville Road, Weston popped the camper on top of the Kombi van, and counted over a hundred and twenty-one geese flying south in the last hour of sunlight and spotted one groundhog at the edge of the woods. He realized Sorano worried more about money than any other facet of her life, a lady who wrongly judged Weston's theory of "building a business on dedication and a dream," ignoring him on most occasions. All he needed was a small break from his uncle and now he had land.

Under the glorious canopy of twinkling starry sky that hung over the dark Shenandoah Valley, was the place where Weston's prayers were answered and his dream became a reality, destined to build a vineyard in his leather sandals. He moved out of the Bed & Breakfast and bought a mailbox for his property on Conicville Road. As he rested flat on his back the only glow in the valley was from Weston's flashlight, shuffling through pictures of lovely Sorano. Sometime after two o'clock in the morning, his eyes closed, dreaming and hoping, and seeing each building and a team of vineyard workers at harvest time.

The next morning was cool and damp, the sun broke through the pillow shaped clouds, and he stacked twenty-one rocks around a wooden post that formed a small pyramid beside a giant oak tree, which was the main entrance to the vineyard, one without a name. In the warmth of the sun on his shoulders, he walked the winding countryside and became full of ideas, seeing, dreaming, and drawing the stream and hillside at age twenty-one. His first night on Conicville Road. Now, he had one more call to make.

Six
Face the Music, 1998

Two decades and ten days after Weston purchased the land, he called Andy Oliver Vineyards, something happened. Jason's pockets were empty. Not a red cent, not a dollar, and nothing folded or jingled inside his wallet or money bowl, either. Eyes closed, he dropped his long face, it was his father's voice, pounding his ears:

"You ended up no damn better man than me, big loser. All that damn college money was spent on a useless degree. I coulda bought a baby blue '66 Chevelle for the money your mother pulled from her retirement to educate your fool ass. College didn't teach you how to save for a rainy day and it rains every damn day, fool."

The cash advancement to write the murder story was gone.

No doubt Weston was playing the father figure over his nephew and for good reason, too. The man had good intentions to overrule a fool. The drunken days of Jason, smoking and drinking, days of disrespect were remembered by his uncle, a good businessman who kept three quarters of every dollar he ever made in the bank. Jason rolled his eyes on several occasions, discounting his uncle's words a half dozen times over until he was ashamed of himself for leaving Florida, where his aspirations faded, and he ended up dead broke in less than two weeks. As a result, Jason returned to Andy Oliver with his tail feathers dragging in the mud and his gas tank begging for a gallon of fuel. He knocked on the door, humbled, hungry, and one big disappointed photojournalist.

"Well, well, well, Jason, have a seat." His uncle flipped his foot on his right knee. "The great prodigal nephew has returned to Andy Oliver Vineyards."

"I screwed up. Now you think I'm worthless, like your brother and bad for the winery, huh?"

He waved his hands and stood.

"You don't have permission to ask questions here or be a bum." Weston slapped the table. "We need to talk, boy. I mean, a serious down to the damn earth talk. One of those Jason come-to-Jesus meetings everyone is talking about on Walton's Mountain."

"What is it?" Jason fell back, sinking low into the recliner, cocky faced and stupid, kicking up his feet up on his uncle's favorite oak table.

"First, hey, get your damn feet off my furniture." His strong arm jack slapped his muddy shoes from their slated position. "Second, I'd like you to move out and not return. Get the hell out, bud, and that's for good, I mean it and make it quick." He turned off the television in front of Jason's eyes. The room was silent for a few minutes. "We can call each other on birthdays and write kind Christmas cards every other year. Heck, send me a muscle car shirt for my birthday, right?" He said the words without a crack or bend on his stone face.

His nephew shuffled in his seat trying to find a lie to tell him. Something he wasn't good at, anyway. He pressed his hands together in meditation, not a nut case, or a liar but planning an attempt to negotiate a deal or just make it right.

Knowing his discipline was the way it was going to be, was the day Jason's life changed and the day he decided to grow up. With a deep sigh, he was dead on the inside when it came to dealing with his father, the same for his uncle, he predicted.

"What? Weston, you are not serious, man?"

"I have no problem with your work. What little you have done at Andy Oliver, and I graded it decently, but on a curve." His uncle thumbed his eyebrow. "But I do have a giant problem with your attitude. I'd like you to leave before we tarnish our family and new found friendship, for good and right now. Here, you have taken advantage of family boundaries and I'm pissed."

"I'd like to stay on at Andy Oliver, sir." Dropping his head, Jason held his face. "Dad, he doesn't care too much for me. My sister believes in me and my mother thinks I could turn water into Pinot Noir."

"I don't know your sister. Your mother is highly intelligent, Jason, and too good for my brother. Your father and I don't get along, not even on holidays and never will." Weston flipped wood into the fireplace. "We talk once every ten years. That's plenty of conversation for both of us. I hope it doesn't get any better."

His feet hit the floor, flat footed, Jason pressed his hands on the recliner, he had no come back to lie. Everything Weston said was true.

"Uncle Weston, I can't go to Germany. To be honest, I can't go back to Florida because I was fired. My work is to freelance articles with no pay from Andy Oliver. I took a big advance from Tommy Hunter on an article I'm supposed to submit in a year but the money's gone. The Braves suck by the way. I'm pretty much screwed, but I'll dedicate myself to the vineyard until Tommy reads my articles next year."

His fist slammed into the door.

"You're not staying with me!" He spun around. "I'll help you get your passport, if you don't already have one stamped." We'll be out of each other's face and content and say we tried." His eyebrows raised to the top of his forehead, twitching and waiting for his reply. "Fly to Heidelberg, Germany, like nothing ever happened. Just say you gave it a good ol 'college try. Admit you couldn't handle the workload at Andy Oliver and drank up all the profit. Tell your mother, I let you go. No hard feelings because we're family."

"I've screwed myself ....now what?"

His uncle didn't tolerate his brother or his punk kids, either.

"Plus, you'll have to pay the advancement back if you fail to produce a decent article for Tommy Hunter. I know the man, let it be a lesson to you, kid. My old college roommate will not tolerate a goat choker from some slack ass writer, one who doesn't give a damn about his performance or attitude."

Jason lifted his hands. "I'd like to stay here, help update the irrigation system which will prevent any more fruit from dying on the vine. I learned how to handle a better drip system in Florida than you have on this property."

"Bullshit." He slammed his beer into the fireplace. "You're here to freelance, live it up and party. You don't care about irrigation and grapes or what I have built here, do ya?"

"I'm here to work. When can I start?"

"Start?" His face was a stone pallet. "You wasted all your money. Pissed it away on beer and gambling at Parker's Bar, I bet?"

"Yeah. How'd you know?"

"I recommended you come here." Weston took a fast pace around his desk and locked the door. "In case the media stumbles onto the steps of Andy Oliver asking a bunch of questions about my involvement in what happened in the Dominican Republic and the murders, I wanted you."

"You want me?"

He brushed his mustache and stared at Jason.

"Yeah. I wanted an educated man who knew journalism, a writer instead of a lawyer to fire back with expert answers, beating them in their own game and it might have given you some street cred. Tommy Hunter said you're the best in the Southeast. I told him I'd make sure you'd write whatever article he needs published."

Sitting up straight in his seat, Jason believed in himself because of his uncle's story and didn't realize Tommy Hunter was a country boy from North Carolina, and good friends with Weston.

"I'll write it." He stood. "I can't afford to give back the advancement, Uncle Weston."

His uncle poured a glass of bourbon and stood in the doorway tapping his silver tone belt buckle, deep in thought. He'd been burnt a dozen times by friends over the past few years, but he could do without a punk kid. "Did Fred Hughes and Tommy Hunter give you the title of investigative reporter?"

He nodded. "Yeah. Here's my business card." Jason leaned forward. "If the media shows up, I'll tell 'em the *Tampa Bay Times* has a man on the inside and that's the only paper Weston Laramie will speak with today. No more questions, please."

"Good. Will you do that much?" He finished his bourbon. "Glad I didn't waste my time on Ricky Plummer, like my college buddy Fred Hughes said to do, if you didn't work out."

"Well, ummm, it's goin' workout," sliding his hands down his throat, desperate to change. "I'm here, ready to work, let's go."

"Don't think you can handle the media?" His uncle turned and walked through the house. "I'll bet my truck that you can't go a month without being a typical jerk kid, making me think of my brother?"

"I don't need your truck." Jason admired his office. "I'd like to bet you something, though." He turned and faced his uncle.

Weston crossed his arms and squinted, closing one curious eye.

"What do you have to bet?" Weston crossed his arms. "That new Jeep? You lost all your damn money. I mean, my damn money. I paid to get your ass here."

"Your money, huh? Oh, God. So, do I owe you?"

"Not really, kid. That was my insurance to get some work out of you. Tommy said you had more wine tasting events than anyone in Tampa. Plus, kid, there's three reporters outside looking around the vineyard. Take care of them, Laramie."

Cold weather had a skiff of snow on the ground in early November. Jason wore his favorite navy blue coat and dark shoes, nodding. Two days and four hours into his new career, Jason had perfect attendance, his uncle marked the chalkboard and laughed.

"Bet I have something in my pocket that you want?" Jason opened his hand.

"You better not be on drugs."

Handing Weston a stack of postcards and letters, Jason grinned.

"Oh, you found more pictures of my Japanese girlfriend. We had the best of times. God, I miss her."

"She's beautiful. You never told me her name."

"Her name is Sorano."

His face brightened. "My brother must've mentioned her."

"My mother actually said you dated a beautiful lady of the Imperial household in Japan, right?"

"Maybe I did."

Thumbing through letters and postcards on his desk, Weston found one that made him take a deep breath and whistle.

"You said you'd tell me, old man." Jason hooked his jacket on the wall, knocking snow off his shoes. "Now what?"

Friendly, Jason sat across from him but didn't dare put his feet on the furniture, pulling back his legs, close to his chair.

"The rules are, what we discuss doesn't get repeated or published unless I read it and sign off in black ink. You got it?"

He stared at the writer to make sure he heard the rules. "Hope you got it, loud and crystal clear."

Jason lifted straight up in the chair, no longer sloppy or belligerent. Mature and astute.

"You have my word on the Bible, King James Version, too."

His uncle slowly transported Scripture into his direct line of sight, a shiny copy of the KJV was under his right hand. Agreement fulfilled.

"I'd be glad to tell you about her 'cause she doesn't travel to Mount Jackson any longer." He poured a tumbler of Cliff's Old-Fashioned, handing a friendly glass to Jason. "She's something special."

"Looks to be a hundred postcards or more in that box and an old camera." The trunk was placed on the oak table, like it was the Holy Grail or some photo shrine. He opened the trunk, flipped the hinges, and tried to remember the last time he was in the trunk. He couldn't.

"There's exactly ninety-three postcards and thirty-two letters from Sorano." He gunned his drink down. "I personally hid them in the trunk about ten years ago when I realized she wasn't coming back to Mount Jackson. I'll tell you a wonderful story about her when you start respecting the great man you call Uncle "Ridge" Laramie. Now let's call it a goodnight."

"Oh, come on." He stood at the doorway between the kitchen and living room. "Tell me something about Sorano. Something I could print."

He pitched a chuck of wood on the fire, grinning and laughing to himself.

"That should keep us warm while you sleep on the damn couch for a week." He poked the fire and laughed again. "You can have your room back when I no longer see my brother's attitude coming out of my favorite nephew."

"Give me one good sentence, Ridge." Being a smartass, he placed a picture of her on the kitchen table beside where he'd eat his next bowl of oatmeal.

Scooping the pictures up with both hands, he stopped in his tracks, under the hallway light and looked over his shoulder.

"She was the love of my life." The bedroom door was ajar. "And her body was so..." The door slammed behind his uncle.

"I knew you could remember."

"We'll start with one postcard a day when you respect my authority."

That night Jason turned the pages of classic novels he'd left on the coffee table. Hemingway. Fitzgerald. Orwell. Men he knew about. Thomas Jefferson's friend, a young man named Peter Leicester Ford, had his attention until he fell asleep each night on the hard sofa.

Something untold and legendary lingered like a vapor inside Weston's home, and Jason wanted to write it, and write it badly, to print a biography. His mother had wanted to write about Weston's story decades earlier and now he could pen the story about his uncle dating a member of the Japanese Imperial family. The man who had made his life and living in the small town of Mount Jackson, Virginia jolted him until his past life became his nephew's obsession. Journaling each day, thinking and writing, in hopes that he'd say something about Sorano or the murders in Santo Domingo. Weston didn't know what was inside his notebook and he wasn't about to tell him everything.

***

The next morning, Weston sat in his recliner and they watched a heavy snow, deer and rabbits crossed the land at Andy Oliver, and maybe it was the name or the view, but Jason felt at home in Shenandoah County. He unfolded part of the story about Sorano which was journaled as fast as Jason could outline the story and take good notes.

HER PICTURES TRIGGERED HIS MEMORY

"We stayed the night in a full board bed and breakfast." Weston stared at the photograph of her, gazing out the wide front window into the distance and then glanced into the small fire he'd built while the wind howled and more snow fell.

He found an empty photo album and began organizing the pictures, year by year, from 1977 through 1980.

"Did she honor her traditional Japanese roots, and sleep in her own room?"

"You're one inquisitive little Army brat, aren't you? You mean... did we do it?"

"I'm all ears, old man. Talk."

"There you are being disrespectful again." He rolled his watch. "You think I'll open my love life to a guy who won't ask Becca Hunter out and take her top off?"

"Becca Hunter?" Jason was surprised he knew his interests. "How do you know, Becca?"

"Top and I go way back, they are like family to me."

"I might get back to Becca, one of these days."

"Scared? First time jitters?"

"Would you tell me the dang story?"

He needed vivid details. All of them. To know exactness made the best stories and what he felt twenty years earlier would be vital. His emotions would be essential to writing the best story, if he cared to share them.

"I hope you will unfold clear and concise images, like origami."

"Life is a song, Jason," he said, "if you leave out a single note or part of the lyrics, the song doesn't speak to the heart of the audience as well as it's meant to be."

"No better words were ever spoken, uncle."

"Here's the story from the Bed & Breakfast: I own the B&B now."

Jumping up, "You own the B&B in Mount Jackson? Why don't I move up there?"

He nodded. "I told 'em not to let you in the front door."

"Why?"

"Well, I have my reasons."

"Tell me about Sorano and the hot nights at the B&B."

"To date, particularly, the night Lynyrd Skynyrd's plane crashed on the 20th of October 1977. We held each other as we watched a mouthy journalist, like yourself, offer The Special Report News coverage on a small black and white TV in the lobby of the Bed & Breakfast and then we went upstairs to our room."

"Did she cry when the journalist told of Lynyrd Skynyrd's plane crash?"

"She was tough in business matters, down to the dime, but inside, she's an emotional lady when it comes to loss of life."

"I bet she still has a big heart." Jason took good notes.

"The story was all over television and the next day we read it again in *The Daily Progress*, turning our stomachs as we were both big fans of the group."

"What was she like?" He prepared a separate page. "As a person, I mean?"

"She noticed things, natural things, such as baby birds and gently flowing rivers, less man-made items. Earthly things other ladies her age might have overlooked, flora and fauna, doves, songbirds, rabbits, crickets and whitetail deer picking grass at the edge of a meadow. Mockingbirds intrigued her, too."

He placed a small green tree inside the hands of his nephew.

"Bonsai?" Jason turned it around and even felt the soil and small rocks inside the flower pot.

"Sorano's favorite little tree. Bet I bought 2500 of these damn things in twenty years, hard to keep alive. I'll have one, if she decides to return, then I'll have her favorite tree in the house." Jason examined the limbs. "I've bought dozens of these trees since she went back to New York City," Weston told him, as he walked around the room. "Every time I go shopping."

"Do you mind if I have one, for my room?"

They walked over to a table where he had several more plants.

"Life, it meant something to her. Even the tiniest creatures were her friends. She knew the names of trees, young and old, by the shape of their leaves and trunks. Take that one by the window, it's full of life."

"She was an explorer?"

"Sorano remembered winding country roads in West Virginia and the warm color of leaves reminded her of Central Park." He pointed to a small Japanese maple garden in his backyard and the backdrop was a waterfall, lifeless in the winter but he made it for her. "Not far from where she grew up in Brooklyn, watching the Yankees, chugging down soda and popcorn, and she hoped to catch a foul ball from Thurman Munson, one day. Once she did, by God, in the summer of 1978, down the third base line, landed right in her glove, too."

"Thurman Munson?" His eyes bugged in amazement. "Munson, Wow!"

LOVE IN THE FALL, 1977

Jason took notes as his uncle spoke.

"She loved sunsets as much as she loved baseball. To sit on a rock, embracing the last hour of the day, kept her smiling. She's simple. Sorano would say, " 'That was an amazing day at its golden hour, like the grand finale celebration of the day, wasn't it? The way the sun glows in the sky, and all of a sudden, hides behind the mountains until morning."

"Spectacular view from Mount Jackson, isn't it?"

"It is wonderful being here with you, Weston," she whispered, leaning against him. "And I have a beautiful time planned for us."

"I opened the door for her and carried our luggage into the Bed & Breakfast. Four bags were hers. I claimed only one, roughed up duffle bag that was handed down to me by my grandfather, for military school or for travel. Her bags were of good material, new and durable. Much different than the bag I carried."

"Tell me about your ideas," Sorano said. "Your plans."

"It would spoil the evening," he kissed her. "One room please."

***

He journaled extensively and with great expectations. The television was off each evening, his uncertainties faded away as to what he was doing became comfortable and routine, natural and pleasant in the Shenandoah Valley. The writer was flawless and in every detail spoke of her extravagant lifestyle in the Big Apple. Much more worldly than he was at age twenty, Weston sat in his recliner as a true storyteller. Wine in one hand and a picture of her in the other. He continued as if he was right beside her again.

***

"I nodded to the clerk," he said as she stood beside him at the B&B. "We walked to the second floor, third room down the hall and opened it with the keys placed in my hands. Built nearly a hundred years before, the place was a relic, old fashioned, but we both liked it and the house beat staying at her second cousin's home on the sofa or in a motel."

"Look at that big window," said Sorano, as she saw her reflection.

"You will be able to see for miles at sunrise." He told her with certainty.

"That will be a beautiful photograph."

"All I see is you," Weston told her.

One night after the '77 World Series they became closer.

"Sorano jumped in my arms, thin and radiant, weighing about as much as two heavy suitcases. I carried her to the bed like we were married, but I'd only known her a few days, by that time."

"Are you always this forward with the men you date?"

She got up from the bed. Her feet hit the floor and she paced around the room, with her arms crossed.

"Watashi ga hayai to omoimasu ka?"

She threw pillows at his head and laughed. He understood her Japanese but spoke English in translation.

"No, I don't think you're too fast."

"You must." She wrapped herself in a silky gown while he sat in a pair of Bufford Lee Boxers. "I made love with you in High Point because I feel something more with you."

"Something extraordinary and rare. Once in a lifetime."

"This is once in a lifetime. Hey, let's order room service." Weston stood, dodging a bullet. "I'll walk downstairs for a menu, see if they have a chef on staff or some good food."

"Even a cheese platter or some wine would be nice," she whispered at that hour of the night.

Weston made his way downstairs, whistling. Rang the bell and waited.

"Hello, is anyone home?"

An elderly lady who stood in a large room quickly answered, "I'll be right there, sir."

She had on a blue dress, patterned in flowers, neat and pressed, full length, a different person than who had checked them in earlier. Did they change shifts?

"How can I help you?"

"Do you have an evening menu?" She searched the entrance table. "Something to eat or a platter of cheese for the lady?"

"You mean the Japanese lady?" She leaned in on the counter. "Your wife, perhaps?"

Weston shook his head. "We're not married."

"Ummm." Disagreement registered on her face. "Fiancé then?"

"Just dating her, too early to tell." He thumbed a Montgomery Ward catalog atop the teller's desk. "Would there be some other place, a few miles away, to grab a bite?"

"Sir, we'll have breakfast in the morning at six. That is our next meal, hence the words 'Bed and Breakfast' on the big blue sign." She grinned to let him know she was teasing and angled her head to the sign outside. "But you are here for the bed and not for breakfast, aren't you, lovers?" Her eyes rolled behind her glasses, and she kept on working and mumbling.

"Ma'am, I just asked for a place to eat." He tugged his collar, "Not to be judged."

She reached for a cup of pens and grabbed the one that had a white feather taped to it.

"Is that a goose feather?"

She held the goose feather pen in both hands as if it was a treasure from Thomas Jefferson's desk collection.

"They fall from the sky on occasion." She rolled the feather in her hand and tested its sharp point on the back of her hand. "Canadian Geese use this valley as a thoroughfare to a warmer and greater south."

"That's a wonderful collection."

"I'm sorry if I offended you, sir." Her eyes were blue and sincere. "Down the street, you'll find a good place to eat, Italian food."

She handed him a piece of paper the size of a small napkin. "Here's the address, young man."

Sorano and Weston held hands as they descended the wide staircase. The stairs and the floor creaked in the colonial home, had to be a perfect building for a bed and breakfast. The baby blue colored walls had few pictures, and the pristine drywall sported a fresh coat of paint, an overlay of the original. Weston felt a sense of pride about being with Sorano, more than any other lady he'd dated. The older lady smirked when she saw them kissing. He wasn't sure if it was their dating or their cultural differences that irked her the most.

"Have a nice time, lovers," she said sarcastically as he held the door for Sorano.

Weston turned to the lady and tipped his head in her direction. "Your door sign reads, 'Virginia is for Lovers' in red, white, and blue paint, right?"

Sorano pulled his arm in a mannerly fashion, tugging the sleeve, edging him outside.

"What was that all about?" She whispered, eyes wide open.

"Oh, nothing." He didn't want to upset her or have her feel uncomfortable because of her culture. Outside New York, things were different.

The desk clerk stepped on the porch, leaned forward and laughed, catching her can-sized glasses on the bridge of her nose.

"Kommen Sie Liebende zum Frühstück?"

Sorano turned around flat footed in the parking lot. "Ich mag meine Eier sunnyside und er mag seinen Kaffee mit einer Milch."

"What were you and the old hag talking about in German?" He opened the van door.

"I told her that you are great in bed." Sorano bent over laughing as he kissed her.

"I didn't know you had graded the experience."

"You are okay, mophead. Not bad," she flashed her eyes and grinned.

"I'll hand you a survey when we leave."

He held her head, planted a giant kiss on her forehead and jumped as he walked around the van to the driver's side.

"I'll be able to tell her in the morning about the details."

"Or you can hand her my survey card about Weston Laramie." He chuckled about how cultured she was in different languages.

***

That evening Weston was amazed to find out Sorano's love for languages.

"At least four and maybe more," he told Jason. "One of her hobbies."

***

"Take me to the restaurant, Weston."

"I'll take you to the Italian restaurant." He grabbed his coat. "Let's go in the hippie van."

Weston rose from his chair, walked over to the fireplace, and chucked a piece of oak wood on the fire. He started down the hall. The grin on his face was hiding a greater story within him, the one Jason wanted to hear and write about.

He wrote a few more pages and stoked the fire after he left with a steel poker, turning some of the logs around on the crate and hoping he'd return to see him, but he didn't witness his efforts.

"This story is hot stuff, Ridge."

With his wire glasses off his nose, Weston turned toward the writer. "I'll tell you what I did." He rubbed his hands together. "She ordered chicken marsala, covered in savory mushrooms, minced garlic and had a hint of shallots, mixed with Marsala wine."

"That isn't what I wanted to hear about."

"Jason, she ordered the damn thing in Italian, spoke the language, like we were seated at a balcony in Lucca or Sorrento or some crazy Italian city."

"Yeah, yeah, yeah. She's an amazing woman." The writer rolled his hand like a roll tide roll commercial. "But tell me the good stuff, the sweet stuff. Ladies like to read curious books with lots of romance, kisses and hot tubs."

His uncle tucked his hands inside his pockets and wiggled his thumbs.

"The Creamy Limoncello Italian Ricotta Cake, it is the sweetest dessert."

On the way back to Weston's home, he was bottled up and didn't say much the rest of the night.

"Oh, come on. I need something to hook the reader."

"See you in the morning, nephew." He turned off the lamp. "You are a great listener. I even like the questions and the photographs on the table." His bathroom light snapped off.

Weston walked from room to room shutting doors, a subtle signal that Jason learned to understand, the noise halted further questions, which concluded all stories for the night. He didn't have to say anything more, nor did he elaborate about Sorano, the silence in the moment was a silver lining to all curiosity and concluded questions. His nephew sat by the fireplace and shuffled through more photographs from the '70s. Not a speck of dust ever covered her pictures.

Framed photographs, a number of them had their own space, some catty-cornered and others hung on nails with small wires or twine from twenty years earlier. One photo captured both of them, one of her smiling and waving. It was Kodachrome paper from 1978, written in a lady's handwriting - Love Sorano.

In that snapshot, Sorano glowed as Weston hugged her on the steps at Monticello, Thomas Jefferson's homeplace, a majestic colonial residence in Albemarle County, near Charlottesville, Virginia.

Stacks of handwritten letters were penned in Japanese and English, stamped from across the globe, from places like Key West, San Francisco, and even Tokyo. More curious about the Imperial lady than ever before he found the picture of the Monticello, too. He wanted to rouse his uncle's attention with it, to hear the rest of the story. But since he also wanted to live through the night, he let him sleep.

Seven
Twentieth Year at Andy Oliver

The Blue Ridge Mountains were dry in the fall of '99, too dry for Weston's plans, who was alerted that possible wildfires would strike a blaze near his big home. Fallen leaves packed layer upon layer, and trees downed from storms and age waited in the forest, like crisp paper in an abandoned warehouse; leaves became fuel.

"All it needs is a spark from a foolish hiker mixed with a swift breeze," said Weston at breakfast, pointing to the prevailing westerlies. "And it will light up Mount Jackson, hillside after hillside, flame after flame, and that would bankrupt us."

"Have you seen the mountains on fire before?"

"In the fall of '82, I hadn't lived here very long when it happened." He stood in the doorway looking at rows and rows of dominant vines, "Late one evening the wind was howling and a piece of cardboard box blew into the woods from a backyard fire. Crews were called out, but not before ten acres of Andy Oliver were burned to a crisp within two hours."

"Rain is the hope that never happens when there's a drought coming to town."

"I've been on watch ever since late last year."

Later, they sauntered over to the edge of a field. His uncle's fears proved prophetic. A wildfire broke out after lunch on the Wednesday before Thanksgiving. Fire raged in Mount Jackson and the wind whipped uncontrollably as the locals wanted the expertise of fire fighters to guide them before they headed into the woods. At the end of the night, uncle and nephew stood black as West Virginia coal miners on a double shift, hands roughed up, dark faces marked in black smoke and smeared with frequent handprints. Clothes charred, boots to headlamps, the men reeked of an unforgettable, deadly smoke. Coughed. Choked. Eyes red.

Weston, Jason, and a dozen volunteers along with several brave forest service workers fought the blaze with everything they had for seven hours. Beaten and blackened, they'd driven four wheelers and trucks to the mountains with only a small amount of water and food between them. They handled the tall fire, made raked lines around the mountains until the fire was controlled. Two hours past sundown, they didn't have a drop of water left in their canteens and Jason's boots began to melt and his pants leg caught fire once. All they could do was watch the woods burn, smoldering cinders, and flames picked up and jumped the fire line behind the hillside and hollow trees glowed, burning from the fields to the mountaintops. The small group was surrounded by a raging fire. Weston stood too far from the stream to save the far end of Andy Oliver Vineyards. Twelve rows of merlot vines were lost, part of his Pinot Noir vines. But thank God not one vine of the three Chambourcin acres were harmed by the blaze. Thousands of dollars in vines and roses were dead.

Jason drove back from the fire, the bravest man of the bunch seated beside him, Weston Laramie. Strapped in and with his eyes closed, his uncle rested his head against the inside of the club cab truck. Jason spoke about the lives of four volunteers who were surrounded by a consuming fire and Weston drove an all-terrain vehicle through the lowest point of the blaze, like some wild man out of a motion picture set with no choice but to live or die on Short Mountain. One of them was the grateful writer who drove him home that night. Without that machine and his uncle, Jason would have huddled in a small circle and possibly burned to death with others in a matter of minutes. They didn't talk on the drive home, but mostly grunted out answers and arched their back and legs from walking the high mountains. Later, they had sandwiches, some chips, and several cans of soda and lots of water. Like a grizzly claw on a salmon, Jason finished his food in a matter of bites.

After earth and smoke were scrubbed away, Weston gave Jason his room back for his bravery and courage. The next morning, his uncle awoke bright and early, and Jason could smell the aroma of a strong, dark coffee pot that slapped his nose and popped his eyes. In lieu of breakfast, his uncle cooked up a good sized turkey, one of the largest he'd ever seen, paired mashed potatoes with gravy, and corn on the cob, a true traditional Thanksgiving dinner, if he'd ever seen one.

They watched professional football and didn't discuss Sorano or the wildfire, yet it was football that occupied their evening and a three hour nap. Fully rested, Jason pecked on the typewriter with what he'd heard up until that point, and what little Weston knew about the murders in the Dominican Republic was in his notes.

Pages of notes stacked on his desk as he outlined chapters. Then when all the games had ended and he was nodding off, he asked, "What do you know about Moby,

Raymond and Myrtle?" He held his pen ready to write. "I need something on paper for Tommy Hunter by Monday. Can you help?"

"Okay." He scooted up in his chair. "Moby Steel was a big time gambler at twenty five, who'd made some money at the table, from Atlantic City to Vegas. He was good."

"He was a bald guy in his mid-twenties, right?"

"Yeah. He wasn't related to anyone at Andy Oliver. Moby was in sales and worked under Sherrill Taylor?"

"Raymond was the younger brother of Sherrill and they were good friends, but had their moments. Raymond and Sherrill argued every day, drawing fists at one point, so much so that I had to reassign Raymond on a daily country route, to keep the brothers in different departments, far apart."

Jason jotted down what he said in shorthand.

"What was Myrtle's job?"

"She had been an accountant for Andy Oliver for five years."

"How was she with money?"

He hesitated to say and rubbed his chin, tilting his head toward the bookcase.

"Myrtle was a good employee, at first."

He knew when to stop writing and listen to him with the utmost respect.

"What happened?"

"The last two years were different and unorganized on paper and in practice. The drawer and safe were coming up short along with how Raymond had moved to the role as a subcontractor and not an employee, it made me curious of the spending until Sherrill figured out they were funneling false jobs when I was out of town and overspending on purchases.”

“Bingo.” Jason tapped his pen as he acknowledged the story. “They were working together in a subcontractor conspiracy to make bank off of Andy Oliver’s good fortune.”

“Raymond was funding Moby’s gambling and their scam was winning them big money.” He walked around the room with his thumb twitching in his pocket. “Backing Moby was going well. In three years Myrtle and Raymond had bought a big house on the river in Lake Holiday.”

The writer found out that Myrtle and Raymond were close to retirement. Raymond had done fairly well in Charlottesville over the years as a civil engineer, but had blown his money on trying to flip real estate at Smith Mountain Lake and a few other lakes. He watered the Bonsai tree as he told the story.

“Sherrill, on the other hand, was conservative to the penny and lived small and was good with his money. The worst day I remember having at Andy Oliver was where they were fighting in the warehouse. I walked in as Sherrill had Raymond by the throat against the wall.”

Jason opened a beer bottle.

“Here’s something to settle your nerves, uncle.” They both found seats. “Why did Sherrill have his brother against the wall?”

“Thousands of dollars were all over the floor. They had fought for several minutes before I rushed into the break room and divided them. Raymond would have died even if I hadn’t broken up the fight and he should’ve, too. Luckily, I recovered the money he'd stolen or he'd taken eighty grand more to the Dominican Republic."

"What happened?"

"Three people are dead over big money. I knew it. Myrtle and Raymond were guilty. I called the police. But all three of them were on a plane by the end of the evening. The police couldn't find them." He put his beer on the table. "Sherrill told me exactly what happened. Raymond ran out of the warehouse after I broke the brothers up, but not before I fired him and Myrtle."

"It is true they were working with Mickey Starr after they left Andy Oliver?"

"That's true. The three of them had been working for him for a while."

Weston took a rubber band off of a legal booklet.

"What's that?"

"Later, Sherrill and I ran the numbers from my books when we began losing money and they'd been stealing from me for about three years before Sherrill caught them."

"After they got with Mickey Starr, what happened?"

"I don't know that side yet." He shook his head and tucked his booklet in his briefcase.

"But they ended up dead because of the amount of money they had."

The day after Thanksgiving, the men he saved stopped by to thank Weston for his good deeds. The local newspaper called Weston Laramie a hero. The Andy Oliver team served them apple pie and leftovers. Weston sat at the kitchen table, and suddenly he came alive with words. Maybe it was the holiday or indigestion, who knew? After the volunteer firefighters left, Jason went through his albums again.

"Where'd you find this picture?" Weston leaned back with the photograph.

"In that stack of books you moved in my bedroom."

He flipped the picture inside his hands.

"I bought her that denim jacket after we visited Bull Run. Cold day."

He handed Jason a bowl of vanilla ice cream and a slice of apple pie.

"The picture was stuck inside a book."

His eyes were heavy and his head leaned backwards.

"*Sons and Lovers*, the D.H. Lawrence novel," he said. "I know the book well. Gertrude is not happy about living off of Walter's meager salary. That's what happened in the book. It was the same with me and Sorano."

"You mean, you didn't have the vineyard off the ground yet?" Jason sat his soda on the table and grabbed a pen as fast as he could.

"That's why you broke up, huh? Royalty versus a no name vineyard?"

His nephew scooted forward on the edge of his seat, his eyes were fixed on the page as he listened to his uncle's interesting stories. Hiking. Love life. Murders. What was next?

"We had our differences about earnings." The air left Weston's lungs in a hurry. "And let me tell you, I lived with her father's face in my mind for years. Resentment is a horrible thorn of pain. She was my beautiful rose."

"That was why she didn't stay at Andy Oliver, wasn't it? Well, well, she didn't understand your earning potential and dreams, did she?"

He nodded. "That was some of it." Abruptly, he stood and carried his half-eaten dessert to the counter. "You finished with the pie and ice cream yet, Jason Laramie."

"All done."

His nephew washed his dessert bowl in the sink.

But Weston opened the door and shouted, "Leave it. Follow me."

"Where are we headed?"

"To the hillside, the part of the woods where the fire missed. I made sure of it, and I'll show you why she left me. Let's go to the hillside."

They walked through the backyard and headed to the biggest oak on his property.

"When we broke up, she brought me a German Short-haired Pointer pup." His uncle adjusted his coat against the windy day. "Best dang dog I ever had, flushed out pheasants and doves and any other birds that moved on this property."

"What was the dog's name?" Because of the chill in the air Jason shoved his hands inside his pockets and walked with his collar flipped up. "I saw a picture of him on the wall when I first arrived at your place."

"Tomodachi. The name means friend in Japanese."

Two stones stood like small statues in Jason's sightline, a large one the size of a mailbox and a smaller rock placed in the near distance. Both situated twenty feet from each other.

"Did you have two dogs?"

Jason raised his walking stick at the flagstone and then a marble stone.

"Tomo, my dog, he's buried here and …."

Weston sat on a wooden bench covered in leaves and cracked acorns. It faced an open place at a point where squirrels had broken nut shells and whitetail deer crossed in a low gap, but it was the most pleasant area he'd ever been. Separated at ten paces or so from where his pet was buried, a flagstone covered in mossy oak and with machine lettering, too. The only stone, made of white marble stone, angled south and had the best view of the great valley.

"What?" His nephew stood in respect. "Here's a small grave."

Elbows on his knees, his uncle opened his pocket knife and whittled as Jason removed leaves from the front of the marked stone. He stopped moving when he saw the name and the dates.

"Andy Oliver Laramie?"

"My boy," he said in a low voice. "He lived four months."

Jason stood beside the headstones with his hands atop the walking stick, listening for him to say something. Then silence.

"I'm sorry, sir."

"Few people know he's even here," Weston went on. "Not the Barkers over there, or the Klebers, the folks who first owned the bed and breakfast and especially not the Vickers who'd tell everyone my business, if they could." Then his dark eyes locked on his nephew. "Don't you speak a word of this to anyone or print it in your dang book. It might mess up my wine business among the locals. They'll ask too many questions. I don't have the heart to rehash questions about Andy Oliver."

"I won't say a word." He bent down to clean acorns from Andy's grave. "I am sorry. Dad never mentioned your son."

"That's okay. The picture at Monticello was taken in the fall of '78. You mentioned she was glowing, and it brought back old memories of Andy Oliver."

There was room on the long park bench, so Jason leaned back on the bench.

"Did you and Sorano get married?"

"She didn't give me time to ask her." He walked over to a Beech tree with his hands in his slacks.

"It's none of my business, but you had plenty of time to make her your wife. The two of you dated for two years, '77 and '78. You tried to work it out for several years." Jason said, as he stood over Andy's resting place. "That's when she got pregnant."

"You are right." He looked across the big valley. "It's none of your damn business. I did have plenty of time, though."

Scanning the grave, he tossed two broken limbs aside from Andy's resting place and raked leaves with a handful of broken limbs. Next, Jason moved over to Tomo's flagstone. His uncle picked the moss off the rock and removed twigs, three feet around each grave where his pet rested in peace near his son. He pulled a blue handkerchief from inside his coat pocket, balled it up, and brushed the dirt and dust from his son's name atop the marble.

"You're tellin' me, it's none of my concern, Uncle Weston." Jason rubbed his thin beard. "Buddy, you had plenty of time to handle the question of marriage with her."

Jason hit a big nerve, his uncle's face turned red. Crouched down beside Andy's grave, he stared at Jason like he was about to kill him with his bare hands.

"Maybe you're right. Maybe I had enough time, more than enough, to talk with her about having a future in Mount Jackson."

"So?" The young man picked a handful of acorns before he asked him what he wanted to know. "What's the real reason?"

He stood on the roots of a Beech tree.

"I asked her, not once or twice, but a half dozen times."

"What was her hold up?"

"It wasn't her, at all." He leaned against the trunk of a downed tree. "She wouldn't marry me because it would dishonor her father's wishes."

"That's what my father said probably happened."

"Bet his sorry ass laughed at me, didn't he?"

His nephew walked over to where he was and looked across the long Shenandoah Valley.

"He says too much and speculates too often."

He stared down the hill back to his home.

"Don't spare my feelings. Let it rip. What'd he say?"

"He said Sorano's father wouldn't agree to have you as his son-in-law because he had someone else in mind that would make a solid business partner in Japan."

"Least he told the damn truth for once."

"Obviously, she still thought about you." Jason set his curious eyes on him. "She sent you all those postcards and letters from all over the world. Why don't you call her up?"

"We haven't really talked in years, plus her family at the Japanese restaurant in town said she was dating some wealthy man from New York City now."

"Some of the postcards were from the same address in New York. You could get in touch with her, talk to her, see what happens?"

"Let's go back inside, warm up beside the fireplace."

His uncle hiked a slightly different path, down the hill and over the stream. They crossed through one of his many fields before something bothered his nephew.

"But she's an American," Jason said. "How could her father have that much power over her?"

"It wasn't that she didn't love me or that I didn't love her." He picked up a chunk of wood for the fireplace. "Her grandfather was killed by the Hiroshima bomb."

"Dad said it was about status in society or some crap."

"When we met, she had three big furniture businesses in New York. Her family owned a Japanese restaurant in town and said she opened a fourth store in Sonoma." He slapped the back of the young man. "I couldn't make her dreams come true in the late '70's, buddy, and I can't do it now either. That was left up to some other lucky guy in a penthouse suite."

Jason organized his freelance investigative skills and readied himself to type.

"You could do it now."

The young man rubbed his cold hands together.

"I'm sure she made a name for herself somewhere between New York and California." He walked up on the back porch and opened the door. "I have been long forgotten in her mind now. She doesn't remember Weston Laramie, anyway."

They walked inside, and Weston said, "Haven't heard from her in years. I'm not up for the drama anymore."

"What are you looking for?"

He opened a small wooden box he had tucked away beside his tools and shotguns on a back shelf under the staircase. He nodded and handed Jason the box.

"Open it up. Back in the late 70s, the world didn't want us together."

"Look at that family picture with the little pup at your feet. Is that you, little Andy Oliver and Sorano?"

"That's little Andy, big as a watermelon in her arms."

"He was a beautiful boy."

"Andy Oliver gripped my hand with those tiny fingers the night I kissed him goodnight for the last time."

"I'm sorry, Ridge."

"He was my only son. I have thought about how strong he would be by now, working in the vineyard, driving the company truck, cutting grass with the tractor, and how much help he would be on pulling grapes at harvest time."

Jason wrinkled his face. Weston gripped his face and exhaled the air from his lungs, walking to the doorway where he couldn't see if he had tears or not.

"He'd be my age, right?" Jason looked at the photograph, all smiles.

"You two would be good friends, Jas." He took his keys from his pocket and chuckled. "Then I'd have two asses to kick out of bed in the morning."

Unhooking coats from the hall tree, Weston said, "How about Japanese food tonight?"

"Yeah, of course," the young man said. "And we could meet Sorano's cousin in town."

The cold air of the Shenandoah Valley was whistling on that particular day. Halfway to the truck, Weston said, "It would be good to see them again and ask how Sorano is doing."

He flipped his collar and fired up the truck.

"Let's eat some miso soup and see about your friend."

"Why would you pay for seaweed soup?"

"Seaweed? Seaweed!" Jason said, laughing. "Gotta love seaweed soup."

At the restaurant, Weston had a grand serving of tempura, dripping the seafood and vegetables in tentsuyu sauce, a good meal, coated in a cold batter and then deep fried. His hope was to find out what Sorano had been doing for the past two decades and how many sweet kids she had and how she was doing in New York City. He must've asked her cousin a dozen questions, folded his hands, kept to the conversation and not the seafood, in respect of tradition and honor, for it was something she taught him, for his memory of her, he did it and Jason followed his movements. However, sadly, the lady didn't divulge any information about their cousin, this is, if she knew the answers, she kept it to herself, for the sake of family.

The next day, Weston and Jason repaired the old bench, the one on the hill, nailing fewer than fourteen boards, including a heavy duty seat, that converted into a lid, to hold more than one person. Adding the feature for Jason, for his space to write, and out of respect for his bravery at the blazing fire, of which, the writer suggested a new angled backrest, and his uncle admitted the idea was worth the extra time and energy. New mulch was placed around Tomo's stone, and later on Andy's grave held flowers. Holding back his emotional side, but only for a short time, Weston felt Andy would have befriended his pet, loved him even.

His uncle mumbled something.

"What did you say?" Jason asked, leaning against a tree. The cool air became cold, so he zipped his thick green military jacket, and gloved his hands.

Weston brushed his eyes and was the first to rest on the new bench. Jason couldn't tell what his uncle was doing with his hands, but regardless he had the right to pay his respects.

"It was my promise to Andy."

"What promise?"

"When it happens, Jason, I'll tell you 'cause I appreciate you being here since you cut those dreadlocks and stopped being a Tampa drunk."

To cope, Jason knew his uncle laughed his way through the broken places in his heart, and in time he dealt with hardships like everyone else, with respect and honor. All of a sudden, twenty red roses were pulled from a paper bag, hidden under his arm, inside of Weston's navy winter jacket. Long green, garden style stems, small thorns, brilliant red petals, bud eyes, and small flower buds, held together with a small rope. Jason nodded. Under the cross on the stone, the wind swept leaves over the carved name and date of Andy Oliver. Halfway down the mountain, Weston had something up his sleeve, grinning. Jason couldn't wait to hear about the perpetual promise he'd made to Andy.

Eight
Christmas Season

On Christmas Eve '99, Weston and Jason bottled orders until their backs were burning and sore, grunting and lifting, case after case, and readied bottles for New Year's Eve. Feet throbbing, Jason packed the Chardonnay and Cabernet Franc in new wooden crates and stocked the famous Andy Oliver warehouse until local customer routed trucks were dispatched from the docks. Another season had ended.

Without hesitation, Weston tabled his first run of Petit Verdot, a man relieved and teeth shone, eyes closed, he fell back on a stack of pallets and rested. The wine's plentiful red color, tannin, and floral aromas turned Jason's palate to his new craft. He wasn't much of a wine connoisseur, but he knew his uncle felt certain his wine would sell in bigger cities such as Boston and New York City just the same as it did in the Great South. With all the work needed, Jason buried all unwary emotions in lieu of his earnestness to help expand Andy Oliver. Commitment. Timeliness. His uncle seemed grateful he was less of a rebel than he was when he first arrived in Mount Jackson. He locked the door to the warehouse, pressing in the dark until the click of the stainless steel locked inside his grasp.

"There's one day in a man's life where others witness the auspicious side of his character. I've seen yours," said his uncle, taking him underneath his wing. "Some people can't humble themselves to find goodness. They'd rather have notoriety, thus they walk vainly, lost in the world. Not you. I see a great deal of wealth in your future, driven by good character, too."

Whatever Weston noticed in his nephew's actions that day, he vowed not to differ from what good he'd given him. Later over coffee and biscotti, they agreed to exchange gifts that same day because they felt the lights and tree made it more traditional at night versus waking up and unwrapping gifts at daybreak.

"My favorite gift," said Weston, "were white chocolates from a market in Charlottesville."

Jason surprised him with a good wrist watch, too, a blue flannel shirt, and a burgundy tie for more formal events should he have the nerve to ask out a lady again. With his name on the gift, boxed and under the tree, Weston pushed a new computer into the hands of his nephew, the best gift he could have shared. In a short time, with the furniture assembled together and to each his own, he stacked a handful of classic books on the shelf. By the handshake and spark in his eyes, he could tell that Jason was extremely pleased. He also threatened to take his life if he dog-eared a page.

"You'll need these things," Weston told him. "If the notion hits you, peck out words, type a letter, one day, just write something good. You'll have it in front of you when the time comes."

"I got you something else, too." The young man handed Weston a small box, which he opened in seconds. His nephew wasn't sure if he'd done the right thing or not with the last gift.

"Where did you find origami paper? Or did you have this art made at the Japanese restaurant in town?"

"Nope. They're original pieces."

"You bought it already made this way? That's cool," he said. "I favor Japanese crafts." He held it up above his head. "See, it goes well with my decor."

"I found the origami in the closet."

"You gave me something I already owned." He laughed and held them up. "This was paper Sorano made years ago and I tucked them away. It's a small purse, a pair of shoes, and a flock of geese."

"I thought you might like to display them on your shelf."

Walking over to a shelf of treasures, he stood beside them, and said, "I will. After twenty years, they're still holding their shape."

"This gift was also in the trunk." Jason handed him a box. "I had it framed for you."

He took the frame into both hands. "This picture was taken in 1977. We were skiing at Flat Top Mountain, a good resort in West Virginia, not too far from here. Neither one of us was very good at the downhill," he chuckled and took a deep breath. "We warmed up in the log cabin, though."

"Didn't you model the cabins at Andy Oliver after the Flat Top cabins?"

"Yes, I did. I remember being snowed in for the weekend by the fireplace." He snapped his fingers. "Check inside your stocking on the fireplace."

The young man removed the red and white stocking from the nail. It felt light and empty, but he reached inside the sock and touched something.

"My passport." He drew it out. "What's this envelope for?"

"A little something special for you."

"Are you kidding me?" He unfolded a smile. "A round trip ticket from New York to Germany."

Weston turned on that natural grin that made people happy, similar to the one he'd flashed when he won forty dollars on a scratch off ticket in Timberville, two months earlier. He'd used the money toward having the Andy Oliver name printed on corks, something new Jason recommended.

"You didn't have to do this."

"Thought you might want to see your folks and sister since we're all caught up with orders for the holidays." He held the picture of him and Sorano in West Virginia beside the baby picture of Andy Oliver, his only son and sang "Silent Night" by the fireplace. "Christmas is a good time to be thankful for family, anyway. I'll drive us to J.F.K. Pick you up in a week in Westbury. There's a few dollars in there for hookers or hamburgers, whichever happens to warm your heart first. Just use it on hamburgers." He laughed.

"There's five hundred dollars here, plus tickets." Jason shook his hand with a hard grip to let him know he appreciated him more than he knew.

"Get packed. You fly out in two days."

Instead he settled by the fireplace with a drink. So did his uncle. Weston told him about the origami Sorano made and a few secrets about his father and how he met his mother. His father was a big drunk, of course. Jason told him how much it meant to him to visit his family in Heidelberg for the holidays. The next morning, Weston locked the wine cellar and the house and parked the company truck inside the barn. They tossed their luggage into the hippie van he loved to drive. Then, Weston pitched one bag beside Jason's luggage and another bag in the backseat with crates of wine. The journalist in him needed explanations for his strange actions and to find out about the promise.

"If I'm headed to Germany, where are you going, old man?"

"I have some business clients to see in Boston and Hartford and then I'll see you in Westbury soon, mister globetrotter journalist."

His face glowed, and he belted out a laugh.

"So my little speech motivated you, huh?" He slapped his uncle's arm.

"Just shut up and get in. It's starting to snow so we need to get started." He slammed the door. "I'll drop you off at J.F.K." He started singing, "You're off to see the Germans. The wonderful Germans of Heidelberg."

The owner of Andy Oliver had his eye on a stainless steel fermentation vessel that would help expand the winery business. However, to sell some bottles in New England would make the determination of the vessel and the extra funds would be enough to secure it. They talked about sports, vacations, and a thousand other things on the trip. There was one thing he waited to mention until they were close to J.F.K, and what he said chilled him to the bone.

"The negative media coverage from the murders hurt profits, Jason." Weston stared deep into New York traffic then faced him with a tight smile. "If we don't land a few big clients, then I'll be forced to sell the vineyard next year."

"What?" Grabbing his face, Jason was devastated. "Shut it down?"

"We'll talk when I get back."

"I have a few ideas myself."

His window rolled up before his words found his nephew's ears.

Worried. Jason lost ten pounds in Germany. Running with his father, his mind elsewhere, coupled with the flood of concern for Weston about if he had to sell Andy Oliver Vineyards or not. He knew he had to do something and fast.

His father felt Weston knew more than he'd said about the murders in the Dominican Republic. Jason disagreed. Now, almost ready to board the flight home, he planned a careful lie before his family.

"Dad, mom, sis," he took a deep breath. "Well, I met a girl in Virginia."

"He's getting married, Victor," shouted his mother. "Thank God."

"Wonderful," said his sister. "Can I move in with you and my sister-in-law?"

"Miracles still happen." His Dad downed another swig of dark German beer.

"You got pictures of her, boy?" His mother held his arm. "Can I see her face?"

"No pictures. Mom, there's no ring and no wedding. We're just dating."

Jason stared at his father who'd ragged him about girls since he was a youth baseball pitcher. He didn't have much faith in his son. Nor did Jason enjoy spending time with him. An ocean wasn't far enough apart to satisfy them ...or him either, when it came to family.

"Yeah, boy, tell me about her." His father kicked him under the table. "Did you find a rich one?" gripping his neck. "Make sure she's a hottie from that big university in Charlottesville."

"I left her picture in my room at Weston's house, but yeah, she is a cheerleader, for sure." He continued to lie like a dog.

"Please marry her," said his mother, grabbing his hand. "Don't take any advice from Weston or your father about women. Your uncle can hook 'em for a few years, but can't reel 'em in and well, he's no good at dating the hot ones."

His mother. High strung. Bossy. He loved her.

"Here's some tea, sweetie, and Victor, our boy will be married this time next year."

"You damn right he will." His father. Drunk. Controlling. True jerk. "We'll make sure he has a nice wedding and a long honeymoon in Europe. Could have it at Weston's vineyard if he wasn't such a tight ass Yankee, now."

His mother paced back and forth and then called her best friend, Rudi, with the good news. She covered the phone with her hands and spoke of baby names.

"I need grandkids," she pleaded. "We'll retire soon and we need grandbabies to watch."

She called Rudi to talk a second time about how pretty the lady was and how she came from Old Dominion Market money and she lived in a mansion with fat shutters, outside Staunton, Virginia and rode horses at her summer home in the Outer Banks. Jason realized what his mother told her friend was no different than his own deceit to get back to New York with his good ideas for Weston, just to make them proud. Both of them were wrong, in the worst ways.

"He's a grown man now and he doesn't need to worry. He'll do fine on his first marriage and better on the next and so it goes," his father laughed. "Your mother doesn't want you to use that strange animal protection they make in other countries before you get married. If you are going to do it, just go with what God gave you, son."

His father was the dirtiest old fool Jason had ever met. He disregarded the advice from him the minute he heard it, a habit he'd picked up from his mother. Then Weston confirmed it. His parents were lunatics who needed to retire overseas, far away from his residence in Virginia or wherever he decided to live.

"Whatever, Dad." He turned to his mother with an idea. "Mom, can I borrow your computer before I go?"

From his mother's computer, he printed an address where Weston wanted to meet in Westbury and tucked the page inside his coat pocket. He looked forward to seeing his uncle in a couple of days. Weston had told him he had a few things he needed to handle on Long Island, a place he'd only been to a handful of times in twenty years. His reason was unknown. The promise, he thought?

Later, his father spoke with Jason outside while his mother napped. He told him that he needed to cut the vacation short and get back to his lady before someone grabbed her on New Year's Eve. He agreed. Plus, he said, he'd left Weston with an awful back injury.

He offered the same explanation to his mother who cried most of the night about him leaving early. Jason sweetened his explanation with a story about how Weston had cases and cases of Chardonnay he needed to truck to Virginia Beach and the Outer Banks by the third of January. He told her how there was no one to help his uncle. Soon, he'd be pushing a walker around the vineyard.

To this day, Jason regretted the tales he told in Germany, but his purpose was in his future. His uncle wasn't a failure, just terrible at dating and closing deals. His words never came out right and he'd gotten worse over the years. He simply needed time, practice and a good win now and then, like the Yankees had had the season before in Boston.

Nine
Lady in Black

As the golden sunset faded away somewhere over the sleepy blue waves of the Atlantic Ocean, Jason's heavy eyes closed and he dozed off. His head tilted backwards, suddenly, the man to his left woke him and shared the difference between whole life and term life insurance. The man to his right on the airplane told of his daughter in Baltimore and his son in Dallas and how his mother was in an old folks home somewhere outside Mobile, Alabama, not far enough from him. He was too sleepy to have a conversation or to make new friends.

The insurance salesman thought Jason's short experience of three months as an apprentice at Andy Oliver Vineyard matched up perfectly for a role in his progressive office in Richmond. His offer was refused. After his two hour spill, Jason's short answer followed, and when he said, "I don't think so mister!" He shut up and a dozen people around him cheered. The insurance salesman turned his head, folded up his proposal and wouldn't talk anymore about his profession. Finally, Jason became a sleeping giant among his new airline friends. Passengers in his coach section awarded handshakes at arrival, and one man wanted to buy coffee for Jason's cool hand answers. He declined, out of pride. If it was beer thirty then the young man might have accepted his generosity. That was his first experience on a 747 and he became a hero. Not a moment too soon, he reached a real New York City coffee shop where his taste buds discovered a mocha frappe, another first for him on the trip. Jason flagged down a yellow cab and found the Radisson. That night, the young man sampled his first chicken marsala in honor of the many stories Weston had shared about fine dining in NYC. His cultural respect doubled with the first bite in the Big Apple.

He heard Weston's raw voice and even laughed to himself about his uncle, a good man, better than his father would have ever given him credit for being. And oh, how Jason regretted lying to his family in Germany, but he was on a mission himself.

The next morning, Jason hailed a cab for the address in Westbury he'd printed from his mother's computer the day before he became a hero.

"Here it is," he told the cab driver. Jason fumbled for cash, paid him, and walked inside the cool restaurant.

"Welcome to Tanaka's Restaurant." A lady in black handed him a menu. Gray streaked her hair, but he recognized her instantly from the photos in Mount Jackson.

"Sorano?"

"Yeah." She searched his face without recognition. "How do I know you?"

"I'm Jason." He stood to greet her. "Your friendship is with my uncle."

"Who is your uncle?" Her lips turned tight.

"Weston Laramie."

Sorano turned and walked over to the bar. She whispered something to another lady of Japanese descent and they glanced at Jason in the doorway. Minutes later, the other lady approached Jason's table and thrust a "Take out" menu in his hands.

"A Bento box, it's a good meal to take home," she suggested, and stood with sincerity. "Please consider it a gift from Sorano."

"I'm dining in. Tell her I pay my own way." He touched the picture on the menu. "Could I have tempura with a good beer, make it Sapporo?"

Jason examined the large establishment and searched for Sorano several times. She'd walked to the back of the restaurant, working out her past, he predicted. The idea of an apology for upsetting her with Weston's name crossed his mind more than once while he waited. The mention of his uncle must have flooded her mind with memories of Andy Oliver's death. Tomo. Mount Jackson. Andy. The Irishmen. Yankee Stadium and baseball games in the 70s, and being wrapped up in Weston's arms at Monticello. Maybe he had done the wrong thing by being there, he thought, and the mention of the Laramie name caused an issue and surprised her.

"Sir," said the waitress. "You have two choices, seafood or vegetables?"

"Seafood, please," he moved to the bar. "I haven't been to New York City before."

"Welcome." The waitress walked him to the dark side of the room where two lights dropped from the ceiling and the place was elegant and open. The long bar faced a horizontal shaped mirror, and a hundred or more bottles of fine wine were racked on silver and glass shelves, positioned for show or for large parties.

It felt out of place to ask for an American beer in her restaurant or a shot of Tennessee Whiskey to wash away his discomfort, a common need of self-appraisal in Tampa, but he was far from Florida. A Long Island Iced Tea crossed his mind. Jason's plan worked much differently in the hotel mirror. Within a few minutes, his food was within arm's reach, and he couldn't believe he was seated in the presence of Sorano Tanaka.

When he looked up, Sorano stood beside him.

"May I sit with you?"

"Please do."

She examined his features, eyes, nose, and short smile.

"I hope you don't mind me saying it, but you look like Weston."

"He's a handsome man, too." Jason grinned at her.

Her eyes squinted when she laughed, just how he'd imagined she'd look. She loosened up and became his friend, relaxing.

"I bet he hasn't changed much."

"More stubborn than when you knew him in the late '70s, I bet?"

"I didn't mean to walk away a few minutes ago." Her dark chocolate eyes from the photo squinted again. "Weston and I shared some great years together. Our jobs pulled us in two directions. Is he still working on that old farm project?"

It crossed Jason's mind, she didn't know about his fine vineyard.

"His land does keep him busy." He gulped the beer. "He's outside all day and works in the barn when he can."

She folded her hands and looked forward, peaceful and grinned.

"He's not one to write or call, is he?"

They both roared in laughter. She covered her face with her hand just as Weston said she used to do and turned, same as in her younger days. In some strange fashion, the man they referred to had touched their lives, and without doubt or hesitation, he was there for him. She had no idea why Jason decided to show up for a meal, out of the blue, uninvited, mentioning an old friend. Intentional on his part.

"My uncle has one ink pen and it's taped to a goose feather." Jason touched the bottom of his chin and chuckled. "And he doesn't know how to use it."

"How is he doing, it's been years? I haven't asked about him at all."

"He's wonderful."

"Good."

"You met Weston the year I was born."

She opened a bottle of Sake and poured two shots.

Holding up the drink, "He still thinks of me, does he?"

She raised her glass higher and so did Jason. Their glasses tapped.

"To Weston Laramie." Her dark brown eyes sparkled. "To my special friend, in Virginia." She closed her eyes and finished the glass.

"Cheers." He slammed the Sake down. "I don't think he ever stopped thinking of you." Jason wiped his lips and mustache clean.

"You're kidding me, right?" She dried her mouth with a napkin. "How many kids does he have now?"

He wanted to say how sorry he was about little Andy Oliver, but out of respect for her and Weston, he didn't. And he liked Weston too much to embarrass him or the lady he just became friends with minutes earlier over a drink.

"He dates a few ladies. Marriage, well...," shaking his head swiftly. "Not sure he's ready to ever settle down." He sampled the beer the waitress left beside his plate. "What about you, and your kids? You got anyone to take this place over when you're ready to move to Hudson Valley?"

"No children, Jason. I closed my furniture store in Westbury a few years ago and moved to Japan for a guy. My parents liked him." She rolled the tiny watch around her wrist and tugged on the gold necklace as if the guy was difficult to discuss. "He wasn't husband material, though. After two years, I moved back to New York City and managed this restaurant full-time. My father felt dishonored about the whole thing. He disliked my independence and we didn't talk for a while."

"You have a fine establishment." The beer and Sake were good, strong drinks, but she needed Andy Oliver wine in her glasses, to make it a place of excellence, he thought.

"How long are you in town for?" she asked.

He looked into her eyes. "One more day or so, then I ..." It crossed his mind. Jason didn't need to mention Weston was driving to NYC from Hartford in a few days. "I'd like to see the city. I'm a first-timer to the Big Apple."

"Oh," she said with a big smile, grabbing his arm. "How about we take a walk through Central Park? The weather is going to be perfect on Wednesday, not like Virginia or Carolina, but fair for these parts."

"Let's plan a trip."

"I'll pack us lunch and tell you stories about your crazy uncle."

"I'd love to hear 'em."

They hugged. She wrapped herself in a long coat and stood in the doorway.

Turning toward Jason, tying her coat, she asked, "Where are you staying?"

"The Radisson beside JFK."

"See you at noon and pardon me, what is your name again?"

"Jason Weston Laramie."

"See you at noon, young Laramie."

He raised his beer, teeth shone, and she left.

Ten
Promising Thoughts

Traffic lined 140th Street. Horns honked. Pigeons flew. Skyscrapers, steel scaffolding, and fresh concrete formed part of the landscape of most urban cities, and New York City, towered no differently than all the rest. Several hundred-thousand people crammed into town for the New Year's Eve countdown and it was that exciting element of cheers at midnight and a few others which caused Jason Laramie to stand on the street pop eyed, and awe struck. The writer knew he was only days away from seeing over 32,0000 glowing lights and counting down as the Time Square Ball dropped, not just another day or year, but a new century, Y2K. The reason he left Germany early. Mayor Giuliani and other celebrities were expected to be at Times Square, to ring in 2000, and Jason felt that's why Weston planned to meet him in New York City and not somewhere else.

At noon on December 29th , he waited for Sorano by the curb in front of the Radisson, a yellow checkered cab wheeled up to his feet and the door opened freely.

"Good morning, Jason." She smiled and took his cold hand. "Come on. Hurry. It's cold outside."

Dark makeup lined her eyes, hidden behind stylish round sunglasses, she looked like a movie star. Her shirt was navy, rolled under her tiny chin was a thick turtleneck, gold and silver bracelets, of some value, he predicted, wrapped around her wrist and forearms. All her fine jewelry matched her earrings and watch, revealing her classic style, just as Weston had said, months earlier. As friendly as anyone he'd ever met, and right away Jason could see why his uncle fell in love with her, as lovely as she was to him. Even in her late forties, she was incredible. More down to earth and social, a lady tailored with class, who made people feel at home and comfortable in her presence.

"Cool weather, but great for a walk in the park." He grinned and turned to her, unfolding his hand. "And where's my Bento Box, you promised?"

They started their friendship with a laugh, a welcoming tactic his uncle had taught him at the vineyard to break the ice with nervous customers, especially those who stood too far away and crossed their arms.

"No Bento Box for you." She pulled off her gloves to welcome him. "Your hands are like ice, how about some warm coffee at Wonderful Ralph's Cafe instead?"

"It's the best in New York," said the cab driver.

"Even Giuliani likes the brew." Sorano waved her hand. "His wife and I are good friends."

He never hesitated to doubt her, not even for a second.

"My treat," she said.

"I'd love a good cup of beans at Wonderful Ralph's."

"Sir," Sorano said to the cab driver, "this gentleman has never been to Wonderful Ralph's Cafe before. Could you drop us off at the cafe on Madison Avenue?"

"Yeah, sure, 888 Madison, Miss Daisy. It's your dollar, Ms. Tanaka." He sarcastically bounced his big head, chuckling. "I'll take the newbie out for beans."

"It has to be better than the motor oil Weston makes in our coffee pot each morning," he said. "That stuff would kill a mountain goat."

The tubby driver peered over his shoulder again, and with a deep Brooklyn accent, said, "Where's he been? Inside a cave somewhere with that Southern accent?"

"Virginia." Sorano adjusted her coat in her lap and nodded. "Shenandoah."

"Yo, Buddy, you a caveman from Virginia, huh?" The driver chuckled. "I should've guessed it with that overgrown hair on his collar."

Sorano rolled her eyes and then Jason relaxed.

"I'll need an Irish Coffee after this bumper to bumper traffic," Jason told her.

Sorano touched his hair and shook his arm.

"Oh, that reminds me, did you ever see Weston drunk?"

Leaning forward, Jason chuckled.

"I've seen him with a bottle of wine but never drunk."

She moved over to the other side of the cab, turned around to face him, and laughed before she said anything more.

"He came to see me, I believe it was in '88, seven years after we'd split up. We'd agreed to give it a second chance over the phone, he said, 'Why not, right, babe?' "

"So, you got him out of Virginia?" In Jason's mind he saw him standing tall beside her again, like in the photographs. "He's stubborn as a dang mule when he wants to be. I respect his privacy, though."

She clenched her hands and twisted her bracelets.

"He had odd jobs," she said, "nothing stable and nothing that brought in big dollars like he wanted or like what I desired of him, when Reagan was President. He worked as a substitute biology teacher, sold insurance and cars, and then talked about flying through the valley on some small plane he was going to make in his spare time," Sorano scoffed. "I don't know if you have figured out your uncle yet, but he has a big, big imagination and is a smooth talker, too."

"Occasionally, he has a good idea and widens his playing field." He took up for him. "And he's a mastermind when he wants to draw an idea on paper."

She touched her chin and leaned on the window.

"Umm, Weston and his night of drinking."

"He got drunk with you in '88." He helped her remember.

"Weston was as poor as a homeless man even after his Uncle Elmer had bought him some farmland he wanted in Mount Jackson. He's a good man but he struggled in every area of his life," shaking her head and watching the cab driver do his job. "He tried in every way to plant vines. I'm not sure if one vine ever lived to produce a single grape," she whispered. "After many failures and a dozen disappointments his belligerent father wanted him to join the Navy as an officer. But his vision prevented him from flight school, so he joined the Army for a stint and his brother was also the G.I. Joe type."

"He's my father, a Rambo-type and you're right. He bleeds camouflage and metal polish runs in his Army veins."

"Oh, it makes sense now." She touched her watch. "Weston wanted to see the Hamptons and that was all he talked about was walking through the rows of vines for inspiration.

Nothing else would suit him. We borrowed my friend's home in Sagaponack and we took a little vacation."

"My uncle Weston hates the beach." He told her. "He's more of a mountain man and lives in the valley, far from the beach."

"On that day he wanted to see the ocean." She opened the window for fresh air, sighing. "Work on his new farm was not going well and his father made fun of him, calling him a loser for being turned down by the Navy, he needed to escape. It worked out for us though. The trip cost much less during the week than on weekends or holidays. He had a small amount of money in his pocket to visit a good vineyard."

"He does like fine vineyards." Jason kept his winery business to himself.

"Weston had three small vines in the ground and one big dream when I left Mount Jackson."

She belted out a laugh and to be hospitable he chuckled along with her, despite knowing more than she did about her old boyfriend. Twenty years had passed and she had no clue what Weston had been doing with his life. He grinned, and thought of his uncle who would have done the same. To Weston, privacy was as important as his faith. To hear her speak, Sorano had no idea that he owned a large vineyard in the Shenandoah Valley, fulfilling his plans year after year until he had satisfied his dream in 1991. It seemed her family in Mount Jackson had failed to mention the winery to Sorano. His plan was to keep Andy Oliver Vineyards a secret for as long as he could. Closed lips. Over the decades Sorano had lost track of Weston and so did her family in Mount Jackson, leaving Virginia to follow her own dream in New York City.

"The vineyard in the Hamptons also had fine brandy." Sorano tied the baby blue scarf around her neck. "I remember the night well," she nodded, "as if it were yesterday."

The cab driver said, "We are getting close to Wonderful Ralph's Beans. Tell the story lady, you got me hooked now," he spat tobacco inside a red cup and sat it down in his console. "Get to the good stuff. I want to hear this story before you go."

Sorano placed her finger on her lips, then her eyes lit up.

"It was when the Yankees had a decent season. Weston was excited about watching the Yankees together in the fall of '88."

"I remember that season," said the cab driver. "That was the year Lou Piniella replaced Billy Martin as Manager."

***

To describe Wölffer's vineyard as a magnificent place, was and still is an understatement, and fortunately her friend's holiday residence was within walking distance, the length of a baseball field. Jason pictured the winery on a grand scale, listening intently as she told of the lovely winery, painted soft yellow in color, roofed in Italian tile, with a huge wooden door as an entrance way. Off of Sagg Road, rows and rows of pristinely groomed vines, acres and acres as far as the eye could see, which seemed endless and picturesque. The vineyard seemed out of place, less than a block from the ocean. When she spoke of the high and wide climbing grape vines that hung heavy, full and robust, handfuls for harvest, the place reminded him of when he first arrived at Andy Oliver, months earlier. She told of the vineyard's logo as a muscular stallion, painted in dark brown above a green color, leafy grapes and twisting vines.

"I know of the Wölffer Estate," said the cab driver. "I've had the Grape of Roth at a party there in '94," raising his hand, "it has a smooth lasting finish and my wife favors it."

"We toured the estate before we walked inside the grand tasting room," said Sorano, pulling on the ends of her scarf again. "Bottles were racked, floor to ceiling, and Weston must've asked a hundred questions before we left Sagaponack. The house was vacant when we arrived, a perfect vacation spot with a view that would make a young Rockefeller or a Vanderbilt become jealous."

Jason turned his head. "I haven't heard this story from Weston."

"I'll tell you." She laughed.

***

"Weston and I sat at a small dinette table made for a smaller couple when he said, 'Can I pour you a glass of Chardonnay?' I said, 'Yes and I'll pour you the Hungarian brandy' and I did."

"Weston has a charming bright smile and I remember him for that, saying 'I'll take a tumbler to the rim with brandy, please.' I can see him pulling his long mustache with something on his mind," Sorano said, "Gripping the tumbler and boxing like Sugar Ray did in the ring."

She continued as if she was right beside him. He took mental notes.

"Here's your Hungarian brandy, Mr. Laramie." She handed him the glass, and he crossed his long legs, twitching his big feet. "Thirty feet off the ground is where we kissed and kissed for a long time. He was a good kisser."

"I'm getting sick up here," waved the cab driver, "and Wonderful Ralph's is a block away."

The men listened politely to Sorano's soft seductive voice.

Weston turned to her in a daze. "I've missed you dearly over the past seven years."

Sorano told how Weston stood and leaned on the rail, half his brandy was gone at sunset and the evening was warm on his face, and warm on the both of them. He slowly wiped his forehead and sideburns, down to his chin with the cold glass, cooling him, deep in thought, and yet, still clammy in his palms, he settled down into his seat.

Walking up beside him on the rail, sipping her white, dry wine, she said, "What are we celebrating, anyway?"

"You have been in New York for seven years and I've been in Mt. Jackson, trying to make ends meet." Turning to her, "I thought this would be a good place to talk."

Sorano sat in the corner of the deck, part shade, part sun, resting the wine glass on her leg and waited to see what he had on his mind, listening closely for the reason behind his random trip to Long Island.

"It has been a few years since Andy died." His face was serious. "Thought we should talk again."

Removing his dark glasses, face red from the strong brandy, Weston said, "Obviously you care about me or we wouldn't be here, right?"

"Sure I care about you, Weston. I've always loved you."

Turning the glass to his lips, he said, "Are you coming back to Virginia to live with me? I need you back and we need a home."

"I live in the city. My father's businesses are close, and it wouldn't make any sense to think of living in Virginia just to watch us struggle on a farm and try to make ends meet when I'm doing well with what I have established in New York."

Later, Weston finished his brandy, stood inside the doorway.

"I came all this way so you could talk about how you'd watched me struggle, and how well you are doing without me, huh?"

Against the railing, Weston held himself up. She walked up beside him.

"New York has everything. Good Economy. Best concerts. Top cuisine. Baseball." She told the men. "There's nothing in the world we cannot get in New York City." She remembered, and said, "My father said he could learn to tolerate a southerner as long as you would do what he says and work under his orders."

He slammed his fist against the metal dinette table.

"Your father wants me to serve him like a Lord until I can make a few dollars and deserve his daughter, right?" rattling the chair at the bar. "Make myself worthy to be in New York!"

Weston stood tall, adjusting his shirt and jeans with one hand in his pocket while he stumbled to the table holding his Hungarian brandy bottle.

"Until you can support yourself, and that's not much to ask from my father."

"Live better and support myself, huh?" He rolled his eyes and scoffed. Weston belted out a strong laugh, wiped his red eyes with his long sleeve and laughed again.

"My father is offering you a better life in New York, Weston. To start, drive a truck and learn from him." She paced and stood. "Deliver furniture to customers or better yet, you can be an assistant manager in one of his fine restaurants. Something like that. Take his generous offer and humble yourself."

"Your father can kiss my southern ass, lady. I will make it without him!" He lit a cigar on the balcony. "Seems you two are in agreement? If you expected this second chance to work with your father's suggestions, you've underestimated me."

Later, the brandy made Weston sick and he switched to beer. Two hours had passed with him hanging over the balcony and they refused to find peace. The man was drunk with his head on the rail. Seated on the sofa, stubborn and unmovable, turning on the television, Weston accidently broke a crystal clear candle holder on his way to the restroom. He trashed the pieces. The television screen flashed the final score of the Yankees, and another disappointing ending.

"Oh, yeah, when you work for my father, you get season tickets handed to you by my father himself." Sorano set the Chardonnay bottle on the table. "And if you humble yourself to him and try, he'll put you to work, right away. Don't be so stubborn and stop drinking so much, Wes."

Clenching his fist, Weston bit his lip until it bled and grunted, then walked out the sliding glass doors into the cold night air and turned toward the ocean, he gripped the rail, still holding his bottle of brandy, and threw it over the rail.

"I-I-I- I hate that man."

The next night, still mad, but dressed in fine clothes, they shared a fine bottle of Riesling and agreed to eat in peace, settle their differences, and Weston complimented Sorano on how beautiful she looked in navy blue. They agreed to watch the Yankees without fighting. Before the game, they were close again, making love for the first time in years. Later, Sorano and Weston cuddled underneath a blanket and shouted at the television, still in agreement as the Yankees lost another big game, twice in two days.

"I'll have my father call Coach Piniella on Monday morning, get the pinstripes back on track," she said, rubbing her face with both hands. "We need Mike Schmidt in New York."

"Let's bring Pete Rose out of retirement. He knows how to hit the dang ball." Weston pulled a bottle of Sauvignon Blanc from the rack. "I know a lot about wine, Sorano." He grinned. "The farm could be a vineyard. Three months before Uncle Elmer died," rolling the glass inside his palms, "he shared his winemaking secrets with me, in private. I have them in a safe in Mount Jackson."

"Working part time doesn't justify you as someone who could make a farm into a vineyard. Much less make a sensible living with some hocus-pocus family secret." She took napkins and cleaned the table. "Visiting Napa Valley during the summers doesn't qualify either, does it?"

"Tomorrow, I need to leave early for Mount Jackson," he said, buttoning up his slacks. "The Wolffer's have inspired me to keep going with my ideas, to turn the farm into a vineyard in Virginia. It's good land and there's good people in Mount Jackson."

"Did I offend you?" She reached for his arm. "Daddy will loan you a hundred grand on Monday." She held out both hands. "You don't have to ask him, I'll do it for you. Be a humble man, Weston."

She took a moment to cool down and change clothes.

"I don't need your father's money or you to criticize, either! This second chance was a bad idea, Sorano. Bad, bad idea. But it offered us closure, didn't it?"

"We could have been great together if you weren't too damn proud to take a good salary and some baseball tickets from my generous father and thank him!" She walked down the hall to her bedroom in her favorite black and pink robe. "Are you coming to bed?"

"I'm sleeping on the sofa." Weston turned on his alarm clock. "I'm getting up at five and leaving. I have a long trip to Virginia."

Placing her hands on her hips, Sorano laughed. "I can't believe you think you can turn some farmland into a vineyard, and you're not like the Wölffer's Vineyard."

***

The cab driver pulled over to the curb on 888 Madison Avenue, and Jason handed him the money, flapping a generous tip before Sorano could reach into her purse.

"That's a grand story, Ms. Tanaka," taking off his hat. "Is it the truth? You stayed in the Hamptons and know Lady Giuliani, huh?"

"Yes, it's all true."

The cab driver spoke in his Brooklyn accent as he counted the bills, "Weston might need another chance. Hell, all men need a second chance."

Gloving her hands, Sorano tapped his shoulder and thanked him for the ride. Stepping into the warmth of Wonderful Ralph's Cafe, whispering about the menu and the deep aroma of beans and bread, Jason let her lead the way. She was undecided.

"I like peanut butter on my bagel, how 'bout you?" He said in a low voice. The writer's curiosity sometimes landed his butt in a heap of trouble. His next question to himself: "Why is she interested in spending time with me, well, unless she wants to know more about my uncle's life?" He turned. "Why didn't you walk away yesterday after we met?"

Her lips curled in a sudden fright, still in line for coffee, eyes brightened, and her hand clutched the handle of her thin purse. He hoped so, or at least; Weston was part of why she befriended him.

"I would be lying if I said I didn't want to know how my friend Weston is doing." She slipped her gloves off, pressed them deep inside her coat pockets. "My respect goes to Weston for standing on his own two feet in life, working on his farmland in Virginia."

Her back was to the counter.

"You are up next, Sorano."

"Could I have your name for the order?" asked the girl behind the register.

"Sorano Tanaka."

"Are you the business lady who owns a dozen restaurants and furniture stores, stretching from here to Montauk?"

"How did you know that?" Sorano turned her head.

"I study business at NYU, and your name came up in one of my courses, and now you are here." The lady at the register clutched her hands. "My father was in Tanaka's Cigar Shop last week and bought Christmas gifts for his brothers."

The hands of each lady met across the counter.

"Great to meet you, and your tag says, Rosalind?"

"Yes, that is my middle name, I go by Rosa, when you come back again, just ask for me, Mrs. Tanaka, please."

"Ms. Tanaka." Sorano eyed the lady and then the menu. "I'll have a double short, nonfat, low foam latte with a hint of nutmeg and a dash of cinnamon, please."

"What size?"

"Medium," she said. "And for the handsome guy...?"

Winking at the college lady, Jason was next. "I'm Jason Laramie, by the way."

She shook his hand in the same fashion but held it a few seconds longer. He thought it was her way of flirting with a Southern guy and then she winked at him.

"Great to know you, Jason." Rosa lifted her eyes. "That southern accent tells me you're from Georgia or Carolina?"

"I live in Virginia now, but I'm from North Carolina." He didn't want to seem overzealous about the beautiful red-head, who's sparkling green eyes and genuine nature had him leaning toward her. He scanned her soft face but pointed at the menu. "Could I have a large mocha frappe and a few dates, I mean a package of dates and mocha frappe?"

"Date? Yeah, sure." She looked at Sorano and smiled.

"These southern guys," said Sorano, bumping him with her hips, "are so subtle, aren't they, Rosa?" grinning at her.

"One cold drink and one hot date coming up." Rosa giggled. "They are easy to read, aren't they, Ms. Tanaka?"

"I've become addicted to hot dates and mocha frappes." Embarrassed, Jason scanned the menu. He asked, "Could we have two bagels, one blueberry and one peanut butter?"

"You might like New York's fast paced lifestyle, Jason Laramie. Ever considered a move to the Big Apple? There's a good company waiting in the city," Sorano bumped his arm. "Ask her out," whispering, "go ahead."

Shoulders shrugged. "She's just being nice, walking around, minding her own business."

"I've been here before and I haven't seen it. You're not like your uncle, are you?" She crossed her arms and nudged him, three feet away from Rosa. "Ask her out."

"Rosa, if you aren't busy later and if you are, it's okay, but..."

"Yes, I'll be glad to go out with you, Jason. Whispering, "Thanks, Sorano."

"My work here is done." Sorano dusted her hands.

"You heard her, didn't you?" He grinned.

"Your southern drawl just stumbled over the words. I'd be an old maid if I hadn't stopped you," said Rosa, easing a bag of dates inside his hands. "What time, by the way, is the date, Jason?"

"I'm more social at dinner."

"Ms. Tanaka wouldn't be around you if you weren't a true gentleman."

Sorano rested her hand on Jason's shoulder. "I dated his wonderful uncle for a few years." she told Rosa. "I think you're safe with this guy. He seems to be the squared away southern type. Harmless. Hopeless and available."

Jason looked stupefied at Sorano. Then caught the soft, welcoming eyes of Rosa, who had her hand on her smooth flush red cheeks and waited.

"We are headed to Westbury, after your shift, Rosa."

"You are in luck," said the young lady. "My shift ends in one hour."

"I'll let you finish your work," his head tilted. "We'll be back after lunch, see ya soon."

Rosa handed out their drinks. And Sorano and Jason found two seats. "I'm more of a mountain man like Weston. Urban culture is too fast paced for a guy like me," he told Sorano. "Have you considered visiting your cousin in Virginia?"

"There's only one reason I'd leave New York."

"What's that?"

"Weston. He's the only man I have ever trusted. I wish we'd..." After she removed her coat, she wept.

"I could tell by the tears, you two had something special."

Unfamiliar with her religion and culture, Jason did what he knew was right and blessed the meal, at least, in the Christian faith. He prayed she didn't get indigestion or maybe she did pray, he was unsure.

"Once your uncle told me, 'When I picture love, you're the only face I see' and I still believe he has a big heart for us.

That's why we met and stayed in the Hamptons in 1988, trying to work things out. He looked so sharp in his summer outfit, I didn't want to let him go. I have not seen him since that trip."

"He keeps a private life."

"He's the only man I ever think about. I did write to him several times but he didn't return a single letter, not one postcard or my phone calls after he left in '88. Eleven years is a long time to wait for him."

"He kept all the letters." Jason stopped eating to tell her the good news. "There's shoeboxes full of cards and love letters, too. I've seen him shuffle through photographs of you. He still has the beautiful picture of baby Andy Oliver, too."

"You know about our baby... Andy Oliver?"

"He had the most beautiful round face and bright brown eyes, still framed on the wall at Weston's home. Yeah, I know the whole story. I'm sorry."

"Sometimes I dream of little Andy and Weston passing a football in Central Park. More than once, this type of dream has happened. We were so happy." She closed her eyes and cried. "It was tough for both of us after Andy died. Our relationship wasn't the same. It was displaced anger and should not have happened. His passing crushed our spirit."

Touching her hand, Jason told her. "My uncle has told me wonderful stories about you and him. I work with him...on the farm and in the field," holding back the name of the vineyard. "Sorano, he misses you."

"Thank you for saying that. But we were never on common ground after Andy was gone. He hates my family. He blamed me and I blamed him. It shouldn't have happened."

In that short time, Jason wanted to jog her memory.

"You had a lot of romance in those steamy love letters, Mrs. Erma Bombeck."

"Stop, you are embarrassing me." She covered her face with both hands and laughed just as Weston said she would do. Personable. Social. Smiled again. "Does Weston have my love letters, seriously, and all the photographs from Virginia, too? He kept all of our pictures?"

"Every one of them." Nodding and grinning, Jason said, "Does the river at Meems Bottom Covered Bridge and the hippie van mean anything?"

"Jason, stop." She covered her eyes again.

He quoted his uncle, speaking in a deep voice. " 'I'll never forget those southern nights in the van." Jason tapped his heart. "She's etched.'"

"You have the same voice as Weston."

"Portland, Dallas, West Palm Beach and a few hot love letters came from Okinawa, Japan, too."

"Stop teasing me."

He glanced around, lowered his voice. "On his wall, a large nude poster."

"You're a jokester, just like Weston." She ducked her head and giggled like they'd gone to high school together. "There better not be a naked picture of me floating around."

Reaching in his pocket, "I keep one in my wallet. Oh, here, it is."

He slid a photo across the table, picture side down.

"How did you get this photo?" She picked it up and adjusted her glasses. "I'm glad it's not a nude photograph of me, though. I love this picture and wondered what might have happened to it."

"Let me get this story right, ummm," warming his hands. "He said it was the first picture of you standing in the big field at Mount Jackson. See the geese overhead and the covered bridge in the background. My uncle said, well… you two made love in his hippie van that day."

"Jason!" she squinted her eyes. "You know he didn't, did he?" She leaned forward and whispered, keeping her eyes on the picture. "I remember that day in the water underneath the covered bridge. We kissed in the hippie van."

Raising his hands, "It's true *Virginia is for Lovers*. He said the geese landed and watched you two make out." Foam from the coffee covered his lips when he told funny stories, just to make her laugh and remember the good times with Weston and the stories helped build his relationship with Sorano, too. "I've seen the geese. In fact, there's still lots of geese in the valley. Last fall, flying in a graceful pattern, flapping and gliding peacefully through Shenandoah County."

"We should finish our food." Her small hands held the picture. "That was a wonderful day with Weston by the bridge when I tackled him for making fun of me, calling me Violet from the cold water. 'You're turning violet again, he said.'" "He mentioned my name, did he?" She chewed, still sighing as she saw Weston's happy face in the photograph. Good times.

"Maybe more than you realize." He took a big bite of food. "I'm sure of it."

"I heard a man mention a restaurant on the plane. It was Cesare Giulio's in Westbury."

"I know the restaurant. It has a Northern Italian appeal to it. But I haven't eaten there in a few years." She slid closer to Jason, maybe as if she trusted him as she did Weston, taking the time to describe the restaurant in more detail. "They have a wonderful selection of wine for an evening with Rosalind, don't you think?"

He examined Rosa without her noticing him, then turned back to Sorano.

"You think she will go with me?"

"I think you'll have her on your arm by eight o'clock," nudging his shoulder as she watched Rosa stare at Jason. "If you are like your uncle and not your grumpy father." She sat up tall. "Both of you will be pleased as punch with your first date and take lots of pictures. Most people forget the camera on their first date."

The thought crossed Jason's mind that his uncle was right about her beauty and classy style. New York City was a great place to have coffee with friends.

"What if we meet you at Cesare Giulio's Restaurant since you've recommended the place?"

"Great. My evening is free." Sorano opened her hands. "We could give it a try." She nodded. "I might stop in and say hello to you because my friend has a home three miles from that part of town."

Her mobile phone rang. After a few minutes, she boxed up her food and phone. Stressed. Lunch at Wonderful Ralph's was over.

"I'm sorry for not being your guide around Central Park today," she said as she stood, adjusting her coat and scarf.

"Work, work, work, pulls me a hundred directions, but I love what I do."

Hugging Jason, she tucked the picture inside his coat pocket and he never knew it.

"Wonderful lunch," he said, adjusting his collar. "Plus, please make it tonight, if you can get by Cesare's in Westbury for a drink around eight o' clock, okay?"

"I might. We're friends now, and any Laramie is welcome to eat at my restaurant, tell your sweet uncle, I said that. "

"He'll be pleased, Sorano. Very pleased."

She left.

***

To him, making friends in New York City was a blessing and to have coffee with Sorano Tanaka at a nostalgic cafe seemed something worth writing about. The opening of the lazy cafe door caused a waft of chocolates, mocha, and roasted coffee to invade his nostrils and open his eyes to the world around him. He journaled, more for inspiration than hunger or thirst, seated pen in hand. Deep sighs of relaxation, and more than once, mixed aroma filled his senses. Patrons gathered, lathered in perfume and various spices of cologne lingered when the door fanned and closed, mixed with the whirling blueberries from the kitchen. He thought it was meant more for a fairy tale, something more grandiose, and part fascination, than that of a cafe.

"Well played, Ralph." He told himself.

Endless possibilities blanketed him, lunch and dinner, and a good Carolina lady, where he credited the still warm friendship of Sorano and Weston. Then there was Rosalina.

The writer jotted in a thin notebook, sketched some too, top to bottom, drafting chairs covered in soft green, glossy glass cases, and committed to memory couples who sipped their coffee and talked as he sketched. Lost in thought for a half hour after Sorano had left he ordered a peppermint hot chocolate from Rosa. She knew he was flirting and told him so.

Elegant and yet modest, he witnessed Rosa clutch the hands of young children and leaned forward to hear the disappearing voice of an elderly lady, who ordered a straight black coffee and a chocolate muffin, her favorite part of lunch she told. Rosalina shared time and concern for others, natural and graceful, in a sincere way, too. Something special. Traits he most admired. From the first sight, she was the one lady he desired to spend more time with, he thought. Moving about her day, she was a ball of fire in his eyes, red hair, sporting a pair of framed glasses, and gentle in spirit. Anticipation was a wonderful thought for a young man spending his first night, strolling in the social life of New York City. He carried promising thoughts.

Eleven
Nights in Westbury

Jason proudly escorted Rosa to her apartment to freshen up and her style impressed him. She wore a dark green turtleneck, rolling her collar several times before feeling confident in the mirror that reflected the man by her side. They hooked arms under the glowing street light, enticed by smiles, grins, and more promising thoughts. Later, he whistled loudly for a passing cab and helped her inside.

"Radiant," he complimented her. "You should be in the movies."

"I know what I like, you and me, and it works," she replied. "I knew it from the start, back at the cafe."

"We do make a hot couple," he raved.

Her long red hair was pinned up, eyes darkened with liner, and she flipped open a small mirror from her purse, and gave her jewelry one last adjustment. Rosa's diamond earrings, two pairs on each earlobe, sparkled like lights on Lemon Creek.

When the cab pulled up to Cesare Giulio's Italian Restaurant, the strong aroma lingered for a block, as Ellison Avenue was packed with tourists. Jason saw his uncle standing in the glow of a well-lit entrance, the place they agreed to meet, was a good idea. He wore black slacks and a white pinstripe button up shirt with his gold quartz watch, the one Jason had given him for Christmas, and when he angled his eyes, he could see a matching pair of round, gold cufflinks clipped to his shirt sleeves.

"O' Lord," said Jason.

"What is it?" Rosa held his hand.

"My uncle has on a pair of black logo-embossed crocodile shoes, and there long as a Cadillac hood."

"He's a flashy Southern man, just like you."

They laughed. His shaved face and short hair combed to the side made Weston look ten years younger, but his shoes didn't help his appeal. The man hiked mountains and worked long hours at his vineyard, but now, fashionably dressed, he appeared to have immersed himself into the cool social ranks amid the culture of Long Island. With Rosa by Jason's side, he walked to the front door.

His uncle eagerly opened the door. "Jason!" Weston hugged him, pulling him inside from the cold night as if they hadn't seen each other in ten years. "Wow! Where did you find this beautiful lady?"

"We found each other," said his date. "Hi, I'm Rosa."

"Nice couple. Too good for you, Jason." Weston slapped his nephew's arm.

"You look sharp, winemaker."

"I'm here on a date myself," said his flashy uncle, stroking his lapel with his ring finger. "Different clothes than my winemaking outfit and hiking boots, huh?"

A friendly older gentleman greeted his uncle at the door.

"Why, Weston Laramie," said the old man dressed in a black three piece suit. "I hope you brought more of your Virginia wine to Westbury?"

"I did. It's great to be back in Long Island." The restaurant had given Andy Oliver wine a try in the fall of '82, the owner said and they'd been with Weston ever since. "Alessandro, you look stronger than a bullfighter from Spain."

"I'm Italian, you dirty grape maker." He laughed in Weston's ear. "You must want outdoor dining, stranger."

He handed Weston a fat envelope. They ribbed each other for a few minutes, amusing Rosa and Jason as they watched the two men catch up and talk business, waiting in the warmth of the foyer.

"Several cases of my wine are waiting for you in the back of my van." His hand tapped the large handle of the door. "I'll grab them."

"Nope. I'll have my grandsons carry in the cases, Laramie. You are off duty tonight."

An elegant lady in diamonds stepped out of the restroom, wrapped up Weston's arm as he stood in the doorway, greeting one another, kiss after kiss, hugging and whispering. Tall and thin, the bleach blonde adjusted her hips, and laughed at everything Weston said to the owner.

"Julianna," he said to his date, "this is Alessandro, he built this wonderful restaurant and this is the only place he's ever worked."

"Great to finally meet you, Alessandro." Julianna extended her hand. "Weston has spoken often of your good food and how he loves your wine selection."

Holding his tie, Alessandro squared his shoulders with pride and winked.

"This is Rosa," said Weston, "and my nephew, Jason."

"Great to meet you both," said Alessandro, a delightful man, who named a long list of famous people who had dined in his fine establishment over the years. "Please, please let me get you folks a table by the fireplace before Matteo gives it away to one of the locals."

Snapping his fingers twice, a young man, much younger than Jason rushed to his side. "My grandson, Francesco, will be your waiter, and he's my next great cook."

"We are in no hurry," said Weston, shaking hands with a younger version of the owner.

"Italians like to make a meal an experience," said Francesco, rubbing his carved chin. "We live to eat meals and tackle dessert with good friends."

A stout young teenager with long legs, dark hair, and a thin mustache, Matteo, moved fast when Alessandro volunteered him to traverse the wet snow to carry in wine cases. Proud of the bottles, as much as Weston was, Jason carried half of the cases, helping the young men to the warehouse and cooler. They unloaded ten cases for Alessandro, who had opened the first case of Andy Oliver in the back of the restaurant, kept the cork, and pressed his thumb across the golden letters on the fine label. While Alessandro graciously checked on other tables, he went to the kitchen, made a drink at the bar for a man and paced around well for a man with years behind him. He told Weston his wine made people happy, but his food made them feel alive.

Weston elbowed Jason's ribs and turned toward him. The twin brothers, Lorenzo and Matteo uncorked two bottles of Andy Oliver at the bar, a 1994 Pinot Noir and a bottle of 1993 Chardonnay. Red and white were served. The two boys handed wine glasses to an elderly couple, who nibbled crackers and cheese at the bar.

"I hope they like the Chardonnay as much as I do," said Weston.

"We have plenty bottled and ready for Long Island," Jason mumbled.

They watched one lady flare her nostrils to wind the fragrance, then she spun the drink in her stemmed glass and finally wet her lips with a taste of Andy Oliver, for the first time.

"Virginia's fastest growing vineyard," Alessandro assured her.

She kept on with her ritual, eyes on the color, lips on the flavor, like she was an expert in how to profile a fine wine. Maybe she was, Weston thought. The lady lifted her head, offered a good smile and eyed the owner with sincerity and assurance, and poured more.

"I'll take a case," she said, having another taste. "That's a good finish. Make it two cases, Alessandro."

Alessandro waved his arm to his grandson, Matteo, the young man stacked two cases at the counter for the nicely dressed lady from Queens to take home after her meal and with one last bite her Semifreddo was gone.

"Did you see that?" Jason pressed his fist; one nod to his uncle's favor.

"I saw that she was pleased," he said, shaking Jason's shoulder, turning a sharp smile on his smooth, rosy red face. Elated. Confidence shared.

"We need Alessandro to triple his order each month," Jason removed his coat after unloading the van. "And you could visit Julianna more often and take over this region, grow Andy Oliver all the way to the Hamptons."

The idea crossed Jason's mind as a promising and lucrative proposal, not knowing if he wanted to remain in the Shenandoah Valley for another harvest season or handle customers in New York City, to visit Rosa more often.

Each season was different in the winery business. Weston touched the cross on the mantle and seemed relieved to see his hard work expand to Long Island and to New England perhaps and the United Kingdom, the following year. He told his nephew how he hoped his Boston and Hartford tastings looked promising in the coming season. So, he had his fingers crossed for the purchase of a new vessel.

Shuffling around from room to room, Alessandro filled glasses with the Pinot Noir that came from the cases he delivered. Arthritis perhaps was winning in his hands, battling with his fingers and arms, bout after bout, making every effort to steady himself in an arched position, to take nothing away from his guests and their fine dining experience.

Jason and Rosa stood in the foyer for several minutes. Alessandro and Weston talked about wine and grapes and flavor profiles and their favorites in each case and how he wanted more bottles in the spring. Rosa and Julianna discussed jewelry and clothing shops in Westbury and where they could snag an Italian leather purse. Finally, Alessandro waved at Francesco and spoke Italian with a stern voice to ready the table by the fire for Laramie and his friends, then the time had come for them to follow his youngest grandson to the most desirable setting in the building.

"O' my wife, Gina, she sure loves your Shenandoah Chardonnay."

Alessandro whispered to Weston, pacing a few steps until they reached the swinging doors at the kitchen. "Wes, can you have fifty cases delivered by Valentine's Day?"

"Wow! Tell her I said she's a sweetheart and I'm pleased she likes Andy Oliver. It's familiar to the '94 profile everyone raves about." They shook hands and pressed each other's shoulders. Weston had a glow after they'd spoken. "I'll make sure the cases are here a week early, in case old man weather bites us in the ass on Groundhog Day."

"That will make her ecstatic." The man slipped Weston a check, prepaying his order for February. "This will cover express delivery before Valentine's Day and there's a little extra green for gas money." Gripping Weston's hands as if to appreciate how far he'd driven to take care of the owner.

"Perfecto," said Weston, touching his lips with a glimmer of hope in his voice.

The owner grabbed a small red bow from the limb of the Christmas tree, still glowing at the entranceway, he attached the Andy Oliver cork from a bottle of Pinot Noir to the tree and bragged about the wine to a couple from Rhode Island. Then found more customers from Connecticut and Maryland. Alessandro left the restaurant in a heavy coat and gloves, and disappeared into the spitting snowfall to meet his wife. He was the key figure to larger distributors from Westbury to Montauk, some of them were his family and others could steer promotions in smaller shops and spread Andy Oliver into New Jersey. Hundreds of Alessandro's friends dined nowhere else when they crossed into Nassau County, standing in line for his dessert and finer vines, braving frigid weather for a spoonful of Marsala wine sauce drizzled over a skinless chicken.

Matteo, Lorenzo, and Francesco spent much of the evening asking customers if they'd like to sample red or white wine from Shenandoah. Most of them lifted glasses and agreed, some were in deep conversations, just waved them away.

Weston walked around and met a few of the people, shaking hands and speaking frankly about his vineyard and grand tasting room. He invited several customers to visit Andy Oliver in Virginia, and fly south, if ever they dared to venture to the Shenandoah Valley.

The four of them stood in front of the fireplace for a photograph, and then they moved beside the large assortment of flowers for a second shot from Matteo's hand. Jason said his favorite picture was the one in front of a square mirror, near the entrance, centered between the grand window and the fireplace, and planned to frame it.

Francesco served table after table with Andy Oliver wine, pouring bottle after bottle into glass after glass, loud and alive, with music piped in through the speakers and the place became an attraction for memories.

They ordered the first course, prima. Looking around the restaurant often, Jason didn't see Sorano anywhere. Maybe she didn't make it out in the snow, he told Rosa, as the slippery roadways caused automobiles on Post Avenue to resemble cotton fields in the Great South.

All of a sudden Jason heard a glass shatter on the tile floor. A lady screamed and cried. He could hear Sorano's voice, close and excited, but Jason could not see who was seated near the broken glass. Unknown to the person who dropped the wine glass, Weston shrugged his shoulders at Jason and did the same to Julianna. His view was blocked by the Christmas tree.

"Hope everything is alright." Julianna leaned forward.

"What happened?" Rosa twisted in her chair to scan the commotion at the end of the next room where Matteo and Lorenzo were intensely working with brooms to remove shards of glass.

"Sorano is here." Rosa whispered in Jason's ear and grabbed his arm. "She's with a man in the next room, seated at the corner table."

"I should go talk to her," he told Rosa in a low voice. She agreed.

Weston pushed Jason's shoulder down as if he'd overheard their conversation.

"Excuse me."

Looking at everyone at the table, Weston stood up, dropped his napkin, and walked across the room. Julianna watched him, and before anyone could get up from the table, Jason knew where he was headed. His nephew also knew he might be in some deep trouble if he found out he'd invited her to the restaurant at the same time Weston agreed to meet him.

"Where's Weston going?" Julianna looked at Jason for an answer.

Huddled down in his chair and chewing bread, Jason didn't know whether to be ashamed or proud. Nonetheless, he continued to sip wine and watch two old friends reunite, leaning and watching what he had created unfold. Moving his chair backwards, the room was clear for his view as the young man observed them embrace and laugh, hanging on to each other's hand, like he had been off to war when he told the interesting story of his Mount Jackson property. Jason's thoughts were about Weston's emotional state, love and regret stamped as if it were printed in front of him on a photograph and if his heart was smashed with memories the moment they touched hands and smelled her perfume. Tomo, the German Shorthaired Pointer. Geese in flight. Nights in the van. The precious face of Little Andy Oliver Laramie and many other wonderful times must have flashed in the minds of the former lovers.

"To meet an old friend," Jason said to Julianna, sitting up tall. "They have known each other since the 70s."

"You mean they dated?" said Julianna. Her eyes beamed at Jason for a response and he could not lie to her at that moment, as she slowly angled her head and reexamined the Japanese lady. "It looks like..." She stopped and tried to place the face of the lady speaking with Weston.

Turning to Rosa, rubbing his red, sweaty neck and adjusting his tie, he became nervous. Jason's unsettled behavior was unknown to his date by that moment, a genuine relief, but obvious. He emptied a glass of Andy Oliver wine; the red matched his face and dry lips, but made him brave.

"Yeah, they were a couple." He told the ladies with certainty. As if wet snow melted on his neck, he felt beads of sweat making a home on his forehead and down his flanks.

"By the way, Jason, they hugged and as quick as he left the table," said Julianna, who turned to Rosa as if he knew more information, something deeper. More private. "They must've been extremely close friends, I bet?" Weston's date pressed for anything else he'd like to reveal. More secrets. She wanted the good stuff.

Rosa whispered in his ear but was interrupted by Julianna who irked and exhaled brushing his date's arm to finish her thought, as if she wanted to introduce herself. The two ladies eyed each other at the table, asking each other questions, twisting and turning, drinking and speaking in low voices. They spoke as if they were sisters contemplating how to take down Weston with a thousand inquiries and bark at him for leaving the table.

"They dated for a few years," Jason said, calmly.

"What?" Julianna leaned toward Jason and grabbed his hand. "Are you saying Weston dated Sorano Tanaka?"

"Long before she became famous in New York City, of course." He checked his watch, Jason tried to hide what little he knew about her. To lie was without strength and to tell the truth was his job as a journalist. "Way back, I'm sure of it."

Rolling the empty glass inside his sweaty palms, he thought carefully before he answered more questions, taking another long drink and surveying what Weston was doing from his angle made what he knew of value and yet, his role as a reporter suddenly became the target of instant scrutiny.

"It was a long time ago, huh?" Julianna spun the wine glass, hand to hand, and poured herself one more round. Then she shined her nails on her long sleeves and patted her lips with her napkin and grunted. In a short time, a red rash formed on Julianna's neck. Pissed off.

"Yeah," shrugging his shoulders with an immovable chin.

Julianna turned her chair several times until she could better examine him and her and what they were doing at the table. She twirled her long blonde hair, and her eyes widened and she kicked her legs back and forth each time Weston touched Sorano on the shoulder. The obvious appeared. Red faced.

"It's alright," Jason told her, but it was no use.

Jealousy flooded her heart, like a tidal wave. The way Weston and Sorano laughed, it looked as though he was getting reacquainted faster than Jason thought, revisiting his first love. Julianna tapped her nails on the tablecloth and was displeased. Since Jason's early arrival to New York was intentional, he'd created a heavy cloud of envy in the air from Julianna's perspective.

Maybe Jason's mission to reconnect the two lovebirds was naive, even selfish. What could he say? Could he stop a moving train? He was an aspiring writer who liked a happy ending and from that moment he had made a valiant attempt to do so. But he also felt it was important to play Cupid, or at least roll the dice on his uncle's behalf before he knew Julianna would tangle the web he weaved to get them in one place, talking again.

Or maybe he needed to stay focused on digging up facts about the murders he'd neglected to explore and what Top Hunter had requested of him while in Mount Jackson? He was way off course and nowhere close to the Dominican Republic to question anyone, far away from a motive or subjects. Off, in the back of his mind, spinning in some giant void, unbeknownst to him was where he needed to be headed, pointing south on the next plane out of town, driven as a journalist.

TO LOVE AGAIN

"Sorano? It's been a long time." She stood to hug him. Weston smiled at the elaborately arranged woman with her prominent eyes. *How did I let her get away?* he asked himself. *Those radiant brown eyes that hypnotize, then and now, are back in my life and have alerted my attention each time I see her.* He ran his hands atop her cold, pale skin, chilled from being outdoors, but in his grasp again, he anticipated warmth. By her slow reaction to wrap up, he noted Sorano was pleased to see him again, placing her small, delicate hand and head on his shoulder.

"How are you doing, Weston?"

"I'm fine."

Slender as a yoga instructor, she was dressed in black slacks, grey sweater, and snow boots. "Weston Laramie, what are you doing in Westbury?"

She looked as stunning as ever when she stood beside him, from her table and in the midst of the room that glowed from holiday lights. Weston admired her, holding her hands.

I'd take a seat beside her if I were alone, he thought, noticing the absence of an obvious companion. *Still, to me, she is the most wonderful woman in the world. The fragrance about her neckline, a bold and fresh perfume, notes of apricot and peach, was one I'd picked out for her in Virginia, years ago.*

Sorano's date had stepped inside the restroom.

"I'm in town for a few days," said Weston.

"We were in Westbury after a Yankees game, in 1980, I believe. Remember, those nights? Dancing and dinner?" She winked.

"You made the weekend memorable, in 1980."

"Remington Bentley," a man said when he approached the table. Turning, Weston noticed he stood tall and thin, the golfing and country club type.

"Weston Laramie." He spoke with a clear voice.

Jason saw Weston accept his hand from where he was seated, patting his shoulder in a short snap, two or three times. The man seated himself, wrapping both hands around his wine glass and drawing his attention to Sorano, who was still standing beside Weston. His eyes were harsh toward the man who befriended his date. Weston's brief acknowledgement of the man must have pissed him off, less alerted to him than her, stepping back in a respectful manner.

"Like the automobile company?" Weston stared at the man.

Sorano watched the two men, angling her head in her hand, lifting more toward Weston's words than the voice of her own date as if she meant to say something more. Finally, Sorano took her seat.

"Same family." Remington raised his wine glass in honor of his own name perhaps and took a drink. "Fine wine from the south, I heard they were serving it today."

Sorano shuffled her legs when Matteo and Lorenzo finished locating all the last pieces of broken glass with brooms and a scoop. The two boys left the dining area and returned to the kitchen.

"This is Weston Laramie from Virginia," she told her date and then turned back to her former lover, adjusting the chair in front of her. "Please have a seat with us."

"Thank you for the invitation, but I have my nephew, his date Rosa, and mine near the fireplace. I must get back to see them. Sorry for the disruption, Rem."

Sorano looked across the room at Julianna, waving at Rosa and Jason. Rosa grinned as if she were posing for a photograph and raised her glass tall, to salute Sorano.

"You have a large crowd waiting on you," said Remington, moving his hand. "You must join us again soon."

***

"Excuse me, ladies." Jason stood.

"We'll be here when you get back," said Rosa, releasing his hands.

Julianna saw Jason's face as he dropped his napkin and eased his chair under the table.

"Don't stay too long," said Julianna, watching Weston like a hawk would a field mouse. "We're hungry for appetizers."

Walking across the room, Jason heard his uncle's voice in the back laughing and taking over the conversation when Sorano questioned him. Then he heard his uncle's not so charming voice ringing like a school bell inside his head. *"Stay out of my business, and don't be a hero reporter, trying to connect all the dots for people."*

Weston introduced Jason to Sorano.

"Hey, Jason, sorry we weren't here earlier, or Francesco may have put us all together by the fireplace, like a big old family."

"Good to see you again." He held her hand in a nervous manner and looked at Weston who carried a curious smile, nodding and knew something was fishy.

"Well, you two know each other, huh?" stepping close to him with a peculiar face, his expression darkened.

Then, she blew Jason's cover, a moment predicted to happen. "We met at her restaurant a few days ago." the young man hummed softly.

That's when the pressure of his uncle's hand dug into the meat of his shoulder as if he was testing the strength of a tennis ball before he served it across the court, turning his head with an imperceptible smirk, then dusting his shirt when he recognized the truth. His nephew stood tall.

"You did? He does like tempura." Weston echoed. "Well, he's an interesting character and that's where he met Rosa, I bet?"

"No," his nephew shook his head. "That was the next day when Sorano and I had lunch at Wonderful Ralph's Cafe."

"Jason?" Sorano lifted her chin gently followed with a sharp smile. "This is my date, Remington Bentley."

The writer reached his hand toward the man. "Great to meet you, sir."

"She's a regular tour guide, isn't she?" rolling his eyes, then handling his drink with both hands. This is a great Pinot Noir from Buffalo, I bet? Medium-bodied and fruit-forward, surprising creaminess and notes of rounded berry. You can't beat Upstate New York wine, gentlemen."

"Well, sometimes you can," said Jason.

Lifting his glass, "Son," said Remington, "you have no idea what goes into making a barrel-aged fine wine this good, do ya? I don't think he does, Sorano."

"Nope," said Weston. "I can't say that he knows all the steps yet."

Ignoring Jason's hand, Remington shifted one leg over the other and reclined, smacking his lips. Instead he flipped his empty wine glass in a commanding way toward the waiter, but the truth was, he was a snobbish Yankee and cared more about his needs than Sorano's friendships or even her needs. Weston scoffed at the degenerate date who was seated across from Sorano and caught an opportunity to smile at her and she did the same.

The lady smelled like sweet flowers, as a spicy aroma lingered when the wide doors from the kitchen and ceiling fan turned and nothing could not overpower the designer scent of a woman. The waiter handed Weston the bottle, he naturally blocked the Andy Oliver label and refilled Sorano's glass as she kindly held it. The lady tasted the fruit of the red wine, examined its bright color, paralleling the wide glass with her eyes, then took a moment to savor its flavor, and tumbled the wine over her palate in a manner that would make Weston wonder about the body and acidity of the profile. She had been around the world, sampled some of the best wine on the globe. The half glass twirled in front of Sorano, where the men watched, unknowingly she had tasted an award-winning wine from Andy Oliver, the land she surveyed two decades earlier. Her brown lips turned a soft smile. That moment redefined Weston, inside his head, a moment of satisfaction for all the work he'd done, colored her lips red, and he was proud of himself, too. Then he poured Remington a full glass, who was shaking his hands like an alcoholic on a Westbury bench.

"This specialty wine is of exceptional quality," the lady bobbed her head, "and it would pair well with breaded pork chops and sauteed mushrooms."

"You're right about that, honey." Remington toasted her.

Weston nodded and handed the empty bottle back to the waiter who left.

"We better get back to our dates, Jason," his uncle said, pulling on the shoulder he'd just crushed with his fingers, three minutes earlier.

The half-bottle of wine she tasted was the bottle Matteo and Lorenzo served others with as well, but the label had been wrapped in a burgundy towel, hidden from Sorano's sight, and the brothers were called away before they could describe the year and origin of the vineyard to their table, who enjoyed the finish. Lips smacked. Satisfied.

"Weston, hmmm?" said Sorano, and in her hand was the wine glass, a small amount was left.

The movement of the wine spinning and whipping caught Weston's eye, reminding him that he'd desired her approval, from the first harvest, from the first bottle, and from her lips. Long journey. Accomplished. Her first sweet taste, the best Pinot Noir Andy Oliver ever produced, pleased her. Life spun in a full circle, slow and easy, motionless, at times, perhaps, and just the way he envisioned it would happen one day, meeting her that way, anywhere. By the size of her sweet chocolate eyes and gentle smile, she approved.

"Hai watashi no ai." Too many years had passed since Weston called her "my love" and meant it.

"Itsumo." She said "always" in her own language. Her and Weston were the only two in the room who understood each other.

Smoke fogged the room, when Remington lit his cigar. "Vintage smoke," Remington said and chuckled, watching the white rings fade away into the curtains. "New York wine is as good as a bottle of '73 Montelena Chardonnay."

Weston agreed. "Always." His message was more to her than to him. Ogling at Sorano, missing her more than he realized. "Let me tell you where that wine is made, Remy."

Clearing his throat with a laugh, "Thunderbird's the word, was my college slogan." Jason snatched a water biscuit from the table and laughed.

"What's the price, ninety twice," sounded Weston, keeping the secret to himself about the region and vintage. "That's what we said in our frat, back in '75."

Smoked rolled from the kitchen.

"Fuoco! Fuoco! Fuoco." the cook shouted in Italian. "Fire! Fire! Fire."

Weston grabbed Jason's shoulder, both familiar with fighting fires, turning to see what was behind the double doors. Heat. Fire and a warm dangerous blaze lit up the background of the kitchen. The cook fanned the hot grease fire.

"Smoke." Jason ran to the kitchen.

"Fire." Blasting the fire, Weston shutdown the hot grill, covering the small grill in a watery foam substance. He became the hero. In a short time, the cook moved to his secondary grill and resumed his post. Jason opened the back doors and positioned an oscillating fan for fresh air. Thanks to Weston and Jason's quick reaction time, the kitchen was in operation in less than five minutes. Alessandro could have hugged his friends from Virginia, for saving his restaurant.

Later, back at Remington and Sorano's table. Remington said nothing.

"Nice job, Wes," said Sorano. If you two are in town for a few more days we could meet here for dinner again on Thursday night, since you're familiar with the place."

"What?" said Remington, sitting up tall in his seat, tugging on the golden buttons of his dark suit, and clutched his hands. "Sorano?"

Jason's eyes bugged. Shocked. Pleased. He turned to his uncle, who hesitated and touched his smooth face, then eyed the well-lit angel atop the Christmas tree, like the figure had answered his prayers.

"I'm not sure what plans we have on Thursday." Weston gripped his nephew's shoulder in disagreement, to halt the reporter's words, and having enough pressure to ward off any of his jumpy remarks. "But Jason and I would be glad to stop by your restaurant for some famous Mochi Ice Cream and coffee, if that works?"

"You won't regret it," said Remington. "She has an outstanding restaurant in Westbury, too, you know?"

"No, I didn't realize that," Weston answered Remington, never taking his eyes from Sorano's face. "But we are staying in Westbury for the next three days, can you join us, Remy?"

"I'll be in London for ten days, old sport." Remington offered a sour face and checked his watch. "I'm flying out early in the morning. Sorano, here, will be glad to show you around town, though. Right?"

She nodded. "Sure, it has changed a great deal since your last visit, perhaps."

Remington obviously had no idea Sorano and Weston once were in love, had a child together or he may have suggested another tour guide for the man from the Shenandoah Valley, who knew Westbury as well as any part of Virginia.

"That's a great idea," said Sorano, puckering her lips and taking the last drink of the wine she favored. "Stop in my restaurant around noon tomorrow for lunch."

"Deal," said Weston, leaning toward her and winking softly at the lady. "Good luck in London, Rem. Bring Sorano back a sparkling wine from Kent. The chalky soil and warm climate in that region, it's a keeper when it comes to sampling Chapel Down's flint dry. But you need some idea how it's made," waving his hand, "Old Sport."

"I'll be in Kent on Wednesday. Good idea. You have traveled and know your wine, sir." Remington saluted Weston's familiarity of southern England, touching his chin with each thought. Then he handled his cigar, gripping his stogie in a self-willed position. Impressed with Weston's culture and wine stewardship, Remington crossed his legs and flipped his wool Gatsby hat on his hat. The waiter placed the meal on their table.

Halfway back to their seats Weston halted Jason in the foyer as if they were at a downtown stop light and spoke with a stern voice, "What do you think you are doing, young man?" He turned to his nephew as if they were admiring the fallen snow and the busy traffic that traveled slowly.

With a brutally honest face, said, "Helping you out." His nephew jammed his hands deep inside his slacks, shrugging his shoulders for a better answer. "I left Germany early to meet her, for you and for her. And you nearly broke my shoulder, back there."

"You mean, you're playing matchmaker? You desired a hard grip, anyway."

"Yeah, but you desire each other. She still loves you."

"That's my business, Cupid."

They stepped outside in the cold, wet snow. "Once I found out she wasn't married, I asked her to be here, for sure. Worked, didn't it?"

Pressing his hand against Jason's chest, "Now I'll have to explain how I know Sorano to Julianna."

"She knows. I told her ten minutes ago."

"Damn it, Jason!" He walked back inside. "I need a drink."

The young man couldn't tell if he was angry or elated or both. His uncle was hard to read when he had few words to speak. Twenty paces later, the two men took their seats beside Rosa and Julianna.

"Great job with the fire, guys. But what took you two so long?" asked Julianna, hugging his shoulder and kissing him more than once. "You know Sorano Tanaka?"

Weston hummed an answer. "Yeah."

Then Julianna whipped her head around to see if Sorano was watching what she was doing or observing her date. The Japanese lady saw everything. She was aware and intelligent enough to read Julianna's game. Sorano waved to Matteo for a second bottle of wine, to cover up the fact she was following her former lover's every move. Weston's eyes angled to Sorano when she went to the restroom, too, and yet, the man she hadn't spoken to since they stayed near Wölffer's Estate, in 1988, was not without a date in her hometown, either.

"We sampled pasta and fruit," said Rosa, slapping Jason's hand. "So you two will need to catch up on the Chardonnay and Prosecco, go for it, guys."

Weston and Jason surveyed the ladies who had helped themselves to a couple of glasses of Prosecco and strawberries in their absence. When the waiter scanned his uncle's direction, he tapped his glass for more wine. The waiters knew Weston well enough to respect his wishes and was excited to see him back in town.

"I'm in the mood for an Americano," said Weston who elbowed Jason, flashing his eyes and curling a good sized grin as if he'd robbed a bank. "Nephew, how about you, can you follow me, old sport?" He laughed at how Remy said it.

His nephew's thumb and forefinger overlapped the smooth fabric of the lapel of his coat and nodded. "You lead and we'll drink with these beautiful ladies all night long. How about that on my first night in Westbury, New York, huh?"

"Good man. Thank you, Jason." His uncle sincerely nodded. Not only could Jason hang with his selection of cocktails, but he enjoyed the camaraderie from a man who was admired by the owner, the cook and plenty of customers.

"What do you recommend, Francesco?" said Weston, checking the menu.

"Milan Turin, sir."

"It's an Americano." Jason turned the page.

"He's a king," said Julianna. "Jason's the king tonight and a brave firefighter. Right, Rosa?"

"He needs a crown," toasted Rosa. "He's having a blast in New York."

"Your date is an exceptional writer, Rosa," said Weston.

His nephew laughed at him as he was sincere with his compliments.

"What's in an Americano?" asked Rosa.

"Tell her, Jason," said Weston, raising his hands and closing his eyes.

To impress Rosa, soaking up the world around him, from what he could remember while standing in the foyer, he said, "Campari bitter, sweet Vermouth, soda," dropping his hands, "ice, ice, ice and don't tell me ..."

Pulling her bangs from her face and clearing her throat, Julianna interrupted his stalled memory for her own flashy conversation, and added her two cents.

"Lastly," she said. "My favorite two ingredients, a slice of orange and lemon peel on top," she slapped her hands, a bit drunk under the sauce of Prosecco and cheered herself on behind her thin rimmed glasses.

Rosa puckered her lips and seemed impressed with her date.

"How about we all have one, Francesco?" said Weston, flipping the menu over and returning the leather book to the waiter. "Line us up, good man."

"Perfecto." The waiter tucked the menus under his arms and walked away.

Three of them ordered an Americano. Julianna held the cocktail menu and changed her selection to an Italian Greyhound, hinted with rosemary sugar. Beneath the rosemary sprig, garnish, sugar on the rim was gin, red grapefruit, and Campari. Both were fruity and the liqueur did the trick and started adding conversation to an otherwise awkward moment among friends.

In a half dozen months, Jason realized his father was wrong about his brother, very wrong about the man. Weston knew the finer things in life and brought out the best in others without asking for anything in return and he was well thought of in many circles. The kind of man he wanted his boys to model, indeed, if he had young men. His dashing uncle made everyone feel significant. Other tables even carried on with Weston and listened to his stories about living in Virginia and North Carolina and other places he'd traveled. A clear sense of excitement stirred around the table, laughing and smiling became a memorable moment for the life of a good writer. One of those rare nights where the moment was cherished and it meant the world to each one, where friends united, settled and happy with food and drinks, Jason noted. Money couldn't buy an evening by the fireplace so riveting, especially that night and they stayed a long while at the table. None of them wanted to call it a night or call a cab, either. Well, New Yorkers knew Weston and if they didn't, the Empire State was only a short season away from knowing Andy Oliver.

After his uncle finished his Chicken tetrazzini, though, he hardly said a word, and Jason carried the conversation and told stories about his time as a journalist in Florida while Weston glanced at Sorano having dessert. Generally his uncle could talk his way through any setting, but his tangled emotions and memory must have gotten the better of him when Sorano ran her hand down his pants when they met earlier that night, raced his heart again. His uncle was full of funny stories, but in that moment Weston was lost inside his own memories; Tomo, Andy Oliver, The Hamptons, and a hundred other things he'd spoken to his nephew about covered him like the warmth of summer sunshine on the trip to New York. None of his closest thoughts were mentioned at the table that night. His uncle limited himself to places he'd traveled and not about who was with him or the good times they had among friends. Personal. Emotional. Unspoken.

Harboring his words, Weston chewed in peace and remained calm, clasping his hand often, until his plate was clean. Photographs and letters from Sorano must've raced into his pounding heart as if the Pony Express were delivering packages in person again. His wounds of their broken relationship had never fully healed and only Sorano could make things different. Wholeness. Sincerity. Love.

When the dessert arrived, Weston didn't say ten words, but only agreed with Julianna about the good taste. His nephew knew enough about him to say he wasn't being stuffy. Thank God, Jason saved the night from dying in an Italian restaurant, bottle of red, bottle of white, and dessert. Out of respect, Jason asked his permission to repeat a funny story his uncle had told him when he first arrived in Virginia.

"You're the writer, Jason," honoring him, "tell the good story, sir." He did.

At a quarter of ten, Remington and Sorano waved at Weston and left the restaurant. Pressing his buzzing uncle down, to keep him from embarrassment, the young man predicted his plight, so Jason slid dessert and Macchiato in front of his face while Julianna and Rosa were in the restroom. They never spoke a word. While their dates were gone, Weston invited Jason to join him at the espresso bar, teaching his nephew the traditional Italian way to drink coffee was to stand. Jason followed him and finished his brew. Red eyed and jealous, his uncle gulped his coffee while Sorano walked by him, and she winked back, on her way to the doorway. Jason saw them flirting.

"Goodnight, Sorano." She said the same and walked outside. He said he wasn't sure if he would see her again. Remington had double parked his luxury car by the curb, but not without a ticket on the window. Through the peerless restaurant window, Weston saw Remington open the door for her. However, Jason witnessed his first Bentley and one of the owners, dusting snow from Sorano's passenger door. While her date removed snow with his gloves, Sorano glanced across the road at a glowing restaurant and she must've seen Weston, her hand brushing a tear from her cheeks, crossed with flakes of snow, was the hope he held.

"Get in the car!" yelled Remington, raising his hand. "Your flirting with Weston Laramie embarrassed the hell out of me. Don't ever let it happen again!"

"He is my friend!"

Weston took off racing after Remington, spinning and sliding in the melted snow, the driver pulled away. Weston halted. Jason stood beside him.

"If he touched her!" Weston said to Jason.

That moment of emotion redefined Jason's writing career, something real and rare, and something he was supposed to experience, caught in the moment, he experienced the truest kind of love.

His uncle had said months prior, one of the most disturbing arguments Sorano had with him was about money and love, more about prominence and style than anything else. Materialism, she'd told him in the early 80s, fed her ego, the finer things severed her love from him. Maybe she'd changed. Her father provoked the argument because of Weston's lower-middle class status, a military brat, raking through life, wasn't enough glue for his approval. Weston stopped trying and his communication disappeared. Though she must've sent him a hundred postcards and letters over the next two years, to say she was sorry and how much she still loved him. Weston knew his role as a husband would be more of a servant than an equal in her father's eyes, if they stayed together, so he let her go.

Gladly covering the bill at Cesare Giulio's Italian Restaurant, Weston sighed, and out of the blue, he ordered a limousine. The driver dropped Julianna off at her home on Linden Place. Being the gentleman, Weston kissed and hugged her goodnight in the doorway of her grand scale home. Julianna had done well for herself as a licensed real estate broker, making principal partner in her seventh year, but Weston's business was in Virginia. Love faded at a distance.

Rosa kissed Jason, watching and waiting in the back of the limo. Weston wasn't in love and neither was she, a blind man could tell that much, but their friendship was one to be admired. The cold night even made the local's shiver in the frigid snowstorm that blanketed Long Island. Later, Rosa and Jason shared a room together, he held her in the same bed.

Long before sunup, Weston had read the newspaper twice, spreading honey butter on his Texas toast when Jason walked Rosa downstairs, arm in arm. His uncle seemed in good spirits despite having seen Sorano with an arrogant man, but seeing her was worth the trip.

"How did you sleep?" Scooping a spoonful of strawberry jam, Weston locked his eyes on the happy couple, mostly on his nephew for a sincere answer.

"Superbly," said Rosa. She wrapped her arms around Jason's waistline, edging her hands around his biceps and brushing his cheek with a soft good morning kiss.

"How about you, lover boy?" Weston crunched his toast. "How was the floor, Ranger Rug?"

"That clicking radiator kept our shoes warm," he grinned, "but my lower back is just fine."

"I bet it was." Weston sipped his coffee. "Sorry, Rosa. If I would've known he planned on having a guest, I would've gotten you a room alone before the hotel was booked for New Year's Eve."

They welcomed each other into a new century.

"Happy New Year, folks, by the way, Weston. I've suddenly realized I'm codependent and now more satisfied with the way things turned out." Rosa winked at the writer. "We have a few more nights left in this big old town."

"You're just as pretty as he described and a bit classier than the German lady he stayed with last week, I bet?" His uncle spread his mustache out with his fingers and laughed. "What she lacked in beauty, she made up for in a wide variety of fish stockings. I'm sure of it."

"I know that's not true," said Rosa, kissing Jason. "It better not be true or he will lose more than a latte and a roommate with me, right, pretty boy?"

"You're right, sweetheart," he told her. "You speak my love language."

Jason bent over laughing as he poured them both orange juice and realized how serious they were about each other. They hadn't discussed the possibility of being in a relationship, but it happened, equally and intimate, too. He saw a giant phone bill in his future or a moving truck. The adventure to Westbury had done both of them some good, and much like thousands of others who visited the city on holidays, they fell in love. At least, Jason felt love and admittedly, so did Weston, who planned to explore the possibility of love again before he left Long Island.

Wondering how long Weston had been downstairs reading the newspaper, Jason watched television beside Rosa while his uncle was masking his thoughts of Sorano with current events, to keep from talking about the night before. Had he dreamed about Sorano or just spent the morning in deep thought as the Japanese lady crossed his mind, the one he'd spoken about for weeks, even months, was nearby? Or did he drift off with her picture turning inside his hand. He did mention her name once at breakfast. But then, he didn't have his normal eggs and bacon, either. Nor did he throw the salt and pepper shakers at his nephew for inviting her to the place they'd planned to meet in Westbury. He was pleased with his nephew, but he wasn't about to admit it to him or anyone else.

Rosa left in a cab around nine-fifteen, and Jason leaned inside the cab to kiss her goodbye. The writer, now a lover, returned inside the bed and breakfast to see his uncle who had folded the newspaper and finished his breakfast. He waited for his nephew, leg over leg, like a sheriff in an old west film, positioning himself after a convict committed a crime but wouldn't discuss it with authorities.

"I got some news for you." Weston glared over his glasses.

Sweat beaded up on the young man's forehead, and he knew his fist was clenched under the table. "Go ahead, let me have it."

"Hartford went well and they're with us. The vessel looks good."

He didn't hit Jason or slam the table about Sorano and her date.

"What about Boston?"

"Boston sucks eggs." Weston gripped his glasses, scoffing. "The Boston buyer didn't think a Virginia Pinot Noir or my famous Chardonnay would sell in a Shiny City Upon A Hill," grunting and moaning, slapping the table top a few times. "However, my customer in Connecticut arranged a meeting with a big time buyer in Georgia."

The waitress from the bed and breakfast handed Jason a hot cup of coffee.

"Thank you, ma'am." Anticipation brewed. The young man gladly took the cup and sipped the black drink, while they talked, turning warm in his hands. "So you are going to Georgia?"

"My boy, my boy, Jason, there's power in numbers and it's safer to travel in a pack."

"When do we fly out?"

"This evening."

The writer shuffled in his seat and loosened his lungs with a sigh.

"I thought we were staying in New York for three more days?"

"I know you'd like to sack the tart from Wonderful Ralph's Cafe again."

Jason chuckled, wiping his lips with his hand and knew it was true. Still, he laughed even more as he cleaned the beverage from his mouth, pulling down the newspaper Weston was reading.

"Sack the tart? He asked. "O' Lordy. What? You spent too much time in England last year." Jason gained a serious face and rubbed his chin once more. "Will I have time to tell Rosa goodbye?"

"You can call her from the JFK airport or from Georgia. We only have time to check out and fight the God awful traffic to JFK." His uncle emptied his cup, reaching for more coffee. "We have to check on the murders with Mickey Starr, in Savannah, Georgia, too. Now it's your turn to click the typewriter, Mr. Journalist."

"This sucks!" He yelled. "This trip sucks ass! Damn it! It's hard to be in Virginia and be in love with a lady in New York, isn't it, Ridge? Travel sucks!"

Weston and Jason stood, toe to toe, his uncle taller.

"Listen, what you did coming back to talk to Sorano pissed me... the hell off at the restaurant!" He lined his finger in his face, gripping his other hand on the newspaper, crushing it. "But I didn't say anything to embarrass you in front of Rosa, now did I, huh? It's time to say it now, though."

"I'm guilty."

He hadn't seen him spitting fire mad since he was drunk the first week in Mount Jackson. Jason wasn't sure what was about to happen, but he deserved his part.

"That was something my fool ass brother would have done to get in my business and cause trouble, like he did in high school."

His nephew dropped his head, defeated and out of line. He sat at the kitchen table and didn't want to fight, for all his uncle had done for him. Weston flopped in his chair and scanned the front page of the paper to cool down.

"That was wrong to think you might actually react from your feelings for her." His nephew confessed, taking a bite of toast. "My bad."

"Hell yeah, it was wrong." He flipped to another section of the paper he'd probably read hours earlier. "Pack your crap, boy, we're going to Georgia. We have murders to explore, keep a notebook, and a good one. By the way, don't worry about my feelings. I had 'em long before you were born."

"I can stay here with the van and Rosa, and you can fly to Georgia."

"Julianna has my van in her garage. It's fine. Rosa can sleep alone tonight."

His nephew rolled the glass, hand to hand, tapping the table a dozen times, and dreaded the trip south.

"Give me that glass, young man." The waitress brushed her finger over the surface of the wood. "Dang it, you're beating up my brand new table."

Weston snickered. For the first time that day, a smile popped up on his face. He loved it when anyone other than him corrected Jason.

"I'm sorry," said the young man.

She jerked the glass from Jason's hands. "The heck you are. You look at my table."

"He'll be glad to pay for it." Weston rubbed his fingers across the wood.

"What about your lunch with Sorano?" His nephew remembered.

"She caught a plane to Buffalo this morning." He curled his lip at the writer's shocked face.

"What?" grabbing his chin. "She's waiting on you today, I thought?"

"I overheard Sorano tell Remington when they left the restaurant together last night. She's scheduled to be in Buffalo today for something important."

"So, she wasn't really going to meet you for lunch, huh?"

"You're learning how some women complicate your life and blow up your hope balloon. Lost Puppy Dog Syndrome. Plug it into your next news column."

"The Lost Puppy Dog Syndrome?"

"She was seeing if I still cared enough to meet her for lunch, pulling me along like a lost puppy dog. That's all. And she'll probably call from the Buffalo Niagara Airport to see if I'm sitting in a corner booth all alone waiting for her Japanese butt. Look, I waited for her at the Meems Bottom Covered Bridge years ago and she never showed up or called my home or office. She had my number. Back then, I waited at her family's Japanese restaurant in Mount Jackson. I was pissed. Sorano had no plans to see the geese fly south or see me again."

Jason hit the table again. "Ruthless. You never told me that part."

"New York and the Old Sport automaker, Remington, have her now. Money has her." He turned away. "From here on out, Jason, I no longer wait for her in Mount Jackson or anywhere else. Our life together is a memory of photos. Thanks for trying, buddy, it offered me closure and answered my questions about her."

He slammed his empty coffee against the table, it made a loud, hard thump. The old lady ran out from the kitchen and squinted her beady eyes.

"You busted my table, Clark Gable. Now get out of here!"

After a pretty decent breakfast the guys felt bad about upsetting the lady and the destruction of the B & B table. Weston called Brandon's Fine Furniture, a place in Westbury he knew well, and ordered her the most expensive walnut kitchen table money could buy. One that would last her through the next war, he told Jason.

On the flight to Savannah, Weston repeated what the B&B lady said, "You busted my table, Clark Gable. You did it again, busting my table, Clark Gable." He laughed and so did the lady seated in the aisle next to him. The guys felt bad about the table, and it stuck in their mind for several hours.

At the Italian restaurant, Jason became familiar with names of drinks and what consisted of a four course Italian meal, what type of dessert to order and so forth. Barely knew his way around High Point and Tampa before he met his well- rounded uncle. It was the first time they were in a place that had anything other than wine, beer or Lexington style barbeque on the menu, for that matter. What the nephew knew about his uncle was converse to what his father had mentioned. He was a man of integrity and respect. He thought, later, Weston may have suggested taking the lead on purpose, a mentor of sorts, until he learned from him without being humiliated for what lack of cultural exchange and socialization was all about. His nephew was eternally grateful for him. His experience as a country bumpkin and Big Guava expert who preferred Willie Nelson over Billy Joel and pinto beans over Garbanzo Beans slowly disappeared in Westbury. In truth, they were inside that restaurant eating and laughing until their stomachs hurt and drank until they were overstuffed. Half of what was on Jason's plate he could not pronounce or spell. Not because he looked out for himself with cocktails and coffee but because some men were without traits and qualities --- none of that lived in Weston Laramie.

Twelve
Meet Oscar Wilde

Settled in his window seat, far away from the isle was the only way to fly from JFK to Savannah, Jason loved the thought of aviation. The tangerine sun fell behind an endless stack of cotton clouds, more than he'd seen on his return from Germany to New York City and he slid the blind down to relax and think about Rosa. The plan was to daydream about the lady he met at Wonderful Ralph's Cafe and left behind in New York while he surveyed the enormous sleepy Atlantic Ocean, seven miles above the surface, headed to the Great South.

He turned to Weston with absolute certainty.

"One question, why didn't we fly first class, put us in the front row, boss?"

He slid his black ball cap forward on his nose and grinned. Clueless to the fact of what a great role model he'd become to his nephew, a man of inordinate nobility.

"Comport yourself in coach or first class is the same, winner or loser, money or broke, you be yourself and carry yourself with immense pride and everyone will honor you with the deepest respect and you will, too, young man."

"If I ever have kids, I hope they take after you."

He fell asleep.

Closing his eyes for a nap, his nephew planned to rest undisturbed on the last hour of a two and a half flight from the Big Apple to the Peach State. However, all the sudden, a fragrance slapped his nose, and he turned. She wore unnaturally colored purple hair, and the young lady had tantalizing green-eyes. A distraction in her early twenties sat to his left and bumped his arm, and the second time was intentional. She read a yoga magazine, dog-eared the pages she liked and intended to return to them at another session. As a writer, the bending of pristine pages drove Jason nuts and he almost stopped her. He watched her instead, and it became his alarm, a writer's nightmare, for sure. Right off the bat, she spoke about dance class and then about how she needed to pick up her dog, a retriever named Smiley, who was friendly and loved everyone with food.

Over the next hour, he learned that her downtown apartment on West Bay Street overlooked Bull Street, the historic promenade of Savannah. He discovered that she walked, cycled, or ran every day until she found her favorite bench in Forsyth Park under the hanging oaks.

When the plane began its descent, she took a firm handle on his leg. As the turbulence increased so did her grip on his thigh. Once the plane turned, she spoke of her time in Lacoste, France, respecting the instructor more than she did her teacher at The Savannah School of Design. The dark liner around her eyes was easy to get lost in while being in close quarters, and he didn't complain at all about her beauty either or her firm grip. Her purple hair, while comical, was stylish and fashion forward, which separated her from most ladies he knew.

"Two weeks with my aunt Jolene and uncle Clay in Brooklyn." She flipped the pages of Frazier's great novel, *Cold Mountain*. "I'm ready to get home to my best friend."

"Your boyfriend?" He was surprised when she kept talking.

"My dog." She showed him a picture of her pet.

"Chesapeake Bay Retriever. That's an excellent breed to have as a pet."

The dog had tan eyes and snow on his head. She must have been in the north or a great storm had blanketed the south, he wasn't sure of the geography or time of year and she never said much about the storm.

"I love to travel," said Weston, jumping in on the conversation. "This time last year I was having a mint green Absinthe in France."

"I've never been to France." Jason handed back the dog's photo. "But I just returned from Germany."

"I studied art for a year in France," said the lady. "My favorites are Van Gogh, Degas, Edouard Manet, Picasso, but not the post-impressionism style of Toulouse-Lautrec."

"France has lots of good wine, too," the writer winked at her.

"The best." She slapped his leg as the plane turned on the tarmac.

"I make wine in Virginia and write a few stories when I can."

"I'd love, love, love to visit Virginia and taste your wine." She ran her hand down the back of his neck as he leaned forward and adjusted his seat. "Has anyone told you that you favor the writer Oscar Wilde." She said as her left eye closed into a wink, flirting, and laughing. The lady ran her hand through his long hair a few times.

Jason remembered reading a famous quote in an Oscar Wilde book that was on his nightstand. "To love oneself is the beginning of a lifelong romance," he told her, pulling on his collar with pride.

"You know Oscar Wilde?"

Weston chuckled and then coughed into his hand.

"I studied him once."

She jotted on paper. "Visit me, please, in downtown Savannah." She handed him the phone number and address.

"Yeah, maybe I can get away to the city."

Her face posed a blank stare.

"I won't hear from you," brushing her purple hair. "hmm..., will I?"

She shook her head with a long face of uncertainty.

"I'll call you later, I promise," said the writer, tucking her note into his wallet.

"Yeah, he will." Weston pulled his bag from overhead. "He's cool."

She smiled as he handed her the carry-on bag.

"Let's meet for dinner tomorrow at seven o'clock." She took off, pulling her bag down the aisle, pacing at a fast speed and disappeared into the crowd.

His uncle, who had heard the whole conversation, from start to finish, grabbed his nephew's carry-on bag and handed it to him.

"Oscar Wilde, my ass." Weston laughed and looked over his shoulder.

"You're jealous and I'm a lucky man." Jason flipped the hair on his collar.

"Let's get you out of here before you start signing autographs, Oscar Wilde." He laughed as they exited the plane and walked to the terminal. "I have one question, though, what was her name?"

"Smiley?"

"No, Oscar, that's her dog's name. You didn't get her damn name, did ya?"

"I'm an idiot."

***

Weston grabbed a rental car and drove "Oscar" to a prospective buyer's home on the outskirts of Savannah. Conversations consisted of wine distribution, the potential for a new vessel, and how he planned to ship products to Savannah in a cost effective manner. His uncle was much more complex and tactful than Jason's father portrayed him to be when he grew up in High Point. Ten miles into their trip from the airport, turning down Tobacco Road, a dirt road with farms and new construction on both sides on New Year's Day. Street lights lined the roadway for a quarter of a mile leading to newly built paddocks and horse stables, seven of them to be exact, and more were under construction.

"This is a big deal, Oscar Wilde. It might save the winery." He checked the rearview mirror and brushed his hair. "Try to keep your pants on, Wilde man, will ya, Old Sport?"

At least twenty-five luxury cars, mostly imported, some he hadn't seen in Mount Jackson before, lined up alongside the barn and in an open field. Waving in cars, busy valet workers stood outside a large tasting room with ice chests and more shrimp and crab cakes than they'd ever seen at Jimmy's Buffet. Weston parked the rental car and pressed the keys to the Lincoln, deep inside the palm of the valet's hands.

"I'm George. Could I see some identification, gentlemen?" The valet examined their faces against the pictures on their driver's license and checked the guest list photographs. "Welcome to the Tobacco Barn!" an elated man spread his arms and smiled. "Mr. Weston "Ridge" Laramie and Mr. Jason Laramie, we've been expecting you two men." Whispering, "This party is for you, by the way. Have fun, but some of us have to work for a living."

"For us?" Weston dropped his jaw.

The two men witnessed a hundred guests walking with appetizers and drinks.

"All the way from Andy Oliver in Virginia, huh?" said George. "Wherever that is?" taking Weston's business card.

"Shenandoah Valley," said Jason, unhooking his seatbelt.

"My boss is waiting for you," pointing to the swinging doors, "just inside the barn," said George.

"Appreciate it, George." Weston tipped the elderly man. They walked past a row of southern pines and trailed down a gravel pathway to where a large crowd danced and music played. More guests. Hundreds had gathered behind the barn.

"Here we are," taking one last glance in the reflection of an imported car. "Are you ready, Oscar Wilde?"

"Big place, Uncle Ridge, and I'm ready."

The Laramie's stood in front of giant wooden barn doors, inside was a crowded bar adjacent to a tall spraying waterfall, misty fans, smooth dance hall, and a fine collection of seven antique cars were roped off from oily hands. A band played rock music in the background. They adjusted their dark sport coats and headed inside to mingle with the large crowd and to find the boss.

"Let's sell Savannah on Andy Oliver wine." Jason turned a heavy grin.

Music pounded inside his chest. Southern Rock. Drums. Guitars. Singers. Dancers. They stood with zeal and looked forward to a good visit to the Lowcountry.

"There's the star of the show." Weston positioned his head slantwise, angling to see a man dressed to kill, who wore a dark Italian sport coat; the kind found in *Fashion Weekly* and a custom-made pair of green alligator shoes were tied to his feet. Weston was certain the man had ladies waiting for a dance, and had good showmanship about himself, too. "The Son of the South."

"As close to American royalty as you'll find since JFK," Jason paced proudly beside his uncle, strolling inside, suits buttoned, like two cowboys in a western.

The Laramie's blended into a large crowd who surrounded them with questions, deep in conversation about wine, for a moment until they played a familiar popular song. Weston propped his foot on a brass rail under the bar and leaned on the front of the wooden bar and waited for his turn to meet the host and find out why he was invited to Savannah. The crowd moved across the floor dancing and smiling while others were seated at large round tables, dipping bright red strawberries into whip cream and tapping their feet. Tall and wide chocolate ran over the rounded edges of a waterfall on the other side of the barn as a lively crowd kept to the beat and watched the band. For some reason, most of the women and men had purple and pink hair and looked alike. Beautiful women danced on the hardwood floor, one as big as a basketball court, and meant for special occasions, too. Men watched and whistled, jaws dropped to the floor and women clapped to the beat. A night meant for persuasion and glamor. Love was in Savannah and the air was warmer in the Great South. Lovely couples, dressed to the nines, moved outside under the hanging oaks to watch the horses and talk about making bad decisions.

His uncle lifted his hand. "Mickey Starr, by God, in the flesh. I've read about you in magazines and thought you were something from Greek mythology, but it's you."

"I hoped my friends from Shenandoah would come."

Thoughts ran through Jason's head, how he loved the pleasant atmosphere of The Tobacco Barn, from the horses to the ten foot carved grizzly bear in the doorway and how it was wonderful to see beautiful people having fun, slowly spinning, and yet something of fascination, was without blemish.

In his head, the writer questioned the situation as reporters often do, "How was Mickey Starr, a welcoming gentleman, who had a guest list as long as his '74 Cadillac, involved in the deaths of three former employees of Andy Oliver? Surely guests would gossip during the party, wouldn't they? He hoped Weston hadn't forgotten about what they'd talked about on the plane, "Keep to the mission of Andy Oliver and just mingle. Don't let 'em know you are a reporter."

The host reached out his hand, and his gold submariner watch caught Jason's eyes, like a shiny star hanging over the Atlantic Ocean, paired with golden cufflinks and a golden bracelet to boot, he became jealous and knew there was a hidden story that needed the thorn removed from the roses at The Tobacco Barn. Everyone wore gold that night but Jason and Weston. Mickey's hair was gray and cut short, and the sun had chapped his face from sport fishing the week prior. The man turned a hefty smile, and had an addicting charisma about him, walking and singing a Sinatra song.

"And you must be the famous winemaker Weston "Ridge" Laramie, I've read about your vineyard, cover to cover, I might add? Good to meet you, sir."

He scanned Weston's height and arms and checked out his attire, picking a string from his right shoulder. He talked about Weston's polished shoes for a minute, long and black, before he looked around. "And this young man is…?"

"Jason Laramie," he replied, gripping hands with him, "I'm…"

Raising his hand, said, "Wait!" Mickey tapped his shoulder and whispered, "I checked my guest list twice, and there's no Oscar Wilde scheduled to be here, young man." He laughed. "I'm just raggin' ya, son. Jason, you met my sweet niece, Melody, on the plane. The young lady was as excited as a kid at a circus when she recognized the names of two gentlemen from Andy Oliver Vineyards and hoped she'd see you again."

"Yes, we did meet Melody," Jason said, looking beyond Mickey's shoulder for her wonderful purple hair, but too many people danced to find her at any distance.

"Glad you men made it. I, myself, received a fax about you, Weston, from my cousin in Hartford." He walked around behind the bar, moving out the bartender with a nod, to handle drinks himself. "Your wine is here and that's why you are here. I flew all the cases he had from Hartford to The Tobacco Barn today, and now they're right before your eyes." He hunted for a bottle underneath the bar. "The good stuff is here."

"Bottles of Andy Oliver... hmm, are here?" Weston rubbed his chin in appreciation of the extra effort he'd made and became curious of his intentions.

"I've gotten nothing but favorable comments about your Pinot Noir in Savannah tonight and there were too many to count from Hartford, as well."

His uncle touched his breast pocket and cleared his throat. Not many people knew that Weston kept a small picture of his boy, Little Andy Oliver, inside his coat pocket, close to his heart at all times. For luck, perhaps. His nephew found he was a sentimental man, just like the writer was, a bit romantic and sincere with words and memories and stories: some remembered the goodness of people for a lifetime.

"I'm not sure if those Yankees enjoyed your wine or not, but I brought you here, to my barn to show off the flavor of Shenandoah County and spread the Andy Oliver name around the Great South."

"I like your style," said Weston, who eyed Jason for agreement.

"Sir, we need to taste that smooth Virginia finish in Savannah." Mickey pulled on his salt and pepper goatee. Three glasses were placed on the bar. "The purpose for this visit is, well, I'd like to get in on Andy Oliver Vineyards. Become a strong partner."

"There aren't any shares available," said Weston. He didn't even ponder the question for a fraction of a second about taking on a partner or selling even one share of Andy Oliver, stepping back from the bar. He eagerly took a seat, resting and turning his body away from Mickey Starr with his eyebrows raised.

"Mr. Laramie," said Mickey, while watching the dancers, from the bar. "Do you mind if we have a moment outside to discuss my proposition?"

Weston's feet hit the floor, opening his sport coat. Jason followed him. He'd ignored his question, and suddenly Mickey was welcomed into a large crowd of dancers. The two Laramie men were no longer impressed.

"I'll be on the dance floor with the ladies," said Mickey, tapping his foot to the beat, "when you decide to talk business, Laramie."

The Laramie's walked outside into a dense fog where a few people were smoking cigars and drinking wine, cooling off, where they could see the yellow glow of a thousand hanging lights and heard the band playing King Harvest. Proud of what his uncle had done, Jason hoped Weston would at least consider Mickey's offer without insulting him, but he didn't know how to say it to him in such a subtle way. Murders. Debt. Media. Jason knew Andy Oliver was in deep jeopardy and he'd talked about selling the winery, days earlier, and maybe even before he'd arrived at Mount Jackson. He didn't know, maybe Sherrill knew his finances.

"I'm not interested in selling shares of Andy Oliver to a wealthy man who will want control of my company in less than two years, and want principal ownership when he decides to bring more money to the table," said his uncle, dazed in a low voice, "and I'll work for him, regretting my decision for a stack of cash."

He couldn't tell from what direction, but smoke clouded their faces from a heavy cigar that rolled past them, a pleasing smell hit Jason's nostrils and made him curious. "Let's listen to what he has to say about the vineyard, Ridge."

"Well, well…. trader," his uncle lifted his head and scanned the area.

"I ain't no trader, Ridge." Jason remarked. "I know you think I'm after Melody or some big story for Top Hunter, down in Tampa, but I'm family."

"Are you hot for Melody, Oscar Wilde?" Weston crossed his arms. "We'll see by the end of the night about your glue to the Laramie family, won't we?"

"We'll see alright." The writer dropped his head.

George opened the next limousine door, and right before their eyes, a long line of twelve dancers, dressed in purple and gold capes walked past them. The last lady touched Jason's face and walked backwards inside the barn.

"Let's have a good time," said Weston, "go dance, Oscar."

Jason didn't expect to be in that position alongside Weston. It wasn't on his radar to sell his business or net stakeholders for any amount of money. Pride. They both were curious as heck about Mickey Starr and had their own personal mission for being at the party. Had feelings been developed for Melody or was Jason after the story of a lifetime that would make him a famous man, perhaps, or did he want to get back to sweet Rosa? Only time would reveal what he desired.

"Let's go find some dancers and then when everyone is gone, we'll talk about the grapes of Andy Oliver with Mickey Starr," his nephew suggested. "How about it?" They stood beside the limo and eased a grin after a few minutes. Then, Jason gripped his uncle's shoulder and in a friendly way pushed him back to the big swinging doors of The Tobacco Barn. Agreements offered.

Weston stood with fortitude and courage in the doorway for a moment, like Sherman marched through Savannah, Georgia, and he had no intentions in losing his vineyard to the man; one that he wasn't certain he liked, anyway.

"Son, let's hear his thoughts, see how he wants to play his cards," said Weston, grabbing his lapel. "Dance and get wild, Oscar."

They laughed and planned to filter out Mickey Starr's proposition, getting lost in a world of excitement when more people showed up. Jason was glad he thought enough of him to include him over Sherrill. Suddenly, out of the shadow a man with long blonde hair stepped up beside Jason, the one who smoked.

A distinctive Georgia accent sounded, "Are you Weston Laramie and Jason Laramie from Virginia? Did you make the wine everyone is raving about inside?"

"If it's Andy Oliver, we do," Jason said.

"I'm Tipp Starr, by the way, Mickey's grandson." He held out his hand.

"Good to meet you, Tipp."

"Glad to finally see this place and meet your folks." Weston gazed at the height of the barn, long and wide, and fifty horses moved on a sloping hill not far from the doorway of the barn, thundering when they ran.

Tipp was Jason's height and weight, a striking gentleman. Though, the writer wasn't sure why he was standing by himself. Was he following them? Could he be a spy sent by Mickey Starr? Or was he waiting on a lady to enjoy what his grandfather had created and said it was for Andy Oliver?

"It's from your vineyard. Here, Mickey Starr serves only the best." Tipp walked up close to Weston, and all three men stood in the doorway and watched people dance and have a good time. The barn was alive when *Country Roads* played.

"How'd you hear about Andy Oliver?" asked Weston with his hands in his pockets.

"Volt Hendricks bought a case for his band in Hartford, and I sampled the Pinot Noir with the former president, who climbed aboard his tour bus two weeks ago. Then the president called my office from Kennebunkport and said, 'Mickey Starr needs a piece of the company,' and he said it that way with a Yankee accent." Tipp waved his hand. 'Buy the whole damn thing' were his exact words. 'And if the President of the United

States likes Andy Oliver better than Napa Valley, then the profile must be better than France, of which, well, Mickey has visited more times than he flew to Robin's Egg, Texas last year. That is how Mickey Starr got involved with you, Mr. Laramie."

"Volt Hendricks, huh?" Jason asked surprisingly. "The singer-soldier guy, top of the charts, right? That Volt Hendricks?"

"The one and only." Tipp took a drink of Andy Oliver, spinning the wine in his glass. "Volt had his big bash concert in Kennebunkport, two nights ago. He should be here in a few minutes to command the stage and raise this crowd."

"It's not for sale!" Weston blurted out as he left Tipp standing in the doorway. His uncle moved inside to watch the dancers perform and seated himself.

"Please excuse my Uncle Weston, he doesn't have all his manners in his brain tonight." He told Tipp. "His mind is still on cloud nine from the plane ride."

"Jet lag disorder?" Tipp took a sip of the red wine, spun it, and took another one, finishing his last pour of Pinot Noir with a bite of thick cheese on a cracker, plated atop a whiskey barrel, grinning from ear to ear, chuckling as if he already owned Andy Oliver.

"He's his own man," said Jason, "a bit of a killjoy."

"So that's why you are here," said Tipp, who raised his hands above his head and got loud. "The news came down from the former president and then a few calls were made to set this party up in style just to meet the classy guys from Andy Oliver."

"Appreciate the compliments on the Pinot Noir." Jason nodded. "I'm a beer man myself. Weston is the one who has mastered the flavor profile since he and Sorano Tanaka broke up in the early eighties." He eyed the gentlemen to brag about his uncle's excellence as a winemaker and how he was well-known. "He learned a few secrets in California; he'll die before anyone sees that notebook in his safe. That's how he wins the awards in Virginia, though, and other places, too."

The writer could tell they wanted Andy Oliver badly, for some strange reason, but he couldn't pin it down to just one reason. The men were curious and jealousy turned in Tipp's eyes. He wasn't sure if his uncle had a notebook full of secrets but he said it that way, to increase the offer they were about to make. Journalists sometimes elevated the topic like a musician, to draw a crowd from larger geographic regions, spanning from one group to the next circle and so it goes.

"Well... hmmm.. You met my cousin Melody on the flight from New York. She's in the Big Apple three times a month, I bet. She has sampled Andy Oliver."

"How did you know that?"

"Mickey could eclipse the moon with astronauts, if he wanted it to happen that way." Tipp laughed. "He has power and influence, more than in Savannah, far across the world. But Melody likes you, Oscar Wilde," he said, slapping Jason's shoulder. "She said it several times today at lunch." Tipp pushed his arm. "Get inside, dance with her, Jason Laramie."

Tipp opened the barn doors even wider and when the song had stopped, he shouted, "Oscar Wilde, he's here!" Tipp angled his arm at the writer, pointing in praise and admiration. Weston shared an obstinate face. Jason was sure the introduction was an act to build him up for an attention getter, but it went flat.

"Look, I found Oscar Wilde!" said Tipp, raising his cigar into the grand opening of the doorway. The breeze moved off the coast, billowing the autumn colored marquisette curtains, in the rectangular windows. "I said, Oscar Wilde, he's here!" Tipp shook the door and changed the dynamics of the party with his flashy introduction and uplifting personality. It worked, like a drill sergeant yelling on the first day of basic training.

Melody, purple and black hair down, angel of seduction, stood like a panther in a black rhinestone sequin dress, fringe flapper, arms draped, and waited for him to speak. She was the only one he knew in the room and some wonderful thoughts ran through his head, "best of the crowd, ...hmm," he mumbled. The lights dropped low as Jason and Melody, hand-in-hand, slow danced, spinning and turning, laughing and he was truly impressed. They held hands and even kissed. To be honest, he had no obligation to Rosa or Melody. No ring, no relationship. So he danced, arming Melody and thinking of Rosa, who was working the closing shift at Wonderful Ralph's Cafe, while embracing Melody.

The crowd stood as Mickey stepped on stage and spoke into the microphone.

"We have a special guest tonight and many of you already know his name. This superstar has been at the top of the charts for over three years now. His song "Midnight Whistler" just went to #1 in the United Kingdom and in Canada and the U.S.A. All the way from Barringer, North Carolina. Ready your hands Savannah, Georgia, for the greatest singer since Elvis

Presley, the pride and joy of North Carolina Mr. Volt..... Hendricks!" shouted Mickey.

Volt Hendricks appeared, dressed in jet black denim, half-dressed dancers rushed to the front stage. Hendricks scanned the crowd. At half past ten, fifty more people showed up in a bus, and The Tobacco Barn opened to welcome them with drinks and more fresh seafood. The singer was just as the radio and magazines described him, broad and tall, eyes like an eagle, and a cousin to Gary Stewart. His brown hair was cut short, especially trimmed on the sides, and a thin mustache defined his face, strapped to a flat top guitar, he sang three songs, then "Midnight Whistler" closed the night. Men stood around the bar. Ladies cheered for the singer. His wife Shasta stood beside Mickey and Tipp and watched.

Mickey and Weston walked outside during the concert. Not fishing, nor talking about southern ladies, nor was there mention of aviation, the war, or classic automobiles. The point of the trip, the target, for Mickey Starr, was the deed on Andy Oliver.

***

At breakfast the following morning in downtown Savannah, Jason asked Weston, "What did the Son of the South have to say about Andy Oliver wine?"

Weston took a bite of his Colorado omelet, chewing on beef and eggs while he thought about Jason's question, hidden behind dark sunglasses.

"Mickey Starr doesn't want cases of wine delivered each month."

"What does he want?"

"The man wants the whole damn thing." His uncle chewed his food. "All the land, seven navy blue delivery trucks, and the ultralight micro plane I just bought in Atlanta," pointing with his fork. "And the three log cabins on the hill."

His eyes bugged as Jason thought about the amount of the check Mickey Starr was willing to write. Throat cleared and hummed.

"What price would he pay, Weston?"

His uncle slammed his fist on the table. "Sum bitch wants my son's name to be removed from the gate and his grave moved, too. His idea would be to sell what we have with Andy Oliver on the label and then he had a big business plan for Mount Jackson, too."

"What?" Jason sipped mimosa. "He's crazy. Andy Oliver is gaining notoriety and he knows the brand must be hurting some of his friends who own vineyards along the coast. Only he has the power to stop us. Melody told me that much."

Weston finished his coffee. "He wants a name change. To beat all, a giant gate would stand tall, doubled doors at the entrance of the property, signs on the interstate would say - Mickey Starr Winery of Shenandoah."

Pushing his plate to the center of the table, Jason dreaded the next few days and what he would do with Andy Oliver. Keep it or sell it?

"For how much money?" Jason raised up. "What did he offer you for Andy Oliver? How bad does he want it?"

"While I was away over Christmas Mickey and Tipp flew over Andy Oliver and observed the property lines from the

223

sky," pushing his plate to the center and only half of the meal was eaten. "I told him I needed four and a half million."

"What did Mickey say?"

Weston didn't answer right away. When he spoke, he sounded...

"He insulted me with half that figure."

"Mickey thinks you'll take his offer and retire, don't he?"

His uncle stabbed the last half of his omelet with his fork.

"Told him to take his money and shove it."

"What'd he say?"

"By that time of the night, you and Melody had left in her car." His uncle's face tightened. Then all of the sudden he removed his sunglasses.

"How the hell did you get a black eye?" He examined his cut face. "Did Mickey do that?"

He cleaned the lens of his sunglasses with a tablecloth.

"I balled my fist up and knocked the hell out of Mickey Starr. Tipp and Volt rushed in and made me pay the price for bloodying Mickey Starr's nose. Tipp kicked my damn ribs and Volt took a shot or two at my head. But I hammered a few shots of my own before I got out of there."

Jason imagined the brawl was caused by a few half-drunk party animals and he always planned a place to meet after a big bash happened. Weston held his own, he said, protecting his image in Virginia. It was Jason's damn fault, and he felt like a heel for not being there beside him for the fight.

"Those bastards! Took three of them to make it even, huh?" The writer's face turned blood red. Ashamed. "I'm sorry

I left you there. Didn't think it would end up like that or I'd been glad to trade punches with those punks."

"Two ladies drove me to their place in the rental car." He smiled behind his orange juice. "Cleaned me up nice, too. Made me drink two whiskey sours that made my eyes cross and my stomach turned over a few times."

"Glad you remembered what I said on the plane about where we agreed to meet this morning." He stared without any movement in his head or shoulders. "And I won't leave a man in a strange place. Happens again.....you and I will trade punches, Oscar Wilde."

"The best part. The two ladies passed out on both sides of me. What pissed me off, huh, they talked about the good looks of Volt Hendricks and Oscar Wilde before they called it a night. The younger lady, Sherrie, wants to meet Oscar Wilde when the purple haired lady disappears, she said."

The writer leaned over the bench laughing and his uncle lost his voice when he ragged him about what she said at breakfast.

"Don't make me tell that story again; it hurts my ribs to laugh," he grinned, and finished his orange juice. "They think your real name is Oscar Wilde."

Three hours later they were on a plane to JFK. Weston stayed warm in Westbury with Julianna for two more nights. Jason spent time in an apartment cuddled with Rosa. No, he didn't mention Melody.

Early on the third day, with coffee in hand and lipstick on his cheeks, Weston drove the hippie van for the next six hours from Julianna's Westbury home to Andy Oliver, in Mount Jackson, Virginia. Weston said, if Jason would have stayed at the Tobacco Barn, it would have been a hell of a fight with Volt and Tipp.

"We would have walked away kings and my ribs would feel no pain." A handful of pictures, not postcards, hung on the corkboard behind Weston's favorite place to serve customers at the famous Andy Oliver tasting room, just to remind them of their first road trip to New York City and Savannah together.

Thirteen
Bows and Letters

When they arrived at Andy Oliver, Jason saw Weston Laramie's name on the gate and a sense of pride rushed through his warm veins and an honorable chill rippled across his skin. A new respect for the founder, far more than when he first arrived in Mount Jackson, months earlier under his infinite wisdom, and now he felt a part of the team, a man justified even stronger than before. Part of his menial task was to walk from the Andy Oliver office to the mailbox, out by the road, for some reason. He knew how much Mount Jackson loved Andy Oliver as the vineyard became an uncommon thread in the Shenandoah Valley. In the winter of 2000, the vineyard was named "Vineyard of the Year" in a popular magazine that inspired Weston Laramie to become a better winemaker as if he were on holiday in the Napa Valley or France again.

Seated in his uncle's office, Jason handed him the volume and sat behind his typewriter. He looked over his nephew's shoulder for a moment to see if he recognized his own picture on the cover.

Weston raised up with the volume in his hand. That day Jason declared himself a freelance photojournalist. He snapped the picture that would later hang above his desk. The flash went off with pleasure. Every time he looked at it, he remembered what he said, "This is the reason why I get up every day, to be wondrous in my field."

His expression marked the first time Weston had been featured on a magazine cover. Before it was newspapers and small advertisements, but not this time.

By that time in his life, high demand and seasonal production had made Andy Oliver the number three favored winery in the country and "the one to watch" in winemaking according to various markets. The article surfaced while they were in New York City and Georgia, ringing the phone off the hook as Sherrill penned 173 orders in four days. He was a well distinguished winemaker, a bit of a romantic who had spread his name from an idea on torn paper as far north as Kennebunkport, Maine and as far south as The Big Guava. A miracle came after Andy Oliver made the cover — more and more people visited. Poised and self-contained with the additional sales, Weston hired several workers with the hope he could pay them by February, but it worried him. Little to do with his success, but Jason encouraged him to come alive in a revolutionary spirit. He did and redefined his career, and was an exquisite human.

"When you pour it," said Weston, "Andy Oliver sells itself. There's nothing else we can do at that point, but to hope it has aged for quality."

He claimed the secret was in the mixture, the mashed and crushed combination of cherries, strawberries, raspberries, and not many people knew his wine contained blackberries from deep in the mountains of West Virginia.

Weston drank more and more red wine and rarely spoke of his popularity, to cope with being without Sorano. As his apprentice and friend, the astute writer noticed how he'd become more romantic and poetic in nature. Days and weeks passed that way. Maybe he had released Sorano, like a fish swam away from the hands of a true fisherman. Then, by Valentine's Day, Weston mentioned Sorano for the first time since Westbury, and out of respect, Jason didn't rag him about what he said or how he said it, either.

"Could you box her postcards and letters back in the damn trunk and lock them up? I don't want to see them again."

"Yes, sir. I was wrong for what I did to invite her out to dinner when I knew you were going to be there." Jason was straight-faced. "What I have done is inexcusable and has brought tension, less trust and conversation, too."

With a bottle of wine in his hand, Weston nodded in anger.

Jason left the room to type more on his story. The writer kicked the black trunk at the end of his bed and bruised his foot. Mad as hell at himself, he opened the lid. That's when he discovered a dark envelope that matched with perfection, hidden alone on the bottom of the trunk. He hesitated to open it, and then walked in the living room and handed it to his uncle, willing to be chewed out for it.

"What's this? I told you..."

Interrupting him, Jason said, "The last letter."

With a swift motion, Weston grabbed the letter from his hands. "Thought I told you to put my past away."

"Read the damn thing; see what she said."

"I know what the freakin' letter says." He closed his eyes and fell backwards on the sofa. "I know exactly what it says. I lived it, didn't I."

"You sure are in love, aren't you Weston Lamar Laramie?"

He kicked up his feet. "Don't ever call me Lamar again? I've lost my good glasses, anyway."

The letter was written by Sorano, dated on the seventh day of July 1981. Beyond that time, the lady only mailed postcards with nothing but general greetings that read hello or hope you're doing well - Sorano.

"I'll read you the dang letter, Old Man Laramie." His nephew grabbed it from his hand as if he was uncomfortable with holding it.

***

Dear Weston,

I had great plans for us, but things have changed and the argument at home was uncalled for. When you visited on the fourth of July, it was my traditional father and his ridiculous remarks about our engagement. Thank God he didn't know about the year we lived together. It hurts too much to even think about Andy's death.

There is no excuse for my father, he is a sick, sick man. He felt you weren't good enough for me. I apologize for him saying "I could find a better man at a homeless shelter." Please take my apology for my father's insults and actions, not allowing me to talk to you, much less marry you. He was wrong in saying those things. I love you but I have to live with my father because of his illness.

To lose his respect would be an insult to my family, especially my mother, brother and sister. He threatened to strike my name from the inheritance if I married you. You are a wonderful man, the best in the world. However, we cannot have a relationship at this time. I have left messages for you. It would be nice if you cared enough to take my calls. To write to you is the only way I could reach you. Call me when you settle down and cool off. I 'd like to talk. I'm still in love and always will be.

Love always,
Sorano

***

Folding the letter for his collection, Weston withdrew. He didn't speak to his nephew until supper time when a bottle of Andy Oliver wine was in his hand and he'd conserved his communication for long enough. The same red wine that was making him soar across magazines had a hold on him, but it wasn't the fault of the wine or the fault of the icy rainstorm, it was his day to reckon with his past, in his own way. He had his own storm, the one deep inside of him, part of him, unsettled, and there was no winner. Sorano lost, and was broken.

Jason pushed an empty glass his way. "Fill it up, bud. I need high octane."

He poured. Then he soberly sat down at the kitchen table with two plates of jerk pork chops and applesauce. "I'll tell you what happened with Sorano's father. Seven years before we met at Wölffer's Estate."

"You don't have to say anything." His nephew hit the pork chop like he hadn't eaten in a week. "You know that. But it might make a good story, one day."

"I have to get Sorano out of my head for good. Since I saw her in Westbury, I can't give up on us. I need to get her off my chest." He turned up the wine. "Seeing her with

231

Remington," he said, shaking his head, "even after twenty years was hell inside my heart. Total train wreck. Deeper pain than broken ribs and a black eye together can't match."

His uncle sat at the dinner table across from him, chewed food and drank, and once he acted like he was going to speak, but clammed up and grunted, like most men do, who pondered memories and lost.

"Let's hear it then." Notebook and pen in hand. "What happened with Sorano and her father that July?"

With little hesitation, he recalled the day.

"I made the trip from High Point to Westbury in record time. Drove like a bat out of Hades to see my future bride. I was twenty-five that year, and the clock was ticking toward what we'd planned for each other. Travel. Career. Religion. Family. It all flashed in my mind along the highway. I knocked on her door. She leaped into my arms. We spun inside her big home. Her hair was dark and long, smelled like a bath of roses. She had the most beautiful smile in the world and we kissed more than we ever had before."

Like a rolling film, he recalled aloud every moment of that day.

***

"Weston," she said, "I hoped you would make it."

"I love you."

"I love you, too."

"You need to talk to my father, though."

"Okay," he took a deep breath and released it.

He told his nephew how it happened.

"We held hands and walked into Mr. Tanaka's study, a library twenty feet tall, lined with hundreds of books, large wall maps and a new computer. A globe sat to the right of his desk. Japan was pinned with a small sun flag. New York had another pin. High Point had a black pin. A grand view of the Big Apple shone through the window on the other side of the room. Mr. Tanaka raised his head up from the *New York Times* and examined my Scotts-Irish skin. He asked Sorano to leave his office."

"Mr. Tanaka." Weston cleared his throat.

"Yes," a stern voice sounded. "Mr. Laramie."

"You know why I am here, Mr. Tanaka."

"You want to cut my grass, young man." His phony laugh offended him. "The mower is in my garage, farmer."

"I want to marry your daughter."

Her father was a Sumo wrestler, and was dressed in a kimono with a hakama on his shoulders. Both were black as coal.

"Your first mistake is wearing American jeans in my house."

"The grass doesn't need mowing and your house is in America, sir."

He stood up, lifting his arm out of his kimono. "You're a dumb Southerner from North Carolina, aren't you?"

"You're a pompous prick."

"How would you support my daughter?"

"You know where I work."

Weston told his nephew what happened, event by event.

Mr. Tanaka walked around the room, touched the globe and then stopped in front of the large window, and said something to the effect of "You are a part-time farmer in North Carolina. Ridiculous!"

"I told him we are in love." Weston told her father.

"I'll have to loan you money every month to make your bills," shouted Mr. Tanaka, "Weston Lamar!"

"We don't need your money to make us happy."

He crossed his arms. Scoffed.

"You think she loves you?" Dragging his Japanese accent, "You think Sorano really loves you? You think she really loves an American?"

Weston wanted to throw one of his books at him or better yet all five thousand of the hardbacks at the speed of a cannon.

"I wouldn't be here if I didn't think she cared for me."

"Why didn't you two Lovebirds run off to Virginia, like the rest of the so-called *lovers* do? That is, if she really loves you."

"Out of respect for her, I came in here to talk this out man to man. This tradition is a waste of my damn time." So, in a rage, he walked out.

"Weston!" he shouted cynically. But his feet were tapping halfway down the hall. "Go ahead and die." Which basically meant go to hell or worse in Japanese. So, Weston kept walking. Sorano's father yelled, "Get the hell out of Westbury, Laramie."

***

With great vigor, Weston shared a second bottle of wine with Jason, and started at the beginning of the story, spilled wine in his lap and cussed like a sailor for the next ten minutes. With flushed cheeks, his demeanor drug leaves and grapes on a ripe vine and he settled himself enough to continue his initial intentions.

His nephew watched him tilt the bottle more than he took a breath of air.

"Slow down on that wine, cowboy Laramie." Jason offered him some crackers and cheese to absorb some of what he'd consumed inside his veins. "Good. Get that mess off of your chest, talk the damn stuff out, and I'm here for you, Weston."

He filled his glass full again.

"By the time you're forty two, like me," his uncle said with a slurred voice, "your dreams are out of reach, smashed like a cluster of grapes on the heels of your feet."

Jason felt sorry for him as he watched him rip out his heart, artery by artery, vein by vein, leaning against the wall eating ice cream and crushed almonds.

"Dream a new dream," he told his uncle, "give life a big finish and if you get the chance, give her all the love she can handle."

"What's left of your life isn't a bowl of cherries or a box of chocolates, Forrest. It's a plate "what ifs, can't dos and a full cup of could have beens." He blinked his eyes and pressed his big mustache against his red face with something else on his mind.

It made him mad as hell when Jason asked him, like a long green thorn, deep in the skin, landing both hands on the table, "What's Weston Laramie's new lease on life, cowboy?" He asked just as if he were sober. "Tell me the damn truth, what's something you need to do?" Yelling, "What's eatin' you, Uncle Weston?"

He loitered around the kitchen.

"One day" said Weston, "A Vietnam Vet said, 'Some big nosed journalist from Hollywood will write my story, and light my way, but she won't know how we lived and died in Long Binh, Vietnam or how long I kissed Raquel Welch with bloodshot eyes on the day I was supposed to die, unless I tell her."

"You are officially drunk, Uncle Wes."

Slamming his hand against the doorpost to the back of the kitchen, Weston made a beeline to the grave of little Andy Oliver. He lifted his glass as if he were sober.

"True to life, the soldier said!" Weston was off his rocker. "It's a flippin' biography, without stories and dreaming with some gifted imagination, it wouldn't be worth a glass of grape juice," he ranted.

He turned and placed the bottle on the bench. Cold. Windy. He sat.

"Pour the liquid that makes you truthful, make it a happy one, Oscar Wilde. Tell me what's your new lease on life, Jason. Tell me about what's going on in your head."

Not happy about it, but he poured them both a round, mixed with bourbon.

"Oh, it's nothing."

"You wish, my boy. That's why Virginia is for Lovers." He grinned and waved his hand like a music conductor. "Love is best told by Weston Ridge Laramie, with a bottle of Pinot Noir, and rounding the edges off a big dream for a companion, back in yesteryear." He raised his hand. "She's in love with an automaker."

"You got a lot going for you, uncle."

Rain fell from the dark clouds and thunder sounded across Mount Jackson.

"I got a lot going wrong for me."

Jason stood, like a good teacher did and flipped his hand at him.

"You taught me to love the finer things in life. Not the despicable, unbearable truths. We can't live off of what we know. It's the unknown pleasures, for our own sake that drive us to dream of more treasured times." The writer sat and finished his drink, closing his eyes from the hard drink. "Remember when you kissed Raquel Welch in Vietnam? You were a bold soldier who did that much."

"I didn't know a kiss was going to happen."

"It was more of a dream after it was over than when it happened, right? You hoped it might happen again, though?"

His speech was slurred. Weston moved his hands back and forth when he was anxious and drank too much, waving and staggering. His nephew pulled him to the bench.

"All I hear are voices in my head, telling me all the things I haven't done right in my life. Goals I kicked aside."

"You taught me the greatest voice lies in your heart," staring at his uncle, "and your fight for it, in business and in relationships. Accomplish one at a time."

"Listen, my heart is a dream machine and best put to sleep. It's the biggest phony bologna canvas in the world and it's an open target for lost love."

Weston left his empty bottle on the bench they'd built several months earlier. Staggering through the backdoor when the rain turned to snow, he kicked off his boots, in his sock feet, jeans, and a white tank top, Jason let him sleep it off. He started typing while the fresh new snow blanketed Mount Jackson. Later, sober as a preacher, Weston showed Jason the new ultra-flyer airplane in the barn.

He just watched him to see what he was going to do with the airplane.

"I need to learn how to fly," Weston said, positioning himself inside the seat. "That's my new lease....to fly."

"When the weather warms up, we'll fly together."

The snow was fairly deep and loose, up to the strings on his tall leather boots, the kind that kept students home from school, pristine and undisturbed, and then the wind gusts caused drifts, from the valleys to the rolling hills, whipping through the dormant rows of vines. For the first time, Andy Oliver was operational for only part of the week, part of the cold snap, giving Jason the time to write and build his novel, and the lapse gave Weston more hours for renovation and new developments. Instead, his uncle worried about Sorano and he knew what he wanted to do next. They examined the two seater micro flyer, covered inside the barn and wondered why his uncle bought such a strange contraption from Atlanta.

Cupping his hands, Jason shouted through the thick valley snow. "We'll get it running in the spring."

Snow fell thicker in places, more in the cold highlands than the slush ice that layered Interstate 81. Traffic moved at a crawl. Weston disappeared. Cottony flakes, big and thick, as Jason locked the barn. Three feet from the door, Weston's big arms wrapped around his shoulders.

"Tomorrow we'll buy some geese for the pond at Andy Oliver."

"Why do we need geese, Wes?" He warmed his hands with his breath.

"I like geese, so I'm buying geese. Buy a dozen or two geese, to make a flock."

"To eat?"

"No, not to eat. To help me fly, Oscar Wilde. Life ain't fiction for me anymore." He stopped on the front porch with his arms open and said, "It's the realm of vision and living inside it, is my new purpose to save Andy Oliver."

"Let's make it a real fun vision, though. We can save the winery."

"We can buy the neighbor's geese. They like me. I'll feed them at the barn. Heck, they use our pond all the time, anyway."

"How much does a goose cost?"

"He favors the Chardonnay, I'll trade him wine for geese."

"I'm in." Strange, but they grabbed hands with a new lease for geese. "Let's trade for some geese then."

The next morning, Jason delivered three cases of Andy Oliver Chardonnay to Mr. Norway. He parted with the geese, and offered to feed them for a week.

Mr. Norway ran off his porch shouting at the top of his lungs, "Get out of here, you damn geese," and slammed the door. He parted with his pets easily. On the other hand, Weston was elated to have them at Andy Oliver. The writer took notes and wasn't sure what Weston had in his strange head. Geese. Flying machine. His nephew mentioned how one of them might make a good meal for Easter dinner.

Very few men eat their pets, though. Pigs. Chicken. Geese. Regardless, Weston owned them free and clear. "Good trade," said his uncle. Seventeen geese were owned by Andy Oliver. Only twelve of them were friendly.

"That's all we need is to make wine and raise geese," he said as he scattered feed.

After a few days Weston appointed his nephew as the designated lettuce chopper, spinach shopper, and pellet thrower. After Mr. Norway's pellets ran out and the geese flocked to Andy Oliver, honking and hungry, the writer named each one of them, but could only get close to a dozen. No more. Slowly luring the flock of geese, Weston threw handfuls of lettuce and spinach, mixed in bags of pellets when he fed his favorite creatures. The first pets he'd had since his German Shorthaired Pointer, Tomo. He stored some of the pet feed on the back of a four wheeler. Rain. Sleet or shine. Mornings were spent driving around the pond spreading feed for geese. They took turns.

"They'd look better with red bows around their necks for the Valentine's party," said Weston, who threw chopped lettuce on the ground. "What do you think?" He asked with a grin.

"I think you're crazy as a loon, old man." Jason held his coffee as he watched his uncle's spirit soar when he talked about flying with geese. "You should have bought loons. It's not too late to fly yourself to Broughton Hospital and check in as a hippie van driver, free-spirited flying loon."

He made breakfast, laughing and waving a spatula at his nephew's head and sipped his coffee.

"I can have the geese form a straight line for their lettuce," he said, then he lined up a salt shaker, pepper shaker, coffee cup, ketchup bottle and mustard, end to end. "Then I'll put red bows around their necks."

"You need to see a doctor. You're not getting enough air to your brain."

Two hours later Jason returned from Mount Jackson with dark and white chocolates, lemon vanilla wafers, and peanut butter for guests to clean their palate after a glass of wine. He declared his uncle to have raw talent, arms marked in red and bleeding as if he'd been punched with the end of a sharp stick.

"Hey, look out in the backyard at the geese," he said as he opened the door.

"Weston, are you flockin' kiddin' me?"

"Couple of snorts of Andy Oliver and we danced and tied red bows."

"Geese with bows?"

"All seventeen geese have bows around their necks, five of them beat the hell out of me, but they had a new lease on life when Sherrill got an axe from the barn," shaping his smile. "Then, well, they stopped flocking around and stood in perfect formation."

"I see your red arms." Jason turned his uncle's arms around. "How did you do that?" He then examined the geese then back at his uncle grinning.

"Don't ask me how I did it."

"You are the Geese Master."

Weston took Sorano's letter and a bottle of Pinot Noir to his room. To be a writer, Jason lived in the shadow of Weston Laramie, but it was not his light to shine on himself, and his day would come, the more time he spent at Andy Oliver.

Sunshine melted the snow in Mount Jackson.

"Goodnight." He stopped midway down the hall, turned his head. "We need to crank up the plane as soon as possible."

"Look it up, Wes, you high flyer," knocking on the coffee table, "you need a pilot's license before you can fly, top gun."

"I know that." He stopped in the hallway. "So do you, co-pilot Laramie. So do you, Old Sport." His light wasn't on for very long.

To this day, his nephew's mind could not comprehend how he tied red bows around the necks of seventeen geese, five of which ran wild and winced. But they walked, all of them trailed in a line through the brown grass and flew high in the Shenandoah Valley, unburdened and innocent, paddling in the river and treading and circling in the pond at Andy Oliver. Locals laughed and were not surprised when Jason told them Weston Laramie made them stand in a line to receive their Valentine bows. With all the media publicity, the credit Jason could not take, Mr. Norway wanted his geese back but his former pets would not return to the likes of a crabby old man, who treated them in a cruel manner. The following day they ignored him. Instead they flew above his home, treaded water at Andy Oliver. Alone and living in his own regret Mr. Norway died, but not before he carved the words "Forgive me, Neighbor" on his kitchen table.

✷✷✷

"The newspapers ran the story about Norway and the geese," said Sherrill. "Well, someone needs to call those *Guinness Book* folks about the geese." Jason told Sherrill, the oldest worker at Andy Oliver as they watched a flock of geese fly over Meems Bottom Covered Bridge in mid-February.

"They wouldn't believe us anyway, Sherrill." The man snapped photographs. "They'd just accuse us of having too much of that good Andy Oliver wine."

"Orders might increase after Weston's secret mixture tamed the geese into a coma so they'd dress up for Valentine's Day."

They laughed on the drive back to Andy Oliver as they trailed with the windows down beneath a baby blue sky with a flock of geese chasing the hippie van. Sherrill figured they thought Weston had more wine for them. Stretching over the steering wheel, Jason loved the humor of Sherrill.

"Rehearsals for the clown show are closed, Jason."

Fourteen
Somewhere Over Shenandoah

In April of 2000, Weston was beginning to trust his nephew's experience on the vineyard. Nonetheless, he still assigned him to follow Sherrill's leadership, a short, stout elderly man. The writer worked with a few other hired hands they'd added after orders increased because of Weston's trip to New England and Westbury.

The freedom allowed Weston and Jason to graduate with their pilot's licenses. They read books on flying and flipped through aviation magazines like they were the daily newspapers. Each evening, they watched television shows that glorified the joy of aviation. And every day, they admired his ultralight aircraft from Georgia.

While Sherrill's team worked the vineyard for several months, Weston and the writer became flyers, adding practice to theory and playing out scenarios on paper with the two-seater, gas-powered ultra-flying machine.

That spring, people started to visit the winery more often than ever before. His nephew wasn't sure how Weston did it, but he did. Maybe it was the new Andy Oliver banner trailing behind his airplane that prompted people to taste his wine? Maybe it was the newspaper articles that tapped into the public market because of Jason's talented craft of writing and how he had expanded the story at a steak dinner, weeks earlier? Who knew?

On Saturday April 17th, a couple of farmers, Fritz and Sophia Claude, wanted to buy a bottle of Chardonnay. As they watched from the tailgate of Mr. Fritz's truck, Weston descended, drifting and gliding and finally rolling across the earth outside Mount Jackson. Mr. Fritz ran to meet the rolling plane at the end of his grassy field, for no other reason than what Weston had in his pocket. Touchdown.

His uncle crossed the green grass field, tipped his hat to the lady and handed a bottle of Andy Oliver to the gentleman, all because they had never tasted his Chardonnay. Like he was a big time stunt pilot in the sky, Weston started doing this whenever he had the opportunity. News quickly spread across the Shenandoah Valley with the help of the neighbors who visited often and a few allied newspapers.

Impressed with what was going on at the vineyard, Jason watched as visitors hiked through the forest while he flew. Often the writer rested on a long wooden bench with his lunch in hand, leaning back with sandwich in one hand and binoculars in the other. He was muffled by distance, carefree above what was happening below him in the vineyard, he scanned the blue skylines on dozens of occasions. His nephew lost count of the times he'd passed gracefully like a soaring bird over Andy Oliver, landing in hayfields and on roadsides as if he were on assignment or in an aviation spectacle.

After an hour in the sky, he would circle back to the barn where he kept his aircraft supplies stored. Anywhere the ground was cleared and level, his uncle made it his landing zone. Life at Andy Oliver became more exciting when the snow melted and the river swiftly moved out of the valley. He loved his small flyer, powered with one large fan blade the size of a small satellite dish, the wing covered with Mylar, the plane was the main attraction in a little country town. Three rubber wheels, two seats were on the front in an open cockpit design, and a wingspan the length of a dually truck helped reach speeds of more than sixty-five miles per hour.

By late spring, Weston was an expert on his flying machine. On April 18th, Jason looked at his uncle with a tilted grin.

"We aren't working today."

"Why not?"

"The two of us are flying." He grabbed the writer's arm. "You are going up with me."

"I don't think so." He scratched his head.

"You'll like it up there." Handing him a helmet and microphone. "Strap up."

"What the heck?" His eyes bugged, "It's a nice day to die."

"You won't regret it."

"If you kill me, and you walk away, I'll haunt your ass." The writer had a long face, but had never flown much. "I follow you, but bring it down in one piece, huh?"

"I hate ghosts, Jason." His uncle blocked the fiery sunshine.

"So make sure we live," he told him.

The two of them charted a course across the green fields and over the river. By noon, his nephew recognized landmarks in Harrisonburg. A strong wind kept pushing them forward, so they turned and headed back to Mount Jackson.

"No different than riding a skateboard." His brave uncle dared to compare such a contraption to a skateboard.

When the two of them landed, Weston tossed the geese pellets and lettuce on the ground while Jason checked the mailbox. Three letters. Germany. New York. Savannah.

Weston started the truck.

"How'd you like the flight?" Dark glasses reflected the passing trees and bright midday sunshine on his uncle's shades. "Not bad, huh?"

When the wind shifted, Weston laughed and thought his nephew may have needed to change his shorts when the plane landed.

He slapped the steering wheel and wiped his mustache.

"The first time I took the plane up, I did have to change my shorts."

"You blamed the geese in midair for that bomb, I bet."

"It was both of us. Ha-ha-ha."

"Hey, look what came in the mail." He handed Weston the letter. "I'll be a monkey's uncle," flapping the envelope. "Letter from Mickey Starr. He's a crap head!"

"Don't trash that letter. Read it," he told him.

"He can kiss my ass." He rolled his tongue and spit out the window.

His nephew grinned, pulled the letter from the bottom of the trash can and slit the end of the letter and read the typed page. Inside the Andy Oliver office, the two gentlemen dropped down in their leather high back chairs, and while Jason read aloud, Weston listened and touched all his fingers together, resting his elbows on his desk.

***

```
    Dear Mr. Laramie,

    Though not much for small talk, I'm large on
understanding my wrongdoings. What happened in
Savannah, the way we conducted ourselves as
gentlemen at The Tobacco Barn, was obtuse. Other
than gunshots, years ago, the confrontation was
the first incident since a lady tried to burn it
down in 1995. From Volt, Tipp, and myself, we'd
like to apologize for what happened this past New
Year's Day. I had too much to drink and things got
out of control. I shouldn't have fired off at the
mouth and caused trouble between friends. Maybe
partners, too?
    On a lighter note, I'd like you to reconsider
my offer. The Starr money is still good on a grand
scale offer for Andy Oliver Vineyard. My plans
will be written in a contractual agreement, more
official and professional, of course, if you are
open to talk, somewhere in the Shenandoah Valley.
My team will increase the production, offering you
a three percent cut of the profit. You keep little
Andy Oliver's name on every single bottle, buddy.
    The Mickey Starr name will be the parent
company. I realize 1.5 million dollars is short of
the asking price. I know a wise man will call and
take the offer, which stands good until the end of
the harvest season, in October.
    Melody would like to visit Oscar Wilde over
Memorial weekend, dance and hike the trails with
her dog, if Jason would call to confirm the
invitation is still good.
```

```
    Time is important. I'll have to withdraw my
offer by the end of October and acquire another
vineyard if I do not hear from you or someone from
Andy Oliver soon.

                              Best Regards,

                              Mickey Starr, CEO
                              The Tobacco Barn
```

***

"Wow!" The writer neatly folded the letter and stuffed it inside the envelope. "That's a big ticket to punch on this property, Weston. You are sitting on the winning numbers. Are you going to cash it in?"

"Throw the damn thing away." Weston changed gears. "What's the other envelope in your hand?"

"Two letters. One from Germany."

"That's to you from my brother." His eyebrows raised up to where he wore his hat. "What's the other one? Open it up."

"Looks like a lady's handwriting from New York." Jason flipped the letter against his broad shoulder.

"Wow. New York, huh?" Weston rubbed his hair. "Well, Julianna, right?"

The writer smelled the perfume on the letter. "Maybe it's good news."

"Does Julianna want to meet in Washington D.C. on Saturday?"

Pushing the letter across the table like a small, paper airplane, Jason didn't hesitate to speed up the process and nodded at him several times.

"That one is for you, Boss. Postmarked Buffalo, New York."

He caught the envelope as it slowed down, grabbed his glasses, and thumbed the postmark with care and hesitated, being a private person.

"Julianna," he said. "She doesn't usually write."

"Your Japanese beauty does have respectful penmanship. Sorano Tanaka is the name on the envelope."

"Where's it mailed from again... Buffalo?" He waved his hand, "You remember she stood me up. Then flew to Buffalo. I would still be choking on a tropical chicken dinner in her Japanese restaurant, but we flew to Savannah instead."

"Sounds like she wants Uncle Weston back. Old Sport must've been kicked to the curb."

"Stop!" With a sad face, the man pushed the letter back to Jason with the same sufficient speed from his fingertips. "Tuck the letter back in the envelope. I'm not up for it."

The writer folded the letter and pressed the glue tight.

"I'll leave it on your oak end table for when you get the balls to read it." He tucked the letter into his pocket and walked to the living room where his uncle kept notes and letters, large to small, organized in a stack.

"If I read it, you'll be the first to know." He slammed the door and walked into another part of the house to avoid what needed to be read and addressed, he thought.

Polish sausage and baked beans were fired up in a pot on the stove after Weston finished his shower. The whole time he was eating, his hawk eyes beamed on the envelope with Sorano's handwriting turned in his direction, positioned by his nephew.

"Why don't you open the damn thing, see what she has to say?" He handed him the letter and a cold beer.

"Put the letter back." He uncapped the drink.

"You need to read this letter, Weston, see what she wants. It could be important."

Weston didn't touch any wine or beer the rest of the evening. He only ate half of the food on his plate and acted like he was reading a book. When Jason left him in the living room, the television was off and he stared at the fireplace. The letter still sat untouched.

***

His memory faded to Jockey's Ridge, Outer Banks, North Carolina, 1980.

Holding a kite loose in her hands, Sorano climbed barefoot to the top of the sand dunes while Weston snapped two dozen photographs of her for his album. He drowsed over her through the lens of a camera more often than he ate or exercised.

She had grown wealthy in her early twenties. Here and there, her fans would recognize her, a sort of subtle celebrity in Boston and New York. The papers loved her adorable smile and lively personality, too. When her eyes were covered by sunglasses and a wide straw hat, she blended in like one of the locals, but she had class and notoriety, as well. That was why she liked the Outer Banks, more than Long Island.

Outside more than she was indoors, her favorite pastime aside from baseball was flying a red Dragon shaped kite in a strong breeze. She loved the thought of flying. They both did.

"Your only downfall is you were not born with wings, Sorano." Weston told her while he watched her stumble, swaying in the rolling hot sand, kite in hand, delicate fingers, and the line tight as a banjo string. "I'm thankful God keeps you grounded, my angel."

A small group of teenagers ran by and pulled her kite string by accident, so he wasn't sure if she heard his words, but he meant them, anyway.

Weston followed her as if he was her shadow, an unassertive figure but a reliable man, half obliterated by her nearness and the spell she put on him with just a wink or a nod would make most men envious. Her features were exquisite, with a kiss of the sun on her skin after a weekend and grains of sand packed on her feet, a delicacy of simplicity among her own gender. The summer breeze and open skies were enough to keep her busy, a lady mesmerized by nautical themes but fully absorbed by flight and the thought of aviation. She liked the Wright brothers. Kill Devil Hills was perfect for parasailing, helicopter rides, and simple things like flying a kite, especially the four designed by Weston for her birthday. She carefully named each one: Tangerine Sky, Red Soul, Blue Diamonds, and one that means "Endless Love," or *Eien no ia,* if spoken in Japanese.

"Weston!" She held onto the string with both hands. "Come up here with me. It's beautiful at the top of the dunes."

"How's my homemade kite?" he yelled from a distance. "Does it work?"

She held on tight. "It's flying, isn't it?"

Children flocked by her side with Weston's kite in the open blue sky. She was a natural mother figure, deep down to her soul, he knew it. Weston snapped a roll of film by midmorning and ate a peanut butter sandwich as he watched her work the kite and play with the children. From the top of Jockey's Ridge, the wondrous view was trifold: Kitty Hawk Bay, Pamlico Sound, and the Atlantic Ocean.

"Ma'am," asked a freckled redhead, "could I try to fly it?"

The kid was in a great hurry to try something new.

"What's your name?"

"Jasmine." Having no front teeth, she whistled her name to Sorano.

"Nice to meet you, Jasmine."

Weston lifted his soda from his backpack and adjusted his hat. The day was in the mid-nineties, but the breeze cooled down the Outer Banks.

"Show Jasmine how to fly and handle the string," said Weston.

Sorano held the strings at first, then she let go and for the first time ever the little girl, with more freckles than most kids, was flying a red kite atop Jockey's Ridge.

"Look at me, I'm flying. I'm doing it!" She held on for dear life and stood on her tiptoes. "I'm flying. My big brother never lets me fly his robot kite."

"You're doing great." Weston adjusted his lens for a closeup shot. "Sorano, stand beside her for a picture and give me a big smile."

Jasmine held the line steady, running and keeping her balance, sliding and falling in the soft sand as the wind kept the kite adrift, even low to the ground. Her teeth were like white buttons popping out of her gums. She was six or seven, at best. Jasmine returned to her friends and thanked Sorano.

Sorano took up with the next little girl who said her name was Abigail.

Weston looked into her green eyes.

"Beautiful pose, honey."

Sorano loved babies but she especially had a heart for school-aged kids, the ones who loved to swing and spin at parks and twirl in parades and dance until they fell asleep in her arms. Weston had an unexpected tender side and a gracious gentleness covered him, as well.

"Abbie?" called Weston.

She looked as if she had done something wrong. "Yes, sir."

"You fly better than we do," said Weston. "I want you to have this red kite."

"I can't take it."

"It is yours now, Abbie." He smiled at Sorano and then turned to the girl.

"Really, sir?" Her eyes brightened and with her mouth open. In disbelief as if he were kidding her, and said, "Are you sure, mister?"

She handed the strings to Sorano and hugged Weston, squeezing him. With the line in her hand, Sorano kneeled down into the soft sand, hugging the girl and kissing her forehead.

"We're sure, honey." Weston winked at Sorano and shook Abbie's free hand. "The kite belongs to you now." Sorano handed her the string. "Take care of it."

"Bye, Abigail," said Sorano.

Hand in hand with Sorano, they stood by the road, in love at Jockey's Ridge. Sorano turned to Weston, her dark black hair moved with the warm breeze and kissed him.

"That was the sweetest thing." Sorano pulled him close.

His deep voice was proud. "She was nice, wasn't she?"

"I was talking about giving away your kite." Sorano eyed him. "It took you two days to make that Red Dragon and cut out the long tail. Why?"

"I do sweet things. Good deeds, too." Weston put his arm around her. "Let's go have dinner at Jimmy's. I'm starving."

She jumped on his back, and he carried her across the highway to the van.

"You're a sweet man," she whispered in his ear. "That's why I'm in love with you, Weston."

"I sure love Famous Jimmy's Seafood." He turned north. "It's not far from here."

"Did you hear me?" She tickled his side. "Hmmm."

"I heard your sweet voice." He grinned at her.

"Why didn't you say anything?"

"Just wanted to see if you would say it again. Maybe a few more times."

"I love you." She touched his face. "There you go. I love you, Weston."

"Maybe we should go back to the hotel, lover."

"Later, take me to Famous Jimmy's." She kissed him at the next red light.

***

From a long distance, Sorano saw the girl, still pacing in the heavy sand, kite flying and drifting, long tail bending and swaying in the breeze. To preserve the moment, Sorano snapped a priceless photo of the precious girl and her long red kite, zoomed in with a long range lens. With one more frame, Sorano kissed Weston under the sign at Famous Jimmy's Seafood, OBX, as a stranger snapped the camera.

***

Two decades later, the edges of the picture, yet rounded and wrinkled, not pristine enough for a showroom, but for his own emotional amusement looked fine. For the most part, he thought there would be time ahead to see her again. His hands held his cherished photo, the jewel among his collection, causing him to master his breathing, rising and falling, with no more anxiety about what she meant to him. Of the hundreds of photographs in his collection, Jockey's Ridge was the one he'd shuffle to find when he thought of Sorano. His nephew saw this happen more than a dozen times since he'd unloaded the trunk.

The yellow glow highlighting the doorframe from his uncle's study turned dark after midnight, letting him know he'd fallen asleep. Then Jason jumped up when he heard glass shatter into a burning fireplace. His door slammed, confirming he was wrong about his slumber. When the writer woke the next morning, he cleaned the glass from the fireplace and brushed behind the hearth, with force and didn't complain.

By sunup Jason had thrown away a second empty wine bottle with a label peeled from the sides, fed the geese, and typed. He'd also cooked enough oatmeal for two.

"Good morning, nephew."

His uncle found his food on the tabletop just as he'd left meals before. His nephew walked by Sorano's letter, and saw it was opened. He didn't touch the white envelope, still perfumed, even stronger on the inside and felt it was something for another day. In time, to get it off his chest, he may say something or say nothing at all. The journalist wasn't about to pry into his emotional barrel of memories.

Twenty years was a long time for both of them to settle down and think of the couple of great years they'd spent together without getting emotional or taking on new possibilities. He must've placed the letter in the trunk himself. He didn't wait on him that morning to feed the geese lettuce and pellets, and more chores were done before breakfast was made.

He walked through the house.

"Thanks for cleaning up the glass." His uncle's voice sounded rough. Jason saw he was clean shaved and sober, brushing his hair with his hands. "I was going to get a broom this morning for the mess."

"Already done."

"The letter? Are you going to ask about it?"

Hands in his pockets, and with sincerity said, "No. Not this time."

"Well, it was important. Sorano would like to see me again."

"That's wonderful." Jason widened his hands. "Is that why you broke the glass?"

"No. I just realized Andy Oliver Vineyard is twenty years old this week."

"Congratulations. I'm proud of my blessed uncle who turned down a million dollar deal."

"You better be. I might keep you for another six months so you can investigate or write something worth reading, one day."

His nephew witnessed a giant smile and a good laugh.

"Oh, man." Jason folded the paper. "I don't like the newspaper today." He pressed the newspaper to the left of his bowl of oats.

"What's up?"

"Look at the front cover in the *Northern Virginia Daily*."

Weston lifted his glasses, roped loosely around his neckline and placed them on his nose, going over the printed page.

"Automotive Industry Expects Growth in the New Millennium. The Yankees lost four straight to the Tigers."

"Read the bottom section, Ridge."

When Weston saw her name in print he mumbled the words, low enough for a dog to hear him but Jason knew what it said and didn't need to read it or hear it again.

"Talk of Marriage: Beautiful Sorano Tanaka dumped Bentley Auto V.P. for the Son of the South, Mickey Starr."

His nephew stood. "Was the letter a fake?"

Within a few short seconds, Jason watched the newspaper, flat and pristine, be torn into a thousand pieces. His uncle's hands pulled on his hair, palming his eyes, then he pressed his temples with his fingers, head and heart ached.

"That's a kick in the ass," he said, wadding the paper up. "Low blow fish suckin' son of a bitch!" He slammed his fist against the wall.

With an idea, Jason snapped his fingers, popping up tall in his seat.

"While we were in Savannah, you told Mickey Starr how you and Sorano dated in the late 70s and 80s."

"That piece of crap Mickey Starr flew to New York, knowing we'd dated years ago. He must be twenty years her senior."

He stood behind the tall ladder back chair, twisting his hand on the rounded final post of the chair.

"Do you love her?"

Weston scooted his chair back from the table as if it were on wheels, beaming in his direction, he crossed his arms, nodded and then with some fortitude, he squinted, like an eagle on a fat rat.

"What did you say?"

"You heard me loud and clear, didn't ya, pilot?" His nephew rocked the chair, waited and grinned and asked him again. "Do you love her?"

Still no answer. Jason raised his voice, pounding his hand on the upper rail of the chair, and targeted him. "Are you still in love with Sorano?"

"Nope."

Was what he said the truth? Did he love her?

"There was a man who told me, 'If you live with me, you'll have to be truthful.' The spoken words of Weston Ridge Laramie." He addressed him with a smile. "Are you telling the truth?"

"I've always loved her, and always will for as long as I live and breathe." He folded his arms tight.

"Good." Finally got to him, he thought.

"Yeah, sort of," he said. "Without a doubt in my heart. I still care for her, young man." He perked up. "Hell, yeah, I do."

He kicked the chair underneath the table and took his empty plate. It was the first time since he'd been at Andy Oliver that he'd expressed himself about a lady.

"Get your damn bags then, young man."

Looking over his glasses, Weston finished hot coffee.

"Why do we need bags?"

"We're headed to New York City again, pilot jackass, who provoked me to read the letter and travel more."

"New York? You mean, Westbury, to find Mickey's penthouse?" He shaped a gun with his hand. "And shoot Mickey, right?"

"No, Hell no!" he shouted. "We're not shooting anyone."

"Why not? I'd take great pleasure in it."

"We both would. But I decided since I called you, man, not a kid or punk or Dreadlock drug dealer, that you wouldn't mind riding in coach again to JFK."

"To stab the Son of the South?"

He grabbed the butter knife from the drawer.

"Only if you use the butter knife on him. Don't buy a damn knife in the Bronx."

"That's a great idea."

After his breakup with Rosa, Jason wasn't sure if he wanted to go, or not but, he was going, like it or not.

"We're not planning on killing anyone." He leaned against the doorway.

"By the way, I called you," he gleamed, confirming, and said, "Young man, not man," nodding, "It's better than kid or punk, right, pilot?"

Casting a hopeful nod, his nephew said, "Keep up the good work and some respectable wits about you. That giant cool attitude will land you on my Christmas card list, if by some miracle, we stay friends until December."

With his arms patiently crossed, wrinkling his forehead, without a knife or drink or gun, he demonstrated, he thought, if only for a moment he conceded to understand his directives again 'New York road trip,' he told himself.

"We leave in three days."

"Westbury or bust."

Fifteen
Market to the Mountains

His uncle once explained how important it was for a man to clean his plate, chop firewood for winter, stack it well, and never skip dessert. And if a person does those things with diligence and pride, the voices in the back of his head wouldn't overturn his belly, chill his calloused hands, or waste his time on procrastination or thoughts of regret.

How he came up with such hideous conclusions, no one knew, but they were effective at accomplishing tasks that needed to be tackled and not forgotten. So the writer took notes and adopted the same methods for himself.

Snow layered the Shenandoah Valley for the next three days, thicker and heavier in the high country versus the valley. Ice. Fog. Cold wind. However, the harsh climate didn't stop Weston from chopping firewood inside the shed and building his muscles for Sorano. The outdoor work gave him time to think of his plan, how it would unfold in New York, and what he would say, to handle the unexpected. Whether he would see her in Central Park, holding a hot cup of Wonderful Ralph's Coffee and a Danish, or somewhere more private, he couldn't say. He just knew he wasn't agile without a plan.

The woodpile was twenty yards from the cabin at Andy Oliver. Less than fifty yards from where his nephew worked shoveling the driveway, parking lot, and walkway to the famous tasting room. The writer carried a square, metal lunch bucket and took breaks to check on Weston.

"Are you troubled, Old Sport?"

He sat alongside "Old Sport" and soaked up the deep blue sky, where the sun decided to reveal warmth in the valley. He looked worn out himself, rubbing his hands and flexing his fingers into a fist, but he couldn't fully clench his hands together from the time he'd spent gripping the axe handle on a cold day.

"What's this bucket for?"

Jason handed him the box with great intentions.

"Open it."

"I'm too tired to eat."

"Unclip the damn latch, you are an old mule, sometimes. A flippin' frog may jump out and piss on you."

His uncle's face lit up when he saw what waited for him inside of the box.

"I'll be damned," he laughed. "You brought me dessert and coffee, didn't ya?"

"You once told me to never skip dessert."

"I didn't know you listened to my advice." He took a bite. "Best apple pie I've ever had."

"I had my dessert earlier. No need to share."

"I wasn't. But I hope you shoveled the walkway to the tasting room. Sherrill is eighty some years old and he doesn't miss work because of snow or death."

"Looks like the runway at JFK airport."

"Good," he nodded and finished his last bite of pie, cleaning the pie from his fingers in the top layer of the icy snow. "Saves me from having to do it."

Rolling snow inside his hands, the writer threw the snowball against a dogwood tree and with some bravery he spoke. "Are you getting back in shape for Sorano?"

"Nope." He flexed his arms. "Just chopping the last truckload of wood for the tasting room fireplace before we leave."

"It's none of my business again, but while we're in New York, I'd like to see Rosa, if you don't mind?"

"I want you to see her. So I can have a few days with Sorano alone before she goes to Savannah."

"Why is she going to Savannah?"

"Weeks before a man gets married, the wife plans to decorate and buy what she needs to make the home look beautiful for guests," the man said, pulling at his gloves. "Sorano will move to Savannah, decorate The Famous Tobacco Barn, paint his yacht and commission a private horse and buggy ride for the media on River Street with her new husband Mickey Starr."

"In the letter, she said she'd like to see you. Why don't you call her and save yourself a lot of trouble?"

"I have tried. Her number is unlisted."

"Good thing you have a nosy punk kid investigative journalist in the family," he said, grinning and reaching for his wallet.

"Oh, no way?" He opened his hand. "How'd you get her business card?'

"Sorano Tanaka and your nephew are close friends, remember?" He adjusted his coat and walked with his cold hands pressed deep in his pockets.

"Do you always whistle when you feel cocky?" He picked up his lunch bucket and followed him. "I'm glad you thought ahead and grabbed her number."

"I learned a lot, not from my father's brother," he said, putting his hand on the man's shoulder. His voice shook due to the frigid chill in the air.

Surprised and timely his uncle became fond of pork chops, baked beans, and cornbread. They were starved. He impressed him with the meal and added "Thanks" and appreciation to the table. His preference would've been a side of sweet potatoes, topped with butter and bacon, lined and spun with a fork until the inside matched the look of whipped mashed potatoes.

His uncle flipped the business card inside his hand, from thumb to forefinger, unhappy and restless. Examining the torn paper seemed to remind him of his bad luck with women. He watched the clock, pacing and debating, as nervous as a man running for public office and excited to meet Sorano in Westbury or wherever he had to chase her down for one last chat before she was married.

He stepped outside to break the silence in a starry night as black as paint. Jason gazed at the street light to the side of the first Andy Oliver tasting room his uncle had constructed by hand, back in '81, when the writer felt as nervous as he was about seeing Sorano again. This time their meeting was intentional.

At a quarter past eight, on the 18th day of April, he walked into his study where Jason worked on invoices. His smile gave away what he was about to do. Half past the hour, he returned whistling the tune to "Put me in Coach" and tapping his hands to a Fogarty hit.

Jason heard him skipping and pecking the drywall with his knuckles at a good rhythm.

"Did you call her?"

"Heck, no, I didn't call her." He stared at a baseball inside a glass case. "Will Call at Yankee Stadium, is holding two tickets to the game against the Rangers on Tuesday. The girl who took the call," he said, slapping Jason's leg, "she's David Cone's cousin from Kansas City. He's expected to pitch on Tuesday."

"I think I can picture him."

"Good pitcher. I sampled some of the best barbecue in Kansas three summers ago and met him."

"You sly dog, flirting with the box office lady to get better seats." He pushed him away. "You got two tickets to the Yankees for you and Sorano. So you are trying to win her back with the men in pinstripes, huh?"

"Two tickets, alright, for Rosa and my good friend Jason Laramie, the best damn sportswriter in Florida, but he ain't worth a darn as an investigative reporter."

"I have never seen the Yankees before. You are unbelievable. Thank you."

"It's the least I could do."

"Don't trouble Rosa with anything other than baseball."

"I'd never go to NYC two days early to talk to an old girlfriend for you or myself, but it worked out didn't it?"

"We will see."

He tossed a chuck of oak into the fireplace, stoking the wood with a second piece, and arranging the grate with a poker.

Sparks flew and the blower kicked on, air shot out as if a giant hair dryer turned on in the living room. He pitched the newspaper with Mickey's picture on the cover into the fire and watched it disappear into a hot orange flame.

"I heard Rosa loves the Yankees as much as Sorano does." He hugged his nephew's neck.

"You sure, Ridge?" He asked him, knowing he'd love to see the game.

"Three rows behind the third base line."

"Hot damn! I may catch a beamer off the bat of Goodwin, if we're lucky."

"The second idea is, oh yeah, get some sleep because we're leaving in the morning, so you can see Rosa tomorrow."

"Where are you going?"

"To the Irishman's Pub." He stared at Jason. "In High Point."

"Who's in High Point?"

He locked the doors, thinking about his trip.

"Let's just say, I have surprised you. I called the number on the business card, and I'm meeting a Japanese lady in North Carolina."

"Congratulations." To his surprise, he did have a new lease on life. "Unbelievable. You have surprised me, for sure."

✳✳✳

Weston closed the book *Pride and Prejudice*, which became one of his favorite novels on the subject of love. For a few years, at least, he had lived his own love story with Sorano. Young and vibrant then, his life lay before him and all he had to do was to follow his own advice, "Put your heart into whatever you do and romance will find you. With enough luck and grace," he told himself, "you can keep it going."

Decades later, he sat in his home at Andy Oliver with the lamp turned down low and his head propped on his hand, Weston fell asleep. And dreamed of Sorano.

***

She dressed in wide, bell bottom blue jeans like other women did in the '70s and a green cowl neck sweater pulled from his closet. Weston wore a striped V-neck velour shirt as if he were at dinner. Sorano loved to sit on the rocks at the Hazel Mountain Overlook, calling it the "Edge of the World" in a postcard, not crammed into a square, but with neat cursive lines. Weston remembered her that way, uncommon and subdued by the distance. They'd traveled and hiked, to see the vast land they'd yet to explore together.

With an hour of daylight left on the last day of October, he'd taken a knee.

"I know we have only been together for a few years," he began.

"Oh, Weston," she interrupted him, wiping the tears from her eyes. "What do you think you're doing?"

"Sorano, I love you." He reached in his pocket. "I hope you know that, and I hope you feel the same way."

"I do feel the same," she said, touching his face and smiling. "I'm happy in love with you."

Weston opened the box, and the diamond sparkled as if the night sky had only one glowing star and it was in that box.

"Sorano, I love you," he said, pulling her hand to meet his face. "Will you marry me?"

"Yes! Yes! Yes!"

Weston towered above her in his boots, and she fell into his arms, sobbing and wrapping her arms around his face. In the midst of nature, she was more beautiful to him than ever, increasing his world with her overwhelming "Yes" to his request to marry him.

He could have never planned to live in a more majestic place or with a more exceptional lady, nor could he imagine himself being the hero in his own love story. Weston wanted the wedding to be in the spring when the rhododendrons and dogwoods were in bloom. He had met love face-to-face in a wonderful place, him and her, and he'd follow her anyway. Loneliness had lost. Weston felt sure of what he had asked her. Soul. Spirit. Love. Togetherness.

He opened the Kombi van door for her like he always did, but this time, she was in agreement with being married to him and it was different. With great excitement, she grabbed him and her eyes sprung to life.

"Sorano, let's stay in the Skyland Lodge."

"Sure."

He was considerate. German made vehicles needed extra time to heat the large interior. Having much more space to move around, layering thoughts of affection in Weston's head, but he knew that wasn't the place or the time. After three years together, he'd left times of deep affection up to her, but the street light seemed to make herself conscious, so he added a long kiss.

The sudden undeniable twinkle in her eye, the shifting movement of her lips, and the way she kissed him again, made him think he wouldn't want to be anywhere else. Weston took off his thick, button-up coat and placed it around her legs. He looked over his shoulder in reverse, not far from Luray, nudging and backing out of his parking space.

"Can we stay the night?" Her voice interrupted his thoughts.

Weston slammed the brakes, jarring them both as he stopped. She winked and smiled. He examined her pale skin and eyes, touching her forehead with his hand and laughing.

"Stay the weekend, you mean?"

"Two days would be wonderful," she said, holding his hand, "and romantic."

He had adopted the same heartfelt emotion, striding in an unquestionable direction and yet falling into temptation with her again.

"Let's find Skyland Lodge, see if they have a place to stay," Weston said.

"On second thought, maybe we should wait."

"Sure." He turned the van around. "You have the ring and my heart. When you are ready, let me know."

***

Weston woke from the dream as if someone had stepped on his foot. Sorano's image was real, as clear as if she was in front of him. Twenty years later, aged but still carrying the same deep ambitions, he rose out of bed, realizing the dream was over.

"Wow! Oh, my God." He caught his breath and looked at the clock. Finally, with some certainty, he said, "Three days in High Point, then she marries Mickey Starr." Weston sat straight up in his bed. "Gone forever. She needs to know how I feel."

***

Weston gave directions and advice to Jason on how to get into the stadium, how to contact Matteo and Lorenzo, and where they normally held seats. His nephew printed the directions and called Matteo. Rosa wanted him to park in the space by the curb with the plan to let him in her apartment, a place he didn't need reservations to enter.

After a terrible night's sleep, at four o' clock in the morning to be exact, Weston packed a few outfits for dinner with Sorano, a pair of jeans, three dress shirts, a pair of leather penny loafers and some hiking boots. His plan was to stay not just one day, but several nights, even five days if that's what it took to speak frankly to her in North Carolina.

He headed to High Point. The town full of so many memories, where he graduated college and met Sorano, would be in the view of his windshield in just a few hours. His vision of The Irishman's Pub was still a good one, a favorable establishment for one who loved beer and baseball as much as he did.

He'd hoped, even prayed, that he could somehow reserve the same two seats where he'd first seen her, angelic and entertaining, walk into The Irishman's Pub. The seats where they watched the World Series in 1977 could cast their magic one more time, he thought.

Sorano's voice on the phone had sounded positive, and he hoped the words in her letter weeks before spelled out feelings toward him. Weston couldn't be sure she wasn't seeking some type of closure, maybe a simple goodbye, a crazy bear hug and a handshake. Since they'd seen each other at the

Italian restaurant months earlier had her mind flooded with emotions about their son, Andy Oliver.

Weston planned to ask questions and spout out good memories to see if she felt about him as he did about her. Would she remember the little girl with the kite at Jockey's Ridge? The half dozen trips in his hippie van from North Carolina to New York? Would those memories mean anything to her? Would the '69 Volkswagen van he still kept running all those years make the long spring trip, down the Shenandoah Valley through the winding country roads to sweet Carolina? The song rang inside his head as he drove and even came on the radio once. Taking the photos from the truck, he hoped, in small premeditated fashion, his photos and stories could trigger her memories, tug on enough emotions to turn her heart to him for one more chance, a monumental one.

Weston checked into The Atrium, a downtown High Point hotel sitting amid the furniture market's hustle and bustle. The furniture market was an annual event that brought thousands of people to High Point twice a year, flying into North Carolina from around the world. He had landed a reasonable room because of a cancellation. At the front desk, he paid for five nights. Like a shooting star something crossed his mind, a longshot but he wanted to know. Maybe the clerk was a kind man, he thought?

"Sir, did you happen to see a Japanese lady check in the hotel today? I'm going to meet her for dinner at The Irishman's Pub."

The clerk tugged at his bow tie and grinned.

"Several Japanese ladies have visited the market and checked in today and yesterday and even the day before."

Weston cleared his throat. "I'm speaking of Sorano Tanaka, specifically."

"She hasn't been here in years. Her newspaper picture with Mickey Starr is on the wall behind you. She's shopping at the market without him," the clerk said with a soft voice. "Yeah, but staying on Main Street, I cannot reveal her whereabouts or if she is even here." The clerk pointed his pen at Weston and whispered, "If you think I believe you are to meet a celebrity, like Sorano Tanaka, then you must be crazy."

"I'm not here to convince you."

"You won't. The slogan "Virginia is for Lovers" doesn't apply in Carolina nor to everyone who has a Virginia license plate and drives a cool hippie van, lover boy."

"I know her well." He brushed his hand through his hair. "I'm Weston Laramie, by the way." He turned his wrist and surveyed the time. "We stayed here before you were born."

"I've never heard of you, but if you want her autograph," said the young man rolling his eyes, "perhaps you could get her to stop and sign a few copies of her new book. I just love her style, don't you?"

"She's wonderful," Weston said, grabbing his business card. "I'll have her sign the book for you by Friday."

"Make sure she spells my name correctly," said the clerk, moving around between the computers. "It's Stacy Callaway."

"You'll have it by Friday."

"You are a dreamer, buddy."

If you only knew, Weston thought as he watched the clerk, all the times he spent with Sorano Tanaka and dreamed of her even more.

***

Sorano's expertise in contemporary style and traditional design first brought her to North Carolina in the late 70s. This time, she had been commissioned by a firm in New York City to upgrade their restaurant furniture, a fresh new feel and look. Nothing too Southern nor too rugged like western furniture, without turn twist legs, and not neoclassical, or Napoleon, for sure. Her assignment was something with a deep top rail, inward and outward, French or Greek, perhaps, curving forward from the back to the legs, made in solid wood, resembling a sword, tapering from seat to floor and made in America. She didn't forget comfort either.

On the phone earlier, she had been excited to find a "Waterloo," she said, or a swept design amongst the masses of furniture makers, which may take only a day or two for her client, but she planned for five days at the market. With her time limited, she didn't have many extra hours to examine the hundreds of manufacturers on the list each market season.

Thank God for maps and vendor lists placed inside businesses to help her navigate from building to building and street to street. It was much different than it had been in the fall of 1977. More often than not, manufacturers generally stationed themselves in the same showrooms, year after year, planning to spend as much time as possible on the streets of Wrenn and Main.

She didn't know what it would take to send her client five options from spirals, Reeding, Cabriole and Scimitar designs. Her familiarity with the market would be a plus as she determined who, where and what vendors had to offer within her budget. Metal was not an option. Time and money were valuable factors.

***

Vehicles from Georgia, Delaware, and the Empire State sat in front of the hotel. Weston had no idea which one — if any of them — belonged to Sorano. He waited, checking his gold watch every ten minutes. He gave himself time to catch a cab so he could meet her as planned at The Irishman's Pub. Monday wasn't a busy time at an Irish pub unless it was packed with people in town to witness the latest market trends.

He waited at a corner table, dressed in a blue sport coat and still slim as he was when they first dated. He'd trimmed his hair and shaved his beard, leaving only a dark mustache.

The door opened, and a couple made their entrance, taking seats at the bar. Then a pale young man and young lady walked in wearing purple. The two of them were from his old university, making him feel comfortable as if he hadn't left college or the city at all.

A nice looking girl walked up beside him in a purple shirt and blue jeans.

"Can I get you something to drink?" she asked.

She shrugged her shoulders and twisted her body to show off her green and gold clothing with her hair pulled up.

"I'll have a draft beer."

"Are you waiting on someone?"

"She'll be here in twenty minutes or so," said Weston, who shook his head in some nervousness of her beauty. "So... maybe I'll be drunk before she gets here."

"Irish beer will help get you there," she said, nudging his arms. "Is it that bad?"

"She's that good."

"Wooo! I can't wait to meet this lady," she said, turning and winking at him. "I'll be right back with your beer, sir."

Raising his hand, Weston said, "Bring her a Pinot Noir, will you?"

"Must be a classy lady."

To the right of Weston, a man with a long well-trimmed beard and a bandana wrapped around his head emptied his pockets and gulped his beer.

"Can I buy you a beer, Weston?"

He squinted his eyes, turning his head to see who had spoken his name. The man was smiling and drinking at the same time.

"I already ordered. Where were you five minutes ago?"

The lady placed the frosty mug on a cloverleaf coaster and leaned over him. "Can I get a name for your tab?"

"This man is the famous Weston "Ridge" Laramie of Andy Oliver," the man said, facing his friend and lifting his beer. "But he grew up in High Point and was a hell of a baseball player. He was recruited by the Yankees and the Pirates."

The winemaker took a drink of his beer. "How the hell do you know me?"

"Is he really famous?" asked the waitress.

"Well known would be a better word." The man reached out his hand. "My name's Monty Moon. Do you remember me?"

"I'll be damned." Weston laughed. "I remember a Monty Moon who trained me how to make wine in 1970 something."

The two men stood and hugged. "Why aren't you in California with the big winemakers or in jail somewhere?"

"Since you last saw me I've been in jail for tax evasion, worked in Redwood Valley, and been married four times."

"Which was worse?"

"Take your pick." Monty gulped his beer and wiped his chin. "I don't want to ruin your hopes with this lady, so I'll keep my thoughts to myself. Like the labels say, 'results may vary,' it's all based on decisions, anyhow."

"You mean, good decisions, right?" Weston asked, reaching inside his sport coat and handing Monty his card. "I could use a good winemaker in Mount Jackson."

The man read the card and placed it in his wallet.

"Saw Andy Oliver on the cover of *Grapevine*. Your Bordeaux is one of the best I have tasted. I'd like to talk more," he said, shaking Weston's hand. "But I have to meet my brother in Greensboro, buddy. I'll see you in a few weeks. Your Bordeaux is one of the best. I'd like to add black cherry and chocolate to your merlot, though." He laughed and adjusted his flat hat.

"I'll see you at Andy Oliver next month," Weston said. "I look forward to hearing your great ideas, Monty."

"For sure." He walked out the door and then shouted behind him. "We'll see if you can afford my counsel, Mr.

Laramie." The man poked his head back in the door. "And don't try to pay me what I paid you two decades ago, either."

"Glad you're alive, Monty Moon."

Weston's first year in winemaking Monty Moon taught him the simple task of how to harvest the grapes and crush the harvest. The man also shared his knowledge of sugar, acid, sulfur, and sulfite with the wine. Now, Weston watched Monty start his truck and drive away.

"Mister Weston Laramie." Her voice interrupted his thoughts. "It's been a long, long time since we jammed in this room together."

He stood, took her hands, and kissed her cheek with some passion. She wore a sleek black dress and silver earrings matched with a stainless steel quilted dial and a silver toned bezel with star-like crystals. Her soft, short haircut remained jet black without the gray that now flecked Weston's hair.

"It's been twenty years since we shared a drink and watched a ball game here, Sorano."

"Is this our table?" She pointed at the spot.

Pulling out her chair, he whispered in her ear, "The place looks good after twenty seasons of baseball, doesn't it?"

"He's upgraded the televisions and the hardwood floor," she said, checking the dust. "Must be bad luck for the Irish to clean the windows, though."

Sorano scanned the memorabilia, covered in old-fashioned green and gold signs, leprechaun art, seats made of solid wood and booths crafted in honey brown leather. Twenty five straw hats were hung, one for each year The Irishman's Pub had been in business. Laughing with a straw hat on his head, Weston said,

"This place brings back lots of fond memories, doesn't it?"

The waitress walked to their table.

"Here's your bottle of Pinot Noir, Mr. Laramie and Ms. Tanaka. The cheese platter is free, and compliments of our new owner."

Weston sat up tall and inclined his chair. "Who's the new owner?"

"The man in the flat hat, Mr. Monty Moon." She placed the cheese platter on the table beside the wine. "It's the new Irishman's Pub, by Monty Moon."

"I know him well. My first job was working for him as a cellar assistant." Weston poured wine into Sorano's glass. "There's no better winemaker in the business than Mr. Moon. You have a great boss."

"Oh, my God, I remember the name Monty Moon," said Sorano. "Mr. Moon ordered a truckload of furniture from our New York showroom when he lived in California. He decorated his vineyard with tan leather and burgundy and green patterns to match his grapes."

"He was one of the top winemakers in the world ten years ago," Weston said, reaching for her hand.

"Stop." She slapped his hand away.

He gazed in her eyes, missing what he once held dear, decades earlier. They were a good couple, he thought.

"I love to tour vineyards, don't you, Wes?"

He nodded. Weston tugged on her ring finger.

"Nice rock!" he said, thumbing the gold and diamonds. "Someone is definitely in love."

"Mickey proposed to me on Valentine's Day in the Bahamas," she said, wiggling her ring finger, twisting the giant diamond around her hand.

"Did he drop it in a champagne glass, down on one knee, with balloons and ponies in the backdrop?" he asked, taking a drink of beer.

Lifting her hand up and down, she said, "Feels wonderful being in love."

"Did planes fly overhead and firecrackers pop, or did he lay red roses on the bed for a hot night of romance?" he asked, grinding and shaking the table in a shuffle of his long legs.

"Stop that!" She grabbed his hands. "He's a traditional man."

"The hell he is. He's a jackass."

He took her hand.

"I proposed to you once too, remember?"

She pulled her hand back.

"On Hazel Mountain." He picked up his drink. "Remember?"

"You had just bought the hippie van."

So she did remember. He tried to flag down the waitress.

"You rejected my proposal, though." He gazed straight into her dark eyes and then a knot came to his throat.

"It was the wrong time in my life." She sipped her wine. "Times were more complicated back then."

She tenderly bit a chunk of cheddar cheese and chewed.

"Hell of an embarrassment to tell my friends and parents that there wasn't a wedding or a lady to marry. My brother, Victor, was laughing his ass off when he found out you turned me down, but here we are again."

"Weston, I didn't come here to argue."

The waitress appeared and grabbed his empty mug. "Another beer?"

"Make it a Stout, please."

"Sure thing, Mr. Laramie."

Tapping the pocket of his coat with intensity, Weston's mind spun off to all the wonderful places they'd been and remembered only the good times.

"The letter said you wanted to see me again. What for?"

She twisted the stem of her wine glass. "I thought I'd talk to you about Mickey."

"You invited me here to talk about another man?" He shook his head. "I don't believe you."

"Well, it's true."

"What part?" Weston stood.

"Where are you going?"

"The Atrium Hotel." He buttoned his jacket and adjusted his lapel and collar.

Looking over her wine glass at her old friend, she said, "It's been a long day. Meet me for coffee in the morning at nine o' clock. We can talk about Mickey then."

"I don't feel like talking about some filthy rich seafood baron from Savannah, Georgia." He threw $50 on the table. "I don't need to stay in High Point. I'm heading home at first light."

"See you at breakfast."

"Nope. You won't." He walked away.

✱✱✱

At The Atrium Hotel, Weston raided the mini bar, munched on chips, ripped candy bars open, and snacked on cookies until his belly was tight as a basketball. He stayed away from sweets on most occasions, but Sorano's nearness and his thoughts of Mickey Starr caused him to mix the soda and alcohol, which crossed his eyes for a few hours. He turned off the television and flipped through the phone book, and found the number he wanted.

He gasped as he dialed the phone, and then fell back on the bed.

"Hello, Mom, it's your oldest and favorite son."

His mother made him smile on every occasion.

"Oh, my God, thank you, Jesus. I was hoping you'd call, son. You always call on your father's birthday. Wes, he has been pacing the floor and waiting for the phone to ring. We even had a civil conversation today, more than yesterday."

"How's High Point treating you?"

"Better than Fayetteville did. Your father didn't care too much for the Bible belt ten years ago."

"That's no surprise. He's watching baseball, I bet?"

"Jason will see his first Yankees game on Tuesday," said Weston leaning back on his pillows. "Tell Dad to look for him down the third base line. Look for a young man with hair like Oscar Wilde. The dreadlocks are gone, thank God."

His mother paced the kitchen with her cordless phone. He could hear her pouring a glass of something, probably

Merlot, and treating herself to a snack that crunched. That would be cheese and crackers, he guessed.

"My grandson, Jason Laramie is at a Yankees game, what? There must be a little lady friend involved or Jason wouldn't be caught dead in Brooklyn?"

"He might be falling for a Carolina gal, too." Weston sat up. "How's his health?"

"Not good. I hope you stop by to see him."

***

Shouting and screaming climbed inside Weston's mind from his father's devilish voice, ringing in his head for years past when he was in high school and before, treating him no better than a stray dog. He was punished, bruised and beaten, and yet worse than punches, the words broke him on the inside. At graduation, Weston remembered the last statement he'd spoken to his father, but since then few words came between them.

"You'll never be anything more than you are!" said his father.

"You'll see, just wait and watch me." Weston told him and left for college.

Slamming the van door with his fist, his son left the free ritz of North Carolina, in a hell bent rage, shortening his vacation to hang out with friends, far away from family, saying 'Goodbye' only to his mother. He didn't regret a single word he'd said to his father and somewhere between July and August '74, he was overcome with an internal peace "it may one day improve," he thought. He made his way to California to see his Uncle Elmer, and halfway back in Amarillo as the sun blazed in the last hour of the West Texas sky. Submitting to hunger, he had an uncommonly juicy steak and buttery potato, and dreamed his brand of wine would reach Slam-Amarillo, Texas. He intended for it to happen.

Witnessing the darker stage of twilight turn black as West Virginia coal mine, less than a half hour into nightfall, a million stars glittered across the galaxy above the friendliest city Texas had. Weston no longer burdened himself with what he'd received from his father, latching to his grandfather's words in California, but time and distance made the best mixture of remedy and reward for his long journey to Virginia. Out of honesty and anger, days and nights, he tortured himself with the ugly memory of his father's numbness and he hoped enough time had passed to reconnect with his father. Regardless, he pledged to overlook the inexplicable strangeness of the past.

***

"Since his heart surgery, he has changed drastically." His mother stammered slightly. "Want to speak to him?"

"Is he still mad at the world?"

"No." She stared through the glass door at her husband.

"What happened?" asked Weston, with a drink in his hand. "Did he get religion?"

"He did accept the Lord, three months ago."

Weston placed his feet on the floor. "I'd like to come over, if that's acceptable?"

"I'll ask him." The phone clattered when she set it down. He could still hear her house shoes slapping the kitchen floor. "Your father will be waiting outside by the firepit. Bring some hotdogs and buns, would you? No beer. We haven't eaten."

Weston slipped his feet into his penny loafers.

"See you in an hour or so."

***

Sorano tossed and turned, a lady more prone to writing than speaking, though she held her own if someone disrupted her day. Early the next morning she intended to impress her first love when she wore a gray dress with yellow and silver flowers, and gray shoes that matched.

At nine o'clock sharp, she parked at The Atrium Hotel. Happiness crowded her heart seeing Weston again, the man she had refused to marry but never forgotten. Sorano rang the bell on the countertop.

"Hello?" She peeked around the room for a hospitable smile. "Anyone home?"

"May I help…" The young man's voice faltered. "Ms. Tanaka! You are joining Mr. Laramie?"

"That's right." She noticed the sheepish-but-starstruck look on the clerk's face. "I'm to meet him here for coffee."

"Your friend said you would sign your book for me." The young man handed her a plastic black ink pen chained to the counter. "It's the best pen I have." Taking it, she opened the book and signed it.

"First book I've ever signed in North Carolina."

Proud to be working that day, the young man bowed to the celebrity, and told his new friend, "You are the best."

"Could you ring Mr. Laramie's room for me, please?"

The clerk tapped the keys on his computer. "I'm sorry, but Mr. Laramie checked out early this morning. It was before sunup."

"He's gone?"

"But I'd be glad to have breakfast with you." He nodded nervously. "Since Mr. Laramie has obviously left you, I'm here for you."

"Well, thank you for the offer, young man." She touched his hand and looked at the clock behind him. "I must find him, though. Did he say where he was going?"

"No." He reached inside the drawer. "Mr. Laramie did leave this business card, though. He said if I ever needed a bottle of good wine, just call him and he'd ship me a case for my hospitality."

She stared at the card and handed it back to the clerk.

Her lips curled a smile and she hugged the guy.

"I know the place." She tugged at the rattling door.

"One more thing before you go," the clerk said.

She stood in the doorway with her ear canted toward the clerk.

"Is it true that you are in love with Mickey Starr?"

"I better go now." She cried when she saw the name Andy Oliver on the business card. Her son. Their son. Little Andy.

She waved at him one last time through the clear glass door.

Sixteen
Rest, Happy Traveler

Business had taken Sorano around the world — to Reno, Buffalo, Austin, Monaco, and beyond. However, she'd found a hidden gem of delicious strawberries, chocolate milk and pancakes, double covered and smothered in butter and maple syrup at PepperMill Cafe in High Point. The lady felt at home in the Great South, ceilinged under an ever changing blue sky, rolling grass fields, friendly people, and more gardens and flowers than she'd remembered. True serenity.

Later, more certain in her heart of what she was about to say and do, she proceeded alone. First stop, Meems Bottom Covered Bridge. She sat, eyes closed, leaning on her palms and dipped her toes in the cold, clear water, longing to draw in the cool mountain air that gently moved her hair. She relaxed with assurance pretending to be in Savasana on her first visit to Mount Jackson since President Reagan took office.

Always a bird lover, Sorano counted cardinals and hoped to see blue jays and certainly geese in the wide Shenandoah Valley. Rock to rock, she decided to walk along the North Fork of the Shenandoah River, in hopes of flushing a painted bunting fleeing from a cedar tree and headed for the dense forest.

Far from the frosty wind of Westbury and car horns and street lights of the Big Apple traffic, here, in the valley of paradise, she felt free and unburdened, even blessed, under thick cotton clouds, in a jovial mood. A gentle breeze shifted leaves on the ends of bitter-berry bushes and vibrated the stems of a Japanese snowbell across the flowing riverbank. Sorano savored the evening aroma.

More positive than she'd felt in ages, she lent her attention to the impressions of the Shenandoah Valley in full bloom. Blue skies ceilinged overhead like a French painting in the shops of Lagrasse. All of it brightened her thoughts especially when rabbits jumped and ran from meadow to meadow zigzagging for cover and dashing beneath the good earth. Like a symphony of animals blessed her ears, as the bark of a couple of squirrels positioned on the branches of chestnut trees caused her to carefully steady her steps only moving her eyes until something else produced an impromptu visit or an undisputed sound.

Although she loved Central Park in other ways. Less urban and curtailed, to compare the two settings would be unfair to both. Mount Jackson was a world apart in beauty and fascination, her concern wasn't about landscape any longer, but more intimate and personal, riveting on the inside. Sorano's courage, yet unknown even to her, built in part on her confidence and pose, was fading as the time approached to search for Weston. He'd ditched her earlier that morning, but his residence sat only a few miles from where she was parked.

Returning to her car, Sorano aimed her vehicle to the address on the business card. Three times she veered off the road into the dirt driving the switchbacks, as if she were twenty years younger and a greenhorn driver behind the wheel, who admired towering mountains. But she wasn't twenty years younger. She was herself. Aged. Matured. There was something she needed him to know about her. Her soul had changed with love many times over. Sorano wasn't afraid to face him or to walk away if she felt uncomfortable, casting away her wavering mind and what was weighing on her heart. What was another decade or two after all? Life raced, she thought, but she needed to find closure with him, for good.

***

Inside the tasting room at Andy Oliver, Sherrill elbowed Russell, a young cellar assistant, leaning his head against the window, peering like awestruck school boys at a slender figure in the parking lot.

"Looks like we have trouble on our hands," said Sherrill as he moved beside Russell.

They both knew when a woman entered the door alone to make time for her needs and be a gentleman about it or deal with the boss. Russell pulled the long string on the blinds to see what his supervisor had been so eager to point out.

"There's only one beautiful Japanese lady I know." Sherrill observed the luxury car in the parking lot, then threw a towel over his shoulder, a man who knew what was about to happen. Russell was clueless. Maybe not detail by detail, but in some odd way, he had a vision of how relationships unfolded when an extraordinary woman came to the front door, especially one that he had not forgotten.

"There goes Mr. Laramie's extra flying time," said Sherrill who attempted to understand unresolved issues after years of being apart, "and he might as well hang up those hiking boots he just bought."

"The only Japanese lady I know married John Lennon." Russell readied himself to open the door. Then, he grinned at his boss. "The lady who anchors the television station in New York City is another one, but this is not either one of them."

The workers returned to their duties, eyeing each other when she walked inside the tasting room. Sherrill ventured to the warehouse and then the cash register to ease his nervousness and curiosity as well. He dropped the golf cart keys in his pocket in case he needed to warn Weston that a Japanese lady was eyeing the tasting room at Andy Oliver.

"Can I help you?" Sherrill asked from behind the bar.

"I'm looking for Weston Laramie." Sorano rolled a bottle of Chardonnay in her palm. She looked up from the label and a slow tear fell. "Do you know where I can find him?"

"Sometimes he walks the grounds, encourages the team and feeds his koi fish on a bridge that arches over the pond. Yeah, he's a busy man." The bald man leaned on the counter. "Other times he is consulting with the sommelier." He nodded, raised his hand, and said, "Or at midday he makes deliveries and thanks his customers. All in all, the man's hard to find, but you're welcome to wait in the famous tasting room, that is, if you have time. He does usually show up for lunch with his crew, when he's in town, for pizza."

After losing much of his hair since the 70s, Sorano didn't recognize Sherrill Taylor after twenty years, but he knew her at first glance. Unforgettable.

"Can I tour the property?"

His beard was gray and his gait a bit slower, but Sherrill shuffled the keys in his pocket and turned to see her admiring the long view of greenery and browns in full bloom; exposed a grand picture of Eastern Red Buds, flowering cherry trees, nestled were the pink of dogwood and azalea, just to name a few. Patches of grass and rows of vines rolled on knolls and valleys were an uncommon feature, in their general appearance, patterned along the road and paralleled as planned on torn paper and part of a napkin, years before at a coffee shop in town. Long stemmed roses, all of it and more, pouring his life into the soil of the valley, Weston colored the ground in a panorama of life. Deep wells and mountain runoff had never run dry on the grounds of Andy Oliver Vineyards, the hills and heavens supplied enough water needed to support the drip lines into the hidden gem of Shenandoah County. The winery and vineyard were crowded with visitors and business was at peak when Sorano arrived but Sherrill felt compelled to talk to her.

"Kind lady," clearing his throat and tapping his watch in eagerness, "Mr. Laramie doesn't allow self-guided tours at Andy Oliver. However, he hasn't denied the travel of a golf cart yet on a midday adventure. Can we roll in the cart?" He stood beside her. "You sound so familiar," shaking her hand. "What is your name?"

"I'm Sorano Tanaka." To greet him, the lady held out her hand. "From New York City."

"I was a much younger man when I first heard your name and saw you here. Andy Oliver was a blueprint of buildings dog-eared on a napkin back then and just a dream when I met young Weston Laramie," said Sherrill who opened the door to where a string of a dozen or more matching green golf carts were parked. "Weston mentioned you a time or two. You may be the very reason he nailed up the 'Virginia *Isn't* for Lovers' sign in the breakroom."

Sharing a thin grin, she touched her face. "Does he still honor that slogan?"

Sherrill grinned and unhooked the cart from the charger. "Until his dying day."

The two of them agreed it was priceless and laughed.

"This vineyard is amazing, Sherrill. Weston has done well for himself," she said, quickly arming the elderly man's sway and walking toward the golf cart. "Azaleas. This vineyard has blossomed like trumpet shaped Azaleas. There's something blooming on every road, just like azaleas do."

"You mean, he has done well to hide himself in the Shenandoah Valley, like a valley box turtle that doesn't go very far from its home."

"I've been gone too long myself."

Turning the key and shifting the lever, Sherrill drove the golf cart down a winding blacktop road, behind the big red barn where he stopped. He told how Andy Oliver came to be in the early eighties from before the first bottle was corked just after she'd broken up with Weston. Next, he quietly turned and beelined for the vineyard's highest point so she could see where her son was buried among the wild flowers and lilies and beneath the oaks.

Suddenly a flood of tears burst from her sweet eyes in a relentless stream of motherly love, for obvious reasons. That was where the lady broke into pieces on the new bench when she saw her son's name neatly manicured on a tombstone. Sorano was reminded of what she had left behind in the Shenandoah Valley so many years before and she spoke of being a good mother. Something she never had a chance to be for very long. In the stillness, he let her have her moment on the hill, shifting her body so she could see the long view of the valley stretching across the countryside, more than she could remember. Hardly anyone knew he was there, but she'd never forget that part of her past as she spoke of feeling at peace beside Andy Oliver.

Sherrill sat beside her, cleaning her glasses. She wiped her eyes.

"I know how you feel." He nodded.

Tears hung on her cheeks. "You can't, Sherrill."

"I do. My wife and I moved to Mount Jackson in 1953. My place is only five miles from here. Benny was born in '54."

Sure enough, corners clipped, but tucked inside his worn out leather wallet was a creased black and white photo of a sandy haired boy.

"Look what a beautiful smile he has."

"My wife's brothers and sisters were at the house," said Sherrill, waving his hand, "people were eating and laughing and having a good time, packed house, three days before Thanksgiving in 1963."

"I was eight years old in November of '63." Touching her chin, "Wait! John Kennedy was shot that month."

"That was the day. Poor as church mice, but we had a television and it was the first pre-emption show I'd ever seen. President Kennedy was assassinated. Kennedy Dies on Dallas Street. Three major stations broadcasted the sad story."

"I was too young to remember. Pictures showed Jacqueline's pink outfit was covered in blood."

"Kids, adults, all of us were watching the motorcade. Then someone noticed Benny was gone. We looked in his room, inside the cars, top of the barn, even in the attic. My wife called the police about 2:45pm that day."

"What happened?"

"It was dark, still no sign of Benny. We searched everywhere. The police found him about a quarter after eight o' clock. Deputy King, he guessed that little Benny was probably hiding from the other kids, running and fell into an abandoned well."

Hugging him as he teared up. "I'm sorry, Sherrill." She cried.

"The worst part, I ran out of nails and didn't finish the well. Told myself I'd fix the well cover after her family left. Sorano, his death, it was my fault. We divorced a year later. I remarried. Carried Benny's picture every day since 1963."

"We're a couple of broken souls, aren't we?"

He nodded, still in pain.

When Sorano stood, hands shaking, Sherrill walked her to the golf cart and they explored the property, and said nothing more about the past.

"What do you think of this vast land?" He lifted his head.

Without hesitation, Sorano turned to him, and said, "I'm not sure I want to leave Andy Oliver. It's home."

"I hoped you might say that. Andy Oliver is a good place for you. New York is too big for the world." He hugged her. "This is your home, Sorano. Take it all in and live here. Not just today but every day. Andy Oliver was Weston's vision. He has made it one of the most popular places in the Shenandoah Valley. When you were here twenty years ago, we spoke once. I gave my condolences and handed you my handkerchief when you were crying just like you are now."

The ultra-flyer caught their eye as the plane descended, floating through the wide valley, tilting and finally, the aircraft was low to the ground.

Trying to shift her thoughts, he said, "Hey, look at that plane how it adds color to the sky." With his eyes bent, he scowled at her. "Are you and Weston courting now?"

"I saw him once in New York and tried to talk to him in High Point." She said, heavily as Sherrill parked the golf cart. "But it hasn't happened yet." She shook her head, gripping the seat rail and smiling as he drove down the winding road. "Weston was with a lady when he visited Westbury."

"Julianna." He turned his head toward her and then back to the road. "A high-end real estate broker, I believe. She flies in and out on her Cessna plane. Not sure how serious they are these days. No wedding has been announced. None that have gone public," clearing his throat, "not like you and Mickey Starr."

She looked at him, obviously surprised that he knew so much about her personal life.

He despised Mickey Starr as much as Weston did.

"The story got out pretty quick," she said.

"The two of you made the media as far north as my doorstep and as far south as my cousin's mailbox in New Orleans."

Dodging the response about the engagement, she replied, "I'm surprised he hasn't asked her father for permission." Shivering from the chilly wind coming down from the mountains, she stuffed one hand under her armpit and held on as he rolled over a small bridge that arched over a stream of water.

"Julianna's long blonde hair is a ray of sunshine." Sorano took both hands to hold on going downhill at a rapid pace, gripping intensely to the cart's handle for balance. "She's gorgeous, but there's no mention of a serious relationship, huh?"

"It's not all hers." Sherrill stopped the cart, removed his coat and wrapped her up as quickly as he could. She shivered.

With less approbation and a cute smile, she continued. "The airplane or the long blonde hair?"

The old man laughed at her humor.

"The wig is not hers. I guess she owns it, though, along with the airplane."

"What else do you know about her?" Sorano asked him, shamelessly.

"Julianna?" Sherrill raised an eyebrow. "She was once married to a ritzy piano player." Adjusting his gloves, Sherrill added, "She has a penchant for the good life."

"Is Weston in love?" Sorano cut to the chase.

"I'm sure it's the same type of love you have with Mickey." His eyes followed her as she turned her head away. "Wow! Nice diamond, by the way. Mickey must really flavor you, I mean favor you. The fishing industry and The Famous

Tobacco Barn must've lured you to the silver-tongued devil of the south or are you in love."

"What type of love do you mean?"

Sherrill didn't answer immediately. He parked the cart, and they walked to a level spot where a park bench angled eastward. The lady examined his pale face with a kindling interest to the rest of their conversation.

"Here and there love is what I'm talking about. You are here and he is there, in Savannah, of course. And there's sincere love but it's distant and evidently fades away like it did with Weston, years ago. Out of sight, out of love."

Sherrill crossed his arms, and was interested in what she was doing at Andy Oliver.

"So, Julianna and Weston?" She hesitated to say it. "Does she stay here much, and sleep with him?"

"She's a free spirit. I'm not sure God made a man with enough patience to live with Julianna."

"She's a pistol, huh?"

Sorano touched her face, laughing into her gloves as if she was freezing and shivering again. She loved the way he told stories, less unction and more fire.

"The lady said marriage is an electric chair and doesn't want to be confined to one residence and especially not Andy Oliver. We're not urban enough."

Turning sideways to see Sherrill's round face better, she blurted, "Wow. She said it that way?"

Sherrill rested beside her on the bench. "Julianna travels and flashes her money around. Yeah. She thinks a marriage proposal is a death sentence, perhaps."

Twitching her hands and standing and blocking the sun from her eyes. Sherrill stood and waved at the ultra-plane flying gracefully in the wide blue sky, walking back to the gold cart. "Glorious plane. We better go. I'm still on the clock."

Shivering again, Sorano scooted back as far as she could in the seat of the golf cart and leaned forward as if she was on an amusement ride, settling herself in the cool mountain air. Her hands moved uncontrollably. Sherrill rubbed his hands together and she smiled and did the same. The old man aimed his hand at a small ultra-flyer plane making its way through the valley, observing the area's newest thrill in the sky. He released the break and pressed the foot pedal eagerly. They went from top to bottom, rolling over the landscape and her eyes stayed glued to the flyer.

"Have they spoken of marriage, at all?" Sorano watched his face.

"They have talked about it especially after Mickey offered to buy Andy Oliver last December." He bit his lower lip in anger. "She told him they'd have a good retirement, maybe in the Outer Banks, and pay everything off."

Her belly churned and she leaned in close to hear his soft voice.

"Mickey made Weston an insulting offer on Andy Oliver Vineyards. Made Weston sick to his stomach." The old man slammed on the gas and raced down the hill. "As old as I am, I would've taken it." He gripped the steering wheel and took a sharp turn where she had to lean hard against the driver. "Packed up my things and moved out to the Lone Star State. If

Weston decided to sell Andy Oliver, I'm sure as hell not working for Mickey Starr, but my boy Montgomery would have to."

"I can't imagine he'd sell Andy Oliver."

"Money bubbles a man's mind when he has a big vision for something else, brews him like coffee percolating on a winter day, whistling in his heart when it's time to change and do something different." Sherrill whistled at the plane dropping lower in the valley. "After you left Weston, I helped him plant the first vine on the 14th day of April, back in 1980. I've always admired him for his dedication over the past two decades. He's done well for himself, far better than most people expected him to do."

"That's little Andy's birthday." She knew the date well.

"Yeah, it sure is." He raised his chin. "Because of Andy, the winery is in its twentieth year." Sherrill stopped the cart on a knoll. "We better go check out this plane."

"Look at the man in the ultra-flyer." Sorano locked her eyes on the aircraft. "The red plane stands out in the sky, doesn't it?"

"He has poured his life into Andy Oliver, even making deliveries in his plane."

"Are you telling me that's Weston flying?" She blocked the sun with one hand to see the plane better.

"I know this golf cart doesn't compare to the plane, but would you like to see the flyer up close?"

"Looks attractive and exciting to me."

"Are you speaking of the plane or the pilot, dear?"

She grinned, eyes nearly closed and didn't answer.

"Weston stood me up this morning in High Point and I'm still pissed off about it." She held herself inside the golf cart as he beelined toward the flat bottom land where the plane was about to land. "By the way, he owes me a cup of coffee."

Sherrill turned swiftly down the rolling hills, taking his favorite part of the drive behind the barn and the tasting room, pointing the golf cart toward the open landing field. He charted a course for the rolling hills and stopped atop the knoll for a better view of the landing area. Together, he and Sorano observed Weston's rough roll where he leaned back in relief when the plane stopped. She waved her hand with the excitement of a cheerleader, but the pilot wasn't attentive to her actions.

To not rush his start, Sherrill inched the dark green cart forward to where the bottom land tapered off and entered the flattest part of land Weston graded a few weeks earlier, making an exceptional runway for the ultra-plane to end its journey. If Weston hadn't bought the plane, he had planned to build a youth baseball field, which would draw a sizable crowd to Andy Oliver on weekends, but he had other plans for flying. For some odd reason, though, the plane had been all he talked about the past autumn, other than making and selling more wine.

Sherrill overlapped his hands on the golf cart's steering wheel and leaned forward, observing what might be sparks between two old flames. He loved a good fire, too.

"On clear days and under baby blue skies," he shouted as she walked toward the plane, "you'll see him making deliveries in the plane." She turned and waved at Sherrill as he motioned her to wait at the end of the bridge. The wind shifted her hair and clothes as she walked to meet him as he unstrapped himself. "Though to refrain from fracturing the glass bottles, he flies with no more than a half case," he added. "The trip keeps him in practice as a certified pilot while adding a little liveliness to the business, don't you think?"

Her focus was on Weston, and she nodded to the driver of the golf cart.

"Yeah, he's fine." She whispered to herself. "And the geese are beautiful when they swim in the pond."

"He raises geese now. Yet, it's another layer of sophistication despised by Julianna. She hates his pets."

Sorano paced over the bridge that crossed the pond where his geese nested to close the gap between her and the pilot of the ultra-flyer.

Weston waved Sherrill over to the ultra-flyer plane. His friend hurried as fast as he could to help him roll the plane to the edge of the barn.

"What's she doing here?"

Shrugging his shoulders, Sherrill beamed at Weston and grinned like a possum. "She didn't say. Sorano might want more than your Pinot Noir, huh?"

"As many questions as I've answered about you," he laughed, "it could be a hot night," Sherrill warned him.

Unstrapping himself from the plane to walk inside the barn, Sherrill kept after him. "She wants her mountain man. Sugar, sugar pie honey-hon. And she doesn't care for the sign in the breakroom, either."

"Stop!" Weston grinned and hid his laughter with his sleeve. He watched Sorano toss the last handful of feed to a dozen geese that had followed her.

"Julianna is a jealous lady, Weston." Sherrill slapped his hands together. "Julianna is as sweet as a sour pickle, isn't she?" stuffing his hands in his pockets. "You have your slice of Sorano pie and Julianna cake," shaking his head and kicking the straw under his feet. "Are you burning the candle at both ends, Old Sport?"

"Julianna is a wonderful woman, sometimes. I have an idea."

"Sorano is a super lady as well, boss man. What are you thinking," slapping Weston's shoulder, "a lady hooked on each arm, I bet?"

He removed his aviator helmet. "Nope!" Weston dusted himself off and watched Sherrill laugh at his complicated situation. "Take Sorano on a delivery to Luray for me, please. Three cases of Merlot are already in the back of the van. Julianna will only be here for an hour or so. She's meeting her daughter in Charlottesville for a benefit dinner at seven o'clock. They will stay overnight there and not at Andy Oliver. Thank God."

"Good plan. I will drive slow and buy you some time."

Weston strapped up. Sherrill fueled the plane. Next, rolled the flyer to his makeshift runway, for a quick getaway until he figured out what to do with both of the beautiful ladies at Andy Oliver. Weston had never been that lucky before.

Saluting Sherrill with a great big smile, he said, "I'll make another flight around Mount Jackson and return, by that time you'll be in Luray."

"I'll take her in the van on delivery as slowly as I can," said Sherrill, who stepped back and paced between the golf cart and Sorano.

Walking up beside Sorano at the fish pond, Sherrill noticed how marvelous she looked amid the bridge, like something from an oriental movie. "Weston is flying away, we'll get going on the delivery, if you have time?"

The plane turned around, and in a short time Weston was only a small dot in the baby blue sky as Sorano blocked the sun from her eyes to watch the plane trail off through the long, wide Virginia skyline as she crossed the bridge back to the golf cart. She stopped one last time to see if she could see the plane darting off again.

"Let's go," Sherrill announced. Sorano jogged to where Sherrill was seated, slapping the passenger's seat of the golf cart. In a rush and on a mission, he said, "We're running late with a big order of Andy Oliver," he added, tightening his lips and leaning forward to watch the plane turning in the distance.

"Where's Weston going and where are we headed?" Sorano asked.

She held onto the cart handle, still watching the plane, a small thumbnail size figure in faint distance.

"I'm not sure what your schedule is, hon," said Sherrill, who released the break and gassed the golf cart. "But, Ms. Tanaka, for the first time ever would you care to assist this old man on a delivery of Andy Oliver Merlot to Luray?"

"I'd love to." She squinted her dark eyes and leaned back when he took off. "It has been years since I've visited Luray. Could we see the Singing Tower?"

"Sure. We'll get a scoop of rocky road ice cream when we get there."

Directions to the customer were in the passenger's seat of the Kombi van, held by Sorano, which, written in Weston's handwriting, made her feel at home. Warming up the van, Sherrill told her the last time he was in Luray, Virginia, July of the previous summer riding with his brother, who he missed dearly. For Sorano, the passenger's seat brought back songs that Weston serenaded her with as they drove through Shenandoah County, and when the radio played James Taylor, she sighed and hoped to see him for dinner.

After spending several minutes walking down the hall and admiring the pictures on the wall along with the hundred and three wine tasting awards presented to the staff of Andy Oliver, Sorano struggled with being absent from the photographs, drooping and shuffling to where Sherrill waited patiently in the van.

On Highway 211, halfway between Mount Jackson and Luray, east of New Market, a natural majestic community, he answered question after question for his inquisitive friend. Overdue, Sherrill rattled off one that was weighing on his heart, "Do you have a place to stay tonight?"

"Thought about the bed and breakfast in Mount Jackson."

A bit tenacious, Sherrill increased the speed of the van on Highway 340 after passing White House Landing, keeping his schedule to the final destination.

"Weston wouldn't let you spend a single night in his B&B when he had plenty of space in the log home at Andy Oliver."

Sorano grabbed his arm.

"What?" She said, swinging her head and arresting his arm. "Are you kidding me? He owns the historic B&B, in town? The one we stayed in twenty years ago?"

"Yeah. On the other hand, he'd have a cow if you stayed anywhere else but in his grand structure, with wooden planked walls, a log cabin built for the amused pioneer," he said. By her widened eyes, Sherrill expected she'd like the idea as much as he did. "Located on an exceptional piece of real estate," he said, touching his chin. "He's probably lit the fireplace, packed the bowl on the kitchen table with tea bags and lemons, and placed oatmeal in the cupboard for your morning meal by now."

"I'm not interested." She stirred herself. "He can find me at the hotel for coffee. Thank you for your offer, though."

"Don't you know? He stopped drinking coffee when you left because he couldn't find anyone who impressed him enough to stay for breakfast!"

"You mean Weston Laramie hasn't drunk a single cup of coffee since he and I were together?" Little white lie, but the old man was the best at it.

"Maybe you should stick around this time, see what's happening at Andy Oliver." Sherrill lowered his voice in regret, and murmured, "I'm sorry. That was wrong of me to try to manipulate and be opinionated about something that is none of my flippin' business."

"You're not out of line." She nodded, examining the countryside. "I'm comfortable with the truth and that's why I'm here, to see if I'm welcomed, to see why everyone keeps telling me to buy Andy Oliver Wine for my restaurants."

"So you'll stay in the log cabin, business or pleasure?"

"On one condition."

Sherrill pulled into the customer's parking lot in Luray and turned off the van to speak frankly. "What's the stipulation, dear?"

"Have Mr. Laramie knocking on the cabin door with Pinot Noir in his hand at eight o'clock."

"Are you planning to seduce my boss, Ms. Tanaka?" he asked as he opened the side door laughing.

Moving to help him with the wine cases, she said, "There's nothing wrong with two old friends catching up, right?"

"I haven't given him the news yet." Too much for either one of them to tote any distance, in tandem Sherrill and Sorano pulled the cases on a hand dolly to the door of the business. "He's going to wonder why you're here and .... if you're spying for Mickey Starr?"

"That isn't why I am here."

"Or why the sweet Japanese lady he once knew is dating a man he hates, and if she is trying to renegotiate a better deal on Andy Oliver, huh?"

"I'm here because of Weston," she said shaking her head, "not for any other reason."

The customer handed Sherrill a check. They inched their way through Luray, scanning the street for a nostalgic store and some great ice cream.

"You'll have to sort all this out with Weston."

Seventeen
It's Eight O' Clock Somewhere

Kind-heartedness was handed down by Sorano's mother, surefootedness and magnanimity, not only at home but in public, spreading good deeds wherever she ventured even with a tactful friend knocking on the door at any moment. Thrilled to be in the Shenandoah Valley, she prepared to render Weston speechless by midnight.

It may take more effort than first expected, but she hoped to find out more of what she'd missed. Her natural ineffable beauty impressed Weston and the fact she was there, staying in town, caused him to guard his emotions after she'd left him a few times in the past.

Weston wanted to trust her, yet he understood the assertive power of love and how she could muscle his heart with the squint of her mesmerizing eyes and the slightest turn of her body, paired with long soul touching hugs, made him helpless. The thought crossed his mind about who she loved. Was it Remington Bentley or Mickey Starr and why was she in Mount Jackson, Virginia? Or did she enjoy the thought of being loved by more than one man? Maybe that idea had crossed Weston's mind more than once, like a thunder cloud sliding off into the far distance or was it the ultimate rainbow that finally appeared after the hard storm of life?

For her part, Sorano prepared for the uncertainty of how he would receive her, leaving behind what had happened, full of life as if the world had started over the day before, for him. At the same time, not a day went by that she didn't hover over the thought of Weston and make a comparison of how her life might be different had she stayed in Virginia versus chasing her career in New York. The one man who continued to impact her heart from afar, was near, planning to liberate unanswered questions for him and for her.

The log cabin Weston built with his own hands glowed like a midnight star on a dark night as the fireplace warmed a seldom used living room, puffing smoke from the chimney in Mount Jackson, a distinction Weston favored.

Driving back from Luray, Sherrill described it as "the mixed architecture of ponderosa and pioneer days." Furnished for a purpose when occupied with the care of good company, or otherwise it was in vain, and otherwise would've made a good hunting cabin for out of towners. The vineyard cabin Weston had poured his heart into had stood vacant for ten years, at least. Something of an extravagance in a wonderful town, it served as a statue the town felt proud to admire both up close and from a distance, an uncommon standout among modern homes. Just like the smoke from the Vatican drew attention, so did a fire from a chimney at an Andy Oliver log cabin.

A hint of majesty happened when the rich oaky smell burned from the fireplace, waltzing with ebbs and flows, a silver trail of aroma billowing across the southern sky, intentional and untamed, curling into nothingness was a powerful opaque ribbon of delight that had never followed with a warmth of her company. Weston kept dry wood by the fireplace just in case Sorano ever visited. She never did and it was something rare and memorable, if only for the night. Why, he asked himself, was she back there now, at Andy Oliver teasing him?

He remembered Sorano liked him in a blue striped suit, so he dressed the part and held a '96 Pennant Pinot Noir, an apologetic Yankees gift for having skipped coffee with her early that morning.

Knocking on the log cabin door Sherrill had assigned to her to board for as long as she needed, Weston took a deep breath, standing as he'd never been there before.

Cheerfully he said, "Anyone home?"

She opened the door wearing a burgundy evening slip and matching shoes, eyeing him, up and down, Sorano raised her head to examine his Carolina blue tie, the style she'd bought for him years ago and followed with a gentle kiss on the cheek.

"Konnichiwa." She added the formal Japanese greeting, beaming in beauty and elegance, and stood optimistic.

In breathtaking admiration for one another, they stared at each other for a moment, in disbelief, perhaps. Without an invitation, she eased her reluctance, and was covered in years of regret, missing what they could have had together and what they might have experienced. Years of curiosity was at her fingertips.

"Hello to you as well." Being a gentleman, he stepped inside and brushed the small parts of his hair with this hand, and something was in the other hand. "Should I take my shoes off, to honor your heritage?"

"Weston! No," she said smiling, winking at him and touching his arm. A gentle rain had settled down, so she pulled him inside from the cool dampness.

Weston handed her a fine wine bottle of Andy Oliver, wrapped in a tall burgundy and gold bag, bow tied above a rope around the neck, and it was a winner among the crowds who had visited the winery. For her, why not, though? She took the rope handle in her fingers.

"You brought my favorite. What's behind your back?"

"Small gift."

"Did you buy me roses?"

"And I made Pinot Noir with you in mind. You've always been my pin up lady," he said, laughing and hanging his coat on the hall tree.

Taking a deep breath, he tucked his hands inside his slacks and remembered when he built the cabin, nailing board by board, log by log, in the fall of '81, the home was always for her, he told Jason while they flipped through postcards and letters, weeks earlier. He told her the same, at that moment. She loved it.

"For some reason, I feel at home in this log cabin." She slid the bottle from the bag. "Spacious. Impressive. From the rugs to the rafters, it screams style." She stepped toward where he stood in the living room. Relaxed. "You have built a paradise in the Shenandoah Valley, Weston Laramie."

"I wondered about you and how you were doing."

***

After Weston's friends were killed in the Dominican Republic, the A-frame log cabin became his getaway from the darkness of the world. He hid out there mostly to avoid the regional newspaper reporters who peppered his primary residence with invasive knocks and left notes and business cards on his mailbox. That's why he'd called Jason into the picture and had him move to Mount Jackson, for privacy and indeed he was a private man. His nephew's purpose, to shield the reporters so he could concentrate on the vineyard being in a number of wine magazines across the country, he wanted to keep the business side positive.

He'd become use to the quiet residence, remembering how the long view of the valley was serene, a sign of comfort and assurance, for better days to come. The silence and relaxation helped him cope with the loss of his friends. Now the lady he'd originally built the structure for planned to stay with him. He hoped she'd stay forever, make it her home and they'd become close again.

The woman in question waltzed around the open living room.

"I see you have done well in my absence."

A thin grin made its way to his face as he uncorked the bottle of Pinot Noir with a stainless steel tool, a two prong cork puller. One he kept hidden, part of Atwater's collection — a cherished southern gift from her years ago.

Lifting his eyes from the raised embossing of the bottle to see her reaction, he palmed the base, thumbed the punt, and poured her a glass of Andy Oliver.

"I'm still the determined man you left behind in the Shenandoah Valley," he said, handing her the wine. "Did you think otherwise, ma'am?"

Milling around the room at some of the gifts he never got to give her and digging through his custom made cabinets she found a set of opaque 18th century twisted, tall stemmed

Biltmore glasses, which Weston had bought from a credible collector in New Market, just a few miles from his cabin. He noticed the sherry glasses she might like to use. The tempered bowl, wide mouth glass rim, was made with such a romantic setting in mind, despite the rounded shape to direct the varietals on the tongue and olfaction of the nostrils. At that time in his life, he was considered as an expert in the field, knowing more than she did about grapes and even stemware and was humbled that she noticed his success.

"Let's keep this evening civil," she replied, toasting him. "Can we?"

Sorano opened the cabinets and admired his decorations and custom design. She even complimented the furniture he'd shipped in from High Point. On the top of a walnut bar, he steadied his hand to pour her a second glass of Pinot Noir, resting the bottle and placing his hand over his heart.

"I'll try to be the peacemaker and do my part while you are here, I promise."

Positioning a stool at the bar, she held his hand and whispered, "Why did you stand me up at breakfast earlier?"

"Our conversation about you becoming Mrs. Starr of Savannah, Georgia upset the cheese and crackers churning inside my stomach." He rolled his hand. "Hope you signed that young man's book while you made a cup of coffee and snagged his homemade apple pie?"

"Of course, I did. Nice kid, and I ate at the PepperMill Cafe in High Point," she said, sipping her wine and blinking her dark eyes in his direction. "And I denied myself a pastry. Thank you very much."

Pulling out a bar stool for himself, he positioned his knees next to hers as he used to do years ago when they dated. Not as calm as he thought he'd be when he heard from Sherrill that she was touring the grounds at Andy Oliver and became even more nervous when he found out she'd invited him over to talk.

"Are you here because you saw the name of our son on a bottle of wine?"

"That's part of it. I cried when I read Andy's name in New York, to be honest." She held up the bottle in the light, examining the geese flying across the blue sky on the label. "I saw you on the cover of *Vineyard* magazine too. I'm so proud of you, Weston. Not at all surprised. You have always been one to watch."

"Did you hear about my awards from your boyfriend in Savannah?" Weston walked around the room. "His ridiculous offer to buy Andy Oliver just pissed me off. Still sick about his Happy Meal offer." He emptied his glass, pushing it to the middle of the bar. "I'm still offended. Sherrill had a cow."

"Sherrill told me today about the offer as we toured the vineyard. I was extremely proud to deliver cases of wine with Andy's name to Luray." She threw up her hands. "I didn't know Mickey wanted to buy Andy Oliver, Weston. Honestly, I didn't."

"You didn't know?" His look of disbelief hurt her more than she showed. "Isn't that why you are here? To make me an irresistible offer with Mickey Starr's money and sweep this conversation under the rug on Mickey's famous yacht for you and him."

He poured them both another serving, where he washed out the bottle for another purpose. Hundreds of times over the past 2c years, he'd thought about what he might say or do if he talked to her again, in private. He wanted a simple evening without a war or a debate. Was it going to happen?

"What do you mean?" she asked, tapping her long nails on top of the bar and beaming at him with her sweet chocolate eyes.

Calmly, he answered, "Aren't you acting as Mickey's negotiator and partner now, perhaps, trying to acquire this place for a song and a little dancing before midnight?" Weston strolled to the largest window of the cabin to rub his mustache, trying to figure her out. "Is he watching you from his dark limousine just down the road?" He spun himself around with a sharp glance. "Are you wired?"

"That's not my plan, at all," taking a gulp of wine and cleaning her top lip. "Stop it!"

"Are you sure?" he said, touching his chin in deep thought. "So you and Mickey can have a big laugh, kicking back in your new Savannah farmhouse saying, "We sure suckered Weston Laramie for a fraction of its worth?" Brag to your new friends at the country club, about how you hooked that big ol' Shenandoah vineyard for the cost of a fishing rod and a used shrimp boat?"

"Damn it, Weston!" Sorano slapped the bar with both hands. Her face flushed. "I'm not *here* for him. I came to Mount Jackson for you and only you." She pulled her hand to her face. "We have a history I cannot let go of, today or on any other day," she whispered. "I see us together today, tomorrow and every day that follows this moment, right here."

Weston felt like he'd been hit with the blunt end of Reggie Jackson's baseball bat in game five of the 1977 World Series. Her declaration was all he'd hoped for, so why didn't he believe her?

He stood tall, both hands wrapped around his glass. "I don't think you have ever been *here* for me. We were in love once and lost Andy. Then you ran away to New York after the funeral, that's the history of what I remember. You vanished and covered your grief with letters. Our relationship was a long, long time ago, Sorano."

"I was wrong." She reached for him. "Young. Foolish."

He turned from her. Steamed.

"Careless, that's the message I got. You fell out of love."

Sorano fired back with sharpness and purpose in her eyes.

"I left message after message after message on your phone and mailed postcards, more than I can count and begged for something different." She threw up her hands. "You wouldn't respond, sulking like a little teenager." She faced him. "I hear you still have the letters and old pictures."

"Who told you that?" Weston snapped his hands and rubbed his chin, taking a gulp of wine. "Jason, my own nephew played your game and told you, huh?"

"Your nephew wants us together. What about you?"

Weston brushed the thought of Jason away with his hand. "Family. We weren't married. Why are you here? Tell me, huh?" His piercing eyes locked on her. "I'm doing fine without you."

Sorano flung her hair and twirled, headed in the opposite direction of the house and stopped. "Wait! Wait! Didn't you send Jason to speak to me last winter?"

He leaned against a post, crossed his arms and tensed up. "The hell I did." He lifted his glass. "That was something he did on his own after he'd seen pictures of us inside my old trunk."

She smiled and dropped her head, long bangs covering her eyes, walking over to where he stood in the middle of the room, twisting the bottle in both hands, whispering, "The old trunk I bought you? Is it full of cards and letters?" She laughed. "You are a sentimental soul."

Sorano was his muse, marveling at her, turning to melted butter when she reached out her hand and grinned at him. Weston opened the large refrigerator to keep from dropping his guard.

"Are you hungry?" she asked on purpose. "I thought we would have dinner here."

"Since you have a high-dollar Barbie doll, street corner dress from New York, New York, well, we could go out for dinner?"

She scoffed and lifted her wine glass with a theatre laugh that he was sure to notice. Weston remembered the first time he asked her out on a date. He'd had less gray hair atop his head and fewer wrinkles around his eyes, but his memory flipped through the past without missing a single day. She meant everything.

"I'm not sure that's such a good idea." She walked over to the tall windows. "I love the details, the oversized recliner and the sectional sofa you have in the living room." She walked over to the pool table, chalking the pool stick, gripping and pulling back, leaning over the table and lifting her foot off the floor. "This wine is going right through me. You are a true master."

"I'll call in a pizza." He reached for the phone.

"I love Italian food," taking a cloth to her sweaty head.

Weston picked up the phone. "We can do Mexican, it's not far from here."

"Pepperoni pizza, *please*." She walked toward the back of the room, gazing back and forth with a passionate glance. "Can we shoot pool or play the jukebox?" She gripped the sides of the music box, selecting a slow song and pushed the buttons, moving her hips to the rhythm, lost in slow motion. "Wes, can you still dance?" She danced her way from room to room, wrapping her arm around a post and twisting until she made it to him.

After he hung up the phone, he chuckled and held the pool stick she'd handed him, examining her body and elegance from across the room. The sureness of her character had always impressed him, handling herself well in any situation, but his curiosity was endless why she landed at his home, acting as if she was on a business trip or was it pleasure, he couldn't tell. Whatever she attempted to do, she loved to win, and he knew it. For the most part, she was always nice to him even when she elected to date the Japanese guy and stay in New York State. That's when it was over, he remembered. That's when Weston earned the name "Ridge" after hiking across the rugged mountains from Georgia to Maine alone, to find himself and discover his purpose, with or without her, still a mystery man.

"Hand me the pool stick, please?" She yanked and smiled until he released the stick into her hands. "Chalk the tip for me." She leaned over the table with one leg pulled back to her butt as if she was stretching as he racked the solids and stripes.

"How do you play again?"

"The first ball must be placed at the apex position," he handled the rack like a pro. "Front of the rack and so the center of that ball is directly over the table's foot spot. Lifting the rack, "a pair of solids and a striped ball fell."

"What happens next?" She rolled a ball in his direction with a great amount of speed and force. He clutched it in his hand.

"It's my turn. I choose solids, this is, I mean, if you want to play by the rules in Mount Jackson."

He needed some luck.

From her position, half-stretched across the table in a seductive fashion, she pulled the pool stick back and forth, turning in his direction. "We could get closer."

"Remind me."

She understood him. "Like we used to do."

His head nodded in full confidence. Dropping the ball in the corner pocket, clipping the pool stick on the wall rack, Weston scooped her up into his arms, and carried her to the bed in the loft.

A slight trembling in her voice said, "Weston."

Pure and honest hearts, intentional and comfortable, destined for her new home at Andy Oliver, the place she belonged. Nowhere else, he thought, fulfilling the promise he'd made to himself, huddled in a karmic relationship. The glow of a scented waving candle on the nightstand, reflected in the mirror and highlighted her shape, sinking slowly into a pomegranate colored quilt, the prelude to her artistry. Few words were spoken, spiritually married, submitting to the passion of a twin flame. Souls no longer alone and tugging on the heartstrings of an oratorio, with faded voices and holiday wishes. Once far from each other, but now, nearness and wholeness existed. Inside they were singing in harmony and humming songs, coupled with past memories of good times. Caught in a world of better love, proceeding to be the truism arch of destiny, celebrating the union of souls, and lost no more as an illusion. Wrapped up in hope of tomorrow, fresh and anew, activating familiar feelings and sharing the best version of each other. Soft hands, legs intertwined, where the gentle collision of spirit and soul were found, beneath the pale moonlight, long awaited, captured in a moment that spanned with intensity into the night, both intimate and unsurpassable. Then she delivered a sashaying outro.

FATHERLY ADVICE

Two hours later, half the pizza was gone and another bottle of wine. Weston threw three sticks of wood into a low burning fireplace to break the bitter chill of the night air from where he stepped on the balcony, gazing longingly into the brightest of the flames, he took in a deep aroma that lingered across the room and he reminisced. The smell of dry oak hit his nostrils, and suddenly, he was a teenager again seated beside his father and listening to his stories.

As his father taught him how to keep the fire chucked, stacking more wood on the grate, Weston listened to his stories, laughing until his gut snapped at his father's crazy jokes, leaning on the sofa amused. Planning his defense against his father just in case he turned ugly, Weston had not expected his father to be calm and rational in his old age. Days earlier, though, the old man had accepted the Lord, and through his newfound heart was no longer crushing the worries of the world with his temper. He loved giving his two cents to his boys, though. Somewhere the Spirit had made him a peaceful man, breaking and mellowing his behavior and words. Rare. Pleasant. Hoping it was his father's new image, Weston accepted his new faith as genuine, transforming the old man into a new ray of hope. The two of them became friends, deeply realizing, for the first time ever, what being home meant.

His father's voice made sense, yet repetitive and logical, expressing his good thoughts about Sorano turned Weston's ear, another first. Instead of a bottle in his hand, he commanded the fire with a long stick and the substitution of sweet tea for his traditional cup of bourbon, making Weston want to visit again. His father was thin, in his mid-sixties, and had grown his beard to the length of a shoebox. He enjoyed the stay as much as Weston did. At the end of a long conversation, his father spoke the truth and it was what his son remembered the most.

"Weston, I'm surprised you decided to visit me," he said with a sharp grin.

"After all the fights we've had over the years. My heart stopped when you called."

"We had debates on cars and more arguments than two big countries about the time I dated Sorano. American versus Japanese automobiles, juggling political and religious differences all our lives." Weston turned his chair to see his father better. "Remember the one where we didn't speak for a week debating which country had the best coffee, Italy or Columbia, huh? Half and half versus vanilla creamer and almond milk? We were stupid fools. I miss those days, Ridge." His father had never called him "Ridge" before, an honor for all the hiking they'd done together in his high school days.

He turned, facing Weston and rested his hand on his son's shoulder.

"Something tells me you are here to talk about the Japanese lady and not about muscle cars or imported coffee tonight."

"Why do you think that, old man?" His eyes popped. "How did you know?"

"You and Jason have spent a number of weeks over the past year running back and forth from Virginia to New York, have you not? And it's usually about a woman. In your case I predict it's true love."

"We have been to New York several times. I have business there. Some pleasure, too."

His father stacked marshmallows on a stick. "Most pleasurable, right?"

Weston wiped his chin. "I can't deny it, Dad."

"Seems to me, you never talk of how the winery business is doing with your old man," his father said. "Whenever I see you, it's been more of a heart to heart, not wallet to wallet talk. Your desires and blue jeans have a common destination in your heart. Perhaps I'm right?"

"Is it that obvious?" He chuckled at his father.

Both men laughed and adjusted their seats when the fire made three foot flames, moving around as they relaxed in their Adirondack chairs. Overcome with a new sense of comradery in the backyard somehow pleased his mother, who watched from behind the sliding glass doors in utter contentment to their laughter and new found friendship even shedding happy tears into the long sleeves of her baby blue nightgown.

"It's the Japanese lady," said his father, "the little siren from Westbury who gets your jockey shorts unstable, isn't it? She's the one, right?"

"She wanted to have coffee today and talk about her engagement to Mickey Starr."

"She is dating that tomcat of a character who built The Famous Tobacco Barn in Savannah?" His father questioned in a lively spirit and walked around the fire. "The Tobacco Barn millionaire, huh? I'll be damned." He corrected himself. "Darned, I mean."

Weston shared a long face.

Watching his son grab his forehead as if his head were acting, his father aimed his hand, and said, "She's getting married to him soon. I read it in the *Charlotte Observer*."

"The wedding is next month. Sorano stopped in High Point just to tell you about it. Son, it doesn't make any sense to me," he said, snapping his fingers beside the fire. He stopped and squinted his eyes. "Unless she doesn't want to marry him and needs someone to rope her in and tell her she's wrong. You tell her she's out of line, she doesn't need to marry him. Say it that way, just like I said it, young man."

Weston placed his tea on the table and sighed, deep in thought.

"Why does she need me?"

"She doesn't want to marry him, Weston," his father said, shaking his head. "She doesn't need him either."

"Why does she need me?"

"She doesn't need either one of you gumball heads to wed her. The lady came from wealth in the first place, and besides, it's not about money to her. Maybe she wants to create some competition, have two popular guys fighting over her. Women are hung up on that medieval crap these days, you know? It pisses me off, the teasing part, the carrot on a stick game sucks."

"I'd have to disagree with you on the competition."

"Well, the only thing that it could be," his father held his chin, "and that would create a bigger problem for you, hmmm, well...?"

His father ate marshmallows and wiped his lips.

"What?" Weston turned to him.

"She wants to see if you still love her before she gets married."

"No way." Weston shook it off. "I don't believe it."

"Listen, I know what I am talking about. Your mother did me the same way. Worse damn time of my life, let me tell you. She decided to disappear for two weeks when we were dating," balling his fist, "and *find herself* in Ocracoke Island, with this guy. I never found out who it was, though. Or I would have Ocra-choked him to death with my bare hands, if I knew where he lived."

"You don't find out these things until they're talked about later or if the lady has the gumption to get it out of her system and open up with the truth. And you might not find out the whole story or the next part, the bit they want you to hear and the less embarrassing part until it's way too late."

"So, you think she's just off on some wild, unruly adventure, to find out who loves her the most?"

"Or maybe she has 'Daddy Issues' as some women do, you know, rebelling, chewing on thoughts of defiance or whatever else they'll deny? Not being tied down just yet, having someone to boss her around, well, but those things don't appeal to a real lady, the type with class, like Sorano."

Weston leaned on the railing, then his father followed him.

"What should I do, that is, considering she does want to start dating again?"

He slapped his son's back.

"Is she worth another heartbreak?"

"Yeah," nodding and finishing his snack. "She's always been worth it."

The dog rubbed up against his father's leg.

"I lost this lovely dog one time." His father bent over to pet the animal. "She was gone for ten days, had no idea where she went, but she came home one day, and never left. In life, love and respect are rare, especially true love. When it comes back, you better know it and never let it go." He petted the dog. "Right, Little Ann?" The half mixed Lab and hound barked twice.

"I see she came home," said Weston, brushing the pet.

"Maybe Sorano is ready to come home," he remarked, holding the face of the dog, "found out your brother was wrong about you being a jackass low-life who fell for a Japanese lady while he and I were out fighting other countries, at war."

"He was right about one thing, though." Weston stared out at the dark sky.

His father turned to him as if he was ready to learn something new about him.

"It matters not where you're from," said Weston, sitting up tall, "but who you are on the inside...that's what matters the most."

"Look at me," tapping his chest, "a crabby old man who changed his life, thank God, and now I know what it means to be the Fruit of the Spirit. And," stuttering in guilt," And I'm sorry for how poorly I treated you and Victor, Weston."

"God forgives. I better go, and see what Sorano wants with me."

His father walked ahead of him, rattling change in his pockets and shuffling his feet.

"Let's go make some popcorn," holding out his arm, "and watch the Yankees play ball, Ridge."

***

After the game, the drive from his parent's home in High Point back to the hotel gave Weston enough time for his father's words to deeply absorb into his mind and settle him down, less rattled, perhaps, at least, stronger in faith, for the moment. Weston fell asleep an hour later in the hotel with a sure fire answer of what to do about his new, fresh relationship with Sorano. Even though he'd hated his father on more occasions than he could count as a young man, what he said on that particular night made perfect sense, and what he needed to hear from him. The next morning he woke at four and rationalized with his infinite wisdom, as his words turned over and over inside his cloudy head caused him to make up his own mind about seeing Sorano again.

Clear as day he heard his father chuckling in amusement.

"Maybe she loves you," he said, laughing, "which is a long shot or….maybe it's some ridiculous competition between you and Mickey. One of those times where she weighs the pros and cons between two studly gents, like you did in high school." He stuffed popcorn in his mouth. "Some female survey that she needs to balance her future with soon." He wiped his hand and shaved. "Maybe it's time for her to come home or she's losing her mind in some weird stage of menopause." His father offered him a hotdog. "Women do that, and they get delusional."

That was what went through Weston's mind after a quick slap of aftershave belted his nose and while he dressed, long before sunup.

***

327

Glowing from ear to ear, she stood by the jukebox tapping to a song, long silken black hair pulled to her right shoulder as she shifted in the form-fitting outfit, and the way she moved was the anticipation of more. The action caught Weston's attention, and he walked up close to her and hugged her, the smell of Japanese cherry blossom lotion made his eyes close. He thanked her for coming to Mount Jackson and silently he thanked God, too.

Later, after the meal, she felt like talking.

"Hope you don't mind," moving her jet black hair into a ponytail, she said, spinning around and her smile became radiant. "Had to slip out of that tight fitting dress after the fireworks, put on some soft blue jeans and your Appalachian Trail t-shirt. I know it's baggy," tucking in the shirt, "but how does it look?" Walking under a dim light, the only one in the room, held a glass of red wine and made herself surreal to him. "I'm much more comfortable now. How about you?"

"I was going to wear your shirt tonight." He chuckled. "You're a ball of fire in whitewashed denim, Sorano." Weston grinned at her as he hopped up on the top rail of the pool table. "You haven't changed in twenty years. Slender. Happy. Full of life."

"You always get me excited, Weston Laramie, especially when you are half dressed and barefoot with that spicy cologne on which turns me ....."

Her features could not be ignored, using every worthwhile trait she'd learned to gain his attention again. Over the years, he'd prayed for her to walk into his world and through some strange miracle she did, but he hoped it was for good reasons.

"Stay the day, a week, or settle in for a lifetime," he told her. "It's not a crush any longer."

"I plan on staying," she said, admiring the cabin and touching the smooth stained logs, dragging her hands along the wood; she turned to him, "that is, if you will have me as your guest?"

"Hmmmm," with his head dragging over the pool table, "Welcome to Andy Oliver and I hope..." He didn't finish his sentence and she never pressed for the rest of his thoughts.

They spoke the same love language, and nothing was more important than having her in front of him. She was home and he knew it, but for how long, he thought, and why? While she was away in the mirror, he touched a prickly pear cactus on the center table to make sure it wasn't a dream, the thin drop of blood reminded him of her reality. He denied the possibility of some game or form of playing Mickey against him or some trivial tactic to make him jealous. Too early to add a conclusion, he couldn't be sure why she was in front of him and kept kissing him, like when they dated.

Often he dreamed of her sampling Andy Oliver wine with him, sharing a California roll, the crab being her favorite part of the meal and doing a hundred other things. Trekking through the high country, scuba diving for lost treasures in the Outer Banks, and a hundred and one other things. For two decades, hard whiskey and smooth notes of oak and caramel weren't enough to wash her memory away. Long work hours. Road trips. Sunshine. Snow storms. Music or fishing. None of it worked to make her appear or disappear from his heart. He felt relieved with her, but for how long? He stood, cursing himself for letting her stay and thanking himself that she was near, making him stronger and more hopeful again. His Japanese beauty was before him, and no longer in pictures and letters. Moments that were hung in the past, but now, flesh and bone, pulsing against each other, he thought.

"Best pizza this side of New York."

"I was starvin' like Marvin." She gulped a soda, then spun the ice in her glass.

The jukebox played Miles Davis, one of his favorite vinyl records, swaying within his arms to the trumpeter. Her attraction to Weston, the man knew music, from Memphis Blues to New Orleans Jazz, and his stylistic appreciation of film and pop songs intrigued her even more. Still warm to the touch, she held his hand.

"Do you want to watch television?" Weston handed her the remote control and a slice of pizza. They spoke about stocks and baseball. She mentioned the Marines that were killed in the plane crash in Arizona. An hour had passed and Sorano nibbled her second slice of double pepperoni, feeding Weston the last bite.

"I have an idea," setting the remote down, and crossing her legs on the sofa. "Tell me about your vineyard," touching his hand. "And we'll talk about redecorating the loft, fashion forward into Y2K, right?"

"Don't you like my Appalachian Trail look," leaning back and laughing, "it's a fine log cabin, though."

"Are you going to tell me about your vineyard?"

"Forty-eight acres of rolling hills, the same land we walked in the fall of 1977. The first building completed was this cabin," holding her hand, "and I hope you find some furniture from High Point and decorate it for me."

"We could match burgundy leather in the living room, right?"

"Yeah." He rested on the sofa. "I met Sherrill in May of '78. He was a surveyor and liked my idea of a vineyard better than his career, so I hired him. We broke our backs, sinking poles, running wire and planted hundreds of vines. When we had energy left, the two of us poured concrete for the tasting room and built the office, and thank God he knew someone in Maryland who had tanks and fermenters for sale. His friendship and connections saved the vineyard thousands of dollars."

"I wish I would have been here to help you."

Not breathing a word of indignation, he just nodded and softly touched her small framed face with the point of his finger, like a minister's blessing for a new believer.

"You were here, all of you," tapping his chest "right here, inside my heart."

"I'm here, for a long while, too." She wrapped his hands. "Itsumo."

"Always." His Japanese had not faded. "That's right. And you can stay, always, and as long as you like."

The log fireplace was warm against her legs. She stood. "The place needs my help, adding a dash of Park City appeal, a splash of Texas, and my attention to detail."

He interrupted her, "And don't forget how I love horses."

"You want that Southwest look in Shenandoah?"

"Why not? That may be our next trip, out in the Wild, Wild West."

Jumping up, Sorano leaned on the banister. He had designed the living room, game room, and kitchen in a grand floor plan. The traditional "A Frame" style log cabin, built with the glass doors and front windows, was staged and positioned east so he could watch the migration of the birds while drinking coffee in the warm morning sunshine. A long row of log cabin chairs sat on the front deck, three had hardly been used, and his favorite chair revealed several coffee rings on the armrest of the chair. Sorano leaned inside his arms, fresh lipstick applied, and kissed him. Later, pulling him to the French doors, they stood beside each other, surveying the glowing lights across the dark valley as the cool night breeze, light and fresh, seamlessly slid through the front yard cedars. He watched her body happily glide across the hardwood floor of the game room in her kimono.

"Why are you here, Sorano?"

"Look at the stars about the mountains and the glow of the vineyard in the fog." She watched the pale clouds rush behind each other, ignoring his question a bit longer.

"Beautiful valley." His hand waved from south to north. "That's why I stayed here."

Weston phoned Kenny, the guard, a half hour earlier to advise him not to let anyone inside the vineyard, so he could lock the main gate to Andy Oliver around ten o'clock, kicking back with a large pizza. Kenny turned off his radio to direct the pizza driver out at the end of his shift. From the second floor of the log cabin deck, Sorano watched the car turn left at a row of cedars, winding a quarter mile as the road divided the lawn and he exited the property. The driver spun in new gravel near the koi pond and then stopped at the end of a string of Japanese maple trees to talk to Kenny, a friend of his who'd delivered to Andy Oliver a hundred times or more.

"Appreciate the pizza, boss." Kenny told over the phone. "Next time, tell that nut pizza driver I said his boss makes the best pizza in Shenandoah County."

"I'll tell them to slow down next time, too." The guard closed the towering gate with the touch of a button. "Thanks again and goodnight, Mr. Laramie."

***

Weston followed Sorano into the kitchen as she carried food and he served up two ice cold mugs of lager.

"And when did you start drinking domestic beer, dear?" he asked.

"When I'm in good company," she said, moving closer to him, "I'm not going to lie, I normally drink Sapporo, but Mount Jackson must be out of stock. Do you remember when the Kelly Brothers teased you about switching from Irish beer to Japanese beer?"

"Heck, yes," he said, "I remember the Kelly Brothers," picking up a handful of rice crackers, chewing and touching his lip. "Meeting you in High Point was the best part of my life." He

333

chewed a thin sausage and tapped his mug against hers, which looked awkward when she used two hands to drink beer.

"We need to dine together more often."

"I usually pack pepperoni rolls and tree bark when I hike," tightening his belly in a laugh, "instead of California maki sushi."

She peeled a slice of pepperoni off her plate and fed it to him. "Are you uncomfortable with me being here? Tell me the truth, Weston."

"I do think it's mighty strange. You date Remington Bentley, invite me to your restaurant, stand me up, fly to Buffalo and a few months later you're engaged and *madly in love* with Mickey Starr; a much older jerk, I might add." He took his beer and grabbed the handle. "Now you are here, drinking beer with me. Strange twist of events. Don't you think this seems odd, just a little bit, and out of sorts for your character?"

Her face turned flush red as she stared at him and laughed, padding her forehead with a towel, netting her brow.

"You think I'm crazy, don't you?" She drained her mug of beer. "Ahhhhh. I'll leave in the morning if that's what you want to happen?"

Her chin lifted when his hand turned her head.

"I think something is going on inside of you." He touched her neck and hair. "We don't have to talk about it until you are ready. You're a bold person and that has always drawn me to you, in some special and out of this world way."

She turned her back to him and crossed her arms.

"Until my meds kick in, you mean. I feel better when I'm near you, that's all." Tears fell down her cheeks, hands shaking in nervousness. She took a deep breath. "Okay," she faced him. "I'm not crazy, but you are definitely an ass to me on this trip. I'm really trying to get us back together, but you won't let us happen. You want to know the truth?"

Making herself at home, pulling out two bar stools and nodding, lacking all gifts of reticence. In a brief moment they were both atop the bar stools as if they were seated in High Point, trying to impress each other with unexpurgated stories.

"I would sleep better if I knew."

"I'm here to meet you and talk about the possibility of us. So, I'm crazy, crazy over you since I saw Julianna kiss you in New York."

"You're jealous of Julianna? I love it. This is getting good."

"Damn it, Weston. Yes, I'm jealous. To be honest, I'd like to spend the rest of my life with you."

"That doesn't explain why you left Remington and now you're engaged to Mickey Starr." He half laughed. "And this *new found love* stemmed from you seeing me with a beautiful lady in Westbury?"

"I have always loved you," she said, seizing his hand. "I'm here, aren't I?"

"You're here for some odd reason. Love isn't it, though. I can promise you that much," he said, waving a mug at her. "Before I can figure it out, you'll be gone. I still think you're a little crazy. I'm crazy enough to know that much."

She walked out on the front deck, watching the security guard lock the gate, and keeping her words to herself. Weston walked up beside her.

"In the morning, you should leave before someone from the newspaper finds out you're here. Not because I don't want you here, but because you'd put your engagement and reputation in jeopardy for a terrific, life-changing one night stand with me."

A big laugh burst out of her small body. Their laughter echoed across the wide valley as they walked inside from the dark hand in hand.

"You said, 'Yes' to Mickey for a reason." Weston snatched a cracker. "And if the pizza guy saw you here, he might tell his father who writes for the newspaper, delivers mail, cuts hair, and makes gossip out of everything else in this small town. But he makes good pies."

She laughed, nearly spitting out her wine. "Small town gossip?"

"It's no different than blasting a banner on the boards at Time Square."

"I'm taking my chances," she said, beaming her eyes at him. "This crazy Yankee gal, well, she's staying the night to see what happens. But you're not getting lucky again."

"It wasn't luck. Well, you couldn't resist it, anyway."

She laughed again. "Just a bit conceited, aren't ya, Laramie."

"I could never underestimate the cool drive of a Yankee gal to get what she wants."

"O' boy, I'd never miss out on a lucky streak."

"Where is Mickey Starr, anyway?"

"I missed a trip with Mickey to the Dominican to be here." Sorano walked across the room to the jukebox to make a selection, then dimmed the lights. "I decided to stay with my best friend this week."

The murders of Moby, Myrtle, and Raymond crossed his mind.

"Are we friends?" He asked with a serious look. "I mean, good friends?"

With the help of Weston, she flipped the switch on the wall to the billiards table, and racked the table. He walked around flipping switches, one by one, until each section of the cabin was dark, and he was satisfied. Other than the bright orange glow from the fireplace, the only other light was the yellow bulb above the pool table. Her eyes followed him until she understood what he was doing.

"Always." She racked the table and gleamed at him. Soft music played.

"We will shoot a game," looking at her, "then I'll see you in the morning."

"Aren't you rocking me to sleep?" She chalked his pool stick. "I mean, stay a little longer, please. There's more to discuss. Don't you have any other questions?"

"I don't want to keep you up too late, and it's been a long day. One we'll remember for a very long time."

Sorano placed her pool stick on the wall, grabbed his, and did the same. Game over. Showing her camping skills, she tossed a stick on the fire, brushed her hands and sat on the big blue sofa adjusting pillows. "You coming?" She stared at him, patting the seat. "This crazy lady isn't talking to herself tonight."

He glanced into the oval mirror of the hall tree with confidence. "Why not?" He leaned back beside her with his arms around her. She rubbed his stomach, holding him and not speaking for a moment.

"I've missed you over the years. All jokes aside, I still love you."

"You are forever on my mind."

Why was she at Andy Oliver? He could not let down his guard and fall in love with her like he did decades ago, without months of assurance and sincere love behind him, could he? Her unexplained engagements, or whatever, he was cautious and reserved. Close, too close, eye to eye, kissing him, reluctantly.

"That wasn't romantic, Weston, I was just getting warmed up." She lifted her body up with her elbows and rolled her eyes. "If you are going to touch me then...do it."

He nervously walked to the refrigerator. "I need something cold." He sat beside her, filled with unanswered questions.

"You need to be a bit warmer." She rolled over on her side, full from eating and drinking too much, and waited.

Placing the bottle on the coffee table, he took a second drink as if he was hesitant to carry on a conversation. "That's better." Weston wiped his mouth with a cloth. His mind was still perplexed. "Now, let's get down to business." He removed his shirt, still in excellent shape, unchanged since college.

She touched his skin with her nails. "What do you mean business?"

If she was going to play with his heart, he would return the favor. No shoes. No shoes. No regrets. His slacks were thrown across the high back chair.

"It's time we cut out the small talk."

Later, sometime after midnight, her eyes followed his hand, and she was light headed. The room began to spin.

"Wait! Wait! Wait!" She sat up and handed him his shirt and tie. "This is how I do business. Nothing more, until we decide to start dating again."

"You're here to seduce me, right? Get a few secrets about good O' Andy Oliver Vineyards? Win my confidence? Or is it some big mistake, spatting a list of reasons over coffee why we can't stay together, and you'll say your goodbyes to me in the morning, leave a note and split."

"Put your damn clothes back on." She threw a pillow at him. "I'm not here to throw myself at you, seduce you and collect secrets. I'm staying!"

Buttoned his slacks, calling her bluff. "I showed up, made love, played along, and now what?" He stopped and stared at her.

"You want the real truth," clearing her throat, "from me?" She looked him in the face. "You want my sincere story?"

"Love to hear the damn truth, doll." He buttoned his shirt. "Make me stop wondering and wishin' we could talk, okay?"

"I'm here to convince you to let me run Andy Oliver with you."

Thoughts crowded his head. Times he'd started before daylight and worked until his muscles couldn't move, sweating like a mule until he sold the first case to a man in Woodstock, Virginia. Two cases to a lady in Manassas Park. Next, he delivered three more cases to a golf shop owner in Chancellorsville.

"Screw Mickey Starr!" He strapped his belt around his hips and slipped on his shoes. "You want to run it to get him some secrets?"

She handed him a blanket and turned away.

"What are you doing, anyway? I'm not here for Mickey. It's for me. I'm the one who'd like to be a part of something as great as little Andy was. That's the honest truth. I swear. This vineyard is only a few phone calls away from national status."

Weston stood, tucked in his shirt tail.

"That's bull crap and you know it. The more you talk, the more you lie."

"I'm not lying."

He sat at the hearth and snapped his fingers. "Okay, what's Mickey want with Andy Oliver?" He locked his arms.

"I don't know, Weston."

"That's what I thought. You're blowing smoke up my ass, right?" He crossed his legs. "Did Mickey teach you these used car salesmanship tactics to try and swindle me out of this vineyard? I've busted my ass to build this place...in the name of our son, by the way."

"This vineyard isn't like all the rest, Weston." Sorano touched his arms and neck. "It's personal, for me. It was built for Andy and that's why I'd like to put my name on it, help as best I can, to remember him."

He whispered. "That's why his name is already on the gate, dear, to remember him, and not for you or me. So, as I said, it's not for sale to you, Mickey Mouse, Mickey Starr, or anyone else."

"Now that we've closed the door." Sorano paced around the room and held his shoes captive. "Let's forget about business and have some fun. Can you do that much? Too many years have gone by and I'm tired."

Hugging her, he said, "I have something else planned."

"Should I rub your back first?" Her eyes squinted. "So we can relax?"

Weston walked to the bathroom to collect his thoughts. Ran water over his face and found himself in the mirror. Pulled up his socks, tucked in his oxford shirt, tightened his belt to a better fit, and combed his hair before stepping out.

A sharp whistle came from her lips.

"Don't you look handsome?" She stood in front of the fireplace, waiting on him. "But you didn't have to dress up for me a second time."

The room was heated from the fireplace, but he walked past her on his way to open the front door. He grabbed his shoes and was ready to call it a night. She followed him with her wine glass, turned off the pool table light, and all the lights in the cabin except the blaze of the fireplace. She stopped smiling.

"I'll see you in the morning, dear." He kissed her on the lips. "Stay as long as you like." His words were sincere. "I built this cabin for you, babe, and hoped one day you'd enjoy it. Please do. The hat room you always wanted, it's upstairs, beside the loft. One hat for every year you were gone, hung and bought 'em on your birthday."

"You have twenty hats upstairs for me, Weston?"

He walked to his van, shouting, "I won't be around until after lunchtime tomorrow."

Sorano's lips tightened in curiosity, glancing upstairs and then back at him.

"Where are you going?" She adjusted her dress. Her silhouette was radiant as the fire flickered behind her. Something he wanted. Still confused. Maybe they both were startled.

He held the van door. "Meeting Julianna and her daughter for breakfast," he yelled, "in Charlottesville."

She stood in the doorway with her arms crossed.

"For breakfast? You owe me a coffee, Mr. Laramie."

"You seem stressed, Sorano. The cabin doesn't have a Japanese "sento", but Julianna said the garden tub makes a perfect "furo" for a lady."

"Are you leaving me alone?" She crunched an apple.

"Be back around noon to check on you, dear." He cupped his hands. "Bring your sunglasses and wear ripped blue jeans. It'll be fun."

"Ripped jeans?"

"Yeah." He tugged at his lapel. "Believe it or not, I just bought you a new hat last November that would match perfectly."

He stood with the van door open.

"You are a thoughtful guy, aren't you?"

"I'll leave a note for Sherrill to give you a grand tour of Andy Oliver's famous tasting room and anything else you may need tomorrow. Feed the geese and ducks, please." He waved. "Enjoy the cabin, it's cozy. There's a hundred good books for you to read. Good night." He grinned.

"Sweet dreams." Sorano drained her wine glass. "I have something else to tell you tomorrow." He drove away, had no idea she was still talking.

Eighteen
The Iconic Kombi

Surrounded by talented artisans, in scholarship and business at the Art of the Shenandoah Conference in Charlottesville, dozens of people questioned Weston about winemaking and how the elevated success of Andy Oliver captivated the attention of the media. When he compared his own talent to the artisans and craftsmen, he was reminded that he could only draw a strawman and trace a dotted line with the help of a fine protractor and a quarter for most of the circles penned. Today, though, he was a volunteer, who served pancakes and bacon in the kitchen for an outstanding fundraiser. Positioned in a humble spot but ideal for witnessing Julianna's daughter, Ginger, take "Best of Show" for her painting entitled, *The Poetry of Provocations in the World of Jazz.*

The charity raised thousands of dollars for special needs children, especially centered around those on the Autism Spectrum. With great appreciation of her artistic talent and after Ginger's acceptance speech, the show asked her to travel with the exhibit to Baltimore, Boston, Chicago, and then to a number of cities on the West Coast. Relieved and punctual, Weston thought of Julianna being gone for six weeks or longer depending on her West Coast schedule and the continuous sponsorship at each event.

He felt the best expression he could add to postmodernity was maintaining his iconic '69 VW Kombi, where he rolled down the windows on a brisk spring morning, driving through the rolling green countryside from Charlottesville back to Mount Jackson. Only one man could claim to have such an engineered relic, with good taste or bad taste, he owned it, free and clear. Then he remembered his guest back at Andy Oliver, he was a half hour from his destination and needed to change out of his good clothes. He didn't want to flash his suit in her face about where he'd been and who was hanging on his arm after the night he'd shared with Sorano.

At noon, the gatekeeper opened the wide swinging gates to Andy Oliver.

"Good afternoon, Kenny."

Weston jumped out of the van, grabbed his leather duffle bag, and headed to his changing room inside the building to freshen up from the smell of pancakes and bacon that had seeped into his good clothing.

"The Japanese lady in the big log cabin was asking about you," said Kenny. He had the most country accent of anyone in the south. "Sonya, I believe, is her name. The friendly New Yorker with the tiny slanted eyes."

"Sorano. What's she want?"

"She called three times and needs you for something important."

"Thank you for the message. Here's a stack of lumberjack pancakes for you, my friend."

"I'll knock 'em out in one round."

Weston walked into the building and thought about what it could be.

Kenny was fascinated with the Kombi van, stroking the new burgundy paint and the smooth gray pinstripes that Weston had added for an accent. In astonishment, Kenny walked around the vehicle, polishing the windows and mirrors, sliding the side door, and ducking his head inside the moonroof. Twenty minutes passed before his boss returned to the parking lot.

"Sherrill already introduced us," said Kenny, who stuck his head through the moonroof. Then the gatekeeper returned to his post at the entrance of Andy Oliver, as he zoomed in on the passenger's side front tire.

Weston jumped in, started the van, and said, "She can wait!"

Running in front of the van with both hands up. "Hold on, Mr. Laramie, your front tire, it's almost flat."

Weston jumped out. "Flat as a pancake in Charlottesville."

"Maybe a nail?"

They both walked to the front of the vehicle.

"I need the van to take Sorano to the mountains."

"You can take my truck. It smokes like a freight train, but it has good power up the hills and through the straights." Weston looked at the tire again, then examined the long wheelbase diesel truck of Kenny's, parked beside the building. Discouraged. "Or, well, then, old man," said Kenny, who rubbed his chin and nodded. "I could pull it inside the garage and fix it for you. Got a spare tire in this hippie wagon?"

Weston slapped Kenny on the shoulder and smiled.

"Hot damn, young man! Tire in the back. Make it roll again."

Kenny fired up the van then leaned out the driver's window.

"Have it for you by two o-clock. Okay?"

His boss started the green golf cart.

"Call me at the cabin when you get it aired up."

"I'll have it in no time flat." The kid took off his hat. "Hey, Sorano and Sherrill have made several trips to town in the company truck. I hope you like what she bought for you."

"Like what?"

"You'll see." The kid gave a candid smile. "You'll see."

***

Weston parked the golf cart, pacing uphill and stopping to survey the log cabin. Something was different. Tall floral curtains were pinned to the sides with ropes. He took a few more steps, where he found seven lotus blossom patterned pillows that weren't there the previous night, some stacked and some flat, in a planned arrangement on the porch sofa. Plants in full bloom were placed on tables and benches, along with a pet.

"What?" Weston rubbed the pup's head. "Who's dog?"

The spring breeze blew through the open door, moving the new floral curtains and she wasn't in the room.

"Sorano?" He walked across the long deck. "There's a German Shorthaired Pointer pup on the front porch, licking my hand and whimpering. The sign says, specifically, NO DOGS ALLOWED because Julianna is allergic to dogs."

The shower turned off. Sorano walked out of the room with a white towel wrapped under her arms. Wet as if she had

347

walked out of the Shenandoah River, dripping water in the back of the room.

"Weston?" She slowly tucked the towel into her chest. "I love taking a shower with the windows and doors open. The puppy loves it here."

He propped himself up at the end of the pool table and wasn't about to discourage the wind from keeping her dry.

"What is all this ..." he said, pointing and waving his hand.

"You meant to say," she changed her sweet voice to mimic his deep voice. "Thank you, Sorano for decorating this place, making it look damn good again, livable even, not like some Shenandoah cave."

With a second white towel, she patted her dark hair down.

"Julianna, did this." He grinned. "She beautifully decorated all the cabins at Andy Oliver."

"I'm sorry." She dried her legs with her backside toward him. The sunlight hit her body as he gaped in admiration.

"Did you tell her today how we dated and that I'm well known in the world of commercial and residential design?"

"She doesn't care about your resume." He turned.

"Does she know I'm here? Where is your *Baby* girl, Julianna, anyway?"

"On her way to Baltimore, Boston, Portland." He gathered a few more towels to remove the water from the tile floor. "She'll be gone for six weeks or so."

"So, so, so sad." Her lips rolled in sarcasm. "You should have brought her here first." The towel loosened from around her top when she moved. She tucked the end deeper into her cleavage. "I'd like to split a bottle of Merlot with her."

"I thought you liked Pinot Noir?"

"I'm not going to share a fine wine with her, like you do, Weston."

Still thin, glamorous and pale as the first snow, a perfect shape, at any rate. Most men would love to see her without designer jeans, tying a pink bandana into her thick hair was a major attraction for Weston.

"You should keep the door closed," moving the blinds. "It isn't summertime yet."

She leaned beside him on the pool table, his heart skipping a beat and he marveled at her.

"I like to hear the birds sing." She opened the blinds up and the ray from the bursting sun hit her skin, just the way she wanted. "Don't you?"

"Yeah. Remember how we explored and photographed the birds, years ago?"

Half-naked, she stood sideways and shared her profile as if she was looking at a Picasso canvas in a museum. He knew what was in his mind, but what was she doing?

Her towel lowered to her feet.

"Mercy," he said. "Can I borrow the towel to wash the van?"

She giggled.

"Here, you go."

"Since we are friends again." She laughed. "I'll get dressed before you have a heart attack." She left wet footprints across the hardwood floor, twisting her hips, pacing and disappearing behind a nontransparent wall.

"Too late."

He hated himself for being so dang disciplined, unlike his father in his younger days who would have done otherwise. But he'd memorized her alluring profile, the smooth and rounded places, sun kissed face and hidden sides, her elegant shape etched in the front of his mind.

"The pagoda lanterns are a nice touch, Sorano."

The towel she'd been wearing flew out from behind the wall and he flinched, grasping it in his right hand.

"Here's another towel for the American hardwood, h-mmm," Sorano laughed, "floors, I mean."

Weston finished off her glass of wine with one drink. "I wonder if she needs another glass," he mumbled, pushing the towel with his foot, drying up the water and thinking about her. He was getting deeper into trouble the longer he stayed around her. Did he want her to leave? Or was he enjoying her company?

Barefoot and dressed in ripped jeans and a tight navy blue Yankees t-shirt, Sorano opened the door, stood face to face with the man and kissed him, closing her eyes and it wasn't a dream to him any longer for either of them. Then she hugged him, pulling on her wet hair and walking to the nearest mirror.

Blow drying her hair, she paused, "I missed that part of you, mophead."

"I have other parts. And I haven't heard that from you since 1977."

"Do you like what I've done with the place or not? Juliana's style was so 1776. I just dropped her relics inside the dumpster, along with the **Virginia isn't for Lovers** sign. I believe I've changed your mind."

"You shouldn't be so cold hearted to a fellow Yankee gal." He picked up a pillow and walked around the room. "Are those yoga mats, I see?"

"Two of them. Mine and yours, darling."

"I don't think so. You can take those with you when you go."

The puppy ran through the kitchen door and licked Sorano's painted toes.

"Lucky dog," he said with a low voice.

She winked at him.

"I borrowed the puppy from Sherrill's house, he's such a cutie pie. His eyes are dark brown." They both petted his ears and rubbed his head. "Doesn't he remind you of our old Pointer?"

"He's just like Tomo," Weston nodded and held the dog in both arms.

Sorano watched them leave the house for the front lawn. With a swift move, she removed the **No Dogs Allowed** sign, dropping it in the trash can.

"I'm not keeping him!" yelled Weston.

"Don't worry. I'll give him back to Sherrill when we leave."

The golf cart was parked on the blacktop.

"Where's your van?"

"Kenny is working on the tire."

The phone rang. Weston grabbed the phone.

"Hello."

"Weston, come quick!"

"Sherrill?"

"It's Kenny," the old man shouted.

Weston turned in shock.

"What's wrong?" asked Sorano.

"He was messing with the tire and broke his ankle," said Sherrill, breathing heavily. "I can't move him. Hurry!"

"I'll be right there."

"His father is on the way to take him to the hospital."

"I'm on my way, too," said Weston. "Fast as I can."

Weston met Kenny's father, Les, on the road between the vineyard and the garage, long before he could drive to Bay Three where the accident occurred. Les stopped his truck, flagged down Weston with his eyes bugged and his lights flashing.

"We're headed to the emergency room. I'll see my lawyer in the morning, Weston Laramie. Sue your rich ass for everything you got."

"I'll take care of any expenses, Les," said Weston, walking to the driver's side of the truck. "You alright, Kenny?"

"Don't say a word, boy," Les gripped Kenny's shoulder. "Save it for the lawyer and the judge."

"I'm fine. I'm tough." He pushed the arm of Les away from his mouth. "I tripped over the tire, that's all, boss. That's what happened, all of it. Nothing for the lawyer, right, Pops?"

"Call us when you know something." Weston stepped away from the vehicle as Les Venable spun his tires and disappeared over the hill. Sorano walked up beside Weston.

"Hope the boy is alright."

****

He remembered how she loved the tall mountains, majestic and wild. "Young or old, the wilderness was for everyone," she once told Weston. Green valleys, trees of a thousand colors, flowery bushes and nesting birds, coveted Civil War landmarks, and well-preserved nature marked the place where she'd once felt at home. Maybe, just maybe, he could flip her mind to the day when they were head over heels in love and what they shared was the most memorable part of his life.

Weston packed apples, ham sandwiches, soda, water, and chocolate bars in his backpack. Pitched the lunch in his hippie van, with the aim to surprise her. She was notorious for flirting and touching him. Weston hoped she would thread that same ribbon of hope into her memory bank, yet sober and sincere. However, a satisfying smile covered his face as he hoped she'd pawn her engagement ring for a fifty year old bottle of Tempranillo, a glorious red he and his grandfather favored in California, in 1977.

He double checked the work of Sherrill's son, Montgomery, and how he handled the tire and lug nuts, spun the lug wrench one more click and pulled with all his strength until he was satisfied with the way it gripped against the rim. After a quick wash from a water hose and a towel dry, the vehicle was ready for the road. The van was a rare jewel he'd bought from a horse trainer in Winchester who had wanted to part with the automobile after his son didn't return home from the war in Vietnam. Weston had felt that as long as he was able to maintain the van, he'd also keep the soldier's memory alive. He intended to keep his word, too.

Two miles from their destination, Weston parked and saw her shivering.

"Take my sweater and cover your eyes," he told her.

"What? I have a feeling I know where we're headed."

"The last time we were here, I had a baby face, fearless and dumb."

They laughed.

"And now you are cautious and well-established, a local legend as a hiker and wine master." She spoke into his sweater. "Back then no one had heard of either of us."

"I'm far from a sommelier."

"Weston?" Her soft chocolate eyes turned to him, and she dropped the sweater. "You have always been my hero. I was selfish and didn't ever tell you how I truly felt about you back then, listening to my father instead. Letting you walk out of my life for so many years was my biggest mistake. I have a life of regret. I can't make it up to you, but I'd like to try, if you'll let me."

"Here, I've blamed myself for being so damn good-looking and I could have blamed you for being careless." He chuckled and kissed her. "Thought we were speaking about wine, but is that why you are here, to talk about us?"

He had waited years — too many long years — to hear her voice and feel her affection. Today, she spoke from the heart, adding the truth without manipulation of wine or her father's words. Julianna shared her heart often, but Sorano was known to lock up her thoughts and emotions and leave. In letters she would say a few last comments, here and there.

"Hazel Mountain Overlook!" she said. "I knew it."

"But why are we here?" he asked, parking the van. "You'll figure it out later. Hang on, I'll get the door." He rushed around the van. "Relax." It only took a few seconds to open her door, a second more to reach for her hand.

"Don't forget our lunch," she said.

With the backpack strapped to his shoulders, they hiked the upward slope.

"We are headed to your favorite rock." He pulled her hand.

"The Edge of the World."

They were close to where he planned to eat lunch.

"I'm uncertain why we are here, though," she said.

He walked further to where the valley opened, and the rock was unchanged. Deja vu punched him in the gut. Should he be angry or discontented because it didn't work out years ago, or should he look forward to what was about to happen, he asked himself? His prayers were answered. She was beside him again.

A divine young lady and a slim young man with dog tags around his neck hiked toward them and blocked their view as Weston imagined a younger version of himself.

"Hey, mister, would you take our picture? It's such a beautiful view."

"Sure, soldier. Be glad to snap it," said Weston.

"You two make the best couple," said Sorano, smiling.

The young couple wrapped their arms around each other as Weston steadied the frame. He was on leave, it appeared. The young lady was a petite brunette with blue eyes.

"Thank you for your service, young man."

Sorano told them to stand in a clear spot where the Shenandoah Valley spread far and wide behind them in a verdant green as the golden sun burst from the cotton clouds. Sorano took the camera from Weston, snapping three shots. Different poses of the couple in love, smiling and hugging.

"Hold up your dog tags," said Sorano. "You might want to come back here twenty years from now and renew your vows."

"You look familiar." The lady said, checking her nails.

"I'm Weston Laramie." He adjusted his collar and puffed a smile.

"I was talking to her," said the young lady.

Sorano teased Weston.

"Wait! Don't tell me. " The young lady touched her hair. "You are Sorano Tanaka, named "Woman of the Year" for New York City, three years ago."

Sorano hugged her.

"Good to meet you," said Sorano with her recognizable smile.

"I've never met anyone famous before."

"I'm not famous."

Sorano handed the soldier his camera. The teenage girl looked at Sorano's hand in amazement.

"Can I see your ring?"

"That is one heavy rock," said the soldier.

"You lucky dog, to get her to say, 'Yes' and she loves the mountains, too." The young man pulled Weston aside. "What did you do, man, other than give her a ring?"

Weston lifted his foot upon a rock and pondered the young man's question, soaked up the breathtaking view and thought of himself as a young man, struggling to impress a lady. Maybe he could say something magnificent. Like a bell ringing in his mind for ages, or a window that opened into the clouds with a message, he tried to come up with something classic for the soldier to share with his unit at Fort Lee. What mind boggling vanity plate of inspiration could he right to his comrades and change his outcome?

"Do the things now that young men adopt, and old men admire." He told him. "And she'll love you for it. Oh, if she turns you down, just hike the Appalachian Trail in fifty-five days. You won't feel any better, but you will have done something that echoes in the newspaper. You'll feel taller and stronger. No one will be there to cheer you on but God. He's enough."

Weston felt his speech was solid on all corners, with enough mojo to influence a change in the soldier.

"Look man, when I was ten, my parents passed away in a car accident in Welch, trying to beat a train on a Friday night. Didn't have anyone to give me the goods in life. I worked in the West Virginia coal mines for a year, then decided to join the Army, see the world and make a difference for my country."

"Good call."

The stout young man stood at ease, a traditional Army stance and listened to Weston.

"Mr. Laramie, you have given me the truth, but will love make you live happily ever after." He shook the young man's hand. "Not always. What's your name, anyway?"

"Specialist Lon Capehart. My pleasure."

"Well, Capehart, here's my card. Let me know how it all works out for you and her and Uncle Sammy. Stop by Andy Oliver, my vineyard is in Mount Jackson, and see me when you turn twenty one. Okay?"

The soldier's chest took in some air and exhaled with confidence. Weston felt like a father. Lon looked as though his questions were answered, more than when they first met, at least.

Lon left to see his lady. Hands stuffed inside her pockets, Sorano walked over to where Weston stood on a rock and scanned the mountains, trailing off into the distance, she'd helped herself to lunch. Her hiking buddy touched Sorano's hand. She held on. The other couple disappeared into the woods.

"You were going to tell me why you brought me here, Weston."

He crossed his arms and glanced across the valley.

"This was where I proposed to you. Remember?"

"I remember what I said and why I said it, too." She faced him. "I've thought about my answer a thousand times and how my life would have been different if I would have said 'Yes,' and we'd gotten married and lived in Shenandoah County."

"It would have been different in Virginia." He touched her face with both hands, kissing her in front of God and anyone else who wanted to watch. "You insisted on living in New York, remember?"

They both remembered. Tears traced slowly from Sorano's eyes onto her dry skin. Weston kissed each cheek as she cried her eyes out. They spoke of deep regrets and apologized for the years they lost in stubbornness and resentment.

"Let's eat lunch on my favorite rock." She paced beside him looking at the pathway. "I recall my decisions. Bad ones and good ones."

"Thinking of the abandoned orchards in the valley." Weston raised his hand. "They make me hungry for apples. What about you?"

He removed the backpack from her shoulders.

"Let's mosey on to our rock, Mr. Laramie." She led the way.

They made it to Hazel Mountain, where they sat down beside each other. Sorano ate half a ham sandwich and finished her water. He sipped his soda and sliced their apples with a knife, leaving behind apple peelings for the ants and bees to enjoy.

"I hated your father." Weston stood up and threw the apple core as far as he could over the deep valley. "I loved you and I still love you."

"I love you too, Weston." She reached for him. "Sit down before you fall off the mountain."

She squeezed him, kissed him a dozen times and cried happy tears.

"You father was why we didn't marry in the first place." He placed his hand on her knee. "He's why you didn't want to get married."

"That's not the whole story."

He turned around with a shock on his face. Weston faced her.

"What?"

"I told you, I would not receive my inheritance if I married you."

"Yeah, yeah. And it would dishonor your family, Sorano."

She dropped her head and picked the corners off her sandwich. Tossed them to the birds. Looked him in the eyes.

"My father was broke by 1980 when Reagan took office. I had to run his business for him when he became ill from being a depressed alcoholic. He lied about the family business, and I hated him because I let him break us apart."

"Broke?" Weston examined her face. "He gave me so much hell for being poor. I told him to kiss my ass. He was no better off than I was. Why didn't you tell me the truth?"

"He was a hypocrite, I know." She cried in agreement. "That's what killed him."

"I am sorry. Did being a lower class citizen kill him? That's what he hated about me."

"No, too much pride." She wiped her tears. "Not being able to buy and sell as he did all his life. That's why I stopped working in the furniture industry. Managed all his restaurants and consulted for five years after his death until I turned the business around. He was gone by that point."

"Damn him." Weston curled a fist and struck the rock. "He cost me a lifetime of regret and happiness! I was alone without you."

"Your hand is bleeding." She softly cleaned the cut with a napkin.

"It's fine." He flexed his hand back and forth.

"People thought of him as this rich Japanese businessman." She dried her tears. "And yet, to the contrary, his life and business failed because he was mean and ugly to me and you and everyone else. He saw value in money and not people."

Weston leaned back on his elbows. "He died of a stroke, didn't he?"

"He had a massive heart attack." She placed her hand on his leg. "Full of anger and lost it all, in the end. Broke as a joke."

Weston remembered every evil word the man had said to him. Nightmares had haunted him for years about their conversations, the one that shattered him, but fueled him, also. Determined to prove him wrong, he realized the reasons were because of indifference and culture. Barriers that needed to be broken in society. Every word was an exaggeration and deceitful.

"The sun is going down. If you are ready?" Weston stood. "I'd like to leave."

"Can we go back to the cabin?" She placed her head on his shoulder.

He pulled her up to her feet.

"Could you take your ring off, so I could admire it?"

She punched him in the shoulder and smiled.

"You are not throwing this ring off Hazel Mountain, like a rotten apple."

"That's why I brought you here, in the first place."

With her hand surrendered, he tugged the ring off of her hand and never hesitated as she handed it to him.

"You brought me here to throw this ring away?" Wide eyes bugged her face.

They started to hike back to the car.

"We could give the ring to Lon Capehart." She touched his shoulder. "He's holding her hand, curled in that special way. Weston, the man needs a ring."

"If you don't love Mickey Starr." He opened the diamond in his hand.

"Give Lon the ring." She assured him. "That will make us both happy."

"It would also surprise Avon."

"It's getting dark." Sorano cheered him on, "Give Lon the ring, please…"

They walked around the trail, scanning the area and the couple had disappeared. Finally, the last ray of light hit them from the west, and heard the two of them arguing by the fence.

Weston ran over to the soldier who was nervously standing against the gate.

"Did she reject you, Lon?"

"Yeah. An E4 doesn't make much money for a gold ring, sir."

Weston knew what it meant to go without. "Open your hand, soldier."

"Take my backpack and hike the App Trail or take this diamond and get her to marry you, right now."

"I can't take your ring. I'm not hiking to Maine, living in regret."

Weston opened the young man's hand.

"Soldier, take the damn ring and that's an order."

"Roger that," Lon saluted him. "Thank you, Laramie."

"If you ever get the money, please do me a favor."

The soldier's eyes lit up, shoulders back, and he stood proud.

"Anything."

"Come back here twenty years from now and tell her how wonderful she is and how much you love her," Weston said, gripping his shoulder. "Don't live in the nightmare of regret, like I have. Let me know when you get out of the Army, and I'll have a job waiting for you, Lon."

Sorano told him he'd done something wonderful for them when he didn't have to, but it was because he cared for people.

From the van window, Weston and Sorano watched that young man take off his cover and take a knee at the foot of Avon, eyes on her, a small framed girl from the hills of West Virginia, who cried when he slipped on the large diamond ring. She screamed "Yes" and jumped inside his arms.

"Congratulations!" Sorano shouted.

Weston parked next to the happy couple.

"You can have the wedding at Andy Oliver," said Weston. "My vineyard will make a wonderful start. Won't cost you a penny, Lon."

The soldier rushed beside the driver's van, overwhelmed and breathing out of control. Sorano and Weston had made new friends. Life was far better than when they woke up.

"Avon wants an October wedding in the mountains," said Lon, smiling and holding her in his arms.

"Thank you again," said Avon. "I like this hippie van. Love the soldier more. Thanks again. "

"We'll see you in October," said Weston, waving with his arm out the window.

The last time Weston saw them was in his side mirror. They embraced, hugging and kissing. Sorano grabbed his hand and was proud of what had happened.

"I just realized something."

Weston glanced over to the passenger's side.

"What?"

"If Andy would have lived," a tear rushed down her cheek, "he'd be the same age as Lon Capehart."

"He would and maybe he'd been a soldier in the Army, too."

"It's hard to think of such things," said Sorano, still crying. "But it's good to have you by my side again to talk about our boy. Back in the iconic hippie van where we made out some many times."

"I'll have a bottle of Pinot Noir for the Capehart wedding." He nodded.

"The puppy can be the ringbearer." She laughed and sniffled.

Weston waved his hand over the steering wheel and squirmed.

"Suppose I'll have to change the sign now."

Sorano turned. "Pets are now allowed at Andy Oliver."

"No." He disagreed. "Virginia is for Lovers and Pets."

She pressed her lips into his cheek and laughed.

"I'll end it with Mickey in the morning."

"If I was a Mormon, I could have you and Julianna, huh?"

"With me, you won't have time for anyone else."

✳✳✳

At first light, Sorano sat, still curled up in the bulk of a flannel blanket. The more time she spent at Andy Oliver, the more distant her hometown of Westbury became. From the kitchen, she saw Weston training the pup in the yard, a dog with no name. Just as the oak table held the morning paper for Weston, folded neatly to a photograph of the Yankees who had swept the Rangers and Blue Jays in Brooklyn. She wondered how Jason and Rosa enjoyed the game and if they'd snagged a foul ball or bought a souvenir.

Weston decided on the trip from Hazel Mountain to Mount Jackson, convinced about what needed to be done. From a corner booth in downtown Baltimore, Julianna called, Weston told her who he was seeing and that it was over, she cried and hoped he'd change his mind. Four days later with more confidence than a bullfighter, Sorano called Mickey on his cell phone while he was sunbathing on the white sands of Punta Cana. He listened to her brief spill, then demanded the ring back in Savannah. She gave him an earful and said, "The last time I saw the ring, it was being admired by the cutest couple, named Lon and Avon on Hazel Mountain, who lived in Fort Lee, Virginia. It's gone and we're over Mickey."

There were times in a young man's life, like Lon, where he had to fall for the feminine, embrace the warmest of love and tenderness, when he moved beyond sex and social expectations, settling down and discovered his manhood. There came a time in a young lady's life, like Avon, who desired the taste of love for the first time and love of her lover, with fewer dreams, more tangible than the intangible spirit where she became mature, made no less equal than himself. For it was God's plan for them to make it personal, with mutual interests and matrimonial intentions whether it was in their native town or eloping to the heights of Hazel Mountain.

Nineteen
Cavalier Tavern

With Kenny's broken foot confirmed, his post was vacant. For one night, no one guided the entrance to the many acres of dormant vines, paralleling across the pristine landscape of Andy Oliver Vineyards. Buildings sat unmanned. The man the devil called his friend was in town. Not even Santa listed this man on the Christmas list for Jesus to forgive. He'd left Germany and made his voice known, in and out of town, laughing at what he'd done, like a ghost, he thought.

Entering Andy Oliver before the roosters crowed, Sherill leaned on the steering wheel and saw a black truck rolling in his direction, he felt uneasy as he slowed his vehicle down to a stop, targeting the trespasser.

"I wonder who that is?" Sherrill said to himself, flipping his headlights three times and rolling down his window, said, "Hey, stop!" He waved his hat at the truck. "Stop your damn truck."

In slow motion, Sherrill's truck passed a man in the driver's seat with a pale white face and a shiny bald head. The old man made an attempt to halt the driver, waving his hand and honking the horn several times, to announce his dislike, but to no avail.

"That's Jason's father." Sherrill's eyes widened and his heart raced. "What's Weston's brother doing back in town?" He spoke to himself often.

From the cab of his truck, Sherrill, who had the memory of an African elephant and could recall every address in the Shenandoah Valley, knew everyone who drank Merlot and who drank Pinot in Shenandoah County and knew those who didn't, too. Not everyone's name popped in his memory, but with faces, a distinctive jawline and military style haircut triggered him the same as a name and photograph did on the sport's page. Sherrill picked out the angry face from the single military picture of his brother that Weston had hung on his wall. As soon as he drove onto Andy Oliver, Sherrill spotted the barn doors standing wide open. Something was out of the ordinary, he took note and walked slowly into the barn, scanning for a burglar with his flashlight. Grabbing the phone off the wall, Sherrill dialed the log cabin where he hoped Weston would be with a cup of coffee in his hand. No answer.

"Try Weston's Big House," he mumbled. "He's got to see this for himself."

Sherrill read the phone numbers on the wall to each facility on the property. Warehouse, Cellar, Tasting Room, Log Cabin, Front Gate, and the Gravity Flow Room. Highlighted in pink was Weston's Big House, his fingers pressed the buttons, Sherrill waited eagerly, like when his doctor spoke about the numbers of his high blood pressure report.

"Hello," said Sorano.

"Ms. Tanaka, could you send Mr. Laramie to the barn?" The man spoke in a rapid country accent. "It's urgent, please!"

Sorano stepped outside in the early morning fog where Weston had the pup on a bench feeding him sticks of pepperoni.

"Weston! Weston!"

"Yeah?"

"Sherrill needs you," she said loudly with a long face. "Kinku!"

Weston, fluent in the Japanese language, knew something was wrong.

"He said it was urgent?"

"You better hurry!" she said, shaking her hand. "Go, I'll watch the dog."

Like a racecar driver, Weston was gone. When he arrived at the barn, Sherrill had already snapped a dozen pictures with a camera he'd found in Weston's backpack. The boss stood beside his friend, pounding the barn doors, in a rage.

"Who in the hell would destroy a man's plane?" Weston whacked his fist on the ultra-flyer. "Who did this? Who did this? Who was here?"

Sherrill walked up beside him.

"Your brother was on the property." The old man nodded as he propped his foot on the plane. "He left Andy Oliver about the time I pulled into the parking lot."

His boss's head turned.

"What?" he asked with an unsettling face. "You saw Victor? My brother, Victor was here?"

Sherrill pressed his hand against the cut mylar that covered the wing of the plane, then pulled down the plastic pieces. The two men walked around looking at the bent and broken frame that once made a perfect aircraft, snapping more pictures on the roll and kicking the dirt.

"I saw him in a black truck laughing, leaving the scene. He flipped me the bird. The man wanted to be seen. I'm telling you, he's an evil man."

Pacing around the aircraft, Weston examined the building and machinery for more damage and checked the lockers for explosives, but nothing else was found.

"He's been a lowlife, dirty sumbitch since he was born," he said, throwing his flying helmet into the ground. "Damn him! But to do this to his own brother, I wonder what's on his mind. I hate the bastard now."

"That pig broke the fan, and punctured the gas tank," said Sherrill, who knew every part on an aircraft as well as his boss did.

Gripping the plane and shaking the aircraft, Weston rolled the flyer into the daylight, halfway between the barn and the driveway.

"Damn that son of a bitch to hell!" Weston beamed down the road for a strange dark truck. "I wished he'd show back up."

"Why'd he do this?" said Sherrill, groaning and grunting from helping his boss roll the plane.

A truck pulled up, and Weston stepped around the corner of the barn.

"It's a miracle, well, well, Jason Laramie. He's back in town, fresh from Yankee Stadium."

"New York was great, a few glorious days, in some strange way, it felt as if I had been gone from Andy Oliver for a month."

"It's not all good news here," said Sherrill.

"Glad you're home, Jason." Weston thumbed his chin.

"I owe you one, Uncle Weston. Heck of a baseball game." He followed the long faces of the men to the swinging barn doors, and as he got close he asked, "What happened to our ultralight?" He asked, touching the frame and eyed the men with his mouth dropped. "I'm stunned and pissed off, right now."

"Sherrill," said Weston, "could you check the inventory on the Pinot Noir?"

The old man nodded. "Yep."

"I need ten cases delivered to Charlottesville, Sherrill," said Weston. "They gotta have it today for a wedding on Saturday evening."

"Is the address on your clipboard?"

"Pink slips are in the shipping box." Weston waved his hand and lifted his head as if he needed to say something then opted against it.

Jason walked around the plane twice, which appeared to have been hit by a crowbar, from front to back, over and over. Weston examined the damage, jotting down what needed to be ordered and replaced, knowing people loved to see him fly through the valley, he was disappointed.

Sherrill drove to the warehouse.

"Did the cameras catch who did this?" asked Jason.

"Video footage." Weston snapped his fingers. "I like the way you think."

He stood in the doorway of the barn, hands dangling idly. He didn't smoke or he'd probably burnt one down, like on the Marlboro man poster. Too early to calm his nerves with a shot of whiskey or he'd emptied the bottle by breakfast. But he needed to find out why this happened to the plane he loved. Jason watched Weston pace around the flyer, blown away at the busted flying machine he assembled with his calloused hands. He'd made the machine hum with perfection, and made himself a student and teacher of the manual, in case more repairs were needed. He'd learned the function of every part on the ultralight plane, how it worked and how to fix it, and now they needed parts. He'd have Montgomery order them.

Examining his uncle's disappointed face, Jason kneeled down to where the fan rotated and the engine once fired, just to see if he could be of assistance. Then he remembered repairing a typewriter and copier, which was about his maximum when it came to repairs. On that day in 2000, he was destined to learn a new trade.

"Uncle Weston?" Making a fist, Jason struck the ground. "Who screwed with the ultralight plane?"

He touched the engine again, moving his lips and stepped back in the doorway. What he remembered most about that day was his statue-like silhouette and reluctance to answer him.

"It's totaled and isn't safe."

Jason walked over beside his uncle, "You going to say who did this?"

He bit his lip and spat, pressing his mustache at the ends, and said, "Your father did this."

"What?"

His uncle crossed his arms, stood tall, stepping back.

"My sorry ass brother wrecked the plane."

"He couldn't have done this." Jason angled his head. "He's in Germany, right?"

His uncle flipped the busted lock on the barn door, rattling metal to metal, he pulled the broken piece of wood from the hinges, so he could have Montgomery repair the damages when he showed up at work.

"He was here early this morning, broke in, busted up the plane, and left. Face to face, Sherrill saw him leave, less than an hour ago." Weston stood beside his tall tool box. "Do you know why he'd do this or what his grievance is with me?"

"Dad was pissed because you sent me to New York, peddling wine and collecting money on the bad side of town. Something you should be doing yourself, he said it that way."

"You lived in the big City of Tampa. Must be more to the story." His uncle paced around the doorway, cussed a few times about his brother.

"So, that's it, huh? He was scared of New York City, the crime mostly, he couldn't deal with it when I went to Westbury with Sorano twenty years ago. He was jealous. I'm not sure why. He's crazy, and still got it out for me."

"I told him you bought an ultralight plane, and we flew on Saturdays together before the tasting room opened and the crowd showed." Jason saw his eyes bug. "He read on the internet where two guys were killed in Virginia in an ultralight plane, and he got pissed at me for being here. Told me to fly back to Germany, but I refused."

"What did he say?"

"He threatened me." Jason told his uncle the truth. "Said he'd take care of the problem the first chance he got before he visited Fort Lee."

"The plane?" Weston said, shaking his head, "Well, it's our main attraction. People drive from West Virginia and North Carolina to see us fly, and people love it when we use the plane to deliver a few bottles of wine."

His uncle stood staring out across the long valley.

"Because of that conversation, the plane is gone!" he yelled. He slammed his head against the edge of the wooden door. "Damn him!"

"Hey, hey, hey, stop it!" He grabbed his uncle's arm. "Your head is bleeding. Sit down. Sit down, Weston."

Picking up Montgomery's grease rag, the best cloth he could find, Jason pressed his cut thumb and applied the cloth. Blood continued to run down his hand and arm.

"Hold this rag," handing it to Weston, "until I find a clean one."

Then he ran water over the paper towel he'd found inside a supply closet. He checked the blood that had spotted the towel.

"You wacked it good."

"I despise my brother." He flexed his red hand. "It happened long before you were born, too. That's why I moved here. Your father hasn't said a kind word to me in twenty years. Hate the man."

Remembering his painful youth, Jason unconsciously rubbed the scars on the inside of his forearms as his uncle examined the plane. Then he scanned the circles on his arms, clenching and unclenching his fist, his face flushed red. He bit his bottom lip as long as he could and grunted.

"Here's another towel, Weston."

"Who burned your damn arms?" He pulled on the long sleeves and exposed rough skin. "Tell me, boy, who did this to you?"

"Who do you think?" He pulled his arm away from his uncle. "The same person who busted the plane burnt my arms with his truck lighter, cut my back and beat me half to death because I wanted to visit Andy Oliver, to meet you." Jason ripped thin clothes from his shoulder, grunting and cussing. "Your asshole brother, that's who!"

Weston aggressively pulled up the back of Jason's shirt. His eyes bugged as he counted four marks on his back and seven circles on the other forearm, and too many marks to count were left on that boy's shoulder.

He grabbed his shoulder and nervously rocked, shaking and fire jetted through his veins.

"Victor?" Weston shouted, "Victor!"

"Yeah." Jason bit his lip. "Hated him for doing this, and for living."

"Listen." He looked tense. "Stay here at Andy Oliver. It's your home from here on out. I'll give you the deed to one of the cabins. Pick the one you want, and I'll get you the key. You never have to leave, son." Fiery tears misted his eyes. "Work here as long as you like. This is a safe place. It's paid for and you are family now, Jason."

He sat to Jason's left. Drained. Sympathetic. His uncle fell to pieces in a matter of minutes. Undeserving as a little kid,

Jason's sorry father had caused a great deal of pain and scars for both of them. Victor was a big man, the kind of cowardly man who controlled with torture. The bully.

"Why did he harm you?" He calmly said it that way.

"Dad burned my glove hand at age ten after I missed a fly ball, making me hate the game of baseball until you bought tickets to the Yankees. A few years later, I believe I was twelve or so, he said my actions embarrassed him during a soccer game. I ran through the house. He finally busted down my door and used a leather horse whip on my backside because I spilled beer on his leather recliner."

Jason heard the chatter of anger through Weston's teeth and red rushed over his neck. "What else happened?"

"When I first learned how to drive I scratched the truck backing into the garage." His knuckles hit inside his palm, remembering him or more abuse. "He made sure I was black and blue for it, too. That time, he used a club to get his point across for my wrongdoings, he said. I missed a week of high school for it."

Hugging him was when tears caked his eyes.

"How long is he staying in Virginia, Jason?"

Weston jumped up.

"Not sure what he's up to." Jason was sick to his stomach.

"Like to find him." Following Jason to the doorway of the barn, adding a hard look, images flashed in Weston's head about how his brother harmed his own son. "I don't have good thoughts, but one is to snap his pride and finish him, for both of us."

In that moment, to settle the score with his father had crossed his mind for fifteen years, at least the same way it brewed inside Weston's blood.

"There's more." Jason told him not to hold anything back. "He said he wanted to hunt down the man who killed Raymond, Moby, and Myrtle."

"He wants to kill someone?"

"Out of the blue, he said you'd pay him big money and so would the authorities. Then he'd be the hero, if he nailed the shooter."

"One shot, one kill." Weston knew his brother was a hellraiser. "That's what Victor said in high school."

"When I told dad, I wanted to write a story on the murders in the Dominican, three days later he arrived in New York, taking his leave from the Army. He wants to be the gun and the trigger."

"Are you serious? Maybe he's the shooter? Now he wants to cover it up, huh?"

"He showed up and strangely, without my mother's involvement or anyone else with him, he invited Rosa and me out for pizza at Domenico's in Brooklyn. My father talked for an hour about being a hero."

"Maybe he's the hitman. Solo."

"He had a hundred and one questions for me, and then when I came back from the restroom he was gone."

"I bet my shrewd brother left you holding the bill, didn't he?" Weston walked to his vehicle, appearing to be in deep thought.

"Pizza and breadsticks were gone." Jason rolled up his sleeves, sat in shame. "Disappeared into a crowd of people, like he'd done it before."

"He has done it before. Two dozen times, I bet."

"He left a gold pen on the table and vanished."

His uncle knew the mind of his brother, inarticulate and lacking admirable traits, shielding any hope to become wiser in his ways and blurring out the baptizing stance of others, in which to prosper from his own toxic merits and lather his mug with American brew and he was an expert in weaponry, too.

"He'll be where ladies and liquor are huddled up."

Jason told his uncle what he knew about his father. The news caused Weston to tense up, widening his nostrils with every breath. He told his nephew that Victor could be a mercenary and was commissioned to take down his vineyard. Victor was paid for dirty work on two other occasions, contracted out his services here and there, nurtured budding friendships with a few bottles of whiskey, and left town. It was rumored he was involved in a grand theft auto ring and a few home invasions before he was transferred from Fort Lee to Germany. He generally took more than he gave, cutting corners and divvying out hundred dollar bills for connivers and sharks to continue himself as the ringmaster among a handful of villains from Carolina to Coney Island. Victor was the new suspect, Weston told him.

***

Ten days had passed since the ultralight was destroyed and Weston's good ideas about flying, the magnificence of being off the ground had ended or at least temporarily postponed. He typed that his uncle wanted the clouds underneath his wings as a big kid desired to climb aboard an amusement ride on a Saturday night and command the wheel, or how a jockey wanted to saddle up his race horse for a Break Maiden in the Bluegrass State. Parts were ordered. Relieved. Three weeks by freight and fixing the damages would be a major undertaking even for the best mechanic in Mount Jackson.

***

That evening on the highway from Dulles Airport where Sorano flew to JFK Airport after her longest stay in two decades, Weston spotted a truck at the Cavalier Tavern, which was parked three miles from Andy Oliver. The dark as night truck was the exact make and model Sherrill described to be in possession of Victor when he was at the barn of Andy Oliver. His blood burned in his veins after he walked around the vehicle. Inspecting the dark club cab, two dented doors, five spoke rims, and a banged up chrome bumper, which could have been a borrowed truck from one of his friends in Virginia. Few people occupied the tavern at Mount Jackson, so he contemplated the best approach, a safe one, he thought. Being a man of evaluation, Weston planned to wait in his cab until Victor made his move and stumbled to his truck. Weston pulled down his ball cap and lowered his face. Two songs passed on the radio, when a second beat up truck pulled into a parking spot in front of the tavern.

"Les Venable?" he murmured. "What the heck is he doing here?"

The same truck Les Venable drove when Kenny broke his ankle was parked beside Victor's truck, a called meeting, perhaps. A short round figure walked through the front door, it was Les. Weston swung open the door and entered the dark tavern. Cobwebs hung from the rafters, and the only light to speak of was neon and blinked, not with lack of power nor connection, but aged and covered in dust, with no pride and dignity of business. Relic or of value, wasn't the question. Two men were shooting pool, the one of military rank and bloodline was who Weston had the beef with, and stood in the corner.

"Hell and all its fire must've frozen over to find my brother inside the Cavalier Tavern on a Saturday night," Victor said, laughing and struggling to stand with a pool stick as a tripod. Six bottles of beer were lined up behind him, Weston noticed.

"I have business to take care of tonight," said Weston to Victor as he examined the men with him.

Raising his hand at Weston, Les said, "My boy's ankle is screwed up. Thanks to that dope smoking hippie van of yours."

The bartender stepped out from behind the bar and grinned at Weston, a smile ran away from his face.

"Your money is good here," said the middle-aged big and tall man with a deep country accent. "Spend it freely, Weston Ridge Laramie."

Weston turned his head, "Do I know you?"

"You wanted to sell your award-winning wine here, but we are whiskey men and beer buddies who don't need corks to feel our pockets."

Victor pulled back on his pool stick to shoot and then stopped. Still bent over, he looked red-eyed at his brother, "Don't think he's here to see you about his wine collection, Sam," said Victor with a smile. He rubbed his smooth face, standing with the pool stick in the corner of the dark room, chuckling.

"I think my brother knows I've found his hiding place," said Weston, who blocked the area. He leaned and cocked his leg in an undignified manner between the poolhall and the dark bar area.

"Here I am, big brother."

Victor took a drink and spit the beer at his brother's foot.

"He knows why I'm here, too." Weston broke a pool stick over the table. "Don't ya?"

They all made slow movements, staring at each other.

"Do you have a long time grievance against your only brother?"

Victor gripped the pool stick with one hand, draining a beer with the other.

"I think it would benefit me if I waited until you were sober." Weston moved closer. "You may want to apologize for wrecking my plane."

"That ain't happened yet and never will," said Victor, moving around the table. "Not in my lifetime or the next one, Jackass."

Les ducked his head, stepping behind Weston and making his way to the larger room where the bartender lowered himself and watched the three men. Each time Weston stepped toward his brother, Victor moved around the black and green pool table until he positioned himself at the shooter's end. Granted Weston aimed for a favored position and planned for the worst, being the sober one. He surveyed the room for weapons. Glass. Metal. Screwdrivers. Hammers. Possibilities missed by Victor who had confidence in the black-and-white side of the eight ball, clutched in his right hand.

Walking by pool sticks clipped on the wall, Weston steadied himself toward Victor, who loosened his neck and arms at the corner of the room, acting as if he knew he needed them. Working them into a corner, Les and Victor, both of tremendous strength, now blocked the only way out of the pool room. Victor widened his arms and grinned as if he had the best position.

"Boys, my brother is here to test my skills." Victor paced to the larger part of the building. He and Les now stood shoulder to shoulder as if they were tag team fighters ready for battle. "You're going to show me who's boss, Weston?"

Easing his brother to the bar area, Weston had moved them out of the smaller room, just as he intended. To Weston's right, the exit, and to his left, a long wooden bar the length of a '69 Cadillac. Tables and chairs sat scattered about in no particular arrangement.

The door quickly opened, casting light from the street inside the building. As the door closed, it became dark as a dungeon again. Suddenly, Sam pulled the switch to see who it was at the door.

"Jason?" said Victor, stunned.

"I'm here," his son said with a harsh voice, stepping inside the doorway.

All his life Jason had worn long sleeves, but not that evening. Forearms and shoulders now exposed to the world what his father had done to him as a boy, and anyone could see the scars. Yet, his arms were solid from shoulder to elbow, scars were visible and cuts obvious, unsettling, even as he had his shirt unbuttoned and draped around him. Skin his father had burned became no longer hidden, but exposed him as a worthless and evil man. Guilty.

"Button that shirt, boy," his father yelled. "Cover those arms." He looked at what he'd done as if he was caught. Maybe he felt regret. Doubt it.

"Not this time, Pops!" Jason pulled his shirt completely off his back and turned, baring cuts, from his neck to his belt. Arms raised. "All of this was at your hand." He squinted at his father in the dim room. "Remember beating me?"

For the first time Jason had not covered his body. Told his friends he'd been in a house fire as a kid. Lied to cover his torment and hide his tormentor. Weston knew he was on his side when he walked inside the building. His uncle shifted to Jason's strong side. Clearly he had the same idea he did in the Cavalier Tavern — set him straight at least one more time, or as often as needed.

Sam the bartender rushed to Jason's side. He rolled the young man's arms back and forth and examined the cuts and scars on his back. Next, he hugged him with compassion, when a God fearing rush of red covered his neck and his eyes were misty.

"You are the same age as my son." Sam flipped on the lights. "Where'd you get the marks on your arms, boy? House fire? Camp fire?"

Victor's face turned worried. Holding out both arms, Jason eyed his uncle as witnessed his scars. He was ashamed of his father and hated him even more.

"Look at my arms."

His father neither spoke nor moved.

"Is this true, Victor?" Les stepped in front of Jason and rolled his arms. "Tell us the truth, son?"

His father shook his head and hands back and forth.

"My boy burned himself," yelled Victor. "He's a real dumbass, I'm telling you."

Les and Weston eyed each other then watched Victor to see if he was going to be truthful as he lit a cigarette. Jason's father strutted and staggered so close to Jason that the young man could smell beer and sweat on his flanks.

"Again, you made it a point to embarrass me, son, not wearing your shirt and screwing with me in front of my damn friends." He walked around the room with his beer clutched in his hand. "What the hell is this all about?"

Sam turned to Victor. "You burned your own son, on purpose and now you blame him for calling your ass out in front of your friends and brother, huh?"

Victor chuckled, scanned the room, and then laughed, smoking in a cocky way. No respect was shown from his fellow man.

Sam cocked his arm back. Before he could angle his hand to belt Victor a good one. Feet positioned, hands ready and with every muscle he had in him, Jason's knuckles had cracked his father's jaw bone.

In a split second, his hand made contact a second time in a rapid motion and instantly, he fell back against the bar. If Jason had graded the blows, undoubtedly his first punch was noted as his best shot. The impact knocked his lights out. Clenching his busted knuckles and unclenching his hand, Jason had landed a heck of a wallop. Pain tingled the length of his arm and adrenal ran through his face.

"I've waited a long time to do that."

Drunk and unbalanced, Victor fell against a set of chairs, hitting a table and then fell against the copper foot railing at the base of the bar. Eyes crossed and head thundering, Victor adjusted his jaw and found himself unabashed.

"You dirty son of a bitch," Victor said, spitting blood and part of a tooth. "What the hell has gotten into you, son?" Eyes blurred. "You just messed up."

"Retaliation," said Sam, gripping his .38 Special. "Justice is served."

"Eye for an eye," said Weston, twitching his shoulder, "and tooth for a tooth, brother."

"He broke his old man's nose," said Les. "Good hit!"

"He's hated me all my life," said Jason. "Now he can hate me for a reason." He watched his father suffer for once.

Stepping up to kick the daylights out of him and break every rib in his side, when suddenly his stout uncle grabbed his arm as if he were the pull string on a lawn mower. He yanked his body backwards from his intended target.

"Wow!" said Weston, gripping his shoulders.

"He should've broken your neck." Sam aimed the gun at Victor's shocked face.

"Ha-ha-ha," said Victor, "grab my hand, Les."

Les walked away.

"You help him, Venable," shouted Sam, "and I swear to God I'll break your legs! Both of you, get the hell out of my bar. Don't ever come back to this side of town!"

Les ran out the door, fired up his truck, and spun his way to the blacktop. Sam swung his .38 Special over the bar in Victor's face.

"Victor!" Sam's hand was shaking, nervous as he spoke. "If I see you again in Mount Jackson, I'll kill you for burning your own son with a lighter." He cocked his weapon. "You are the worst piece of crap I know!"

Having new respect for his nephew, Weston's silence spoke volumes to the force of the fighter. His uncle clutched his shoulder and stood in agreement beside his nephew, thumbing his thick mustache and nodding as he eagle-eyed Victor who paced out the door in a rush.

"You need to confess your sins, old man." Jason shouted. "Take your own punishment and get the hell out of my life."

The door slammed behind Victor.

"Glad you showed up, Jason," said his uncle, lifting his fist. "I believe you could have whipped Les and that crappy father of yours with two right crosses."

"I know he could," said Sam who grinned all the time. "He's a badass young man with a thunderous right cross. Saved me from bustin' my hands on Les and Victor's ugly faces. That's for sure."

"He's the best man, I know." Weston picked up the tables and chairs from the aftermath of the fight. "Hell of a worker at the vineyard, too."

Sam walked behind the bar, slid his gun inside a leather case.

"Sit down, gentlemen." Sam grabbed a cold mug from the cooler. "How 'bout two beers on the house?" The owner chuckled and spoke like an Irishmen. "We don't carry fine wines and fancy goat cheeses at my bar." He laughed. "But we got other types of liquid fire from the hills, just for men who deserve a strong drink."

"How about some bourbon?" Jason asked the bartender. "I'll have Cliff's Old-fashioned, if you have it. I gotta have a chaser, too. Soda."

Sam gripped the string and rang the bell, filling the glass with bourbon and laughing. "Cliff's Old-fashioned is my favorite beverage, young man. Orange peels, bitters, water, muddling sugars, brandy or bourbon, and lastly a cherry, served in an old-fashioned glass."

"Do you have a North Carolina brew?" asked Weston.

Sam pushed the whiskey bottle to one end of the bar and opened the cooler.

"You got it." Sam returned to where Weston was seated. "I hear the best looking women drink wine and eat fancy goat cheese at Andy Oliver."

"You heard right," Jason said. "Lots of them visit Andy Oliver, too."

Tilting his head, Weston perked up.

"I'd like to change things up, here and there," Sam nodded, "and carry some of that fancy Andy Oliver wine that people are spouting about in town."

"Jason, listen to him. He's a good businessman," said Weston. "Don't you think we have room for some of Sam's craft beer at Andy Oliver?"

Jason nodded. The men had giant smiles. Sam was lively.

"Good deal," he said, reaching out his hand. "Weston Ridge and Jason Laramie, thank you gentlemen for helping me get rid of those creeps."

"Looks like we can set you up a bar at Andy Oliver," Weston stood. "See me on Monday, and we'll have a place for Cliff's Old-Fashioned, and for those popular Sam Copperpot t-shirts that we've been seeing in Mount Jackson, my friend."

"You two are good men," said Sam, round face in a glow. "I think I'll lock up early and hug my wife and my son before dinner. See ya on Monday."

Each one of them shook hands with the other one. Sam admired Weston's hippie van. The vehicle was without blemish. Every ten years Weston upgraded the upholstery and paint, the iconic Kombi was a treasure in a small town.

"Your tire has been cut, Weston." Sam bent to examine the rubber.

"Call Montgomery," Jason said, grabbing his face in anger. "Who's damn knife is in the tire?"

Weston examined the weapon, pocketed the blade. He and Sam laughed as if anything else could go wrong.

Come to find out Victor had gotten flushed out of Germany by some guys who wanted him dead. He'd been knocked in the head during a confrontation — dazed and confused. Sam Copperpot passed onto Weston and Jason what Les Venable told him while they waited on Montgomery Taylor. Beyond that point, it was unclear whether or not they were American or Germans, who chased Victor abroad. Nonetheless, he had been hiding out in Virginia and West Virginia and had traveled even further south to find a new hiding place.

Twenty
The Knife and Pen

Weston had an idea from a downed oak tree that must've been a sapling when Lincoln was shot. Three weeks later, he hired Sam Copperpot and his son to saw up the oak into a good sized coffee table, headboard, kitchen table, and coveted hall tree for Sorano. From the timber came enough wood for one more piece of furniture, a custom-made roll-top desk. Weston gave Jason specific instructions to use the desk for writing about the murders of Moby, Raymond, and Myrtle. Three of his best friends, he said.

After a year Jason was ashamed of himself; three chapters on paper, one still incomplete, was all he could report. The desk was the last piece unveiled "For my nephew," he said. Sherrill was so impressed with the designs of the Copperpot carpenters, he brought his wife over for dinner to Weston's big home. They walked around running their hands down the smooth edges and bragging about the workmanship of each piece and especially the workmanship of the desk.

"Marvelous," said Sherrill's wife, Peg.

"Exceptional," Jason spoke in fascination. "This is a one of a kind collection. It's complete, but my writing is not even close."

"Weston, all you need now is Sorano to tell you what color drapes to hang," said Sherrill, "and how important it is to decorate colors that match the seasons."

After dinner Weston walked over to the grand living space with a glass of Pinot Noir and ran his hand down the tambour in deep thought. Something ate at him. Jason noticed it first. Later, others remarked on his strange silence.

"You haven't been this nervous since the IRS visited Andy Oliver four years ago." Sherrill paced toward his boss of twenty years. "What's on your mind? You ain't right, Wes. Your hand has been moving and jumpy for a few weeks."

Brushing his mustache, Weston smiled.

"It's the knife and pen I found."

Sherrill took a drink of his Irish coffee.

"There's a good doctor nearby or better yet an insane asylum about a half day's travel by ultralight plane, but I wouldn't trust you to fly, much less walk around Mount Jackson to a nut doctor."

"I have a hundred pounds of wacky weed in my hippie van," said Weston in a serious pose. "I need to take it to Florida for a buyer." A weird grin ran from his face as serious as a minister's sermon on Sunday morning.

Both men stood without moving a muscle and stared.

"What the hell's in your head, Weston?" Sherrill held his coffee in both hands. "You don't do drugs, fool," pulling his head back laughing. "I have enough shares in this company to send your ass for a drug screen."

"I'm kidding you, Sherrill." The boss told his right hand man.

The owner of Andy Oliver grabbed his side, landed a cramp in his stomach from the joke about driving weed to Florida. Suddenly, he grew serious.

"Follow me." Weston puckered his lips. "I'd like to show you something."

They left the room, and Jason tagged along behind unseen and unheard, looking at pictures of Sorano on the wall. The two men walked ahead of Jason over to the roll-top desk. Weston pushed the tambour into its hiding place and closed the door.

"Why do you have a knife and a pen staged on a piece of paper?" Sherrill examined Weston's eyes. "People already think you're crazy for hiking the trail in under two months. Now what's this pen and knife about?"

"Look closely."

Weston brought the items under Sherrill's glasses. Sherrill clicked the pen.

"It works fine," said Sherrill who gripped the knife, rotating it in his hand and under the bright lights. "Nice blade. Sharp."

"Notice how the writing symbols on the pen match that knife, old man, huh?"

Sherrill closed one eye and examined the inscription.

"Dominican symbols and written in Spanish?" asked Sherrill. "Wait! Raymond, Myrtle and Moby? Is this knife from the Dominican, too?"

"Victor plunged the sharp blade into my tire a few months ago."

"Where did this pen come from?"

Weston nodded.

"You don't forget much do you? Jason's father had dinner with him last year and left the pen on the table."

"Notice the knife's inscription matches the pen," said Weston handling the instrument. "Look, it's Mickey Starr's Tobacco Barn logo on the wooden handle. Made in the Dominican Republic."

Sherrill picked up the knife again, put it back, then twisted the pen.

"Might be a big coincidence, don't you think?" said Weston. "Sam Copperpot signed off on this furniture with the same pen. Mickey Starr gave it to him last week when he was inside his tavern on the last day."

"Hell, no!" said Sherrill. "He's planting instruments to torment us. What about a knife like that one?"

"Best blade I've seen in a long time." Sherrill took the tool in his hand. He whispered in his friend's ear.

"Jason brought the pen back from New York after he had dinner with my brother." Weston stood in amazement. "Wonder if he met Mickey Starr in Brooklyn, too?"

Sherrill shrugged his shoulders, sighing. "He would not meet Mickey Starr, would he?" He held the knife. "Planted objects on purpose, huh, to get our attention and get us talking?"

"Three items were left from Mickey Starr's inner circle of men," said Weston who sat in the chair at the roll top desk. "All items were left as a message to us that Mickey Starr is lurking around." He scratched his head. "We might need to take a trip to the Dominican Republic with Jason."

Jason saw Sherrill and Weston talking low in the next room, ear against the door, and tried to listen but couldn't determine what they were saying.

"That young man has been here a year now, Ridge." Sherrill leaned against the wall. "I wonder if he recognized the knife and pen came from Mickey Starr's collection. It's a deliberate link, but I'm not sure why he's dropping clues."

"I'll find out." Weston scratched the back of his neck.

"The more people I meet," said Sherrill, "the more I want to live on an island with coconuts and a half naked woman."

"Get me a ticket," said Weston, grinning.

"Do you think Jason is a clever mole?"

Weston stood.

"A spy, you mean?" Weston shook his head. "Can I tell you a secret, Sherrill?"

Sherrill turned his good ear toward his boss, shoved his hands in his pockets.

"You know you can trust me."

The two men took a seat inside Weston's office and closed the door. Jason crept closer to the door. His uncle spoke in a low but clear voice.

"I hired Jason to move here from Tampa as an investigative reporter."

"To investigate what?"

"The murders of your brother, Raymond, his wife, Myrtle, and Moby Steel."

"He should be in the Dominican Republic, not New York or Germany or Mount Jackson, pissing valuable days away as the case closes. Each week the blood trail gets cold as ice, son."

Jason heard a positive grin in Weston's voice.

"I have a plan to connect a few dots and solve the murders."

"It's about time." Sherrill sniffed. "Raymond was my best friend and a good brother. I loved him very much."

"Somebody knows something," said Weston, rubbing his hands.

"Then it would help if he questioned a few people now and then instead of flying around in a damn pancake plane and crushing grapes."

Sherrill held his forehead in disappointment. Twelve months had passed since he'd lost his brother and sister-in-law. He didn't care for Moby Steel, not the least, but he didn't want him dead, either.

Picking up the pen and the knife and placing them in a drawer, Weston was eager to map out a plan to help Jason, following the wisdom of Sherrill. Nodding his head and walking up beside his friend, he said, "I believe the criminal will return to the scene of the crime and boast about his actions either sober or drunk."

"I have a use for my nephew."

"I heard you say Jason writes like Walt Whitman and Oscar Wilde combined." The old man worked his wrist back and forth. "Let me be the one to cut Jason's throat, well, if he's working with Mickey Starr, please pick me, boss?"

"Wait!" said Weston. "Jason isn't a criminal or a damn two bit spy. He's on our side."

The old man paced toward Weston and sat on the corner of his desk.

"My brother is dead because of some piece of crap who's connected to Mickey Starr. I don't have the money to truly investigate this case, well, like you do, boss," said Sherrill, clearing his throat. "The police in the Dominican have quit after one week of questioning, I'm sure of it. They could care less about three dead Americans from Virginia."

"I'd bet my good-for-nothing brother, Victor, works for Mickey Starr through the internet from Germany and meets him from time to time."

Weston reclined in his leatherback chair. Watching through the window, he pulled Sherrill to the front porch by the cuff of his jacket. Both of them surveyed behind them to make sure no one had followed them or was listening through the door.

"The geese are flying south soon, if you know what I mean?" said Sherrill, winking. "The fourth quarter is usually our best-selling season at Andy Oliver. When are you leaving, to find out about my brother's death?"

Weston crossed his arms.

"Don't tell your wife or anyone else what we are working on. When the time is right, I'll take Jason and we'll fly to the Dominican Republic."

He hit his hand against the post several times. "I can cut his throat right now." Sherrill held up his hands. "Let me give him a name for his tombstone since that bastard has taken your money for a year and not investigated the first damn thing."

"Hope it wasn't a mistake hiring him." Weston petted his dog. "I'd never seen him before he showed up asking for work."

Sherrill fell back in a panic, trying to prevent an anxiety attack.

"I bet it was those Ernest and Julio boys in California, who sent him as a mole, to spy on Andy Oliver and copy our Top Secret wine profile, huh?"

Both men watched the first flock of geese move across the Shenandoah Valley sky that evening in a V formation. Migration of birds had started. Fall. Geese. The cool nights had rolled into town.

"And now we have a winery and a brewery," said Sherrill, turning to his boss. "Should be a great end of the year in business for Andy Oliver and Sam Copperpot."

"Jason loves beer," Weston said. "Sam has a hoppy beer coming out this week with a fruit slice flavor on it."

Out of respect, Weston had listened to Sherrill's ideas for twenty years. Tonight was no different.

"In recognition of his valiant effort working with us in the brewery," said Sherrill, pacing over to the end of the porch. "I'll tell Jason the wine season is at an end when geese fly south for the winter and Andy Oliver will not need his services any longer."

"Let me manage my nephew." Weston nodded. "See how this pans out first."

"Then will you let me cut his throat if he screws up or if I find out he's with Mickey Starr?"

The old man cleared a patch of hair from his arm with his razor sharp pocket knife that he rarely unfolded unless he had something on his mind. He stood deep in thought.

"Negative." Weston spoke in a deep voice. "We'll get him drunk, and he'll tell us if he knows anything about the murders, who was involved and if he's hiding any information we need to be aware of for evidence."

Jason walked outside to where his uncle and Sherrill were talking.

"Who's getting drunk tonight?"

"Damn it, boy," said Sherrill holding a knife to his throat, pressing the blade against the young man's neck. "Don't you ever interrupt two men when you see them in private conversation!" He eyed the boy, biting his lip. "You got that, Jason? You hear me? Stop spying around, son."

"Yeah, Mr. Taylor. I hear you, sir." Jason walked into the personal space of a raging psycho. He didn't move and glanced at his uncle.

The old man whispered in his ear.

"Who wrote *The Importance of Being Earnest?*"

"Mark Twain?"

Sherrill pressed the sharp knife blade to his neckline, watching blood drip onto his clothes.

"Sherrill!" yelled Weston. "That's enough!"

The old man pushed Jason against the wall one last time, scoffing and walking away. He raged when his brother was mentioned and since Jason wasn't investigating the murders like he was supposed to do, he was pissed and suspicious, too.

"You certainly ain't no Oscar Wilde, young man."

Jason adjusted his shirt as he flashed a deadly look into the old man's eyes. He combed his hand through his hair, Sherrill spit off the porch into the dry leaves.

"Get your wife a bottle of wine and get out of my face." Jason told him, smearing the blood on his neck.

"We are not done yet," said Sherrill, humming and singing. "It ain't over until it's over, Tampa Bay trader."

"Jason?" Weston yelled at him.

The writer wiped blood from his neck. Angled his eyes at Sherrill, detesting him for what he'd done. Jason marched to the Jeep, rolling down his window.

"He's a freakin' nutcase!"

The dog growled when Jason raised his voice.

"Jason!" Weston stepped off the porch. "Get back here."

In a rage, he aimed his hand at Sherrill. "To answer your question, Sherrill, who wrote *The Importance of Being Earnest*, well, I have to see Gwendolen," tipping his hand.

Sherrill started his truck and yelled, "Jason, you double crossed us with Mickey Starr. I have my good eye on you, kid."

Walking down the pathway, Weston tossed the last drink of coffee into the yard, walking toward where Sherrill was parked, "What the hell is the book *The Importance of Being Earnest* about, anyway?" asked Weston.

The old man owned over eight thousand books in his home. He didn't have one that he could not recall the plot of the story or the names of good characters.

"Two identities," said Sherrill, who spat out his truck window. "The boy has two identities. The main character has two identities. It's Jason, Ridge, the boy is as guilty as sin. He is here as a mole. That's why he hasn't typed a damn thing."

Weston slapped the truck mirror with his hand and hoped he was wrong. Later, Jason cooled off and spoke to his uncle about what happened on the porch. "I'm not familiar with the story," said Weston, "but I believe you made it clear to Sherrill that you know it well."

"I know the story and he's wrong."

A few days later at breakfast, still in hatred toward Jason, Sherrill told Weston, "We've fallen for the Bunbury Trick. I think Jason works for Mickey Starr and until he proves different, my thoughts are against him working at Andy Oliver. That's my two cents and I'm too old to care about other opinions."

Twenty-One
Autumnal Spirit

Three days after the party, Weston invited Sherrill to breakfast at Danny's Cafe for scrambled eggs. The cafe was an aged place, built in the late forties and owned by a WWII veteran who cooked the best garden omelets in Shenandoah County. Weston ordered the omelets for Sherrill. He favored Virginia grits, topped with homemade butter on his toast instead of in his bowl, eating at a slower pace just to pass the time until his friend arrived.

Long after the agreed time to meet had passed, Weston was on his third cup of coffee and Sherrill's eggs had grown cold. There was no sign of the old man. Weston finished his serving, wrapped Sherrill's food, and decided he'd deliver the meal to his doorstep.

Worried. Puzzled. Sherrill had not missed a meal with Weston in over twenty years, excluding the day Raymond died. He'd stayed in bed and wept. When the clock struck twenty after eight, Weston knew something was dreadfully wrong, so he decided to investigate. He thanked the lady for the generous portion of eggs and paid the tab.

A dozen times he checked his watch and his heart lifted into his throat as Weston drove the winding roads, turning and twisting through the countryside to Sherrill's home. The last time he'd seen Sherrill was Thursday after work and the next morning, Sherrill called in sick. Two cars sat in Sherrill's driveway. Weston knocked and then heard his friend's voice through the screen door.

"Peg, could you get the door?"

The gray headed lady walked slowly from the stove to the door.

"It's Weston."

"Let him in." He waved at her to go ahead.

"Good morning," said Sherrill, adjusting his wheelchair. "Have a seat, my friend."

"Hello, Peggy, Sherrill." Weston removed his hat. "What are you doing in a wheelchair? Did you fall off the ladder again?" By their silence he knew something was wrong.

"Coffee?" asked Peg, turning to her guest.

Weston touched his stomach, "Had three cups already."

"Hungry?" Sherrill extended a plate.

"The lady at Danny's Cafe made enough for two. Stopped in to check on you. Only the second time you've ever missed breakfast and I missed you blessing the meal." He tried to use some humor to get them talking.

Peg stood next to the pantry.

"You doin' alright today, Weston?" asked Sherrill.

"I'm fine. But how'd you get in a wheelchair, my friend?"

Sherrill looked at Peg, then down at his coffee-stained shirt.

"Every once in a while I have a bad day." Sherrill spoke from behind his coffee cup.

"Go ahead." Peg used a tissue on her eyes. "Tell him."

Sherrill rolled across the floor in front of Weston.

"Yeah. Yeah. Yeah. Peggy, honey, could you let me talk to the man?"

Peg closed the door behind her. Sherrill grabbed the remote control, turning off the television.

"What's going on, Sherrill?"

Weston found a seat in front of the large wooden desk. "Talk to me."

"I need to retire, Weston."

"Is it your leg?"

"Right leg is broken in two places." He touched his shin. "Hurts like hell."

"Did I do something to make you mad?" Weston edged to the end of the chair and leaned forward. "Or is it your health and wellness?"

Sherrill clicked his pen, as nervous as when the storm dropped two trees in his backyard after Labor Day weekend.

"No. No. No." He waved his hands. "Les Venable broke my leg."

"Today's paper reported that Les Venable was found dead beside the road in New Market. Did you kill, Les?"

"No, but good for him. I love it. He needs to be dead for what he did to me. Did the paper say he had any money on him?"

"Money? No, why? Did he do this and then take your money?"

Tears welled up in the old man's eyes.

"Les is the freakin' devil, I tell you. He's the devil."

"What did Les want with you?"

"Raymond called the night before he was killed and let it slip that he was drinking with Les Venable in the Dominican. Raymond was shooting off at the mouth with the help of a Pina Colada, blabbering that I had fifty grand in my safe at home." He muttered. "Les was here two nights ago drunk. He told me if he didn't leave with the money, he'd burn Andy Oliver to the damn ground and kill Peg for the fun of it."

"Let's call the police, tell them how that bastard held you both hostage, see if they found any money in his truck."

"I'll call the police when you leave." Sherrill rolled his chair in nervousness. "Now that Les is dead, it could be random or could have been a trap?"

"We need the mastermind and the killer," said Weston, now pacing around the den.

"Do me a favor, Weston?"

"Yeah?"

"The day before Raymond left for the Dominican we had coffee at Danny's Cafe. He said he planned to make a quarter million investment down there. My brother never returned. Find Raymond's killer and stop this damn circle of murders before more people die."

"I'll do everything I can, Sherrill. Make a few trips, see if I can find a few leads. By the way, Victor was kicked out of the Army. My brother may be involved."

Sherrill raised his head.

"That was our last penny in the world, Ridge."

"When I get back from the police station, Jason and I will start investigating ourselves, police or no police."

"Take that Mickey Spillane character, Jason with you. See if he can take a few notes while he's there on his Trapper Keeper and typewriter and do something with that damn kid."

Sherrill leaned forward and outlined a plan. For an hour, the two men collaborated behind closed doors in the den about who to contact and who might be involved and even drew a timeline. Weston wanted to involve the police. With every surge of pain, Sherrill wanted to take an eye for an eye and a life for a life.

"Go old school on them," Sherrill said, who was a WWII veteran.

FACE OF AN OLD FRIEND

Prominent eyes and a delicate touch, one true love weaved a ribbon of hope in Weston's life, the same lady he had been chasing in his dreams since he graduated college. An avid pilot, he watched every plane cross the sky, day and night, like blinking stars with a destination in mind. Thirty thousand feet above Virginia, the lady who had fascinated his heart for years was on her way to him. Thoughts of her raced through his mind, absorbing his time and he loved the anticipation of her being nearby.

In a private conversation, he said, "Jason, I am fixated on this lady and now, Sherrill and Peg are involved, and their money's gone."

"What can we do?"

"All I can think about is her," said Weston. "And this is the closest we have been in twenty years, how can I balance this and not have everything fall apart?"

"I'll work twenty hours a day, for you, and you know that."

Pacing around his office, Weston met with Jason. "At this moment, I need your commitment, so get ready to take out whoever is involved in this bloodshed."

"What's your plan?"

Jason noted, word for word, what he said.

With their hands bonded together in brotherhood, nephew and uncle made a pack to find the leader and pull the trigger on him if they had to handle it themselves. Weston had his hands tied with Andy Oliver, trying to replace Sherrill and now keeping his promise to search for the killers in another country, was a daunting task. Jason was shocked when Sherrill offered him his pickup truck, free and clear, if he'd dedicate himself to the case and quit Andy Oliver for good. Jason couldn't tell if he wanted him gone or cared sincerely that he would be a great contribution as a journalist. Maybe save Andy Oliver from more scrutiny?

He was referred to as "the writer" of Andy Oliver, though he had not written much of anything. With his father out of the Army, the murders of Moby, Myrtle, Raymond, and now Les occupied the forefront of his thoughts. Jason wasn't sure why Peg and Sherrill were brought into the picture. Unless the thieves thought the old couple had more money hidden in their house or in a personal bank account. While Sherrill's son,

Montgomery, repaired the plane and had taken an interest in aviation, Weston traveled locally, and Jason made calls about the investigation and his typewriter was humming to meet the deadline he'd promised Fred Hughes and Top Hunter he would write. The world was unforgiving and relentless, at times, and it was truly evident those involved with Andy Oliver were not spared.

Weston said it clearly to himself, "If she cares for me, Sorano will be in Mount Jackson to see the colors of fall and see the geese fly south, camera in hand and we will be together."

If she made trips to Mount Jackson over the years, he did not know of it, but the prospect of autumn appealed to him. Sorano had reconnected with him, closing the gap of geography between Virginia and New York. He repeated a number of times, "If she cares for me, she'll be here." He planned to woo her, sending roses and letters as he once did, writing often and calling her once a day. "If men did this more often and in a special way, it would never lose its sense of appeal in relationships." That's what Sherrill had preached when he spoke of Sorano, how it would be great to have her in his life again, the man began to soften up.

Months had passed since he'd seen Sorano. Without hesitation, he picked up the phone and initiated the prospect of an autumn visit.

"Sorano's Japanese Restaurant. This is Amber, may I help you?"

"Yes, good morning, Amber. Is Sorano available?"

"She left for Virginia on a plane this morning."

"This is Weston, by the way. We met earlier this year."

"Weston Laramie, the winemaker from Virginia. Well, you are the man she's flying to see."

"Wonderful."

"It's supposed to be a surprise," said Amber. "I love surprises, don't you?"

"I was going to have roses delivered to her restaurant, but I could do it in person."

"You could. I'm not supposed to tell, but she's in love."

"With whom?"

Amber laughed.

"You, silly."

"Well, you can never be too sure."

"Sorano bought a pashmina for the autumn days in Virginia." Amber shared the secret, being in favor of Weston. "A certain lady would be elated if you showed up at the airport with roses, wearing those tight jeans she likes."

"I'll have flowers, my tight assed jeans on, and my hippie van will be parked in front of Dulles International."

"She might rock your world, Weston." Amber giggled.

"I hope so."

Large crowds made it difficult to hear through the phone in Andy Oliver's Tasting Room, where people sampled Woodstock goat cheese and Ridge's famous Pinot Noir.

"One more thing," said Amber.

"Yeah?"

"Sorano spoke of that little bed and breakfast you own. The one you stayed at in 1977."

"Nice place."

"Would it be possible to reserve the third floor where she can look out over the Shenandoah Valley and watch the geese fly south? She said there were hundreds and hundreds of geese flying south for the winter. You know women, it must be memorable. I think she'd love it that way."

The man knew exactly what she was talking about.

Weston whispered, "And she favors tempura."

"Make it a homecoming for her, Mr. Laramie. And wait a minute, here's an extra printout of her itinerary. I have it somewhere, and it is Delta, though. Flight, arriving at 3:12 pm."

"Amber, you're a wonderful person. I see why Sorano speaks so highly of you. I'll do as you say. I will let her rock my world." He chuckled, and said goodbye.

Weston knew what he needed to do for her, crossing his mind everyday about what to plan if she ever decided to consider being in Mount Jackson for more than a few weeks. He rushed to grab his jeans and van, wrapping himself up in his favorite dress wool trench coat.

Kenny, Montgomery, and a team of others were pouring samples and packaging wine as fast as they could. Weston walked behind the counter to check on Sherrill who was working part-time, in his wheelchair. He was pouring wine and serving cheese. That man was never going to retire, he thought.

"I have to go to Dulles Airport, Sherrill."

"Why?"

"Sorano."

"Oh, yeah," speaking with a deep smile. "Your lady friend is coming to town, and Virginia is for Lovers."

Weston buttoned his top button, flipping his collar down.

"How do I look?"

"You need a shave and haircut. Trim that beard back a few decades." Sherrill shook his hand. "And you're starting to look like Bigfoot. Well, go do the best you can, caveman."

"I'm a man of vintage and taste," Weston laughed, "one of a kind."

"You look sharp. Now get going."

The boss of Andy Oliver stood in the doorway with the sunshine at his back, just a thin silhouette of a once stout man, who had begun to worry too much about his relationship and getting down to the Dominican.

"I'll be back tonight." The bell rang on the top of the door. "Kenny, don't rent out the top level of the Andy Oliver Bed and Breakfast."

"But I have some people asking," said the young man.

"Tell them, Mount Jackson is for lovers, and you just booked it."

"I hear you, Romeo." The young man grinned. The German cuckoo clock struck noon.

"Have fun," shouted the customers, smiling and cheering with their Andy Oliver wine glasses above their heads.

"Call the B&B, if you need me."

"Roger that, boss," said Kenny.

"Weston!" Sherrill yelled and whistled, seated at his favorite tasting table. He took fresh flowers out of the vase, wrapped the stems in paper, handed them to Weston, and smiled in good nature. "Here, take these roses," said Sherrill, excitedly. "Make sure you leave the lady a nice tip for the room." He laughed at his friend. Only when Sorano was around did Weston move with spirit and a smile.

"If the world shouldered your kindness, people would never go without consideration for others." Those were the words Weston told Sherrill.

"See you in three days or so," said Sherrill, clinging to the bench.

***

Dust clouds rolled behind the hippie van on a curvy dirt road until Weston hit the hardtop. Like no other man could have done it, he pressed the gas and turned north on highway 81. Knowing his own capability he gripped the wheel and was unsure of how fast the vehicle would go or how fast it had been driven since it first rolled off the showroom floor, he gunned it. His life was generally routine and practical, thriving on simplicity, coloring between the lines, so to speak, that is, as the anticipation of Sorano made him do unusual things. Run. Hike. Love. Travel.

Shenandoah County was in his rearview mirror. Dulles was an hour and a half drive from Andy Oliver, but Weston's eyes never lifted until he reached the arrival sign at the airport. The van ran fast.

He had sung along to every song on the 70s classic rock station, it was just the type of music she enjoyed as well. He hoped *All The Leaves Are Brown* would play on the radio once she opened the door. Weston questioned why great singers took photos in a bathtub for their cover album. A thousand strange things crossed his mind as he drove, including his father's advice. However, the image reminded him of Sorano in the tub. Using his new cell phone to call the B&B at Andy Oliver, he had Samantha arrange the tub in scents of vanilla and ginger. Already chilling inside the refrigerator were slices of Creamy Limoncello Italian Ricotta Cake, which she favored, alongside chilled red and white wine, and several bottles of Moscato from his cellar. Samantha had Kenny, the truest servant among his workers and the guy who refused to sue him, deliver the gifts.

Under the arrival sign at Dulles, Sorano stood and waited for her driver.

Weston spotted her walking from a distance as he stood outside his van. Her short, jet-black hair, bounced as she pulled her luggage as if she was on a mission. He chuckled witnessing her humming and singing, lips parted and swinging her arm amid an ocean of people.

Sorano spotted his hippie van while she waited. She waved and smiled, clearly surprised to see him.

The prospect of her was personal and reserved for no one but him, he'd hoped, neglecting his previous self-infliction and doubt. Her obscurity with Mickey Starr had not vacated his thoughts. However, she had been so wishy-washy over the years, so Weston decided to enjoy each day as if it were his first time with her. His small inventive voice had worked as a clever tool, but when love hit him, he endured.

He stood in his jeans in front of the van.

"What are you doing here? How did you know I was here?"

She reached the door where he stood, savoring him for a moment inside his arms. Four months had seemed like eternity for both of them. Weston held her to where her feet left the sidewalk. The harsh whistle from the traffic guard caught up in his vocation, followed by a stern eye on his pale skin and an aggressive arm motion reminded them of where they were. He loaded her luggage in the side door of the van.

"I'll tell you later," as he kissed her cheek and grinned.

She whispered softly in his ear. "I've missed you."

He grinned again, with immediate satisfaction, a definite feeling he'd waited a long time to hear, which came effortless and genuine from her. So many nights he'd wondered if she'd ever come home or how long she'd stay when she did? Would they ever spend their lives together or was he wasting his time? She was no longer abstract but now, the lady was tangible and vivid.

"It has been too long. Missed you dearly," he said, "I have plans for us."

Her eyes sparkled when she spotted the flowers. She opened her door, and the roses made her smile.

"Let's go." She said, "My schedule is wide open, and the leaves are at peak. I want to see the countryside with you."

He kissed her and touched her leg, changing gears and weaving in and out of traffic, making his way to the interstate.

"Do you mind if we go through Warrenton, Washington, and Luray?"

The man leaned to survey the sky, the warmth of what was left of the evening was drawing to a close.

"Are you wanting to visit the caverns in Luray?"

"No," shaking her head. "The Maze." She turned into him. "Can we see it?"

The end of the day for attractions was near. He wasn't sure how long she could stay, prying wasn't his nature. Nor did he want to rush her time with him, so he tried to think of something "social" in an element of surprise.

"They close at 4:15 this time of year." That is what he saw on television the day before, he remembered. It had been years since they were there.

She fell against the back of her seat, curled up, her eyes closed. Weston pulled over and removed his trench coat to cover her up. He imagined something heavy was weighing on her mind or she was relaxed being close to him after a long time apart. Her beautiful Japanese features captured his attractions. She appeared to be at peace but drained. Within a few minutes on the highway, Sorano dozed off.

Weston lifted her hand and kissed her fingers. Small hands and thin bony fingers stuck out of an oversized sleeve, arms bare of gold and silver, wrapped around her neck was the pashmina, just as her friend said. Subtle and attractive, resting in the arms of his van, he snapped a photograph, like many others he'd taken over the years. In his shirt pocket, the first picture snapped of her in a long while.

He parked the van.

"Sorano, hey," he said, touching her soft hair. "We are here."

Opening her eyes after the hour-and-a-half drive, she raised her head. The landscape alerted to the fact the valley that stretched before her was mostly golden in color, but yellow, red, orange, made the mountains a canvas, a special place and time to her.

"Where are we?"

"I brought you to an Italian restaurant in Luray." He opened the door for her. "I thought you might be hungry. Did they serve you anything on the flight?"

"Peanuts and a soda, that's all."

He held her hand as she stepped down. Folding his coat over his arm, they walked arm in arm.

"Wanted to see you again," she said, holding both hands in the doorway. "I'd like one of us to make a decision tonight, not tomorrow, whether or not we're going to live in New York or Virginia."

"That's easy." Weston became stern. "I'm not moving to the city."

Wrapping her arms around his waist, Sorano closed her eyes.

"Good," she said, kissing him. "I'd like to stay here, in the log cabin."

"What?"

Touching his hands to her smooth pale face, Sorano's eyes lit up. A dark haired man walked them to a table. There was hardly anyone there on a Wednesday evening.

"Let's have a glass of wine, and we'll talk it over." Weston helped her with the chair. "I'm hungry, handsome."

Unbeknownst to who he was serving, the young waiter poured Andy Oliver wine into a twisted stem glass, and served it politely with cheese and crisp crackers.

"Cheers to us. I'm finally moving to Mount Jackson."

Words he'd longed to hear rolled from her sober lips of red.

"Cheers to us." Without flinching, he asked, "What is all of this moving to Virginia and when did this idea hit your heart?"

"I've always wanted to be with you."

She lifted her glass and smiled. Surprised that it was about to happen, he emptied the glass in one gulp.

Turning to her with gentle words, he said, "We do have some unfinished business to address."

"You mean, we have some love making to catch up with?"

They laughed, talking about where they'd been and the best foods they'd found from New Orleans to Nashville to Asheville. Sorano called it, The Southern Triangle of Comfort Foods.

"We could drive to Asheville in the hippie van, then to New Orleans, up to Nashville, back to Asheville and be in Mount Jackson by Christmas Eve." She waved her wine glass and twitched her arms. "What do you think?"

He never felt ungrateful in her presence, nodding in delight and surprise, a little shocked and taken back by what she had said. For twenty minutes he said nothing. All he did was gaze into her eyes and listen. She spoke less about television shows, less about people and headline news, or what others had to say about music and food, she had his attention. More about the places they'd like to see together, traveling and staying at the beach, vacationing in the Poconos and the Adirondacks. Her eyes followed his smile when he spoke of riding air balloons in Statesville and Albuquerque and other places in the south and southwest, she'd planned for them to do.

In a sincere voice, Weston said, "Let's do them all and then I'll die in your arms when I'm an old man." He held her hand. "That's what I want to do."

Tears trickled down his long pale face. With a towel he wiped one away and then another thinking she was lost in their big plans together.

"Weston, I have ALS."

Rushing to her side of the table, he hugged and kissed her face. Tears flooded her eyes before he could kiss her a second time.

"Oh, honey." He closed his eyes and prayed. "God help us."

"It's ALS."

"Are you sure, Sorano?"

"It's Lou Gehrig's disease. I had an electromyogram, nerve conduction study, MRI, blood and urine tests, spinal tap and muscle biopsy in Buffalo. I've had it all, and I'm exhausted. Not sure if I can do this for five more years."

He wept against her face, staring directly into her eyes.

"I'll take you to Charlottesville, Duke, or Wake Forest. I have a good friend in Utah who can recommend the best doctor in the country."

"Yeah, I know you have a big heart."

He leaned in, pulling her as close as he could.

"Everything and anything we need to do, we can."

"My second evaluation came from Dr. Richardson at John Hopkins."

"I'll take care of you," he said, pulling her inside his arms.

"You are why I am here." She kissed him. "You are a good man for me, Weston Laramie."

"I love you."

"I've loved you since our first night in High Point." Smiling, she raised her hand and shouted, "REG-GIE - REG-GIE -REG-GIE."

"That World Series night has never left me, crossing my mind often, if not once a week."

They spent the rest of the evening crying and talking about hospitals, the best ones in Utah, Houston, and Saint Louis. He spoke of calling upon nearby doctors who'd offer a referral or who were experts in the field of ALS. He cleared tears from her flush face as quick as he saw one. Then an idea popped into Weston's head.

The waiter delivered what they had ordered. Chicken marsala and a slice of pizza, which wasn't as appetizing after she'd shared the severity of her health with him.

"Sir, young man." He choked back a lump in his throat.

"Yes, Mr. Laramie?"

He pointed toward the office. "Could you bring me the Charlottesville phone book from behind the bar?"

"Do you need a taxi or a tow truck?"

"No, just the phone book, please."

Flipping through the stained yellow pages, one by one, he hoped she was wrong. A sober recognition of her words, scanning and praying as he turned the pages again and again. He hoped she was wrong, or by some low percent the doctors had misdiagnosed her. Often he'd prayed for her and this time it was for a rare miracle. Her hands and arms twitched as she helped him locate names and he read aloud. Only two bites of pizza were eaten by Sorano, and he'd chewed only once.

He boxed the meal up. Sorano spoke of being tired, and with no argument, he carried her to the van. Cherry blossom pillows were her favorite, a dozen of them lined the back seat of the van, having picked them out for her months earlier. It was ninety-one miles back to the bed and breakfast in Mount Jackson. She was tired.

On the way back to the B&B, he palmed his face, checking on her through the angle of the rear view mirror. She'd fallen asleep on the drive home. He knew the road, like the back of his hand, but still was careful to keep her settled and comfortable at a steady pace. Resting in the back of his vehicle, just as if she was in the log cabin, Sorano would put her life in his hands before anyone else. The lady often referred to him as a saint, dependent on him in uncertain times as much as her minister in Westbury.

Twenty-Two
Good Riddance

The colored leaves of fall, hot cocoa and apple cider of Mount Jackson attracted folks from all over the country to the Shenandoah Valley. Thus, every parking space at Andy Oliver Vineyards was taken. Busloads of guests from as far as Memphis and Carbondale held glasses and mugs in the famous Andy Oliver Tasting Room, sampling and purchasing, having a good time. The year 2000 was outstanding for Weston Laramie, happier than he'd been since Jimmy Carter was in office.

From his post at the gate, Kenny counted 250 people a day coming to the restaurant, the B&B, or the trailhead. With the new addition of Sam Copperpot's Brewing Company, one more level of goodness captured the attention of patrons. As a result, Weston made several trips a day to Mount Jackson and Timberville for food and supplies.

Montgomery failed to show back up for work at Andy Oliver, totaling $25,000 he'd carted off from the safe at Andy Oliver and left town. Sherrill and Peg were ashamed of their son.

"Another worker unaccounted for. He can be someone else's problem for a while, washing his hands of the boy," said Weston. "Good riddance."

Weston was saving that money for Sorano's hospital bills.

"I yakkai hai or good riddance," said Sorano in tears.

Other than stealing money, Montgomery had been an exceptional maintenance man, but greed got the best of him. Dozens of times, Weston asked himself, 'Who was behind the recruitment of men from Andy Oliver and who was paying workers to spy and steal from the vineyard?' but he didn't have the answers.

Weston and Jason discussed the case files from workers who had left Andy Oliver as the writer journaled about each employee. Even after a small collection of notes, he had only a few pages of vital information, still no conclusion about the murders and disappearances. Then one morning before anyone arrived at work, Jason walked up beside his boss, who was examining the ultra-flyer plane. He had not started the engine in a while.

"Boss, you got a minute?"

An elevator of rage flipped a switch in Weston's head, moving his hands faster than he thought he could move, reversing Jason's position against the wall of the barn. He slammed him against the barn.

"I got a minute to kill you!"

Jason didn't have time to finish his thought and speak his mind before he could feel boards and nails tapping his back when Weston lifted him off the ground.

"What has gotten into you, man?"

"Yesterday Mickey Starr bought the vacant Cavalier Tavern from Sam Copperpot who closed the doors on that place months ago."

"What's that have to do with me?"

His shirt collar was released from his uncle's hands, and he pushed him to make sure he knew his uncle was watching his every move.

"The rumor is your father will manage it for Mickey Starr." His face flushed red as a maple leaf, and slowly stepped back from his nephew. "Sherrill thinks you are involved in this circle of corruption and murder, are you?"

Staring him down, Jason asked, "What do you think, Uncle Ridge, huh?"

"I know you're on our side." He rubbed his chin and sniffed hard, still pumped with anger. "I just needed to hear it from you and not some rumor."

"With all these men forming an alliance with Mickey Starr, I know Sam, Kenny, Sherrill and several others in town are on your side including yours truly."

He stepped back with his hands up, then paced around in front of the door. Jason slumped onto the bench of the picnic table, hair and clothes disheveled, having less confidence than when he first arrived at work that morning.

"I need the truth." His uncle walked around the straw floor but stayed fixed on his nephew's every word. "Do you know more than you are saying about the murders?"

"I don't know anything about the money or the murders, Ridge."

Someone thumped the barn door with some aggression. Weston opened it. The bald man stuffed his uncle's arms with a heavy backpack and walked inside.

"What the heck?" Weston yanked a gun from his belt.

"Who are you?" said Jason.

Weston closed the door, but not before he checked behind to see if anyone had followed him. Alone.

"Who is this guy, Weston?" Jason turned toward his uncle. "What's inside the bag?"

A slim young man with a shaved head walked inside the room.

"I'm Moby Steel," he said, catching his breath.

"Newspaper said you were dead." Weston unzipped the bag. "You're making this crap up! Are you trying to plant something on us?"

"Every dollar of your money is in the bag. There's $50,000 from Sherrill and $25,000 from Montgomery," said the young man, still trying to catch his breath, smiling and laughing. Everything was a joke to him it seemed.

"Are you freakin' lying to me again, boy?" Weston asked, waving his gun and realizing what came out of his mouth. "My money? You mean, Sherrill's fifty grand and my twenty-five grand." Weston Ridge unzipped the backpack and examined the bills, running his hands over the edging of the paper. He claimed what was his part and jammed the rest of the money back inside the sack.

Pitching the bag back to Moby, he yelled, "You'll take every penny back to Sherrill or you will go to jail. Les broke his leg over this money!"

"That is your damn money," said Moby. "Raymond and Sherrill were stealing from you. I got it back for you. Here's every dollar."

"What?" Weston sat beside Jason, crossing his arms, staring and listening at the boy to see if he was a liar, a thief or just damn nuts.

"I did it, alright," the boy said, lighting a cigar. "I'm the freakin' hero, here." He raised his cigar at Weston and laughed. "You owe me, big time, Weston Laramie."

The young man walked around the room, circling the plane, then sat across from Weston at the table. Weston lit a cigar himself and blew smoke into Moby Steel's face.

Jason's eyes darted from Moby to Weston as he tried to figure out what the heck was going on, still confused and deeply interested. The kid's story made no sense in part nor in whole.

"You recovered the money for me, Moby." Weston puffed on his cigar. "Before we never talked or knew each other for more than a week? You did this out of the kindness of your damn heart, huh?"

"Sherrill wanted to take his wife on a fancy retirement vacation and needed some extra spending cash for the road," he said, dividing a deck of poker cards on the table. "Live it up!" said Moby. "Plus he had his eye on a lime green mint '71 Barracuda in Manassas. He wanted to buy it for Montgomery. Something of great value before he died. I don't remember the details."

Weston stared at Moby, thumbing his thick mustache, then said with a deep voice, "If you are lying to me, I swear. So help me to God...your name won't be a misprint in the Obit column next time!"

The guy placed his hand on his heart, and said, "I'm not lying to you. This is the damn truth." He cocked his head as he stopped dealing the cards. "Every penny is in the bag and every word I say is the truth."

"Who is looking for that money, in Savannah or the Dominican?" Weston poured coffee from his thermos and worked his cigar. "Want some coffee?"

"No coffee for me, Dad!"

Slamming his hand down, "What the hell do you mean, Dad?"

"Is this your son, Weston?" Jason laughed.

"My full name is Richard "Moby" Steel. He placed a stack of cards between them, looked directly at Weston and said, "You knew my mother from college, back in 1977, in High Point, North Carolina."

Rubbing his chin, grinning, teeth shone at Weston.

"The hell, I did."

"Anita Remley." The young man's eyes opened wide. "She went to college with you. You two dated. Now do you remember her?"

"Jason, this is the great liar, Moby Dick, or whatever the hell your name is." Shaking his head, Weston said, "I never slept with your mother. Hell, we never went out to dinner."

"My mother found a bottle of Andy Oliver on the shelf in Barringer, North Carolina and she mentioned dating Weston Laramie, years ago, still grinning when she hears your name. That was your face on the label. My mother said the Laramie Brothers were dressed up on Halloween night, like the Belushi Brothers. You drank wine back then too, Dad."

Taking it all inside his ears, Jason listened and knew he had a heck of a story to write once the ribbon was adjusted on his typewriter. In the meantime, the writer jotted down the details of what was said between the two of them as they smoked stogies. Weston looked like he needed a drink, but he didn't take one.

His uncle smiled and spoke of his younger, wilder days in college. He said how he and his brother dressed in two piece suits, black tie, and off-white oxfords. They slipped on All Star sneakers and went to a block party.

"How could I forget that time?" Weston stared at the plane, recalling his college days. "Yeah, yeah, yeah," he said, nodding a few times. "I remember that night."

Moby stood and turned sideways.

 "She said, 'I slept with Mister John Belushi' and that's who my father is."

Moby unfolded an Andy Oliver label from his leather jacket, slapping it on the table with a fat smile across his face.

"And that's my father's face on the wine bottle. Look at my chin and your chin, Weston."

To elevate matters, Jason said, "Father and son, chinny chin chin. Would you look at that chin, it's a perfect match, Weston," chuckling.

"I hate to disappoint you, big guy, but Moby, well, I dressed up as Jim Belushi." Weston brushed his hands on his chest. "And I never dated your mother or slept with her, and I didn't even know her….but I know who did."

Snapping a photograph of Moby's long, sour face, Jason aimed the camera at him and Weston inside the same frame and grinned. Priceless photographs were taken.

"I saw pictures of my dad," said Moby, nodding, "dressed as John Belushi, though."

Moby shuffled the cards. Then boxed the deck inside his shirt pocket. Pissed. Head bobbed, staring at Weston.

"Wait! Wait!" said Moby, rubbing his hands on the table. "I was hit in the head and shot in the leg, but my memory is perfect."

"Jason, well, well, well, meet your half-brother, Moby."

"Why would my mother make something like that up, Weston?"

"If that's the case, my brother, Victor, he's your *real John Belushi* father figure. Not me and this gentleman, Jason Laramie," grabbing his shoulders, "he's your half-brother. Victor loved John Belushi and he loved your mother very much." Weston tucked his gun back inside his pants. "I'm so glad I dressed like Jim that night. Wow! The Queen of Hearts was always my brother's best friend."

"No way!" shouted Moby. "She never mentioned the name Victor Laramie," he said, slamming his hands on the table. "You're lying! Victor is not my dad? You are joking, right? My daddy is the wealthy Weston Laramie. I got the money back playing cards when everyone thought I was dead, to impress you, Weston."

Weston walked over to Moby.

Flipping his hand in Moby's face, "Your mother was drunk off her ass one night at a big fraternity party in High

Point. My brother Victor and your mother were hanging out, so I dropped Victor off at her home. She dated my brother that night. Congratulations." He grinned. "Tell you mother the face on the bottle is your uncle. I'm your new uncle though, if that helps draw a line in your ancestry book?"

Moby shook his head. "Oh, hell no, that couldn't be possible. That crewcut, slick-faced Army jackass in the Dominican is not my father?" said Moby. "Hell no!"

"Are you saying Victor Laramie was in Santo Domingo when Raymond and Myrtle Taylor were shot?" Jason asked the young man politely.

Taking notes, Jason eyed Weston to see if he was telling the truth and he did.

"Yeah, he was there, and after I left, they were killed."

Weston was caught with a surprised look, sighing, said, "Bingo!"

"My brother could be your father. Your mother and him dated for three weeks after the Halloween party. Plus, I got two dead people and a hell of a lot of questions, Moby Steel."

In a nervous place, Moby didn't want to make a confession to Weston and knew Jason worked for the newspaper, and heard all about him from his father.

"Maybe you and your father will want to play a game or two with the Feds?"

"You won yourself a father, brother, and uncle," said Weston. "You also recovered the money, and resolved your family lineage. I need to go and check on a few people this evening myself." Weston looped the backpack on his shoulder.

"Good to see you two brothers playing together outside the sandbox at Andy Oliver. Don't go far, Moby."

Moby stood, still shocked. "You are right."

Weston took his cell phone number to investigate on his own.

"Now you have a new nephew and your money back," Jason told his uncle.

After Moby left, the barn doors were pulled shut by Weston as he stared at the ultra-plane for a moment and talked to Jason.

"I should sell the plane."

"No way."

They walked from the barn to the tasting room.

"I need to speak to Sherrill," said Weston, "get his side of the story. Find out what's the truth and what's a lie?"

"He still hasn't returned full-time from his injury," said Jason.

His uncle was never short on words when it came to money or to resolving conflict. If he had to go inside a bar or knock on someone's door or get inside someone's head to do it, he would.

***

Sherrill was watching a football game when the phone rang. His face cringed as he lifted the receiver and heard the voice on the other end.

"Weston?" Sherrill whispered to his wife.

"He's on our tail," said Peg, talking to her husband in a low voice.

"Yeah?" said Sherrill. "Weston, what do you need?"

"I need you at the coffee shop in half an hour, my friend."

Sherrill adjusted himself in his wheelchair, sniffing in certainty of what it meant.

"I'm in a little pain. My leg is acting up again."

"My wallet is in a lot of damn pain, too," said Weston, pulling on his pocket. "If you know what I mean, my friend." He thought of his options. "I'll be right over there, just give me thirty minutes. I'll bring enough egg biscuits for the three of us. How about that?"

"We appreciate breakfast, but we've already eaten, young man."

Jason heard his uncle slam the phone down inside his office.

"An unnecessary evil has robbed me of my money and my time with Sorano," Weston spoke to Jason in confidence.

His nephew turned around to go with his uncle, but he was gone. Drove off.

Did I sift through rights and wrongs, Weston thought, trying to draw an accurate conclusion? Who should I believe? Who could be trusted? Who to fire and who to knock out?

The boss spent the greater part of a week chasing the truth. Jason typed and noted the men and women who drifted from friendship to corruption.

Weston hoped Sherrill wasn't involved with Raymond. More than brothers, they'd been friends a long time and if he knew anything about the situation or if he'd seen him conjuring up a plan to steal more money from Andy Oliver, Jason would soon know as much as he did. They agreed to include it in his story. Weston had nothing to hide.

Weston arrived at Sherrill's home and they spoke for an hour about what he knew and it was the same story he'd told Jason two weeks earlier. He loved the Taylors and Sherrill was more of a father to him than his own dad. The old man was on his side. Both of them were locked in an alliance until the end. Best friends.

If Sherrill did take the money, then good riddance to him and Jason would have a big story to write for Top Hunter and Fred Hughes, but there was no truth to the idea. Weston wondered how much money workers had been robbing from him over the years, from the safe to the cash register and onto the tips left behind in the jar for the kids. He suspected workers had been stealing from him for years, since long before computers scanned money and products into their state-of-the-art computer system and warehouse, even dodging cameras. That's why some workers were against the cost of installing cameras in the most vital part of the building and barns. Weston's recommendation was to keep it original and traditional, not like a cave hidden from the modern world. However, it was Moby's word against Sherrill's story, a tug of war for the truth was what Weston needed from each man.

***

Laughing on the drive from Sherrill's home back to Andy Oliver, a vivid image of a young man in a John Belushi mask making love to Moby's mother flashed through his mind. They were drunk. That dreadful image he could have done without. Victor must've looked funny, at any rate.

The list of things he needed to do overwhelmed him. Find Raymond's killer and meet with Sherrill, for sure. But at the apex of each day was to spend time with Sorano and contact her doctor if her health declined. Something caused him to stop laughing when he slammed on the brakes and coasted into a parking spot behind a row of Leyland cypress trees.

The burgundy hippie van was the only one of its kind in the Shenandoah Valley. Weston suited himself in a ball cap and dark glasses, parked in the shade, scanning the coffee shop and to his surprise spotted two men. His eggs and grits rolled over inside his stomach when he realized who was at Danny's Cafe, in Mount Jackson for breakfast. Someone he didn't care to see again in ten-thousand years, had both hands wrapped around a cup of coffee. Weston's blood pressure spiked to the moon.

"Mickey Starr," he said to himself. "You dirty thief." Balling his fist, Weston hit the steering wheel several times. "What's he doing here?" pulling down his visor to block the sunshine and spy on his enemies. "There's Sherrill across from him, who has lost what dignity he has left with me? He's turned into the devil, just like Victor and Mickey Starr."

Weston watched the men for a few minutes.

"What am I worried about other than revenge?" he asked himself. "I need to make this bank deposit." He reached for his backpack and felt the floorboard. "Where's my damn backpack? Where's the money?" Opened the compartments and all the doors. "Nothing!" he shouted. "Gone! Robbed again. God is there anyone in this town I can trust?"

He spun his tires and headed down the street. Then discovered Moby seated in a truck with Georgia tags. Hidden in an alley, he watched Moby Steel in the truck, angling his eyes toward Mickey Starr and Sherrill Taylor, still conversing inside the restaurant. Examining the area for anyone else, Weston eased close enough to smell Moby's cigar. Breakfast became brunch and then a plan popped into Weston's mind. Banging his head to loud music, Moby was buzzed on beer. Wrapping his black trench coat over his arm, ducking behind trees, Weston slid behind Moby. His long arm extended.

"Where's my money, Moby?" His voice was deep and dark. "Your ass is in debt to me now," said Weston, pressing the barrel against his neck.

"What money?"

Moby turned off the radio.

"You and Mickey Starr double crossed me, didn't you! Buy out my employees, one by one, until I decide to sell Andy Oliver, you dirty sumbitch!" shouted Weston, pressing harder, giving a deadly look. "You all stacked guys against me from here to Santo Domingo, planning to screw me over?"

Moving the gun, Weston pressed the barrel against him.

"What was that click, Weston?" Turned and begged. "Don't shoot me. Please don't shoot." He cried. "You goin' kill me, aren't you?"

"Reach me the damn backpack in the seat," twitching his mustache. "Hand it real slow, Moby, or Mickey Starr will have blood inside his truck."

Moby didn't blink. Weston was in no mood for games, watching him push the bag outside the window, reaching in slow motion.

Weston slammed his jaw. Moby groaned in pain.

"Good day, jerk," he shouldered the backpack. "What are you doing here with Mickey and Sherrill, anyway?"

"Business investments."

Weston busted his mouth.

"Answer my damn questions!"

"Screw you, Weston!"

"Want another one, jackass?"

Weston hit him in the face with all he had.

"Okay! Okay! Damn you, Weston!" he yelled, holding his bloody nose. "Wait. I'll tell you the truth."

"Step out of the truck," Weston shouted. "Now!" the gun waving. "You got two seconds to say something, boy!"

"Sherrill and his son, Montgomery work for Mickey Starr, but I don't remember exactly why. Myrtle, Raymond, and Les are dead. I know that much. Money, maybe?"

He lifted the gun between Moby's eyes.

"Wait!" backing against the truck. "I remember now!"

"Speak up!"

"Mickey Starr wants to break you down and buy Andy Oliver. Sherrill's been depositing in Mickey's account since Raymond died." Mickey said, 'Being broke is no better than being dead' and that's what he lives by."

Moby had a smirk on his face.

"All I've done for Sherrill." Weston tightened his face. "Who else?"

Weston unzipped the bag, lifting up the shoulder strap.

"The bag is empty. Damn you, boy!"

Moby Steel chuckled.

"Don't think I'd carry around all my money, do you, Uncle Ridge?"

Weston ripped open the bag.

"Where's the rest of the money?"

Ten middle school students walked toward Mickey's truck, and strapped on their backs were the same colored backpacks, red and black.

"Maybe one of those kids stole your money, Ridge Laramie."

Weston hid the gun in his belt.

"Damn you, Moby!"

The kids walked up to Weston, the tallest one said, "What are you doing with my backpack mister?"

Weston turned around and Moby Steel was gone, like a ghost. Vanished. Weston surveyed the scene, circling the truck and stood in an open area to see better. Nothing but more students. No one was found.

"I trusted you!" he shouted. "You piece of crap!"

A familiar Southern voice sounded from the tailgate, lurking behind him, said, "Weston Laramie, we meet again. I love reunions."

Weston zipped up the bag when he recognized the man's voice.

"Well, well, well," said Weston, turning around to face the man, who stood at the far end of his black truck under his own volition. "What's the 'Sum bitch of the South' doing in Virginia?'

"Didn't you get enough of my boys at The Tobacco Barn?"

Mickey Starr lit his cigar and blew smoke, laughing and coughing out smoke.

"Your boys fight like school girls." Weston threw the backpack over his shoulder and closed the gap toward him.

Two middle school students admired Weston's hippie van.

Mickey stepped toward his opponent. Ten feet separated them. Their eyes locked; muscles tensed. Enraged.

"How's my peach, Sorano, anyway?" he said, smiling and laughing, "I sure do miss that Tokyo treat."

Weston rushed him and swung. Two young boys saw what happened. One strike was landed. Laramie's hand launched at Mickey Starr, like a rocket into space, he was flat on his back.

"Little birds were flying in circles," said one boy.

Weston drove away. Two boys ran to where Mickey was stretched out on the ground, poked his arm with a stick, but he was knocked out. His cigar was found twenty-seven feet away, still smoking. One little boy clenched the stogie in his teeth.

Justified. Overdue.

Weston later told Jason to type the story that way. Then Weston said he walked down the street with a backpack on each shoulder, headed to his van as if he was motivated to start the first mile of the Appalachian Trail barefoot. That afternoon, no one else got punched or knocked out or kicked in the head. No blood was shed nor teeth broken that Weston spoke of at dinner.

The story was told that the round boy knelt, and said,

"Mickey Starr's head was wacked. That man must have surely seen stars."

"Is that a dead person?" The little kid with the stogie stood over Mickey Starr and stole his lucky gold watch.

"Look at his high-dollar shoes," he said, removing them from his feet. "If he's not dead, my mom's boyfriend would love to have them brogans?" They laughed.

The round boy lifted his hand and swiped more cigars. Acted like he was smoking and blowing rings into the air, waving his Cuban diplomat. Then shuffled his feet and kicked his legs.

"If he's dead, he won't mind us eating a pizza on his dime. Take his wallet, Red, and get his hat, too, why you're at it."

The round boy wrapped the large watch around his small wrist. His eyes sparkled and bugged knowing it was made of pure gold and ended in an "x". When they saw the stack of cash that popped out of Mickey's leather tri-fold they hid behind a tree and split the money.

"Count your blessings," the thin dark haired boy said.

The round boy doused Mickey Starr's face with a bottle of water. "Mister? Mister," he said, looking at his friend. "He's dead. Let's call the police," said the boy nodding his head. "Wake up."

All of a sudden, after being jolted a dozen times, Mickey Starr's eyelid moved. Then the other eye struggled to open to see who spoke and shook his arms until his mouth moved and poked him twice with a fat stick.

"Old man, are you still paralyzed?"

He woke like he'd been in a coma. Then they saw his wrinkled face when his head turned, and laughed, taking each arm to pull him up. The afternoon sunshine alerted Mickey to the fact he'd been out for a while, checking his dry cracked lips and finding a firm stance on his feet. The boys were long gone by the end of the day. Mickey climbed inside his truck. Ironically, Mickey Starr found a handwritten note resting on his steering wheel, chastising his own famous method of personal communication.

The note said, "The knot on your head will go down, but look at that tennis ball in the mirror as you drive south. Ain't that a peach, Georgia boy?"

From behind the wheel, Mickey Starr crushed the note with both hands as Weston's voice echoed inside his pounding head, especially when he read the next line.

"I don't want to ever see you in Mount Jackson again. Now get out!" Signed Weston "Ridge" Laramie.

Mickey Starr looked for Moby Steel and Sherrill Taylor who had abandoned his truck, betraying him and leaving him empty handed. On the long drive back to Savannah, Mickey stopped twice, one time for coffee, and a second to get ice for his throbbing head. He checked his injury several times in the rearview mirror.

Twenty-three
Into the Sky

Weston planned something big for Sorano, something only a few people in the world would attempt. The owner of Andy Oliver was certain about the man who could repair the ultra-flyer plane right inside the barn, redeeming himself before the crew. Weston didn't believe the lies Moby Steel had spread about his trusted mechanic. None other than a longtime friend, a certified pilot himself and qualified airplane mechanic, Montgomery Lee Taylor, a descendant of General Robert E. Lee, at sunrise, would be returning to work at Andy Oliver. The parts arrived by air mail on the last day of October at half past ten in the morning. He intended to help repair the plane at first light when the colors of the mountains drew the most beauty in autumn and the Into the Sky - Color Run was in full swing over Mount Jackson.

Like two aviation instructors in dark glasses, Weston and Montgomery met and planned the five mile route over the valley and how it would happen, just as Weston envisioned it in his mind, months earlier. Two hours later Montgomery offered his boss two thumbs up from across the room as Weston stopped eating his lunch and walked over to his mechanic with great appreciation. The long-awaited ultralight plane was repaired and ready for the sky.

Weston geared up. By midday, Andy Oliver Vineyards had a crowd of one hundred and fifty people. For weeks, Weston had been practicing on a friend's plane in Timberville.

When the event was over and his plane touched down, Weston planned to unveil a new wine for his customers. A long line of cars entered the vineyard, guests huddled around the parking lot, and to his surprise a half dozen cameramen and newspaper reporters from three states collected footage and interviewed guests with Jason's clearance.

Weston, Sorano, and Jason were having a discussion in the log cabin that overlooked the long, beautiful valley. From Weston's cabin, the river, covered bridge, the vineyard and the highway thrilled visitors under a clear, blue sky.

"Andy Oliver Vineyards is about to make history," said Weston. "We're introducing a new wine, and Jason and I are flying at a new altitude today."

"Why is that?" asked Sorano, who was eating an egg sandwich and digging into a jar of sweet pickles.

Jason turned to answer. "For some odd reason, large flocks of geese are using the Shenandoah Valley this fall, flying south for the winter." He waved his arms into the open air where they were eating breakfast. "I have been watching the geese for weeks now."

"Jason and I are going to fly through the valley and then we will release this year's Riesling around three o'clock."

From the mountainside, the three of them watched more and more cars enter the valley from country roads and off highway 81. That was the largest crowd at the vineyard since Sorano's arrival a year earlier. In a nervous manner as if he needed a smoke, Jason laughed watching Weston pace around the room in anticipation.

"Jason and I plan to soar and do a 180 in the sky, like a large mechanical creature, trail behind a V formation of geese and follow them through the valley as they make their way south. Mount Jackson is the main thoroughfare, a place of warmth for thousands of birds who fare much better in warmer weather."

Beside Sorano, Jason watched her muster enough strength to walk over to where Weston stood on the deck with his coffee in his hand.

"How close can you get to the geese," she turned to Weston, "I mean, without hurting them?"

Curiosity ran through his mind.

"For a photograph, you mean?"

"I've never attempted to push them or edge them too much in the air."

Finishing what little bit of coffee Jason had left inside his cup, he walked over to where they stood in the center of the log cabin. "Sorano?"

"Yeah?"

"Would you take my seat in the ultra-plane today? I'm fine being a photojournalist from the ground." holding his camera. "Just for you, I'll write something about it in the newspaper. A beautiful story and print a photograph, too."

"Sorano is scared of heights, Jason," Weston squinted at his question. "Please don't ask her to fly."

"I'm sorry." He put down his camera. "I didn't know you were scared of heights, but you've flown on airplanes across the world. Japan. Tuscany. France. I shouldn't have asked that question. I apologize."

After breakfast, they stood outside. Sorano hugged Weston and without a warning, her footing and legs gave way as a result of her ALS. Her eyes were in Jason's line of sight. He noticed her weakness. Sorano closed her eyes in a slight disappointment, hugging Weston's side like she was meaning to wrap him tighter than usual. Weston turned to the wide valley, missing what had just happened with Sorano's leg from the disease. She became weak.

Jason moved closer, just in case it happened again and to assist her. She stood between the men, held the deck rails in limbo, head dropped, eyes closed in embarrassment, perhaps.

"Sorano!" Jason held her up on one side for support. The lady shook her head and gripped his hand for him to remain silent. He nodded and did, out of respect.

Weston had no clue what had taken place. His uncle moved and leaned, outlined the valley with his hands, planning the pattern of his turn, and described the mountains to the valley as Sorano propped herself up onto Jason's shoulder and just smiled at Weston.

"Jason, the geese make a V shape in the center of the valley. That's when you can plan your best photograph as we fill the void behind the geese." He snapped his fingers. "A shot of that quality will land you on the cover of National Geographic."

"Weston?" said Sorano. "I'll fly with you. Take me into the sky. If you will have me ride with you, that is?"

"I'd love for you to be with me." He kissed her. "Having you in the plane would mean the world to me."

"Sign me up."

Jason snapped his camera to capture the rare moment, which was something Weston had coached him to do, collecting smiles, and happy moments, of Sorano at her best, and so he did.

With the camera around his neck, Jason held her right side as she leaned against him with her right hand, and moved whenever she needed his strength.

"That's wonderful news, babe." Weston kissed her forehead. "I can't wait to have you with me. Jason will snap a photo for Andy Oliver Vineyards and we'll hang it in the office."

She moved inside the cabin, held Weston's coffee and stood composed and full of strength. She had her moments of courage and loved Weston for being near when she needed him. She pulled him close enough to kiss.

"I have only one condition, though," she said.

"What's that?"

The writer examined both of their faces when she spoke.

"Weston," she said, "I want you to pull up close enough for me to touch the feathers of a wild goose."

He held her face and kissed her.

"That's dangerous." He smiled after he said it. "But I love the idea. You are brave, Sorano."

When Mr. Laramie hugged Sorano, that moment defined him and her, and Jason wrote how he wished little Andy could have witnessed what he'd photographed instead of him.

"I've been watching you fly for weeks." She held his hands. "I'm so excited to be with you today."

With a glow about her, some hope, some fear, but Sorano walked out into the warmth of the sunshine, and he followed her. They sat in love and petted the dog that had walked between them. The picture was taken.

"I'll do it. I can see you touching the feathers of a wild goose." They held the dog in their laps. "We'll do it together."

"You're an expert pilot." She squeezed him. "I believe in you."

"I think it's a wonderful idea," Jason said from the doorway.

Counting the incidents, few, yet enough to be noted from the perspective of a journalist on sabbatical or just the kindness nature of another person. From early on Jason was sympathetic to Sorano's ALS, knowing her strong willpower and own ability, he was attentive and supportive to her strength, a true friend. Her only incident was dropping a spoon while eating a bowl of vegetable soup and her foot giving way, a few times. Other than a small limitation, she exhibited no others. While Weston walked downhill to Andy Oliver Vineyards, Jason drove Sorano in the hippie van to where he prepared to fly the plane. A crowd had gathered to admire the contraption and speak to his uncle about his flight and Sorano was amused by Weston's hobby.

Sorano walked over to the plane with a coffee cup in hand.

"Good afternoon," said Weston, pointing at his flyer. "Here's the plane."

She walked over beside him. "What did you name your plane?"

"What's the name of the plane? Name? Name," said Weston, tapping his head. "I haven't given the plane a name yet?"

Using video, Jason stood and recorded them together.

"You need to pick a name, Uncle Weston," he said, holding the camcorder. "I have a great idea. Let Sorano pick the name, right?"

"How about Andy's Dream?" She touched the plane.

A cool wind swept through the crowded valley, overhead the sky was blue and clear, sun bright and stunning, Weston acted as though he wasn't blocking the light with his hands, but his eyes were as misty and red as hers.

"You hardly speak of Andy," he said, putting the helmet on her head, snapping her collar and headset around her chin. "Andy's Dream, huh? I love it."

"I love it here, Weston."

"It's home."

"Because I don't mention him," grabbing his hand, "doesn't mean I don't dream about him."

Twenty minutes later, Jason moved inside the doorway of the barn, took a new angle on his knee, snapping a half dozen shots of them as they rolled the plane to where Weston needed it to be en route to the soft grass runway. Even in poor health, Sorano pleased the camera, navy slacks, slipover jersey sweater, and a thin zipped jacket. Weston stood beside her, tall and proud, shoulders back, goatee, and a contagious smile of confidence covered him and her.

Looking at the plane and her, turning his head to the hill where Andy was buried, he sniffed and thought of the possibilities, "Andy could have bought me a beer this year."

They chuckled and wiped each other's tears with their thumbs.

"Andy would've bought Yoko Ono a beer on behalf of John Lennon, too," said Sorano.

"I would've bought the next round." Weston rubbed his chin. "Here, let me strap your microphone on a bit tighter. We'll need it to communicate."

"Andy's Dream? I will paint it on the side next week." Weston checked the plane and grinned. "I never thought of naming a plane before."

Jason smiled and handed him a black marker, shoulders shrugged.

"What's the marker for?"

"You should write the name on your plane." Jason told him and started the engine.

Weston stared at the plane and handed the marker to Sorano.

"Sign it." Kissing her pale cheek, he whispered, "Andy's Dream."

Before the first letter was written, tears flooded her eyes, sighing and adding the name in cursive to the side of the plane. The crowd cheered when she finished the two words. The writer proudly loaded a fresh roll of film, snapping pictures of a large crowd, who had no idea why she was crying. Only a few people knew of Andy Oliver Laramie. Many just thought it was

Weston's middle name or his father's name and others never questioned it. They just loved it.

"Are you okay to fly?"

She smiled through her gentle eyes, hooked on dark glasses and nodded.

"Yes, I'm ready."

"You want me to take you up then?"

"Yeah, why not?" She kissed him. "You have flown with Jason, Sherrill, and Montgomery this week. Why not with the love of your life?"

"Well, I didn't think you liked my plane?"

"I see myself with you. That's all I see."

Jason helped her inside the plane.

"Lean back." Jason buckled her in. "I'll lock you in the seat."

He checked the dark glasses over her eyes.

"Make sure I'm snapped inside Andy's Dream."

Weston climbed inside, double-checked his snaps, and offered a thumbs up to his nephew. Then Sorano raised her hands to a large crowd, screaming and cheering.

"This is your last chance to climb out," said Weston.

She spoke into the microphone for the first time.

"I've always been flying with you since The Irishman's Pub."

"You are serious about flying, aren't you?" He adjusted his straps one last time. "I thought you were scared of heights."

"I'm not afraid anymore." She said with certainty. "But this will take my mind off of things. I'm happy when you're happy."

The moment fascinated the crowd and Jason captured it on camera. Even as a reporter in the midst of sports and main events, popular and unknown, he highlighted that moment in the Shenandoah Valley, as one that would eclipse them all. Above the crowd, zooming at top speed, all of a sudden the geese his uncle had raised from a small pond followed them into the sky over Mount Jackson, in beautiful flight. He'd been working with the geese for months, but on that day, the geese did as God intended for them to do. They flew, in and among good company, too.

Some of the geese were tame, others wild, and a half dozen were called pets. In flight, it was difficult to identify their past behavior. The red Valentine's Day bows were long gone. Something that happened once. Ten of the geese flew with them and kept them company.

The geese she had fed at sunup helped Sorano to be more comfortable as the co-pilot. From what little he knew about the disease, Weston didn't like how it took the strength from her muscles, where she wouldn't be able to run, walk, or make origami for her favorite customers. The pilot turned the plane around about a mile in the valley and the geese stayed right with the plane as other geese followed, from other flocks, moving south at a fast pace. Within minutes, there were several flocks overhead, like dots dabbing a baby blue sky, gliding and flying, as if they were on assignment.

"I love flying," she said, holding on for dear life.

"It's fun, isn't it?"

On the fifth mile, there were geese everywhere migrating south for the winter. Sorano raised her arm as Weston guided the plane to the end of the V formation. Above Andy Oliver Vineyards, Jason turned the video camera on when she reached for the feathers of the goose, touching the feathers of the highest goose in the sky. The moment was the most surreal event not only in her life but in the life of the many spectators. The pleasure was hers. Both glorious and humble, the one-of-a-kind day belonged to Sorano Tanaka. The day was something to write about. The writer felt like the world stopped spinning, for a cool moment, but it didn't, and she handled a goose at sixty miles per hour at maximum flight over the town. Jason zoomed in and snapped several close up shots of them moving at high speed across the valley in a small aircraft called Andy's Dream.

"It's been my dream to have you here with me," said Weston with a soft voice, he spoke into the microphone.

"I'm glad you came to New York looking for me."

"I've believed in you ever since '77 when you cheered for the Yankees that night at the pub, was when I fell for you."

She moved her hands from the grips to the straps on her chest and waved.

"Move me closer to the end of the V formation again, close as you can," she said.

In full flight, high above the Meems Bottom Covered Bridge, she reached out and did what only a few people in the world have done.

"I touched a wild, beautiful migrating goose again, didn't I?"

"You've done a rare and wonderful thing in your life." He said following the birds. "You've lived and followed your heart. Few people in the world have that type of courage."

"It was soft on my hands, too. Like a silk pillow or a sheet." Through the headset, Weston heard her say, "Fly me close again." And he did. He got a chance to experience life with her. Something he'd planned long ago.

"I can't believe I touched the goose in flight."

"I think the geese liked it as much as you did." He laughed. "Let's head back home."

***

The following spring, Jason collected his notes and started to journal more about what had taken place since the day Sorano touched the wild goose. He jotted down what the doctor in Charlottesville said and how the progressive degeneration in ALS caused the motor neuron in Sorano's brain to die. He scribbled the details of the final minutes of her life down on paper. He was there when Weston kissed her lips and forehead one last time and thanked the nurses and doctors circled in her care. They had become family. Her parents had passed away years earlier and her brother and sister would not leave Japan to see her with an American man. On the long and quiet ride back to Andy Oliver Vineyards, Weston stopped and found a little cafe in Ruckersville.

They were seated promptly.

"I had to stop here, sample Sorano's favorite dessert."

Surprised when his uncle spoke. The bright smile that appeared when he mentioned her name was a clear sign he hadn't fallen into some deep depression or wasn't going off the deep end without her by his side.

"What dessert did she like?" Jason held the menu. "The high-stacked New York style cheesecake, I bet?"

"She adored the chocolate mousse in the peanut butter pie. The crust of the graham crackers and that tasty cream cheese is a rare treat," he said as he read the menu. "She would eat it with a cold glass of chocolate milk and licked the fork clean at the end."

"She was a fine lady. The most caring person I've ever met. She loved that dog and the plane grew on her."

"Last time, you and I went flying in Dayton," he said, waving the fork, "she ate the whole dang pie while I was gone. I thought our dog had gotten the pie until I asked her what happened to the dessert. Then she got up from the sofa and started to cry on one of her foodie guilt trips."

"No way? She was a sweet woman." Jason laughed as hard as he did. "That small Japanese woman ate the whole dang pie."

"It's good pie, Ridge."

"Those are the great things I remember about her."

His nephew read the dessert menu aloud again.

"Let's do it."

"What?" His uncle turned.

"Let's order the same pie with some chocolate milk, just like she did?"

"You got it! Let's eat one pie each, in honor of Sorano." He slammed the menu down. "Can you do it?"

Jason nodded. "I can do it if you can."

He flagged the waiter over to the table, requesting what he saw on the menu. His uncle told the nice lady why and she cried, too. The pies were a free gift from the restaurant.

"It's difficult to talk about Sorano in the past tense." Weston's voice was broken and rough.

"It doesn't seem real to me yet," Jason sighed.

"She made this past year the most memorable one in my life."

They finished the pies and spoke of other things they had to do at the vineyard. He gazed out the window. Lost. Broken. Alone. He said no more words the rest of the trip. So in her honor they each enjoyed the best peanut butter pies in the Shenandoah Valley at the Blue Ridge Cafe, ordering a hot coffee to go. His uncle left a hundred dollar tip and Jason followed with the same heartfelt deed.

He dropped Weston off at his cabin.

"What time shall we meet in the morning?"

He shook his head and finished his cold coffee, by that time.

"I'll call when I wake up."

His nephew parked the hippie van and then walked to his place. The writer stayed up later typing, he saw Weston touching the bonsai trees on the front porch and feeding the geese, who'd made Mount Jackson his home along with the rest of the workers at Andy Oliver. His uncle kept her traditions around the cabin. Jason predicted his evening chores were not without her memory or gratitude. His uncle fell in love with the beauty of the valley and the high mountains, but most of all it was Sorano that made Andy Oliver special and inviting for a number of people from friends to customers.

***

The next morning Jason did receive a call from Weston Ridge at ten after seven. He asked Jason to call the employees for a short mandatory meeting. Twenty-five people worked at Andy Oliver Vineyard by the spring of 2001. Men and women Jason had only known for a short time became friends, but he had grown to love them just the same. Men removed their hats. Women huddled and hugged amid the famous Tasting Room to hear the boss speak. By the time his uncle unfolded the newspaper, with only a few hours of sleep, his dark eyes held back a flood of tears.

"Sorano was as vital to Andy Oliver Vineyards as I am. She contributed her time and money to increase our staff and double our production, just as I did. Twenty-five years ago I attended the University of California, where I studied Viticulture, for only a summer, then I worked part-time for Monty Moon in North Carolina at a winery. I learned all I could about running a vineyard." He scanned the employees who were locked on to his every word. "After visiting Meems Covered Bridge, it was Sorano who loved wine from Virginia. I thought North Carolina would be a better choice. She won, but felt my money would not last long enough to buy a mailbox." He laughed. "I think we have done a wonderful job and have the best crew in the country. She loved each one of you. And she loved Sherrill, who has confessed and we have resolved our differences, at any rate."

His team laughed and knew he was stubborn, rubbing the old man's shoulders. Workers wept and huddled up. All were in tears, Jason included.

"Sorano left us with a letter. The muscles in her body due to ALS were gone when she thought to translate it, so I did it from her voice. These are her beautiful words, not my own."

"Sorano was a special person," one lady spoke up.

Weston asked his staff to take their seats. They did. He stood.

Sorano's Letter

Dear Friends of Andy Oliver,

When I first came to Mount Jackson, I expected to only stay a few days and then fly back to Westbury, New York, a single lady again. But the longer I stayed, the more I wanted to stay, and somehow weeks turned to months, strangers became my friends and then I felt at home nowhere else. I knew Weston had grown stubborn and would run me off, but that never happened. Lucky for him. Though we never got married, I never stopped loving him, ever. However, he has seemed to mellow out, less crabby over the years and became a giant in my love life. I wish I would have listened to my heart in High Point, back when Weston didn't have two nickels to his name. Listen, being without the one you love isn't living, it's just existing and dreaming. Next time you are walking around and minding your own business, just make it a practice to listen to your heart.

I thank each of you for a sincere welcome to Andy Oliver Vineyards. I will miss you and love you and hope to see you again soon. Take care of my Weston Ridge and keep making Andy Oliver wine, it's the best place in the world - made with love. May God bless all of you.

Love Always, Sorano

***

The day after her death a candlelight vigil was held at Mount Jackson to remember Sorano Tanaka and the love she shared with her close friends at Andy Oliver. One-thousand-three-hundred and four people attended. Others wrote gracious letters and sent beautiful flowers.

Twenty-four
Pleasantries on the Trail

In the spring of 2001, redbuds and Virginia bluebells bloomed alongside dogwood trees in the Shenandoah Mountains, and the long rainy nights had given the wide valley a glorious green color and the streams were no longer dry. Just as the fall had gained the attention of tourists, so did the spring add its own array of color and blooms to the valley. Months had passed since Bill Clinton announced accurate GPS would no longer be restricted to the United States military, so Weston requested that his nephew be in his office early for some odd reason, and his idea may have had something to do with such technology, in the high country. He hadn't flown the ultra-plane since Sorano petted the migrating geese in flight a year earlier, so he predicted he wanted to fly the friendly skies again.

His face was pale, and Weston was tired and worn out. Weight had fallen off of his body since Sorano passed away. He had been spending more time outdoors, taking in the fresh mountain air and less time in the winery. His relationship with Sherrill was mended after he had begged for forgiveness for meeting with Mickey Starr to find out information about his brother.

Jason sat down at ten minutes till eight, before the morning whistle sounded.

"What's going on, Weston Ridge?"

His uncle folded his arms behind his head.

"I've got something I need to do."

"Do you want to learn about GPS tracking systems to pinpoint the suspects we have on our list?"

"No. Why?"

"Clinton's ping on GPS, it might be the key, right, to tracking these guys to their next meeting?" Jason was charged. "GPS can track anything, anywhere, and at any time. Ridge, for example," nodding, "we could tag a piece of luggage or a car, just like the Feds do it, following suspects on the computer, they say."

"I don't follow Clinton. So, no, I didn't hear the report. I have my own geographic plan. We might use your idea, though, down the line. Listen, someone could tag out backpacks with a GPS carabiner, just the same."

"You seem anxious. Andy Oliver is hopping with more customers, and guests have signed the book from Moab and Saint Louis."

"Sherrill, he's the man who has increased sales and widened the territory since he was trying to find out about his brother from Mickey Starr. Not me."

"Is everything alright?"

"I've been thinking about the ultralight plane, of late. With you being a certified pilot, Jason, you can fly the machine now." He looked him square in the eyes. "I'd like you to be the proud owner of Andy's Dream."

"I love the plane." He shook his head. "But I can't take it."

He grinned with dissatisfaction.

"The Kombi is yours as well," said Weston Ridge. "I have sent off for the titles in your name. It's too late to turn me down."

"Are you dying?"

He pressed the keys in Jason's hand. " I'm not dying but I'm going to hike the trail again. Look." Handed his nephew two hiking backpacks, two polypads mats, two knives, and two flashlights.

"Hiking, huh? Why do you have twice as much as you need?" He examined what he had placed in the chair. "What do you mean giving away your plane and the Kombi to start hiking again?"

He nodded, pulling out a small hand map from the drawer of his desk.

"I've decided to hike the Appalachian Trail again."

Weston had done this when Sorano broke up with him in the early 80s. He'd hiked the trail in fifty-five days, which was something crazy. Some say he hiked into the night air with cougars and owls as his guides. To know what he was going through was impossible, a road Jason hadn't traveled down, and …to lose a child, to say goodbye to Sorano, and to be robbed of his close friends. All of this was enough to send anyone into the high mountains, the writer noted.

"When are you going back on the trail again?"

"It's not just me on the trail." He turned around and then tipped his hat. "We are going on the trail together." He flipped a canteen on the flat of his stomach. "You're in good shape."

"You got the wrong man for hiking a trail."

He unfolded his map. The route he'd taken years earlier was right before his nephew's surprised eyes, the one he'd heard about as a kid. Running his fingers from Georgia to Maine seemed an impossible task. Heck, checking his email was tiresome. Lifting the flag on the mailbox took his wind. Writing, it made his fingers bleed. A hike of that magnitude was insane.

"It's only 2192 miles across fourteen states."

"What?" His head fell backwards. "You are a nut. There's not twenty-two hundred miles in these legs!"

"I've hiked every step of it once. Some people have turned around in Maine, hiked it back to Georgia. Yo-yos. Super-hikers. That's what I call those people. Crazy. Death-wish hikers." He raised his hand like a preacher did on Sunday. "And if we hike forty-five miles a day, it can be done in only forty eight days.

"Forget this damn trip, Ridge! I'm not a hiker."

"Why not? By God, I have stuck my neck out for you a dozen times over the past few years. Plus, that would beat my old record by a week."

Jason bit his tongue and hoped he was kidding. "This is damn stupid, Ridge." He stood. "Screwed up."

The long-legged man sat atop his desk and let that information simmer in Jason's soul. His nephew could already feel his feet aching, back pain, and count timber rattlers. He hadn't even slipped on hiking boots yet. His uncle waited for his response, holding his coffee cup near his chin, and eyes of curiosity and anticipation.

"Let me put this in words even you can understand, Weston," leaning so close he could smell his aftershave. "No."

Weston chuckled.

"I believed in you when I didn't even know if you could work on a vineyard or write a damn note."

"I mean it, Uncle Weston," he said. "It's not for me."

"Is that right?"

He divided the miles on a calculator and placed the contraption inside Jason's hands along with the Volkswagen keys he'd just handed him.

"You can hike it. That is, if you put your heart into the trail, take no less for yourself than the goal inside your mind. That's what GPS is all about... find yourself and make it a journey." He said it with some spirit, tapped his temple, and raised his voice. "While you have your ability to move, use it. Look how fast Sorano faded away with Lou Gehrig's disease. Sherrill can barely hike to the front gate. Walking, running, hiking, it was all gone in a short amount of time. I'd ask Sorano, but she's hiking in heaven right now."

His nephew paced the room, saw photos of Weston's first hike, observed an even older photo of Sherrill's first hike on the App Trail window, and examined the many acres of vines and mountains on both sides of the Shenandoah Valley.

"It would be good for my career as a journalist to hike the Appalachian Trail. That's for damn sure."

"So, are you in?" He raised his fist for his answer and took a deep breath. "Are you a Laramie hiker?"

Looking at the number forty-eight on the calculator and examining the long trail map on the wall, he fell backwards in his chair and his feet flew up. Then he folded the map and handed it back to him.

"There's a great story in these mountains." Jason closed his eyes. "I've said it more than once, but never considered being a hiking photojournalist before."

"You could be the one to write the story."

"Let's do the damn thing. Hiking photojournalist on the Appalachian Trail and I'll write a good story about it one day."

"Hot damn!" He stood. His uncle wrapped him up.

"You're going to love it," he said. "I promise you, you'll never forget a journey of this magnitude, rolling hills, long valleys, game, lakes and rivers."

"Can we handle the hike in forty-eight days or longer?"

He cleared his throat, and without blinking, he said, "Rain, sleet, snow, hunger, pain, farms, streams, valleys, and we'll become *thru-hikers*. Others will call us naturalists and "purists of the woods." He filled his lungs full of air. "We can hike the trail in forty-eight days flat... if you want to, that is?"

Jason imagined it would be a great time to remember.

"We can point our shoes northeast each night, like Japanese slippers, to mark our direction on the trail."

"Sorano and Andy would like your idea," said Weston.

Drawing his fist against his chest, "I-IIIIIII hate myself sometimes!" Jason screamed. "This world takes more than it gives. But this is good for me."

"Weston, buddy? Weston! I like your idea, man. Listen. You're onto something with this hike." The writer wasn't sure if he said the right words, but it settled him down and he caught his air. "This is good stuff. I like it and I'm in. Let's go, huh?"

They shook hands.

"I dreamed of Andy being a young man with us. I hope he'd be as good of a man as you are. Let's get ready and plan this trip."

Hunting for a pen, Weston wrote "May 2001" in black ink atop of the map. Then he pinned the map over another map and ran his pointer finger from Georgia to Maine in one continuous movement, dragging his finger along the turning points of the App Trail, peaks and valleys, and then he reached the end and saw himself as a conqueror. The route was a snail dragging trail, weaving through a pattern of staggered drunkenness, and yet, to him, it was exactly the trail that lay before the both of them, only a week away from the start of the journey.

Tacking the map into a corkboard, Weston highlighted some of his favorite spots with a star. He stood with his hand on his nephew's shoulder, humming and imagining the miles and miles of continuous hiking and photography. A larger scope seemed impossible to accomplish, but Jason readied his mind for the topography. Checks and stars from decades ago were fading into the map and needed to be restored, Weston told him. The trail meant the world to Weston. Every eleven days equaled five hundred miles on the hiking trail, to his prediction, and on day twenty, they would reach the one thousandth mile marker. Northbound hikers would reach Pine Grove Furnace, Pennsylvania, the halfway point of the Appalachian Trail.

"They make digital cameras now, Weston. Much lighter than the 35mm rock you carried around on your neck. A true advantage for a hiker, having the capacity to hold three hundred pictures or more, but batteries and electricity will be needed along the route," he said, stabbing Fontana, North Carolina. "Plus, I got you a belated birthday gift."

"You remembered, sort of?"

He took a box the size of his hand from the cabinet.

"Here, what do you think?"

His nephew opened it.

"Hot damn, a digital camera! You are first class, man. This is nice, Ridge. Thank you. It's not heavy and will save my back, huh?"

"Yeah, for sure. Let's be ready on Saturday. Sherrill has agreed to drive us to Georgia and seven and a half weeks later, he'll meet us in Maine."

"I'm ready now."

"Good." Weston's eyes were confident in his nephew. "We have some work to do before we go, my boy."

***

The deep mountainous tranquility fascinated Jason and scared the wits out of his soul at the same time. The trail would be the worst and the best thing he'd ever tried, hedging on wild and wonderful. To ponder the idea of hiking cross-country seemed ridiculous. However, it was crazy enough to make perfect sense for a photojournalist, who needed to write an article or a novel or pen something down on paper. Writing a story of this caliber would be an outlet to understand being free of burdens for a while in his life, to think and to dream under starry nights.

What if they hiked to Virginia, broken and blistered, and all of a sudden he decided to branch off and quit? Hike home to Andy Oliver for a glass of wine at the bar in the air conditioner? Conclude what Jason had set out to do? The writer assumed hundreds of others had done the same thing, saying he'd had enough of the wilderness. A hundred questions crossed the rookie's mind before he'd even started the trail. Some questions would go unanswered until he hiked and ached on a mountainside somewhere with a hill spur or twisted ankle. Regardless, he decided then and there, he was in, one hundred and ten percent committed to hiking, end to end, hoofing the Appalachian Trail with Weston Laramie.

At daybreak on the 8th day of May, they stood inspired under the rock archway as Sherrill snapped several pictures at Amicalola Falls, Georgia. Smiling and eager to watch them command the 600 steps to the tallest waterfall in the south, Sherrill insisted the trail would take its share of weight from Jason's fatty bones. It wouldn't take long to do it either, he ribbed the young man.

Sherrill, 84, hugged their necks, like men do before war, made suggestions, and remembered his time on the trail after WWII sent him home. Then without a doubt, he had influenced his uncle to hike the trail twenty years earlier. In 1960, Sherrill, thru-hiked the trail again, who became known as a "yo-yo," wearing his t-shirt to Georgia to prove his feat. Something that only a few hundred people in the country had done in his day.

"Old man, we'll see you at Mount Katahdin, Maine, in forty eight days."

"Boys, you sure will," said Sherrill.

Ridge turned his walking stick north.

"Don't be late, Sherrill!"

Like a ghost, the "yo-yo man" was gone in the van.

"I'll be there, Sherrill," Jason yelled.

From the tears in the gray-haired man's eyes, he wanted to strap up his boots and lead the way to Maine. Age and lack of mobility were against him, the long drive to Mount Katahdin in two months would be enough to remind Sherrill of the miles and miles of rugged terrain between the Peach State and the Pine Tree State.

***

Seven days into the trail, trees, forest, woods, but Jason couldn't divide the difference in his mind nor in his sight for the rain and sweat burning his eyes. He thought his spaghetti knees would buckle from the tens of thousands of steps on callused heels. Following Ridge was like chasing a cheetah on crack-cocaine or some high-powered sprinter in a track and field race, who didn't realize his legs needed a break. He had to wait as he took pictures and glanced at every flower and rock formation, noting the height of the mountains on both sides of the river in his journal.

"Let me catch you up to speed on something, Jas," Weston said sitting on a hollow beech tree. "If we miss one mile per day for forty eight days, we will be forty eight miles from the end. Sherrill, the "yo-yo hiker" will have a nervous breakdown at Mount Katahdin thinking something went wrong with our trail plan."

"Sorry, bud. I'll pick up the pace." Jason nodded seeing his point. "That's well put."

He snapped photos at White Rock Mountain (4206' elevation), North Carolina, where the view spans across a half dozen mountain ranges, typically green by the end of May, too. "Stop taking so many damn pictures, Jason, start hiking."

"According to my calculations, we have forty days of hiking, sixteen hundred miles to go, and lots of foot tracks to make," he said, pacing ahead of his uncle.

Jason hiked ahead of him for the first time, and for the rest of the journey, he tried to catch up. The following day, Jason did take pictures again and for good reason. On a foggy morning at Grayson Heights, Virginia, two wild ponies, one black and white, the other one brown, popped out of a thicket. The white pony stood broadsided and became the focal point. He hoped to see more wild horses, but there were none or he would have captured the animal on film.

Later, at Annapolis Rock, Maryland, they rested for twenty minutes and had two protein bars each and some water. It was one of the highlights of the trip, a peaceful view, one that could not be described in words. Though, Jason would not have been disappointed to have caught a cab back to Mount Jackson, Virginia, which had a warm bed and a hot shower calling his name.

"We are over halfway, Jason," he said pointing at his belt. "You are slimmer for some dang reason." He grabbed a tree branch and chuckled. "What?" Air left his lungs in a deep laugh.

"Have you been hiking off some of those apple pies you enjoyed at Andy Oliver?"

"The end is farther, just keep hiking, hero."

"Hero?" He said softly. "What happened to you and the New York gal, Jason, anyway?"

"Oh, here we go again. I guess the distance between us was the same as what you and Sorano faced. It was just too much to maintain a good relationship, right?"

He wasn't sure if mentioning Sorano's name was a good thing or bad idea, now that she had passed away. Ridge didn't speak or question his relationship the rest of the day.

At bedtime, Ridge brushed his teeth, and said, "Go after her, boy."

The rookie hiker remembered opening his eyes and slapping his fist into his palm, shocked as hell at what he said, "You are damn right, Uncle Ridge. I can't let love get away, not a lady, sweet and intelligent, who cares for me, just the same."

"When this hike is over, you find her. Don't let your past be a big regret." He combed his hair to one side. "Sherrill will have several cases of Andy Oliver in the van with him to celebrate our accomplishments. We'll make a stop in New York City, close the gap on your geography, and Jason, stay as long as you need with her. Okay?"

That's the thing about the forest, Jason wrote, "You listen for voices and lean on the right voices."

"I can't afford to hike for two months then hang out in the Big Apple without working and making some money."

"Take as long as you need. Listen, your job is safe. I'll get you a few dollars when you run low. Sorano was gone too long.

If your lady friend likes you, there's a job for her at Andy Oliver too, and you tell her Ridge Laramie said so."

The more time his nephew spent with Ridge, the more he realized the trail wasn't about hiking and sightseeing, but more about healing and recovery. Weston told him how important it was to find out who you are in life and be that person.

***

At Denning Hill, New York, 1400 miles from where they'd started, Ridge's right foot started bleeding. He changed socks, taped his foot for good luck, and proceeded. Whether or not he was in pain, he didn't say.

"Why did you get into flying in the first place?" They had a minute to rest, and the question had been on Jason's mind for months.

"Sorano liked geese and for a number of years, she'd send pictures of migrating fowl flying south from wherever she was, the Hamptons or Hudson Valley. I received postcards from as far as Temple, Texas and Park City, Utah."

"What?" He chuckled, leaning over on his side. "Did you think flying would bring her to Mount Jackson?"

Ridge clammed up and stared over the Hudson River as if they were enemies. Bingo. Jason found him, he thought. Weston became sullen and then snapped as if his nephew were prying his heart with a can opener from his backpack. The writer wanted to get inside his head, deep down, at times, he wanted to have his courage and be admired, just like he was.

"Is the heat getting to you, boy, or is that some smart ass, snide comment, to hear some heartwarming story, you can plug into your journal at night?"

468

"If you don't want to talk about her, I'm sorry." Jason realized what seemed to be rude, was careless words. "It was more out of a question about being in the mountainous air together," he said, standing tall. "Not because your attempts had failed and you were looking for another answer to get her in town again."

"I'd seen a man in France training geese and flying with them in an ultralight like the one that you now own," said his uncle. "What he was doing looked fun. I knew how she had a fetish for geese. Nevertheless, I thought it might be a clever way to see if she wanted to fly and she did."

"It worked." He realized what he'd done with the geese at Mount Jackson and earning his pilot's license paid off, something of value in Weston's mind. "She loved you. I could see it in her eyes at Westbury, when you talked to her at that Italian restaurant. Julianna was a jealous lady that night. She was hotter than the fire we put out."

"It wasn't right to stay so long at Sorano's table and abandon Julianna, though."

"You had to find out for yourself, Ridge." He rested at a Beech tree. "It was a worthwhile talk." Jason turned around to tell him. "Something worthwhile for her, as well. She never stopped loving you." His voice echoed atop the mountain. "She didn't want you to leave that table."

"Why'd she fly to Buffalo and leave me at the restaurant waiting?"

"Rosa said she had a doctor's appointment and wouldn't discuss anything about it with you. You weren't her main squeeze at the time, anyway."

"Don't give me that crackerjack grin."

His nephew saluted him just like the boy on the caramel-coated popcorn box.

"What was the millionaire Bentley's first name again?" He changed his voice like a lady, "Was it Fonzie or Richie Rich or Remy? Oh, Remington, is that you?"

"If I had a Remington shotgun!" he shouted. "I know where I'd stick it."

"I guess in the end." Jason stumbled forward as he pushed his back. "Sorano liked the hippie van better than the luxury first-class vehicle."

"I'm having second thoughts about giving you the van now."

Jason stopped dead in his tracks. "Oh wait!" pointing his trekking poles at his uncle. "You gave me the van so you could buy a Remington Bentley car, I bet? I get it now."

"Let's get going or you'll become the first hiking casualty today in Connecticut," he told him. "Watch your step," he started laughing, "or you might get pushed off the mountain."

"Can I drive the Bentley car when you buy it?"

"I might buy a convertible MG and drive to Key West, but I'm not buying a damn Remington Bentley!" He yelled.

Twenty-five
Isabella Beautiful

Ridge and Jason unloaded their gear and rested for the night at Mount Algo, a wooden lean-to, hidden from the elements, half the size of a two bay garage. A lady fiddle player dressed in blue jeans and a flannel shirt had the same idea to conclude her hike before them and she played well, handling her instrument with passion, too.

The Laramie guys grinned at each other in amazement and applauded as she ended the song. She smiled and dropped the bow and fiddle in her lap, rolling the copper rings on her fingers, ran her hands through her long blonde hair, exposed her tattoos, and examined her two newest fans.

"That was a wonderful rendition," said Ridge. "May we join you?"

"Please do." She pointed with her bow in hand. "That is, if you are friends of West Virginians and the Yankees?"

Being the closest to her, Jason shook her hand first.

"It's perfect harmony," the writer said with a colorful grin, "pinstripes and coal dust."

Ridge found his position at the front of the lean-to shelter and rested.

"Where did you learn to play like that?" inquired Weston.

"As a young kid, I studied at Julliard in the late 80s and then at Marshall University, in Huntington. Later, I played with the Huntington Symphony Orchestra and led the London

Symphony as a violinist." She curled her lip and adjusted her gold necklace. "I've traveled a bit."

"I'm Isabella Edmunds, by the way." The lady stood at the edge of the building beside Ridge. She was older than Jason, by just a few years. "Who are you?"

The winemaker brushed his unshaven face, then bellowed something to the effect of, "I'm Weston Laramie. This is the infamous photojournalist, Mr. Jason Laramie."

They answered questions for her about black bears chasing hikers in West Virginia and wild ponies browsing the trail in Virginia. Jason told her they'd seen a cub with her momma and two wild ponies and that was all. Twenty minutes later, the fiddle player tuned her instruments for a session that lasted for hours. The writer realized, then and there, that all people weren't created equally, and some were brilliant and humble; she made both of his short lists. Others wished they were cut from the same intellect and musical cloth as that lady.

"I'm taking a break from the road of music to rediscover my passion in the wilderness. Find my next adventure in life, so to speak."

"On the trail was where I found my passion," said Ridge.

"What passion is that?" she asked in a soft, low voice that was hard to understand at a long distance.

"Wine," said Ridge. He stood beside her in the open air. She offered him what water she had left. "I thru-hiked the App Trail in the early 8os when you were a toddler, I bet. About a week after completing the trail, it was evident for me to start Andy Oliver Vineyards and a week later, I did."

"Are you Ridge Laramie, the owner and maker of Andy Oliver Wine?"

"He's the one and only," his nephew told her.

She poked his arm. "No way. I've tried your fancy Chardonnay. It was after a concert at Carnegie Hall and I made love to my boyfriend by sharing a second bottle."

They laughed as if they'd heard the telling of a story, something similar, a time or two before. Proud of what he'd heard, Weston brushed his mustache and cleared his throat.

"Glad to know Andy Oliver keeps the Big Apple polished."

"Would you guys excuse me?" She disappeared into the dark. "I must find a Hilton oak tree restroom soon."

While she visited the hillside oak tree, Ridge nicknamed her, "Isabella Beautiful."

"She's better than any talent we have had at the vineyard," Jason told him. "We should have her sing at the July 4th Wine and Fireworks Festival."

"Isabella wouldn't perform at Andy Oliver. She's world-class, Jason."

"I can hear you two talking and I'm not beautiful," she yelled. "See, the gift of a true musician is to have a keen ear for music and voices."

"Jason, would you apologize to the lady for considering that she'd play a Shenandoah Valley event after Carnegie Hall and her world travels?"

"Let me play a few more songs. I'll see if it matches what you like." Isabella winked at Ridge. "I'll call you in a few months, when I make it to Springer Mountain, Georgia."

"That would be an unbelievable concert in Mount Jackson, that is, if you could fit it into your schedule."

Jason's eyes opened wide, turned to Ridge as she considered it.

With pounding feet, Jason untied his boots, fell back on his pack, and said, "She could sell two thousand tickets in one day."

"I'll play another hour or so and we'll call it a night."

Alluring eyes of green, like a pair of emeralds dancing and swaying in the moonlight, blinked and glared. She whipped her sandy blonde hair and delivered a show made for a much larger audience.

The shame of the night was that thousands of people deserved her voice, the sounds and arrangement of Cajun music, klezmer, Irish trad, switching to classical and jazz, at times. At a half hour before eleven, her voice left her after thirty songs. Jason checked his watch, in respect, but not in boredom. She had played for three solid hours. Ridge and Jason thanked her from the bottom of their hearts.

With her voice cracked and hoarse, she said, "Gentlemen, I'm exhausted. My violin has asked for a break."

"Isabella, we are grateful for your friendship, especially for your talent, tonight," said Ridge. "I, for sure, appreciate the violinist even more than the instrument."

"It has been the best part of my trip," Jason said.

Still sitting down, she leaned to kiss each man's cheek and hugged them. Jason could still smell her perfume, a sweet floral scent that lingered in the air afterward, even when he closed his eyes. Happiness flared in her face, and she blushed.

"I feel I've made two lifelong friends on this trail. Hope you guys feel the same way."

"We agree." Ridge nodded. "The trail has made my feet far more calloused on the second trip than it did the first time, hoofing as a man in younger clothes," said with a high spirit, "but I recognize the power of a true colleague when I see one without becoming maudlin."

If the writer hadn't watched her eyes brighten up when his uncle said it, he wouldn't have believed he'd impress a symphonist from West Virginia, by way of Julliard, who had played at Oxford. But she had refused to play at Princeton, she told the men, because of their dislike of F. Scott Fitzgerald. Jason dismissed stereotypes, especially rugged mountaineers, portrayed as less talented and undereducated citizens. He called Isabella a friend, gaining even a greater respect for strings and West Virginians from that day forward.

As Ridge and his nephew watched her turn her hand to the left, he spotted a Japanese saying on the inside of her wrist. Isabella let her fingers drop into position, as the tip of the bent thumb made contact with the frog point, gently curving her fingers over the top of the violin bow stick. Her middle finger was opposite of her thumb as she played, no less than if they'd paid for front row seats to see her perform at Carnegie Hall.

When the horse bow was worn to mere stands and fragile strings hung, she was sweating in the cool night air, letting go of whatever she had on her mind to entertain two men. No one else.

"I love to play, but my arms are like noodles. There's one more I'd like to sing for you, Ridge Laramie." The lady stared into his eyes, angling her bow into his chest.

"For me?"

"Here." Jason handed the lady a drink. "Have some water."

Keeping her eyes on Ridge, she finished a small bottle of water, wiped her chin, and pulled back her hair in a ponytail to prepare herself to conclude.

"I'll sing a John Denver melody, *Perhaps Love*."

Ridge leaned back on his elbows in the direct line of a true, seductive serenade. The battery in Jason's flashlight dimmed about the time her song ended. Exhausted and yet delighted, mesmerized in her company, they listened to a true artist at work. Noting the composition in his journal, Jason was in heaven, caught in a rare and unusual way, he made a bet with himself that a moment like that would never happen again, and it did not. Her voice was clear and sharp, lows and highs, as if it were a lullaby underneath a high hanging moon. Isabella's presence was like an angel in the wilderness without wings, a glorious lady gifted with bluegrass and classical music, having no preferences by the night's end. But Jason believed she mustered up enough energy to flirt with him on more than one occasion before her eyes closed.

The next morning, the lady from Huntington, "Isabella Beautiful", the violinist who they only knew for the night, the most memorable part of the trip had packed up her instrument and hiked south, leaving behind two desserts and a note in the corner of the lean-to:

Dearest Jason and Ridge,

"I'll bet we see each other again someday, and I'd bet my violin against your hiking boots on it. Be prepared to guide me on a three-hour personal tour of Andy Oliver Vineyards soon. Thank you for all the good laughs and the kind standing ovation, storytelling and sincere applause. I'll be in touch. Be safe thru-hikers. Hike on. There's two thousand hard miles to go, and my average is only thirty five miles per day. Hint-Hint. Perhaps ...I'll count on you being at the other end? Say a prayer for me regardless. Remember the last song, Gentlemen.

Your friend,
Isabella "Beautiful"

Jason read the letter and nudged his uncle's arm, and pointed to where Isabella had her sleeping bag positioned when they went to bed. By sunup, her footprints and memories were the only evidence that she had ever truly sang in the dirt that night.

"She left some food for us, too." The writer handed him an almond dough roll. Two bites, he dusted his hands for the ants. Good start to the day.

"They're called Bird Rolls. Japanese." Ridge remembered.

Jason watched him smile as he packed. Then he snapped a shot of her footprints, for his own proof and for the record.

"A Daifuku would have been nice."

"Ridge?" Jason yelled. "You know a lady from West Virginia doesn't do Daifuku on the first date."

They couldn't finish packing up their gear for laughing.

"Do you know what that word, Daifuku means, in Japanese?"

"You have my curiosity piqued since she's Isabella Beautiful."

"Daifuku Mochi is a Japanese confectionery." He said, "They take a whole strawberry, wrap it in Carmel or ice cream, and layer the treat in crushed rice."

"Give me fifty of them, and I'll eat the heck out of them."

After watching Cool Hand Luke a dozen times, Jason said, "I bet my boy Ridge can eat fifty Daifuku Mochis for breakfast?"

He put his arm around Jason's neck. "You are a damn nut, you know that?"

"If hiking with you makes me a nut," he said, grunting, "I'm truly insane."

"You might learn something from hanging around me."

"Isabella did her good deed to share her fuel with us. She's a considerate lady." Jason turned southward down the trail where she headed and where they'd left her trekking. "She's a kind person, too."

"I'd share a bottle of Pinot Noir with her. That is," said Weston, "if she brings the Daifuku."

"Perhaps, you would."

Turning around, Jason angled his pen north and did the math on the back of the note, dividing 2000 by 35. "She'll finish in 57 days, Uncle Ridge, perhaps?" He stumbled. Laughed.

"Perhaps?" He grinned, pushing Jason northward and back on track before he trailed her perfume southward.

Every sentence Jason said that day began and ended with *perhaps*.

"Perhaps love, Jason pie?" He yelled from the mountaintop. "I couldn't resist that one."

"It's still not too late to fall off the damn mountain."

They talked about her music and her unforgettable face until sundown as the men left Connecticut behind them. The sky was a blaze in June, orange and sky blue, and clouds drifted across the horizon, still talking about her until nightfall.

"I miss the music, don't you, Ridge?"

"Something tells me we'll see her again by summer's end. Hikers sheltered in the south are in for a real treat when they meet Almost Heaven, Isabella."

"I bet she could play *Country Roads*, don't you?"

Ridge started to snore. The writer remembered the air being clear and pure, filling his lungs for the final miles of the trail. Maybe he was getting used to the outdoors or nature was getting used to the way they smelled.

Several days later, resting at Bigelow Mountain, Ridge pulled Jason's shoulder to encourage his forward march to Roundtop Mountain. "You are a blessed hiker and great nephew."

His nephew nodded because he didn't know what to say. To leave behind the view of the mountain was something out of a dream, with Avery Peak and Flagstaff Lake in the distance, he watched a bald eagle circle overhead, gliding and ascending, hardened to the fact that anything coexisted with the creature to harm it, rounding and circling, lost in an atmosphere of its own glory.

"We are standing on mile 2000," Ridge said.

"2000 miles?"

"We made it, Sorano!" Ridge shouted into the clouds.

He watched his uncle's teeth shine as they left the post. Then he broke open in a big, glorious, giant smile, where he started singing songs, the ones Isabella had sung a few nights earlier. They looked like two regular guys from The Irishman's Pub, doing their best to entertain the flora and fauna with what lyrics he could remember. Their voices echoed across the long green valley that seemed endless and vacant, yet full of game, large and small. Weston knew when they reached that part of the rugged trail, three to four days were left before Sherrill drove up in the Kombi van and the journey would end.

"I predict Kenny and Charles are loading up five cases of Pinot Noir for Sherrill in the Kombi van, as we speak," said Ridge, who rubbed his hands together, more for anticipation and celebration than for warmth. "My eyes and feet will love to see him with his smiling face as much as my stomach will enjoy a good steak. How about you?"

"Perhaps, I'll let my uncle buy me a prime rib."

Fourteen states drifted slowly in the past, miles and miles, connected by one trail that required endurance and patience. Before the hike, Jason dreamed of snakes and bears. The last night of the hike, vivid and real to life, he dreamed the end had a warm spa and a line of beautiful women ushering hikers under fireworks and balloons. Southern sweet tea, pork and beans, mixed with cornbread and barbeque was flown in for the "Laramie's Celebration" at the end of the trail. Months had gone by since they'd tasted a good barbeque, so Jason hoped it wasn't just another dream.

The writer woke to the reality of one more day of hiking until they met Sherrill at Katahdin Baxter Peak. The landscape was something from the Rocky Mountains, not near as tall as the Great Smoky Mountains, but just as promising a view and definitely as rugged as anything they'd seen in North Carolina.

At midday they crossed the finish line and the trail was over. Without anyone to meet and greet the two thru-hikers, the trail concluded. That was it. No balloons. No fireworks. No one to greet for a celebration, either. Two conquerors stood proud.

"Take a picture of me, Ridge, while I make the trekking poles into a cross."

He snapped several photos from behind the brown sign and the last sign, white lettered and glorious, was positioned at the end and called Katahdin.

"Here, it's my turn. I'll turn the trekking poles into a bow and arrow."

From the profile of his thin frame and solid build, it looked as though he had a true bow and arrow in his hands, shooting into the endless blue sky at Katahdin, Maine.

"My turn again," Jason shouted.

"What?"

"See if you know what this is?"

He danced and tapped his foot.

"Are you making a fiddle and bow?"

"Perhaps, I am." He laughed. "Perhaps, I love this trail, my friend and uncle."

On that particular afternoon, they sat at the sign until another thru-hiker needed it to celebrate her long journey. That's when he told Ridge about his dream.

"There's no barbeque," he said. "No beach bunnies or half naked women, hanging from oak branches, serving protein shakes and power bars. Only you, me and God make three. I never travel alone."

"Not hide nor hair of Sherrill, either, I've noticed."

Ridge paced around the park for an hour. He asked if anyone had seen an old man in a hippie van, but no one had admitted to seeing him or Jesus yet. A few people thought he was delirious from the trail and one lady handed him money to see a nut doctor. It sounded hysterical coming from a scruffy man who hadn't attempted to shave in seven and a half weeks.

Ridge was worried for his friend.

"He'll be here."

The van hadn't pulled up at six o'clock that evening. The trip was finally over and they had not made a toast yet, not even with two bottles of water. Jason fell asleep in the shade and dreamed about Rosa greeting him in Katahdin when he crossed mile post 2178 or 2192, which was up for debate in summer of 2001.

"We beat my old record."

"You pushed us pretty hard once we got out of Georgia."

"Some hikers turn back before they reach Tennessee and miss out."

Jason shook hands with the man and thanked him for pushing them through in under fifty days.

"This is something to live for and tell my kids and grandkids about. I won't forget you, Ridge Laramie."

"Perhaps neither one of us will forget this great time."

"Perhaps?"

At the end of the trail, Ridge gave him some good advice.

"Perhaps, it's time for you to find Rosa. At least, tell her how you feel."

"Perhaps...well, I will once we get to Mount Jackson and rest."

MAGNIFICENT OBESSION

What Jason discovered while journaling on the trail was how difficult it was to keep paper dry, so during the precious hours at night between exhaustion and sleep even a man's flashlight needed a break. In the beginning Ridge reminded Jason campfires were illegal, he penned the natural beauty that could not be differentiated from state to national park in his journal along with photographs, and he became obsessed with writing again. Words could not explain, even in part, how the trail slowly became a "Magnificent Obsession" and a life-changer for two hikers. The more they saw the wild, natural and pure, the more Jason wanted to see, the more he imagined.

Being a thru-hiker became vital- even a magnificent obsession as well. To reach the end and see Maine, Jason felt, was within his grasp after he'd hiked beyond the halfway point.

He could visualize the last day of the journey as the writer crossed mountains to valleys and more mountainous regions again. For the first time in a long while, something attainable and real was evident in his scope. Though he had other obsessions, his dedication was to finish the trail, like Sherrill and Ridge both did, a rite of passage, so to speak. The trail was where he became a man, not before as he first had thought, but at the end.

His next obsession was with Rosa. Her words before he left echoed inside his mind each day. The best part was, to know someone believed he could go the distance with and for, still existed. Jason pushed his legs even when he wanted to quit. He had seen Rosa on holidays and during long weekends, but on the trail, he found it wasn't enough to satisfy his days, she encapsulated him. At night under the moonlight he imagined them riding in the Kombi van, together and happy. No different than Weston and Sorano were, hand in hand.

Several vehicles were parked at Baxter State Park where the trail ended. To be transported was now an option. Seventeen Fords, seven Chevrolets, and the rest of the automobiles came from other countries. None of them had the circular Volkswagen logo, burgundy and white in color, and Jason was obsessed with driving the van back to Virginia.

He walked up beside Ridge. "Maybe we are in the wrong spot?"

After he read the words of Percival P. Baxter, it said,

"Man is born to die, his works are short-lived. Buildings crumble, monuments decay, wealth vanishes. But Katahdin, in all its glory, forever shall remain the mountain of the people of Maine."

Thousands of hikers had made the trail their magnificent obsessions as well.

***

They caught a ride in the vehicle of a park ranger named Ernest Woods who gave them a quick tour of the park, swinging by the golf course and park headquarters, too. He finally dropped them off at the lodge.

Ridge was positioned in the parking lot.

"There's your Kombi van parked outside, Jason. Sherrill has put polish on the paint."

The two men walked inside and basking in the warm pool water sat the old man, Sherrill. Jason could say how great it felt to hear "Hello, men" from a fellow thru-hiker. "I knew you would find the van sooner or later." The old man climbed out of the pool to greet them, welcoming Jason to the club with a bear hug. That day of events and photographs never left the young man.

"Sherrill," holding out his arms wide, "I've waited forty eight days and five hours to see your beautiful face." Jason squeezed the daylights out of him and he did the same. "Love you, old man. Glad you made it."

"That's enough from you, Sherrill!" Ridge was pissed for some unknown reason. "Damn it! This is not where we agreed."

Jason pushed him back against the wall. He was mad as hell. Sherrill raised his hands in guilt and shame, yet in truth, he stood and dried off and cooled off on the first day of July.

"Let's get some dinner and beer," said Sherrill. "He's a freakin' idiot, Jason. Has he had his medication yet?" waving his hand in his face. "I see I have driven into a hornet's nest, and before we have even had food." Drying his arms, "I want to apologize to you both. I'm truly sorry for not being at the end of your journey with a camera crew and the Barbie Twins, but the pool was my grotto."

Ridge relaxed and Jason hugged the old man, who became emotional.

"We are hot and exhausted," Jason said. "Let's get some rest and talk."

The two hikers walked into the elevator, like cowboys with a half-naked old man as a hostage. Jason leaned against the wall and closed his eyes in the cool breeze of air conditioning.

"Would you rather hike the stairs?" asked Sherrill.

"Nope," said Ridge, dropping his head against the elevator mirror. "I'm not hiking ever again. That is my final trail."

The rare fraternity of men laughed, bending over and grabbing their thin bellies, being grateful to experience the true glory of nature. Sherrill's eyes were red and bloodshot after driving nearly nine hundred miles to the rendezvous point the day before. Regardless of the tension between the men of Andy Oliver, they were together again. Three heroes, perhaps. After they'd completed their "Magnificent Obsession on the Appalachian Trail" and loaded the van, Sherrill mentioned the unfinished business in Santo Domingo. Ridge and Jason glanced at each other, knowing their next journey would take them abroad.

Twenty-Six
Live on the Edge of Prominence

Four days after they'd completed the monumental feat of hiking the wonderful Appalachian Trail, Sherrill's arthritis kept him down and Weston took good care of him. The trip Ridge and Jason had planned where they'd finally stamp passports was postponed, out of respect for Sherrill, and he would have done the same for them. Rubbing mountainous dirt from his journal, the one filled with thoughts and sketches on the trail, Jason began penning the novel that flooded his head and needed to be in a dust jacket before the geese flew south in the fall.

Driving the hippie van to Virginia, Jason was jovial. The next evening Jason boxed up the modern keyboard, purchased an Olivetti Lettera 32, and started writing again. Not much at first, but the pages grew into the development of paragraphs, blooming with good prose. The first chapter of a book followed within a week.

Little-by-little, like the minister in Mount Jackson prepared his sermon each week, the writer strengthened part one of the book with an unknown title to the work. With the help of a green banker's desk lamp, his own shadow on the wall befriended him at night, keeping the novelist company over a typewriter. The craft became satisfying, until a writer's block prevented the shadow from movement, reveling with Ridge between chapters when possible.

At the dinner table over seasoned pork chops, Ridge encouraged him at the typewriter, page after page, making the story sing as a novelist. His uncle wanted to read passion and masculinity inside each chapter, just as "Isabella Beautiful" played the violin, driven in movement from her heart. So much so he felt compelled enough to organize an upscale office on the newly designed second level at Andy Oliver. He subscribed to books and newspapers, the ones he needed at his fingertips to make progress and absorb inspiration as he typed.

"I will get what you want now and order more, if needed," said his uncle.

At a considerable celebratory dinner Sherrill had planned for Labor Day in Charlottesville, Ridge explained that he wanted Jason to prioritize his writing over his apprenticeship at the vineyard. Jason disagreed. His uncle and Sherrill overruled his rebuttal. The two of them were vital in funneling time into his day so he could refocus on the last chapter. For their kindness, Jason planned to return the favor, a small gift of gratitude, for their belief in his work. Ridge offered a toast, lifting promises of support that were pivotal and prudent early on in his career.

Standing in front of an excited crowd and with all eyes on him, Weston raised his hand in his nephew's direction.

"Jason, you can't be an equal in society because I won't let you become mediocre like us. Your writing will one day sound the bells and whistles of modern literature, making the noise in a line of novels, where others will follow because of your influence. People will be eager to find your column and read your books." Weston stood behind a podium. "Some will want to pilfer your material and rewrite your quotes."

Weston was truly an influential man. He spoke from the heart, and though he wouldn't admit to it, he was a bit of a romantic himself.

The CEO of Andy Oliver sipped his wine and read his notes.

"The key to greatness is to live on the edge of prominence in the zone of gonzo journalism, like it's founder. In your career you will include yourself in the midst of amusement, for the depth and width of your stories will be remembered over meals and your writing will be spoken about for generations."

Everyone stood and joined in applause after he spoke.

Then Sherrill raised his glass with a sense of charm and dignity, adding his own contributions of encouragement to the evening.

"Type a thousand words each night, in time we'll read them in newspapers over coffee the next morning. From a simple act of dedication, your work will fill the shelves of libraries, where people start a conversation with 'Have you read the book by Jason Laramie?' and then the lady will proudly say 'Why, yes, I have, I read it twice. I know him, he's my friend.' People will say."

Laughter exploded through the dining area and the audience adored the elderly man's comedic personality, but he believed his novels were worthwhile and in the beginning were Veblenian goods.

He told Jason to write so that readers in coffee shops, breweries, and the classroom find emotional depth and width in storytelling again.

"And someday in this country and other places too," said Sherrill with a strong voice, "people will parallel your stories, frame them as classic literature and true journalism." He lifted his glass higher. "Make us proud and stay humble, of course, Jason Laramie. We know that book will sell wine and make babies."

Neither Sherrill nor anyone else knew he'd finished the book. Jason raised his hand and accepted the support needed to put a dust jacket around the novel.

"You got something to say, writer?" asked Sherrill.

The writer stood and scanned a group of beautiful people.

"*Symphony of a Lady* is finished," he said, toasting Sherrill and his uncle. "The book is done."

"Yes! Yes!" Ridge followed. "Your talent is undeniable. The sin would be to keep you from your gift, so it's our moral obligation to fire you as my apprentice."

"What? Not again." He said this among friends.

"Wait! Wait! Wait!" Weston grinned. "And hire you back as Andy Oliver's first photojournalist," cussing the unknown and then hugging his clarity, "our minds are made up about Jason and we'll need someone to be our wine taster as well."

The next week Jason submitted an article to the *Kansas City Star*. They rejected it, and he was heartbroken. Still, he kept emailing newspapers and calling editors about his story. In confidence Jason mentioned his book *Symphony of a Lady* to his former boss in Tampa Bay, Top Hunter. He called his sister in New York City, who called the protagonist, Isabella, the violin player from the Appalachian Trail. Word quickly spread with the support of the *Tampa Bay Times*. The novel took off, like a wildfire in the midst of autumn leaves. Then the phone rang.

The writer answered.

"Jason Laramie, guess who?"

"Isabella Beautiful?"

"No other," she said with great laughter. "I'm humbled that you included me in your novel. Newspapers printed that fans of Jason Laramie should read the book and expect to buy popcorn when the film releases."

"The honor of meeting and hearing your music marked the title and penned you as the main character." He was sincere. "Hope that was acceptable."

They talked for thirty minutes about her finishing the trail where she realized fully the direction of her life, as well. The Appalachian Trail offered hundreds and hundreds of "thinking miles" to play and replay life, building momentum for whatever was on the horizon.

Weston walked through Jason's office door to check his progress on promoting the novel to find the writer on the phone with the violinist. Jason flagged him down.

"Who's that?" he asked.

Jason handed him the phone. "It's someone of real prominence."

His face cheered.

From that time on Jason lived on the edge of prominence, noted because of the push of *Symphony of a Lady* in the column and on shelves. Emotional riffs of journalism and substantial mind boggling events guided his work to endless avenues by summer's end. Far beyond what he had ever planned on the trail, Jason was accepted as a novelist with the help of Sherrill, Ridge, Isabella, and a handful of others.

His uncle was in a daze that Isabella wanted to play violin or as it was called in the south, flex her fiddle, at Andy Oliver. Whether it was for the crowd, the free wine or for Ridge Laramie and the news media, they'll never know. Maybe it was friendship, but it was about to happen. The write ups and anticipation of *Symphony of a Lady* brought great promise for branding the vineyard where crowds would gather alongside classically trained Isabella Edmunds. Of all the people who returned to Ridge Laramie, Jason wasn't surprised when Isabella read the write up in the *Huntington Gazette*.

With his glasses dragging on his nose, Weston asked, "When you live on the edge of prominence you'll remain humble, right?"

"Of course."

"*Symphony of a Lady* and sweet Isabella will be here at the End of October Festival at Andy Oliver in wonderful Mount Jackson."

"To see the fall foliage and release a bottle of wine from the Shenandoah Valley, perhaps."

He hugged the heck out of him.

"In honor of Sorano, the wine to be released is a Pinot Noir, her favorite red dry, originally from the heart of France."

"May we have a drum roll please?"

He hummed and thumped his hands.

"The name of the wine is When Geese Fly South."

"Sherrill told me yesterday that's the name you had decided to use."

"That old-timer leaked out about Vitis Vinifera."

They had another big laugh about it.

***

Somehow things were starting to come together. Nothing seemed hopeless or disdained as long as Ridge was around, the opposite of what his father said about his brother. Many people depended on Ridge's intelligence and enthusiasm, chomping at the bit to imagine life bigger and better by adding measureless value, like Jackson and Munson did for the Yankees of New York. His uncle, typically flamboyant in his approach, laughed and smiled, cheerful with step. The unexpected friend he had gained in Isabella brought out the comic actor in him. Sherrill loved to see him coming, whistling and humming, shining a new light of confidence. Songs he'd heard at Mount Algo, unapologetically trying to copy what Isabella covered. Halo or not, she'd composed most of the material without wings. But Jason had a different point of view about her. They pursued their own kind of friendship as student and teacher.

In the fall 2001, the small town of Mount Jackson, Virginia became populated when events were held at Andy Oliver Vineyard. Hundreds of people walked the wooded trails, snapped photos of the covered bridge, enjoyed carriage rides, and some even proposed in the rows of ripe vines when the fall foliage was the most impressive, proving the slogan, "Virginia is for Lovers."

The novel *Symphony of a Lady* released the same day Isabella Edmunds played her event at Andy Oliver. Five thousand people came out to witness the spectacle of a true violinist, some said it was a once in a lifetime event, in the Shenandoah Valley. From the reaction of the crowd she was destined to bring the utmost of pleasantries and a pounding impulse of momentum to the vineyard and the community.

As promised, Isabella, the sandy blonde from Huntington, West Virginia, a lady with a voluptuous body and a personality to match, accepted a tour of Andy Oliver, arm in arm from yours truly, Jason Laramie. Friends. From the start, he told her the story of little Andy Oliver, who passed away only months after his birth, shared pictures of his German Shorthaired Pointer, Tomo, and explained that even though she was gone, that Ridge was still and would forever be in love with Sorano Tanaka. Isabella heard how the Taylors' and a man named Moby Steel were involved in some conspiracy with Savannah's own Mickey Starr, and how while working for Mickey there was alleged corruption.

Jason sat at dinner with Ridge and Isabella when his uncle told her about rejecting Mickey Starr's offer on the vineyard. She wasn't surprised. Ridge spoke of how pleased he was to live in the Shenandoah Valley, holding onto something beautiful and preserving the heritage of wine making in the valley. His uncle was not vain, but he cherished happiness. He called it "a visible truth that could be read in men and women, far and wide." Hysteria rooted in people like Mickey and Moby, who muddied up the lives of others who denied them of what they desired, so they tried to drip dirty turmoil into society. Ridge stepped in when he was close enough to club the delusional.

Everyone fancied Isabella and indeed she was beautiful. Her contagious smile stirred new ambition within her friends, unfolded hearts like a paper doll and under a radiant sun Jason escorted her to Meems Bottom Covered Bridge, where they made love. That evening they visited Woodstock, Virginia and he bought her shiny jewelry as she considered a move from West Virginia to Mount Jackson. They had dinner every night. She was moonstruck by the small town. Like a true gentleman, he dropped Isabella off at the Andy Oliver Bed & Breakfast.

Early the next morning Jason escorted her to Dulles Airport, violin in hand, headed for San Francisco to a grand symphony herself that would last over three days. Then she'd return to Virginia. After seeing the planes take flight and land, Ridge was powered with the idea to test his skills and fly the ultralight again. Isabella had enjoyed seeing the wings on his leather jacket and him soaring through the valley of Mount Jackson excited them both. So, he did it. He uncovered the aircraft.

"Are you sure, Ridge? It's been a year or more since you've been up there."

He inspected the machine, hopped inside the cockpit and took off.

"Maybe you need a refresher course," he said. "Let me fly it alone, to clear my head? I've got it, Jason." He smiled under his goggles. "I have to be up there when the geese fly south again, for myself, for Sorano."

They shook hands and his uncle was in flight, a beautiful smooth take off, and then up, up and away, out of sight. In just a few minutes, there they came down the valley, headed south, working their wings and picking up speed. From the north, there must have been a hundred or more geese beside him, flapping and honking. His nephew cheered them on from the grounds, snapping photos from Andy Oliver.

If the wind is right, geese can fly 1500 miles in just one day. To join them, Ridge spread out his arms crystalline, in a radiant blue sky, taking the plane as fast as it would go, far faster than he'd ever seen him fly.

Eight hours later, Isabella called to check on Jason and to say she'd safely arrived in San Francisco. Her voice revealed her excitement.

"Isabella, after you left Mount Jackson, a flock of geese headed south and my uncle soared into the sky with them, faster and ridding himself of ulterior pressure, free and glorious as a man could fly," he told her. "Twenty minutes later, I received a call from a farmer in Timberville."

"Tell me," she said with her voice cracking. "I need to know where he is." Her voice broken and spirit gone. "What hospital is Ridge in?"

"Isabella?" Jason lifted his head, eyes flooded. "Ridge didn't make it."

"Oh, Jason!" She cried, "I loved that man as much as I love you."

Wiping his face, Jason's voice cracked.

"So did I. So did I," he said. "Everyone did. No one that met him could say a bad word about my uncle."

"How did it happen?"

"The authorities are not exactly sure."

She cried into the phone and screamed.

"Something went wrong, real fast, the farmer said the plane came down like a rock. I'll fax you a picture at your hotel desk."

"I will be traveling, so I can't make it to Virginia."

"I understand. You can send flowers to the vineyard, please. I'll see that they serve their purpose."

"My tour takes me to California, Texas, Georgia, and the Dominican Republic. I'll be gone for two weeks."

"Thank you for your prayers and condolences."

Three weeks later, Isabella called to see how he was doing and if Jason needed anything. They talked for several minutes about Ridge. She spoke of how the business was doing on Thanksgiving. Then she started crying again. Talked of all his accomplishments and how he made the best wine in the country. He spoke of meeting her on the trail and being smitten.

"Listen, Jason."

"Yeah?"

"Who owns Andy Oliver now?"

"Ridge wasn't married and had no surviving children, so I guess he left the vineyard to me in his will, why?"

Men were speaking Spanish in the background of her phone, partying and dancing, and others whispering words he could not comprehend.

"You do? Wow! Congratulations, you big business man. That's wonderful news." She covered the phone when the crowd cheered at the fiesta.

"One more thing...ummm"

Jason became curious.

"Yeah, of course?"

"I don't know how to say this or ask you, it may not be the right time yet. I'd be in the market, that is, if you'd ever consider selling Andy Oliver Winery, coupled with the Bed and Breakfast in Mount Jackson. That would allow you to become that famous journalist I've read so much about, plus stack your bank account with several million dollars. Like I said, you think about it."

"How would I reach you, if I decide to make a deal?"

"How about I email you as the new CEO? My contact phone and address will be in Santo Domingo."

"You are in the Dominican Republic?"

"Yeah. I'm staying with friends for a while until I decide on my next endeavor. I hope it will be a winery and bed and breakfast, of course. Hint, hint."

He thought for a moment on what he should say.

"Just realized my new role as owner. It hasn't settled in yet, the business side, that is, losing my uncle and heavy emotions go with loss."

"Well, ummmm, check your email and give me a call. We'll talk about operations and distribution a little more on another day."

"Where are you staying?"

He opened his email and then jotted down the address.

"It's worth strong consideration."

In Jason's research he found Isabella was fluent in Spanish and Japanese, and spent much of her time at her residence in Santo Domingo. The lady enjoyed fine wines of the Great South and traveled the world. Her pet peeve was the media, and newspaper journalists to be specific, and she said, "the god awful internet" was the worst invention.

The writer spoke with a close friend of his from the Investigators and Reporters, Inc., who wanted to take a holiday in the Dominican Republic, an international experience he needed as bad as anyone else. Instead of Punta Cana, they decided it was time to have a few margaritas in Santo Domingo.

"Sounds like a fiesta," Jason told his friend over quesadillas and beer at the Palacio de Texas, a good sized Mexican restaurant in Mount Jackson. "Muchas damas."

Finally it was agreed and packed for the Dominican Republic. Jason knew it was time to discuss a few things with Isabella while they were there, the true reason for the trip actually. Personal. Private. Maybe seeing the famed violinist and the protagonist of *Symphony of a Lady* onstage would be beneficial. The passport he used to travel to Germany and Puerto Rico two years earlier while on holiday as a freelance journalist for the *Tampa Bay Times* would look "bueno" with a Dominican stamp between the pages.

Jason met his friend at the airport in Santo Domingo, checked a hotel and then caught a cab ride in a '55 Chevy. The driver claimed the car was once used as a getaway car for the Latin Kings. The one common thread of Santo Domingo over America, men smoked cigars over cigarettes. Neither his friend nor him smoked much, but recognized those who did enjoy tobacco. Shops on every corner sold tobacco, the good stuff not that cheap stuff no one wanted. Straw hats offered shade from the hot sun, and most men in the city wore them. Women were beautiful, and it was easy to get caught staring at them.

"Lead the way," his friend told Jason. He followed him, wearing a dark blue suit and sunglasses. With his thin dark beard, he blended in among the locals.

"Can a newspaper investigative reporter bypass the crowds?" Jason flashed a badge and received clearance to see Isabella backstage before she waved, and said, "Vamos."

Jason stood tall in a jet black three-piece suit and paced to the dressing room, like a rocket to the moon to see Isabella.

"We bypassed the first level of security like agents, amigo," Jason told him.

Jason Laramie recognized one of his bilingual friends from Tampa Bay who was on an assignment in Santo Domingo as an investigative reporter. The man knew someone who knew someone who could get them next to Isabella backstage, just like they were rock stars, if they needed to bypass the enormous crowds for an up close and personal interview or to snap a photograph. So Jason called his number, playing his cards and tooting his horn, "living on the edge of prominence" in a foreign country as Ridge once suggested.

"I see her." Jason told his friend.

"Get us as close as possible to Isabella Beautiful." He said as he looked over the long line of people who had the same idea, to meet someone famous.

"Hola, dama Isabella." Jason told her.

Her face dropped in shock. He was the last person she expected to see in Santo Domingo.

"¡No Americanos!"

One guard announced with a dark brown fedora, smoking a long cigar, tubby as a third rate wrestler in a small town to take on Tiger Mask for the title.

Isabella turned when she heard Jason talking to the man.

"What are you doing at Hotel Jardines Teatro Santo Domingo, Jason?" asked the violinist.

"You are truly Isabella Beautiful," he said. "Look at you and all of this glory."

"You didn't answer my question?"

Unexpectedly, a man walked past Jason with a handful of roses, handing the bright reds to Isabella along with a big kiss and a good hug.

"Signor Mickey Starr," Jason said. His beard was thick, hair colored and cut.

Isabella grabbed Jason's arm and told Mickey. "This is the man I was telling you about on the trail, the writer."

Inside the crowded hallway, Isabella introduced Jason to one of her friends, a nice looking lady, who played a sample of

Pable de Saraest, whipping the bow like it was her ponytail. Jason knew she'd be surprised, shocked was the best word, trembling even in the area she kept private for herself, and warding off anyone who didn't have a tag around their neck. Jason's friend had disappeared into the crowd and had gotten lost, he predicted. Jason recognized the next person who walked up to kiss Isabella.

"Buenas noches, Isabella and Signor Mickey."

"Ridge Laramie," said Isabella. "What, I thought you were...?"

Mickey threw the first punch, which Ridge blocked with his left forearm. Then Ridge followed with a powerful right cross that would have leveled Mount Katahdin. Isabella turned to his uncle, her eyes as big as the center of a coconut and she passed out cold.

"That's one for touching my plane, Mickey Starr, another one for killing Montgomery Taylor, Raymond and Myrtle Taylor, another for that wannabe rapper Moby Steel, and one for my peach, Sorano."

Ridge flattened Mickey's nose and knocked two teeth from the Mouth of the South. Mickey's face bloodied his own tuxedo while Isabella was carried away by her friends. In some crazy panic she didn't realize Ridge had traveled a long way to see Mickey Starr's face. So he was kind enough to take his picture while he was out, resting in the corner of the room. Jason snapped a picture of his wrist, just as Ridge planned for him to do.

The next day Jason's photograph of the fight between Ridge Laramie and Mickey Starr made the *Tampa Bay Times* and *Charlotte Observer*, accepted by many media outlets as a headliner among southern newspapers. However, "The Light of the Coastal Empire and Lowcountry" refused to print the article that others praised as a top international story, where authorities rushed in and pinned Mickey Starr with the murder of Montgomery Taylor, the only son Sherrill and Peg Taylor had, who had taken his turn inside the plane that crashed thought to be piloted by Weston "Ridge" Laramie.

Anniversary Celebration of Andy Oliver, 2002

Three years had passed since I first visited Andy Oliver. Neither Ridge nor I had heard much from Mickey Starr, who was known to wear bright orange behind bars, while Isabella Edmunds continued to tour the world. Ridge and I kept up with her on the internet, seeing her accomplishments and travels were made public.

"The truth," Ridge said, sipping wine, "never came out about Isabella."

"Yesterday, I found out she's dating the judge that dismissed her case."

"Love Perhaps." Ridge toasted my glass.

I had a question weighing on my mind while I was on vacation from the *Charlotte Observer*. I just had to ask my uncle.

"Do you think Isabella knew Mickey Starr had tampered with the fuel tank of the airplane? Thank God for new surveillance cameras and GPS tracking at Andy Oliver back in 2001?"

"I'm not completely sure. I've never asked her the question. However, at the Andy Oliver Festival was the day she wanted another Japanese tattoo on the inside of her forearm." He said as we finished a bottle of wine. "That was what tipped me off, got me thinking about Mickey, Isabella and the Dominican Republic, so I had you call my friend in Reston, Virginia. That's when I encouraged you to join the Investigative Reporters and Editors."

I crossed my arms and leaned back.

"What was up with the Japanese tattoo?"

Weston drew a picture, exposed the inside of his skin, dark markings made no sense to a man untrained in deciphering the Japanese language. He steadied his arm and revealed what was written.

"Is that the exact tattoo that was in your photograph of Mickey Starr?"

"Yeah."

"Was that the exact tattoo on Isabella's arm?"

"The same language and markings I've seen before."

"I saw it on her arm at Mount Algo, years ago."

He walked over to the bar, cut a slice of orange and opened a jar of cherries, poured two Cliff's Classic Old-Fashioned, dropping in the fruit one by one over the bourbon. I knew my uncle well enough, seeing him nod, as the bearded man handed me what he had made in his famous "toast of the tumblers" among men. Something he knew would catch on in the Great South.

"Isabella Edmunds was ten years old when I first met her in 1988. Her parents brought her to New York to study strings at Julliard."

I sipped bourbon, not because I liked the taste but for his honor and out of respect for my uncle; for his own keen investigative reporting, of which he studied while in undergraduate school.

"The best of the best attend Julliard, and Isabella is one of the best in the world." I told him as I struggled with downing the bourbon, which would kill a goat in my book.

Regardless, Cliff's Classic Old-Fashioned was his favorite beverage.

"Isabella was the best violinist West Virginia had ever seen. There was a small problem. Her father worked as a certified welder for a steel company in Huntington and was a sharpshooter in the Army. He taught classes for extra money, the cost of Julliard was still more than he could afford."

Ridge sat in Sorano's favorite chair. I could see the bourbon blasting his eyes in a tint of red, making him sniff and sigh.

"She couldn't afford it," I said, "could she?"

"Not many people have the funds to cover that many years of education and classical training on strings and keys in New York. That was the year, well, Sorano and I dated for a short time, trying to make sense of the distance and our past, just to see if we had a future together. We met once or twice in 1988."

"You sent a postcard to your brother and I read it. I used to ask my mother where you traveled each year. "New York, New York" was her answer."

"Sorano was known to sponsor students at Julliard when financial aid and funds ran short. She valued talent and educated students enough to aid Isabella Edmunds, one of the "Flying Birds" or tobutori in Japanese."

"I'll be," I yelled. "That wasn't in my novel, *Symphony of a Lady*, either."

"Sorano was a saint. An angel without wings, I called her." Ridge slapped his wrist again. "Very few people knew her tattoo meant "Flying Birds," it just looked like bad artwork to most people except the Japanese and the students at Julliard, of course."

"Does Top Hunter know how good you are with telling stories?"

"No. But when Isabella graduated, she was introduced to Sorano Tanaka. I happened to be at the ceremony when they hugged. Isabella never met me. In the lobby, I shook the hand of her father, the steel worker in flannel and denim, and didn't see her mother. Later, Isabella visited Sorano in the hospital in Buffalo. In her honor she must have tattooed her arm in the same cool Japanese words."

"Flying Birds, huh?"

"Sorano favored migrating birds especially in the fall at Meems Bottom Covered Bridge." He cleared the lump in his throat, coughed into his hand to hide his eyes.

That's why I wrote this novel in honor of Weston "Ridge" Laramie and his endless love for Sorano Tanaka, the most beautiful couple I'd ever seen. Every autumn in the midst of the golden leaves and under a pale blue sky I meet him at Andy Oliver, in Mount Jackson, Virginia. The past year, the two of us reminisced about Tomo, Andy, and Sorano, and Sherrill too, who had passed away in the spring.

Last fall, my uncle read my latest novel, *When Geese Fly South* until the warm evening sun slowly faded behind the grandeur that formed the glorious Shenandoah Valley I love so much. Still today, I can taste the spicy stir-fried Japanese eggplant and cucumbers I made that day. We laughed until we cried.

***

In November of that same year, Weston bought Sorano another flowering, hand-woven birthday hat. At sunrise, he dusted the beams of Meems Bottom Covered Bridge, in the heart of Mount Jackson, left the straw hat and a timeless note, that read:

If you love the lady, fly to her, buy her that hat,

buy flowers, and diamonds too, if that drives you;

Why not you?

Then travel to her, hike mountains, walk country roads,

If you love her, she waits for you.

Till the end, be her thoughtful giver, her proud traveler,

buy her that hat and dinner too, if that drives you;

Why not you?

Young or old, see the coast and Shenandoah too.

If you love her, take this beautiful hat, she waits for you.

Why not you?

--- Weston Laramie

About the Author

MATTHEW "PETE" LESTER, PhD, was born in 1970, in Welch, West Virginia and educated at Concord University, Liberty University, and Tennessee Temple University; after service with the U.S. Army, he moved to North Carolina to earn his living in logistics and penning novels and short stories. His first novel, *The Tobacco Barn* (2019), earned him international popularity as a notable American novelist. *Saddles of Barringer*

(2021) was published in the midst of a pandemic; upon completion, Pete had written another timeless and masculine novel. Six months later, his third novel, *When Geese Fly South* (2021) was published, establishing his torch as a gifted writer. Known for his humorous and inspiring personality and his passions for hiking, boating, traveling, and love for classic cars, his poetic and powerful imagination continues to draw enthusiasm to his transforming characters, vivid settings and readers are transported with a dynamic prose and external geography. Pete is a member of Romance Writers of America, Hemingway Society, the F. Scott Fitzgerald Society, and the Thomas Wolfe Society.

In 2021, two of Pete Lester's fictional novels *Saddles of Barringer* and *When Geese Fly South* were approved by the Pulitzer committee at Columbia University, New York, New York, and proudly accepted as entries for the Pulitzer Prize competition. His first flush of success, *The Tobacco Barn*, earned Pete critical and commercial success, but in a short time, the aforementioned novels will captivate the masses, adding style and value to classrooms, with a playful polish in literature, illuminating the depth of pure love and how it impacts cultural stereotypes within society. For the reader, the Hearts & Heroes series is a valuable collection and worth observation, to ponder meaningful stories; upon gaining deep intuitive understanding of human condition; upon shining a delicate light on self-appraisal; upon reflection of his own generation and the good fortune of the next, fanning the flames of a soon to be great American author.

Carson's Story

www.tastypicklesbycarson.com

Carson has a passion for PICKLES! He also has autism and is learning disabled. When thinking about his future, Carson feared that he would never be able to get a job. His crippling anxiety about the future and dread of limited workforce abilities encouraged him to begin thinking about being his own boss. Inspired by a school project, Carson started his own pickle business.

Carson's pickle adventure has given him an incredible sense of pride and has helped him to not only grow in confidence but to also improve both academically and socially. We are thrilled for Carson and his success! Our hope is that Carson's story will help others find their niche in life and hearten others to believe in and support DIFFERENT-ABLED individuals.